# JOVARI THE BLUE

## BOOK 6 OF THE DRAGONWALL SERIES

MELISSA MITCHELL

*To everyone who has ever been the one left behind, who watched others find their place while wondering if yours would ever come. Keep faith. Your light isn't just coming, it's already shining, waiting for the right person to see it.*

DRAGONWALL
Dragonfire Sea
Shadowkeep
Belnesse
Eagle Lake
Mistport
Redport
Squall's End
Three Horned Man
Shattered Islands
Kastali Dun
Bay of Bandu

The Kengr Gate
Northedge
The Gable
Forest
Kaljah
Lincastle
South Sea

# PROLOGUE

Irelia Drakos stared at the television, her mouth agape. She blinked, but the footage remained the same, replaying on a loop. She blinked again. It didn't change. A woman that looked so familiar, a face she could never forget. But...how?!

The breath whooshed from her lungs. She stepped backwards, then sank onto the sofa as her aging knees gave out. Newscasters began speculating about the woman, tossing theories around. "I think it's alien abduction, if you ask me. Just look at the marks all over her body. How else do you explain her disappearance? There's no record with any airline—all her belongings including her ID and wallet were at home—confirmed by her parents, according to our sources. She simply vanished from the United States, only to appear in France?"

"Not to mention, she can't remember getting there."

"Exactly, the whole thing screams of aliens."

One of the newscasters chuckled. "Conspiracy theorists are going to have a field day with this one."

Irelia hardly heard a word. Her gaze was transfixed on the footage instead.

A mob of French police escorted the woman and her family into a private car from the American embassy to take them to the airport. Irelia's gaze fixed on the markings covering the girl's skin, peeking from beneath the sleeves and collar of her shirt. Turquoise, luminescent tattoos. Spriten markings. Markings she'd once seen on her mother, from a time she'd almost forgotten.

She covered her face with her hands, her *gnarled* hands, and rubbed her eyes. When she looked up again, the footage had looped back to the beginning. She glanced down at her chest, then pulled on the collar of her dress, ignoring the sight of her sagging, wrinkled skin in favor of the single, luminescent marking she carried just above her belly button. A pattern of swirls and dots. They were dim, but every once in a while, they flared to life.

The tattoo had appeared long, long ago, when she'd desperately needed hot water. Long before kettles had been invented. Back when starting a fire was more of a chore. Since then, she could warm anything with a single touch, a single desire. She'd kept it hidden, mostly because it was strange. But, she'd always had reasons to hide herself.

Now people marked themselves in all manner of styles. Tattoos of different colors and images. Now her marking was more believable, even if there was no tattoo artist in the world who could replicate the markings of sprites.

She took a deep, fortifying breath, then stood, shuffling into her kitchen to put on a pot of tea. She didn't use her magic. She liked the mundane aspect of going through the motions, heating the water in the kettle, adding the tea leaves, letting it steep, pouring it into a cup, inhaling the steam as it rose. She let the chore calm her.

When she sat down at the table, she reached for her tablet. Another *marvelous* invention that had taken time to adjust to. Technology. She'd seen too much change to be surprised by the bounds of human civilization. Gods, so much change throughout her many lifetimes.

She unlocked the device and began searching for flights. Murine would need to take Darcie, the cat she'd adopted off the streets. She glanced at the feline, snoozing in the sunlight. Perhaps this was a bad idea. She was too old to travel, her bones weary, her body all but spent.

But...no. There was something tugging her, tightening her chest. A need. One she hadn't felt for...how long now? Two thousand years? Perhaps she was mistaken. She was getting ahead of herself.

She glanced down at the list of flights and picked one. She went through the details, making sure she picked the closest airport so she wouldn't have to rent a car. Ride shares! Now that was another amazing addition to human civilization. She hated transporting herself anywhere. She used her phone's ride share app almost exclusively, whenever she needed food at the market, to meet her friends for tea, or attend weekly bridge night.

She hesitated, giving herself one last chance to back out. Before she could talk herself out of it, she entered her payment information. She clicked purchase, blowing out the breath she'd been holding. Then she stood and shuffled about her home, clicking off the television. On the way to her bedroom, she glanced at the framed photos lining the hallway wall. Generations of family come and gone. She'd been a part of their lives only briefly, often as a grandmother watching over them, until the time came to extricate herself. Otherwise, there'd be too many questions.

Photos were a relatively new invention. For the more ancient family members, there were paintings, portraits commissioned to remember them by. She kept those tucked away, occasionally donating a few to museums. They'd be too suspicious if left out in the open. Draw too much attention to her and her age.

There were other aspects of her long life, too, filling storage units, tucked away in the spare room. Items she was fond of. Garments from another time, jewelry from another era. Things to keep her memory intact.

She entered her bedroom, groaning as she knelt to retrieve her travel suitcase. Her arm gave a painful twinge as she reached beneath the bed. Gods, she was too old for this.

As she stood, her knees nearly gave out. She plopped her suitcase on the bed and unzipped it. Then she just stared inside its empty depths. How much would she need to pack? How long would she be gone? Should she really be doing this?

Her chest gave another twinge, of longing and fear. Something felt different about this. A nagging intuition driving her into motion. If she left her life here in Greece, she might never return. But she *had* to go. She needed to do this. Even if it meant answering difficult questions. Questions that were better kept secret.

It was time to return to the world she'd left behind.

CHAPTER 1

# THAT NIGGLING FEELING

*Battle Ground, Indiana*

Claire stepped away from her bedroom mirror and went to stand before the window. Her gaze dropped to the chicken coop, catching sight of her mother. Alexandra Evans was kneeling in the chicken run with a handful of feed, clucking and cooing at her pets as they pecked food from her palm. As if sensing her stare, her mother glanced up. Their eyes met. A flash of concern filtered over Alexandra's features before she replaced it with a smile and waved.

They had the same blonde hair. The same nose and mouth. But her green eyes had come from her father. Her mother's eyes were blue.

She waved back, offering a weak smile in return. She continued to watch as her mother showered the chickens with affection. *Chickens...*

A strange feeling stole over her and she pushed it away. She'd had a lot of that lately. Strange feelings, a nagging sensation at the back of her mind, a distant voice urging her to remember. Yesterday she'd felt it during dinner, while looking at the *Starry Night* painting on the dining room wall. The one that hung over the

5

hidden family safe. Earlier this week, she'd had it while changing the sheets in the guest bedroom.

Movement on the gravel drive caught her attention. Her stomach plummeted. Her mother noticed at the same time and called out for her father. Michael Evans emerged from the large red barn opposite their house. He wiped his hands on a towel hanging from his tool belt. He followed her mother's gaze and a frown appeared on his lips, morphing into anger.

The news van came to a stop in the driveway. A crisply dressed female and her male counterpart emerged. Her father was already striding for them, face contorted. "What don't you people understand about *leave us alone*?!" he snarled, voice drifting up through her closed window. "We don't want you here!"

The female reporter said something, her voice too low to carry.

Claire stepped out of view, putting her back against the wall. She closed her eyes. A tear oozed from beneath her eyelid, dripping down her cheek.

She sucked in a breath. It sounded more like a suppressed sob. An entire week had passed and they just kept coming. Like she was some kind of freak show. A small part of her hoped it had been aliens. That was easier to explain than *nothing*. She simply couldn't understand how she'd ended up in France, dressed like a knight from a historical drama, with strange glowing markings covering her skin. No one else could understand, either.

With the wall at her back, she slid down to the ground, burying her head in her arms.

The faint crunch of gravel singled the retreat of the reporters. A few minutes later, there was a quiet tap at her door. "Claire, honey? You okay?" Her mother.

"Fine," she called, trying to infuse calm indifference into her voice.

A long silence, then, "Okay. I'm here if you want to talk."

"I know. Thanks, Mom."

When Alexandra's footsteps faded down the hall, she allowed herself to think back over the last week and a half. *The Ordeal*, with a capital T and O, because of how serious it was. Appearing in

France, somewhere randomly in the countryside. Being taken to the French police without a single form of identification. Discovering that her parents had filed a missing persons report two days prior, after waiting nearly a week because of a supposed note she'd written—a note she didn't *remember* writing, despite it being *her* handwriting. A note that told them she'd be gone for a while, but not to worry.

Well, they'd worried!

The French authorities had run her name through a database. She'd been found. News outlets around the world had erupted over the details of it. The days following had been a blur of media, accusations, and confusion. Of tears and exhaustion. Of hiding.

It still felt like a bad dream. She kept willing herself to wake up. To remember *how* it had all happened.

The drug test had come back clean, so it hadn't been a wild bender. There'd been no bruises, nothing to suggest a concussion, or that she'd been kidnapped. They couldn't even find travel history to prove she'd booked a flight from the United States to Europe.

It was simply...unexplainable.

She glanced across her room to the upright mirror beside her door, taking in her reflection from afar. The marks had faded. She could no longer count the amount of times she'd studied them, staring in fascination. They'd been so bright that first day in France. Now, they'd faded into a dull turquoise.

She lingered on the necklace at her throat. Another thing she couldn't explain. The beautiful silver chain. The glowing pendent. The pearl strung beside it. Was it some kind of charm? Where had she gotten it?

The crunch of tires on gravel made her flinch again. She held her breath until—

"Honey, I'm home!" came a crisp, sing-song voice.

A burst of laughter broke through her melancholy. She wiped her tears and crawled to her knees, peering through the window. Her best friend, Leah, stood in the driveway, staring up at her, holding something in her hand. She dragged the window open. "I thought you had work?"

"Got off early. Thought you could use a distraction." Leah waved the case of Blu-ray Discs in the air.

Even from here, she could make out the cover on the case. A smile pulled at her lips. "I thought you were joking when you threatened me with that?"

"Oh, come on. When's the last time we had a LOTR marathon? It's been ages! Besides, you got any better ideas? I didn't think so."

"You girls can take over the living room," her mom called, stepping off the porch to make her presence known. "I've already got the popcorn started."

Of course. Her *mom* had called Leah. That's probably why she was here before her shift was technically over. Still, she couldn't be mad.

"Thanks Miss A," Leah said, grinning as she strode for Alexandra and wrapped her in a hug. It was *impossible* to fight the warmth in her chest at the sight of them. Leah, especially, had been her rock since she'd gotten back from France. Between grocery store runs and late nights on the couch, she'd been there for whatever Claire needed—whatever the Evans Family needed. None of them wanted to go out in public. Not for a good long while. Not when questions followed their every step.

"Fine, I'm coming down!" she called, slamming the window shut before skipping out of her room. She ignored her reflection. Ignored the fact that she was wearing a long sleeve shirt despite the summer heat.

Downstairs in the living room, they got cozy on the couch, stretching out with blankets and pillows. Her parents hadn't said anything, but she'd noticed the thermostat. Noticed that her dad had adjusted the temperature, clicking it down several notches after she'd taken to covering herself so thoroughly. Just another little adjustment they'd made in the wake of *The Ordeal*. Even if they weren't really talking about it.

Leah didn't do anything by halves. They were in for the

extended edition of LOTR, not just the standard. One year, they'd even watched all the filming extras.

"Popcorn and sugar!" Alexandra called, breezing in from the kitchen with a tray. "Claire? You okay hon?"

She blinked, pulling her gaze from the tray. "Yeah. Just... I'm good."

There it was again. That niggling feeling. That she wanted to remember something but couldn't quite do it. She cleared her throat. "Do you...is that a new tray?"

"Nope. Always had it. Just don't pull it out often," her mom said. Both her parents had stopped reacting strangely to questions like this. Especially after their first reaction had brought her to frustrated tears.

Their virtual family therapist—because she'd refused to go out in public—had assured her parents that it was okay for her to ask questions like this. That she'd have them as she tried to regain her memories.

Alexandra set the tray on the coffee table. It held a bowl of popcorn, slices of cheese and salami, two glasses of pop, and a couple of boxes of Sour Patch Kids.

"This is perfect, Miss A. Thanks," Leah said, grinning before she attacked the candy first.

"You girls have fun."

"Sure you don't want to join us?" Leah asked.

"Nah. Michael needs some help this afternoon in the barn. I'll see you two later, but come find me if you need anything."

"Your mom's the best," Leah sighed.

It was impossible not to smile. "Yeah, she really is, isn't she."

They settled in to watch The Fellowship of the Ring, quoting nearly every line in various character voices. Leah was absolutely Team Legolas while she'd always be Team Aragorn. Even if they did have a mutual respect for each other's love interests.

They were switching over to the second movie when she said, "Thanks, by the way."

Leah turned with lifted eyebrows, pausing before slipping the next disc into the outdated blu-ray player. They probably could have just downloaded everything on iMovie, but there was something so satisfying about the old tradition of shuffling discs. "For what?"

"Coming to my rescue today—every day. Not pushing and asking questions I can't answer. All that."

"Aww. Clairey. You'd do the same for me."

"I would," she agreed. Not that Leah ever needed saving, now that she considered it. Leah had always been outgoing, strong minded, emotionally mature. They'd grown up together, both determined to get the hell out of this place when they got older. Except, they were both still stuck here, long after they'd hoped to be. Leah hadn't left because her dad had gotten sick. She'd never had the chance to go to college. Then he passed away.

Maybe that's why Leah was so strong. Caring for a parent. Seeing them through numerous oncologist visits. Chemo. Surgery. More chemo. Being there through the hard days, then surviving the grief afterward, when none of it worked out the way it should have.

"I'm so lucky to have you," she blurted, watching Leah's face soften at her words. "I really missed you," she added, before realizing how absurd that was. Except, she felt deep inside like there'd been a time she really had missed her best friend. Like they'd been separated months, when really she'd only been gone less than two full weeks. Apparently.

Leah brushed it off. She slipped the disc case onto the coffee table then plopped down on the couch for a hug. They stayed silent for a few minutes. "You know," Leah said. "When you do remember, because I know you will, even if it takes time, don't forget that I'll be here for you no matter what. No matter what happened to you, I'll listen. No judgement. Just support. If you want to tell me— that is."

"Of course I'll want to," she managed, her throat tightening. Leah's face swam in her vision as she blinked back tears. "You'll be the first one I tell, if I do."

"When you do," Leah corrected.

"When I do," she amended.

The music for the second movie started. They both grinned before settling back in to watch Gandalf's battle. Summer days were long. It would be hours yet before darkness truly fell.

Yet, it felt like it had already arrived. It felt like she was living it, day after day. Like she'd never remember what had actually happened, and that this cloud would follow her. This fear.

Her parents were clanking around in the kitchen, chattering in low voices as they cooked dinner, when the doorbell rang. She hadn't heard any vehicles through the loud volume of the surround sound. She and Leah shared a wary look as Leah paused the movie.

"Want me to get it?"

She exhaled. If she was going to get past this, she needed to grow a backbone. "No, I'll do it."

Her mom popped her head through the doorway between the kitchen and the living room. "You sure, hon?"

"Yeah, it's fine. I got it." She was already working up the courage to tell whatever reporter it was to eff off. She caught sight of the blurred person at the door. The glass panes distorted them, but it definitely *wasn't* a reporter.

She hesitated. Her mom must have felt it because she gravitated closer into the living room. Even Leah had come to her feet.

She reached for the handle and pulled the door open. It was an old woman, stooped with age, and yet, there was something familiar in her face, her hazel eyes, especially. A strange sense of deja vu washed over her, which didn't make sense because she'd never seen her before. "Uhm. Can I help you?"

A presence materialized behind her, her mother, followed by a shocked gasp. And then—"*Grandmother*?!"

The woman's wrinkled face split into a wide grin, her aged eyes darting between them before saying, "Alexandra Drakos. I see so much of you in your daughter."

"You didn't tell me you had a great grandma," Leah said, coming over to link their arms together, oblivious to the shocked silence that weighed heavy in the air.

"Because I never knew I had one," Claire murmured, chills

racing down her spine. She tried to step backwards, only to find her mother was still there, frozen in place.

Something flopped over in her belly, a keen sense of importance and wariness. For a moment, the old woman flashed young in her mind's eye. Her white hair turned sandy brown. Her face lost its wrinkles. She frowned as the image appeared, then disappeared into the recesses of her mind, inaccessible. She recognized this woman, or a younger version of her. And yet, she couldn't say how. She'd never *heard* anything about having a great-grandmother. Or had she forgotten that, too?

"Well," Alexandra said, still breathless. "You'd better come inside. Michael will get your luggage. You can stay in our guest room."

Leah had to pull Claire out of the doorway so that the old woman could step through. Her father was there in an instant, ready to take the suitcase, rolling it into the other room. "Have…" Claire cleared her throat then tried again. "Have we met before?"

"No, dear. I'm afraid we haven't."

"Grandmother lives in Greece," Alexandra explained.

"And I didn't meet her when I visited all those summers ago?" Her brow furrowed.

"No," her mother said, eyes narrowing. "Because she was *supposed* to be dead."

"Dead?" Claire squeaked, frowning.

"Dead," the old woman confirmed, right as her face split into a mischievous grin. "Looks like I've got some explaining to do."

CLAIRE BLINKED, trying to make sense of things. "So you *are* my great-grandmother? Or you're not?" she asked. Alexandra looked as if she was struggling too, trying to understand the newcomer's claims.

They were sitting around the dinner table. Her father sat at the head, watching everything in silence. Leah had joined them, claiming that they'd finish their LOTR marathon later. She was wearing a positively gleeful expression as words volleyed back and forth. The food went untouched.

"It's easiest to explain it like that," the old woman said. "I look like a grandmother, don't I? Many generations have come and passed. I always insert myself into our family before disappearing again. If you wanted a more technical explanation, then you might call me your great-great-great-great-great..." Her grandmother frowned. "I'm not sure *how* many greats, actually. I lost count. But the fact remains. I'm slightly over two thousand years old."

A breath whooshed out of Claire's lungs. "But that's impossible."

"So is disappearing and reappearing on the other side of the world, covered in turquoise tattoos."

"Touché," Claire murmured.

"Are you suggesting," Alexandra said, "that your impossible age and my daughter's disappearance have something in common—?"

"There's no *way* you're over two thousand years old," Claire interrupted, at the same time her grandmother said, "Yes."

Silence fell around the table.

The old woman sighed. "Let me try again, perhaps from the beginning, this time. I am not from your world. I was born...elsewhere. In a place your daughter is more familiar with than she realizes—or remembers. I came here for my own reasons, but I stayed. I didn't have much choice, actually. The portal I came through didn't have an obvious twin on this side of our world. Finding my way back was impossible, even if I'd wanted to. I didn't. I made a life for myself in Athens. Learned the language. Fell in love. Had children. But...I didn't age. Not normally, anyway. I am not human. I was born a hybrid, the first of two races, if you will. I'm part spriten and part drengr."

Claire's mouth dropped open. *Spriten. Drengr.* The words ricocheted in her mind, foreign and yet...not. Like she'd heard them before.

The silence around the table was broken by Alexandra, who said, "If I didn't have so many memories of you while visiting

Greece in my childhood, I'd force you to leave my house for speaking such nonsense."

"Nonsense." The woman harrumphed, then came to her feet. She lifted her shirt. There, on her sagging, wrinkled stomach, was a luminescent marking.

"It's the same as yours!" Leah gasped, covering her mouth with surprise. The rest of them couldn't manage words.

"It's a sprite marking," the woman explained. There was that word again. *Sprite.* It clanged around in her mind. "My mother had them covering her body. They represent magic. I never wanted much to do with magic, and left my world before I could learn. Though, I did stumble upon it after coming here. Because of that, its presence in my life has extended my lifespan. I'm not human, after all. And you might think *I'm* old, but my mother was thousands of years older than even I."

Claire couldn't stop staring at the turquoise tattoo, even after the woman dropped her shirt.

"Grandmother..." Alexandra said, like it was a warning, or a plea.

"You said—" Claire stopped herself but it was too late. Every pair of eyes was trained on her. She cleared her throat. "You said your mother had those markings covering her body. Like...like me?"

"Exactly like you." There was a gleam in the woman's eyes, like she knew something else too.

"But...does that mean I'm not, like, human either? That I have magic?" She certainly hadn't shown any magical abilities.

"Indeed." The woman sank back into her chair. Her expression changed, eyes gleaming with suspicion. "*I* think you found a way into that world, and whatever happened there earned you those markings. You certainly *aren't* human, now that you have them."

"This is preposterous," Michael finally cried, right as Claire said, "And then I came back?"

"*Apparently.*" The woman lifted her brows. "Minus your memories."

"What else aren't you telling me?" Claire hedged.

"I like to think I have an excellent memory," the woman said. "I was young when I came here. Thirteen. But I remember my mother's face. You could be her identical twin, down to the very markings on your skin. My mother was Queen Isabella—queen of the sprites. In that world, that kingdom, I was born Princess Irelia Drakos. I took my father's surname. King Eymar Drakos, first king of the drengr monarchy."

A chill raced down Claire's spine. She gaped at the old woman. *Irelia Drakos.* The name picked at her. There was recognition in it. She knew it, somehow. And yet, the memories surrounding it were just out of reach, like a word on the tip of her tongue.

She wanted to scream in frustration—

"But that would make Claire a princess too, wouldn't it?" Leah asked, eyes wide as she looked between them. "If she's like your great-great-great…whatever."

"Yes." Irelia said, eyeing Claire with curiosity. "It would."

Her parents appeared at a loss, shooting glances at each other like they couldn't decide whether to shut this discussion down, or keep it going, if only to solve the mystery of Claire's disappearance. "We should eat," her father blurted. The food had long gone cold, but they dug in nonetheless. She was almost grateful for the distraction. She needed to process this—the absurdity of it.

Magic? A princess? A parallel world?

All her life, she'd never been anything but ordinary, down to her basic college degree, her bartending job, and even her pathetic love life. Yet, as she glanced down at the marking that peeked beneath the long sleeve of her shirt, she couldn't help but wonder if maybe she was something special instead.

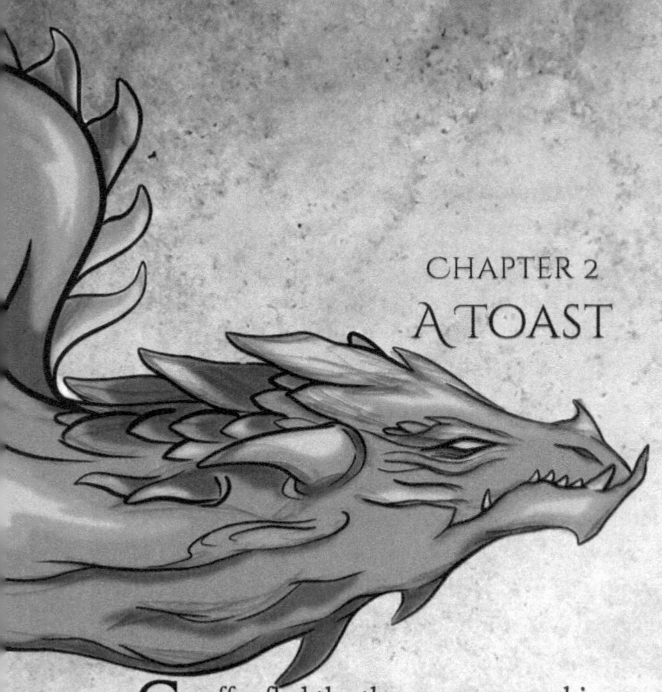

# CHAPTER 2
# A TOAST

Kastali Dun

Saffra fled the throne room, pushing past the crowd ambling towards the dining hall. Court hadn't been a complete disaster, thankfully. Nothing like the first few times, anyway. Jocelyn fell into step beside her and said, "Desaree went out this morning with Aithlin Naeris and Jassin Orythra. So I don't expect her back for a few hours." Saffra hummed distractedly. "She offered to fetch you the herbs you needed, so I gave her a list."

"Oh. Good."

Aithlin and Jassin would be protection enough for Des. With Claire gone, her spriten guards had taken to whatever other duties they could squeeze themselves into. Protecting Claire's friends was one of them.

"Still fretting over your vision?" Jocelyn asked, making her blink.

She exhaled. "Is it that obvious?"

"You have been distracted all morning. Might as well just tell everyone so you can come up with a plan."

Jocelyn was right. But their king—their *stand-in* king—had enough on his plate. She almost dreaded telling him as much as she often dreaded telling the real king. And *that* was saying something.

She quickened her step, Jocelyn keeping pace. They beat Reyr to the tower, where she took up a position near the sitting room to pace. It was empty. The servants had all been dismissed shortly after Talon had left, under the pretense that the king and queen wanted privacy. Everyone probably assumed they were hard at work making an heir—Saffra almost snorted at the thought.

If only they knew...

Taking a deep breath, she swallowed down the guilt threatening to destroy her. Whenever she let it, it reared its ugly head and tried to pull her into a deep pit of depression. This was *her* fault. The others kept telling her not to blame herself, but because of her, because she'd allowed that servant to lead her astray—

The door opened and Talon strode in. She blinked, coming back to herself. No, not Talon, but Reyr. He'd been enchanted by the sprites to look *exactly* like King Talon, down to the very last scar and the messy head of hair holding his crown. Week after week had passed, and she was still struggling with the contradiction. Reyr was an opposite to Talon in so many ways.

He glanced at her, then changed direction and went straight to the liquor cabinet. A sign that he already sensed what was coming. Or, perhaps he was buckling under the pressure. Probably both.

"You're doing much better," she pointed out.

He glanced her way. "But? I sense a but..."

She sighed. "*But*, you're still not grouchy enough. You had no business granting that compensation request without pressing the merchant—"

"I'm trying my best, Saffra," he snapped.

"Ah. There. See? That's *much* better. More in character." Even a little frightening, but she didn't say that last part aloud.

Reyr's features relaxed. He rocked his jaw from side to side, studying her. When she said nothing, he snatched his drink and dropped into Talon's favorite armchair. The scowl on his face deepened. If she had not known, she would have believed it, seeing him there.

The door opened to reveal Bedelth and Koldis. Her stomach swooped at the sight of her mate. Their eyes locked before Bedelth gave her a wide grin. "Should have known I'd find you here," he purred.

"Bedelth, tell your mate to stop lecturing me," Reyr groused.

"*His mate*," she said, "is doing what her queen bid of her. I'm the glue, remember? I'm to make sure all this goes off without a hitch."

"Where are Dallin and Verath?" Reyr asked, completely ignoring her words.

"They had that business to deal with in the dungeons," Koldis said, striding across the room to take a seat. Bedelth, however, came to stand beside her. His fingers brushed hers in silent greeting, sending sparks up her arm.

She'd forgotten all about the business in the dungeons. After the battle with the Osheans, a number of opportunists had turned to looting throughout the city, taking advantage of Kastali Dun's weakened state. Those caught were rounded up and punished by example. It kept the city's guards and even the king's shields busy.

Jocelyn shot her a look that said, *Get on with it!*

The door opened again and Prince Feowen strutted in, hand-in-hand with Jeanine. She smiled at the sight of them. "Ah," Feowen said, "not too late for the meeting?"

"There is no meeting," Reyr-not-Talon snapped. Gods, he was embracing this whole moody-king persona.

"There is," Jocelyn said, "because Saffra has something to tell us."

Saffra shot her handmaiden a glare. Jocelyn merely shrugged.

"Then shouldn't we gather everyone?" Feowen asked.

"I suppose we should," Saffra sighed, massaging her forehead.

This was how it had been since Talon departed. Claire had brought so many of them together. The king, his shields, her queen's guard, and her closest friends. She'd been the uniting factor. After her disappearance, those who remained had grown even closer. All of them wanted this to work.

"I informed Verath and Dallin," Koldis said.

"Desaree's at the market with Aithlin and Jassin," Jocelyn said.

"That's fine, we can fill them in later," Feowen said. "I'll go track down the others."

Jocelyn poured Saffra a goblet of wine, though she didn't usually drink this early in the day. They got comfortable on the sofa, Jocelyn on her left, Bedelth on her right. He leaned in and said, "Are you all right?" His breath against her ear sent shivers down her spine. She glanced sidelong at him and nodded. Whatever he saw in her worried expression made his brows pinch together. He took her hand and laced their fingers together. The action made her heart drum faster.

Feowen returned with the remainder of Claire's guard. They took up positions near the wall to observe, Jeanine with them. Feowen, on the other hand, planted himself in an armchair. A few moments later, Verath and Dallin appeared. They grabbed open seats.

Bedelth squeezed her hand.

"Well," she said. "I've had another vision."

"I gathered as much," Reyr drawled. He said it so like Talon would have, that she had to blink at him.

"Right. Uhm. So, just as we guessed, Kane is making a play against us. I think he believes that with Claire gone, Talon is weakened—*you're* weakened, I mean, since you're supposed to be Talon—"

"What exactly did you see?" Reyr said, impatiently.

"Don't interrupt her," Bedelth growled, a challenge in his gaze. Gods, mates were so overprotective.

"He's collecting the stones he previously hid away from us—or he will be. Soon."

"But, what would the point be in that?" Dallin asked.

"Because he wants them under his protection, most likely," Koldis mused.

"Right, but doesn't he need all five if he wants to use them against us?" Dallin pointed out.

"Could he be making a play to steal the ones hidden in the

forest?" Elyon Marquin asked from where she stood against the wall.

Feowen looked thoughtful. "I wonder if my sister has seen this." Koldis perked up at the mention of his mate. Taylynn had left weeks ago to check on the hatching grounds with Fright. There were already eggs warming in the sands, hidden in the mountains south of the Gable Forest.

"Regardless of what she's seen, I think we need to take my vision seriously," Saffra said. "We don't want Kane to have even a single stone. I know we've worked with Claire before she left to pin-point their locations. I think I have the remaining details, from what I've seen, to find them."

Reyr-not-Talon blinked. Gods, it was just so damn strange to see him like this. "Are you suggesting that we send someone to retrieve them?"

"I'm *suggesting* that you send me to do it," she said.

Nearly everyone in the room began protesting at once. "You cannot be serious," Reyr said at the same time Koldis said, "That could take months." Then of course Feowen brought up the unicorns, and how the sprites had ways of moving quickly—more quickly than dragons could fly. So, it ought to be *them* who set out.

"If you think I'd let you do this alone—" Bedelth growled into her ear.

"I don't," she all but gasped at the feel of him so close, at the warmth that spread over her. "I was hoping you'd be with me."

"Oh." A slow smile crept over his face. She felt heat rising to her cheeks. The others were still arguing. "I think I'd like that. An adventure, just the two of us—"

The room fell quiet.

"You will not be going," Reyr said.

Bedelth lifted his brows in challenge. The two of them had been at odds lately. Probably because she'd been inserting herself into Reyr's business more than usual. He had a persona to uphold, after all. "I'd like to know why you think my mate is unfit for this task," Bedelth demanded.

Reyr expelled a long, suffering sigh. "I need you here, Bedelth. We—"

"You have Talon's other shields," Bedelth pointed out. "You have Claire's guards. You really *don't*. Much as you think you can't do this, Reyr, you can."

"What about the unicorns?" Feowen said.

"They are in the forest," Jeanine said, piping up from her vantage point.

"Right but—"

"We'd have to travel to the forest *first*," Bedelth pointed out. "To retrieve them. We'd need an envoy to lead us to wherever they are. Who knows if they'd be willing to carry us. Saffra alone has seen the places where the stones are hidden, the landscapes and terrain. We can pinpoint that to the guesses we've placed on the map, and go searching. It could take some time, regardless."

Feowen exhaled. "You're right. Besides, we should be here in case our queen returns."

Saffra chewed on her lower lip. "As long as Bedelth is willing to fly me, then I am going."

"I am more than willing," he teased, sending her a flirty look.

Reyr huffed, as if to say, *mates*, with exasperation. "Fine. If you insist on doing this, I'm not exactly your actual king—"

"But you are, while Talon is gone," Saffra pointed out. "So we'd rather have your blessing."

"Yes. All right. This is important. So...I give you my blessing to go."

"You're really going all by yourselves?" Desaree chided, after she'd returned from the market and heard of their meeting. She had deposited a basket on the table, laden with rare ingredients that Saffra needed for some of her brews. Saffra sifted through it while they talked. "Verath and I should be going with you."

"You're needed here," Saffra said, though that wasn't necessarily true.

Desaree hated being left out—they all knew that. But…"I want this time with Bedelth, just he and I. I know it's selfish. That I shouldn't even be thinking of myself during a time like this. During a situation like this. The stones are our priority, yes. But, I want some time for the two of us to solidify our bond. Not—not like that. Don't look at me like that."

"You're still intent on waiting?" Desaree asked, staring at her with disbelieving eyes. It was easy for her to judge, seeing as she and Verath weren't mates. They had been enjoying each other's beds for a while now.

"Bedelth, like Koldis, is trying to be honorable. They both want to wait until the king amends the law before they take mates…officially speaking."

"Ugh, but how can you stand it?!"

"There are…" Saffra's cheeks warmed. "There are plenty of *other* things we can do."

"True." Desaree's eyes glittered with mischief and a knowing smile spread across her face. "Well then, I suppose the two of you will certainly enjoy your alone time."

Saffra snorted.

Jocelyn bustled into the room, a stack of clothes in hand. Her face was hidden behind it, but her muffled voice carried as she said, "Quit being a bad influence on her, Des. She needs to stay focused. They need to find the stones."

"Yes, yes," Desaree said, waving a dismissive hand. "She'll find some stones all right."

There was a gasp, then the pile of clothes in Jocelyn's arms tumbled to the floor as they all burst into raucous giggles. They moved to collect everything and spent the remaining time together speculating.

Jeanine joined partway through, to keep them company. "How long do you think you'll be gone?" she asked.

This was one of the things that left her with misgivings. "I really don't know. Could be a month, two, six? Do you think… Do you think Claire will be angry with me for leaving you when she asked—?"

"Oh, stop!" Desaree said, chiding her. "We all know how important this is. Even Claire—"

"She was going to treat the task as a honeymoon," Jocelyn pointed out, trying to lighten the mood.

"Regardless," Desaree said, "Saffra has seen the locations, even if there isn't some kind of written signpost saying *'blue dragonstone here'* with the name of a cave...or what have you."

"You're the only one who can do this," Jeanine assured her, helping to calm some of the turmoil in her stomach.

She took a deep breath, then nodded. "Hopefully I can be quick. But, until I return, I'm relying on the three of you to keep them in line, yes?"

Jeanine let out a very unfeminine snort before shooting Desaree a knowing look. "That shouldn't be an issue, since we've got at least two of them wrapped around our fingers."

"Exactly," Desaree agreed.

DINNER THAT NIGHT was held in the king's tower dining room. They decided on a more intimate affair as a way to bid her and Bedelth farewell. Servants filled the table with platters of food, and they enjoyed a small feast. Sprites, drengr, and humans alike ate in companionable comfort. Though the sprites only partook in the non-meat options, of which there were plenty.

Their meal wasn't anything like it could have been, had Claire and Talon been present. Their absence cast a dark shadow over everything. But they tried to lighten the mood with stories and jokes. Bedelth often reached for her knee under the table, giving it a reassuring squeeze.

She was both nervous and excited for the journey to come. Usually, her visions were things she relayed to others but didn't act upon. This one was different, and she was going to help everyone by playing her own part in their fight against Kane.

Her eyes collided with Desaree's across the table. Verath leaned in and whispered something in Des's ear that made her grin. Saffra couldn't help but smile in return, at the sight of them—

A clanking filled the room as Reyr-not-Talon used his cutlery to gain their attention. "I would like to propose a toast," he said, his voice solemn. He stood and lifted his goblet. The rest of them followed. "You cannot choose your blood, but you *can* choose your family. I have found mine. I would fly into battle with every single one of you." His eyes flicked around the table, holding each of them captive. Even the sprites. "So, to family found and family kept. To fighting for a world free of a sorcerer who would try to ensnare us, to Saffra's quest to regain the missing dragonstones, and to our king and queen, wherever they may be, whatever they may be doing, may they find their way back to us."

"Hear, hear," they all echoed, clinking their goblets before drinking. Every eye in the room was glossy with emotion. Saffra blinked away her welling tears and caught sight of Desaree doing the same. Jocelyn bumped her shoulder in solidarity, offering a quick, reassuring smile. Then, Bedelth squeezed her hand. She was surrounded by so many people she cared for, even loved, Bedelth especially. Reyr-not-Talon was right. A person couldn't choose their blood, but they could always, *always* choose their family. While she loved her own family dearly, Bedelth hadn't been so lucky. But her mate had found a new family in the people surrounding them and she couldn't have been happier about that.

# CHAPTER 3
# HER MOTHER'S COOKING

*Austar Wilderness*

Saffra exhaled with delight. The sight stretched out below her was both familiar and unfamiliar all at once. Austar. Her homeland.

They'd been flying for days. She'd done what she'd been too afraid to do the first time she and Bedelth had taken a journey together. She'd gone ungloved and allowed him into her mind.

She appreciated the pace they set, flying by day, resting by night. In the air, they exchanged thoughts and memories and stories. At night, they exchanged gentle caresses, kisses, and heated moments. Her cheeks burned whenever she thought of the way he touched her, the way he left her gasping and satisfied.

*"Are you excited to see your family?"* Bedelth asked. Her stomach swooped. *"I'll take that as a yes,"* came his reply. She wondered if he was likewise excited to meet them. *"I am quite excited. But also..."*

*"Nervous?"* she finished for him.

Sharing thoughts was still new. They finished each other's sentences. They said a lot without actually saying anything. They shared emotions, and sometimes it was hard to discern whose was whose.

*"You'll get used to it,"* he said.

*"Oh? Speaking from experience?"* she teased.

A draconic grumble vibrated his chest, the sensation reverberating against her legs. *"Careful with that smart mouth of yours, mate."*

*"Why? Are you going to punish me—?"* A squeal broke from her lips. They were suddenly diving, plummeting headfirst towards the land far below. "Okay! Okay! I'll be good," she screamed, her words mixed with laughter and the rushing wind that whistled past her ears. Her heart pounded and adrenaline flooded her body. "Bedelth!" she cried, when he didn't pull up.

The ground surged up to meet them. Her heartbeat came faster and faster. She tightened her grip on his neck spikes.

*"Relax, mate."* Bedelth would never hurt her. She didn't need him to say it. Still, it was hard to be rational when it looked like they were seconds from certain death.

A heavy pressure, like hands pushing down on her shoulders, pressed against her as he finally pulled level, swooping mere feet above the land. "If you *ever* do that again!" she screamed, smacking his scales, which hurt her hand and did nothing but amuse him.

*"Then, what?"* he teased.

*"Then...then I'll stop talking to you."*

He made a sound in the back of his throat, a growl more than anything. *"Little mate, you realize that when we are mated and begin training together, you will have to do a lot more than dive."*

She licked her lips. *"Like...like what?"*

He sent her a projection of a rider jumping into freefall, only to be caught midair. She gasped. *"They're called trust falls. Every rider must perform them as a part of training."*

A prickle of unease chased its way down her spine. *"I... I don't want to do that."*

Bedelth let out a low growl. A dominant warning. It set the hairs of her arms on end with eagerness and curiosity. *"You will, because you are my mate, and my mate fears nothing."*

But he was wrong. There were plenty of things she feared. He knew that too, because he could see into her mind. Still, he didn't push, didn't say anything about it.

Taking cues from her memories, he navigated them to the cottage that had once been her whole world. It had been more than a decade since she'd lived here, on the outskirts of Brushbridge, near one of the gates. She wondered, not for the first time, where in Claire's world the Austar gate led. Wondered what would happen if they abandoned their mission to locate the stones and instead, went to Claire's world to bring her back.

*"Trust that our king knows what he's doing. That he will bring her back safely,"* Bedelth said. She wanted to. She really did. But so much time had passed. *"We have our mission, Talon has his."*

Bedelth was right.

The heavy thoughts were pushed from her mind as the sight of her family's beautiful cottage grew larger. They descended towards it. A cry erupted from below. Her mother waved to them with a towel in hand. She'd been hanging laundry, from the looks of it.

Such a simple life, those days where she worked alongside her siblings and helped her mother prepare food, wash dishes, hang clothes. Now, Saffra had servants to do it all. Her parents could have opted for servants, too. She sent them home a healthy portion of her earnings. But they didn't want that kind of life for them or their children. They took pride in doing everything themselves. Instead, they squirreled the money away for emergencies.

Bedelth landed and her mother ran towards them.

She was sliding off Bedelth's back, breaking their connection, before she could process her movements. She sprinted straight for her mother. Soon they were locked in an embrace, laughing, crying. Her father strode out of his detached workshop a few moments later. When he saw what the commotion was about, he grinned and picked them both up off the ground, twirling them around in a crushing hug.

He set them down, his eyes twinkling with delight.

"Where's Jordi and Rana," she asked, glancing around. She'd hoped her younger siblings would come out to greet them.

"They're at the market today." Her father glanced up at the sky. "Should be home in a few hours."

A throat cleared behind them, snapping her out of her hazy

excitement. "Oh, right," she breathed, suddenly hesitant. "Mother, Father, I'd like you to meet...my mate." Her brief hesitation didn't go unnoticed as Bedelth lifted an eyebrow in challenge. As if he was *daring* her to introduce him as anything less, when he was her *everything*.

"Mate?!" her mother gasped, placing a hand over her chest, wide-eyed with delight. "A king's shield, no less," her father said, chuckling. Because everyone knew who Bedelth was. Especially in this part of the kingdom. Both her parents knew what had happened with Daxton. There wasn't an ounce of judgement in their gazes.

Her father was the first to reach forward. "You can call me Ali, and this is my wife, Sahir."

"A true pleasure," Bedelth said, grinning as he clasped forearms with her father and then pulled her mother into a warm embrace that left Sahir's brown skin flushed. He already knew her parents' names. Had even met them in her memories. But he treated this as if it were the first time.

"Come, come, into the house," her mother tsked, ushering them inside where she poured tea and served little honey cakes. "Tell us what brings you here."

Saffra was content to scarf down cake after cake, relishing in the memories of her mother's baking. The food in Kastali Dun was said to be the best in the kingdom, but she would challenge anyone who dared, because Sahir's food was unparalleled.

Saffra slurped down an entire cup of mint tea before pouring another.

Bedelth did the talking. He told her parents about their journey, keeping the majority of the truth hidden. According to him, they were flying through Austar on business for the king. Their journey would take them north afterward, and then up to the farther reaches of the kingdom. They didn't mention the stones or any of the other sensitive information.

"And you will be staying with us for the night," her mother asked. Except there wasn't a question in her voice. It was too stern for that.

"I have a feeling we don't have a choice?" Bedelth chuckled.

"None whatsoever," Sahir said, satisfied. "You'll take our room. Ali and I will have Saffra's old room."

"Nonsense, we don't want to put you out," Bedelth growled. "We're happy to sleep under the stars as we have the past few nights."

"I will not speak of it," Sahir admonished in true motherly fashion, making Bedelth sink a little lower in his chair. Ali and Saffra chuckled, used to her tactics. "You are our guest, and a shield, no less."

Saffra couldn't help but notice the stark contrast between her parents and Bedelth's. Not once had they questioned the idea of them being mates, even though he was a king's shield. They never questioned his honor at stake. Never once judged the situation.

Instead, they beamed with excitement and even pride.

Not for the first time, Saffra was grateful that she had them, even if she almost never got to see them.

They chatted a while longer before her parents went back to their chores. She spent the rest of the afternoon showing him around. First through the cottage, then the property, and finally, her father's workshop. Bedelth was enamored.

Her father was a bowyer, the finest craftsman in the region. He had customers for hundreds of miles who came specifically for hand made, custom bows. He also took his wares to various markets, sometimes even as far as Kastali Dun. Not often, though. It had been too long since she'd last seen him.

Bedelth asked Ali question after question about his process, going so far as to assist on his current project. Saffra was content to sit back and watch them work. Bedelth was a quick study. More importantly, he was respectful, reverent even. He never once acted superior despite their differences in status.

Jordi and Rana finally returned, stowing the cart in the barn and letting the horses out into the pasture to graze. "Oh, my gods!" Saffra cried upon seeing them approach the workshop. "When did you both grow up?!"

"Saffra?" Rana lifted her skirts and ran to her. They collided in a hug, spinning and giggling, clutching each other for dear life. "But, what are you doing here? Is everything well in the capital?"

"We're just here to visit," she explained, ignoring the second part of Rana's question. "Passing through on the king's business."

"And who is this?" Jordi asked while she and Rana were still clutching each other. His voice had grown much deeper—almost like her father's. He straightened his shoulders, puffing out his chest to look more formidable. Which was really just comical, considering he was no match in size for a king's shield.

"Oh, Jordi!" She moved from Rana and pinched Jordi's cheeks, just like she used to when he was a boy, because it had always irritated him so much. "Look at you. What are you now? Seventeen?"

"Eighteen. Gods! Please stop," he cried, swatting at her hands, his gaze darting between Saffra and the shield looming nearby. "Are you going to tell us who that is?"

"This," she said, grabbing Bedelth's wrist and dragging him forward, "Is Bedelth. My mate."

Jordi made a choking sound. "Your—your mate?!"

"Lord Bedelth? As in, the king's shield?!" Rana breathed. She was just a year younger than Jordi. At seventeen, she had grown into a stunning beauty.

"Yes, the one and only," Saffra teased.

Bedelth reached out and grasped Jordi's forearm before doing the same with Rana, who blushed furiously and looked at the ground.

"You'll be staying a while?" Jordi asked, a hopeful glint in his eyes as he furtively continued to glance at Bedelth. She could already picture it, the way her younger brother would idolize him.

"Just for tonight," she said, sighing wistfully. "Time is of the essence, I'm afraid."

"Well, we will just have to make the most of it, won't we," Rana declared, linking their arms together and dragging her away, leaving Jordi to bask in Bedelth's presence.

❧

DINNER WAS SPECTACULAR. She and Rana helped their mother prepare chickpea bowls with rice and diced vegetables. It reminded her so much of her childhood. The entire house smelled like spices. She was especially excited for the flatbread that Sahir made on occasion, especially special occasions like this. They even enjoyed a dark celebration tea with their meal.

"We don't get food like this in the capital," Bedelth managed, all but shoveling spoonfuls in his mouth. Thank the gods her mother had the sense to use such a large pot for all of them. He'd eat them out of house and home, a male of his size. Her mother only beamed and encouraged him to refill his bowl not twice, but a third time. Jordi looked like he wanted to keep up, but gave up after two.

"It's true," Saffra said. "There's a mix, of course, from different parts of the kingdom. But food like this?" She ate another forkful and sighed. "The offer stands, Mama, if you lot ever want to move to the capital. I could eat like this for days and days."

"Oh! But that would be wonderful," Rana began, her expression brightened. Saffra made a mental note to invite her sister to the capital once all this business with Kane died down.

Sahir tsked. "Nonsense. This food is only special because you don't get it often. As soon as you eat it every day, you'll be dying for your capital city faire."

Ali chuckled, throwing his wife a loving look.

"So," Sahir said, clearing her throat. "When can we expect an invitation for your ceremony?"

Saffra choked, swallowing down her mouthful and washing it down with a gulp of tea. Bedelth huffed and said, "Once the political climate calms down, Sahir, you will receive the first invitation we send. Saffra and I are waiting until the king amends the law. He's got more important matters at present, as do we all."

Sahir nodded, understanding. "Of course, what with the war and all. Well, whenever it is, you can expect all of us to be there. We are so proud of you my love," she added, reaching over and squeezing her oldest daughter's wrist. "We never expected you to have such a life, to move to the capital, work for the king! Your father brags to everyone in the village every chance he gets."

"Me?!" Ali sputtered. "How about you, woman? With all your little hens when they come over for tea. It's Saffra this and Saffra that!"

Saffra's cheeks turned hot.

"Oh, gods, here we go!" Rana muttered. Jordi elbowed his sister.

Sahir harrumphed. "Well, *now* I'll have even more to brag about. Your father and I never expected you to mate a drengr, a shield, no less." Sahir shared a look with her husband, who nodded in agreement. "I would've been happy to simply have you home with us, to raise you to womanhood and watch you follow your heart. But this? It makes me burst with happiness."

Saffra's throat tightened. She blinked back tears. "Thank you Mama, Papa," she managed. Bedelth ran a reassuring hand down the length of her back.

"Gods, we'll never live up to your greatness," Jordi teased.

"Oh stop." She reached out and managed to pinch his cheek again before he swatted her away. She couldn't help but laugh.

After the meal was cleared, they sipped more tea and enjoyed another round of cakes. Bedelth, Jordi, and her father talked in hushed voices beside the fire. Most of their conversation was about the war in the east, the goblins and how they'd raided so many villages. They also shared stories, mostly Bedelth, of some of his more daring fights during his long lifetime.

Saffra's lids were drooping by the time Sahir emerged from the bedroom and announced that the bed was made up and ready for them. Only then did she realize what it meant. She and Bedelth, for all their kissing and touching, had never actually shared a bed together. Sure, they'd traveled and slept under the stars, side by side.

This was different.

"I'll be along shortly," Bedelth told her. She got the impression that he wanted a few more minutes with her father and brother, so she left them to prepare for bed. She spent a few quiet moments with Rana, taking in the way her room had changed over the years.

She was crawling beneath the blankets when Bedelth appeared. He glanced around the cozy space before his gaze fell to her and heated. The way he stared sent hot tingles shooting straight to her belly.

"Is this…going to work?" The bed was rather small, certainly not made to accommodate a drengr male.

"I'll manage," he all but growled. Then he began shedding his weapons, his tunic, his boots. All that remained were his pants. He was aware of her gaze raking over him. How could she not look?! Especially when she noticed his growing arousal.

Oh the cruelty of it!

Their first experience sharing a bed together and she would die before she so much as kissed him in her parents bed, beneath their roof with them merely in the room next door, and her siblings a couple doors down. The effort of keeping her hands to herself would be torture.

She scooted all the way to the edge, giving him room. He climbed beneath the blankets, his feet hanging off the end. A giggle erupted at the sight of him. "You know, I send home a handsome stipend to them," she found herself saying. "You'd think they would buy a bigger bed."

"I think I know why they haven't," he said, chuckling.

"Oh? Do tell."

"How about I show you instead?" With that, he blew out the bedside candle then wrapped his body around hers. Oh. Of course. Small bed meant only one way for sleeping, fully entwined together. His thigh was nudged between hers, his breath hot on the nape of her neck. The feel of his warm skin against her bare arms left her covered in gooseflesh.

"Relax," he grumbled. "Sleep, mate. This might be the last bed we get for a while."

She exhaled, willing her muscles to loosen. He nuzzled the back of her neck, left a soft kiss there, then fell into a steady breathing pattern. She lay there a long time, listening to the sound of him, to the sound of her parents and siblings settling down. Eventually, the house quieted and she let Bedelth's gentle breaths lull her to sleep, with a smile on her face and happiness in her heart.

# CHAPTER 4
# JUST A GLIMPSE

Jovari ignored the strain of his wings, pushing himself past his limits. He flanked King Talon on the right. They'd set a relentless pace. No, *Talon* had set a relentless pace.

The initial leg of their journey had been the hardest. Finding ways to communicate with humans, learn the geography of a new world, navigate it. Most people didn't use paper maps anymore, apparently—which was preposterous!—because they relied on tiny hand-held devices called *phones* for *internet* and *GPS*. Things that were absolutely foreign to him. He'd only gotten a taste of this world the last time he'd been here. That hadn't prepared him for *this*.

Talon was adapting surprisingly well, even if he couldn't reach Claire's mind. There was a barrier of some sort. Spiderwebs, he'd called it. Like her mind was locked up tight with a sticky substance he couldn't cut through. Whatever Kane had given her—whatever he had *done* to her—had closed her off from them.

Jovari's blood boiled every time he considered it. Every time he thought of what Kane had done to his queen. His perfect, selfless queen. If he allowed himself to dwell on it, he'd do something reckless. It was already taking a great deal of strength to keep Talon in line.

*"Let's land in those hills,"* he said. *"We can afford a few hours of rest, my king."* Talon's answer was an annoyed growl. The king would starve himself, fly until his body stopped working, literally kill himself to get to her, if Jovari didn't step in, which he'd done repeatedly over the past week.

The worst had been crossing the ocean. It had taken two days, riding the wind currents without rest. They'd both collapsed onto a deserted stretch of beach after reaching land, stolen a few hours of sleep, only to take to the skies again, flying north-west.

He descended toward the hills in the distance. Roads stretched and curved across the landscape, with tiny vehicles traversing their lengths, headlights casting white pools of light across the otherwise dark landscape. They found an area that looked mostly uninhabited before dropping through the trees, low enough to transform and land on their feet. Dawn was approaching, but it was still dark enough to remain in the shadows. They'd have to be more careful now that they'd arrived in the United States of America.

Claire's home country. They were close. So close.

He spotted a nearby dwelling, its lights shining like a beacon through the dark trees. He got Talon's attention, motioning with his head. Talon hesitated, then nodded. They crept over to it, quietly ascending the back porch stairs. *"This one doesn't have cameras,"* he noted, relieved. They'd learned *that* the hard way early on.

Cameras. Little devices that recorded pictures. Those pictures then showed up on a thing called a screen. People could even view the recorded pictures on those hand held phones they carried in their pockets. The cameras alerted homeowners about intruders, which, both he and Talon obviously were. Not that they meant anyone harm.

The wood on the old porch protested the weight of two grown males, so they moved cautiously. As they peered through the back window, they caught sight of a television. Jovari's shoulders relaxed. He heard Talon's relieved exhale beside him. They shared a look, before returning their gaze to the television.

Humans loved watching these shows they called *news broadcasts*, especially in the morning. This discovery had gone a long way in acclimating them to Claire's world. First, by orienting them as to their whereabouts, and second, by helping them understand where Claire had ended up. That she'd been a popular topic for news stations around the world had worked in their favor. Though, it hadn't always been easy. They'd come across many languages on their journey halfway across Claire's world—from Greece to the United States—unable to understand most of what they saw. But pictures didn't require explanations, and that's what they had relied upon.

"...our sources are still working to uncover the latest surrounding the girl with the glowing tattoos," came the muted voice of a newscaster. At least they could understand what was being said. "Marshal Whitley attempted to make contact earlier this week. Claire Evans and her family were not interested in offering a statement."

A man holding a coffee cup padded into view, standing in the kitchen. He lifted a remote, turning up the volume. The dial on his kitchen clock showed it was 5:30am. He was half dressed.

Jovari ignored him, instead focusing on the television.

An image of Claire flashed across the screen, followed by footage of her home, a camera crew being escorted off the property by a local sheriff. A low growl left King Talon's throat. *"I'll shred them to pieces,"* he said, his body nearly vibrating with tension. *"How dare they make a spectacle of her?!"*

Except, that's all the public had done. Talon was close to snapping. Jovari took a sideways step, offering the king comfort. *"Can't shred them if you're not there with her."*

*"I'll be there soon enough."*

*"Then we'd better get some rest so we can resume our journey, my king."* Jovari put a hand on Talon's shoulder, squeezing. The king hesitated, then nodded.

They crept away from the back porch and back into the trees, looking for a place to catch a few hours of rest. The sun was already peeking up over the horizon when they finally sank onto the bed of pine needles littering the ground. The woods were wild, with vines of lush growth overtaking most trees—a mix of pines, oak, and some other variants unfamiliar to him. The canopy overhead was a good shield, even if the bugs were near unbearable.

Birds were already chirping. The drone of cicadas created a perfect background of white noise. Soon, the heat would be near unbearable, the humidity, too. They'd take to the skies then, if only to cool off.

"What if she can't remember me?" Talon broke the silence, gazing emptily into the woods. A question he'd asked too many times. They'd discussed it at length the first time the news had broken, when sources had claimed Claire couldn't remember anything about her ordeal. Couldn't remember how she'd gotten from Indiana to France with a body covered in luminescent tattoos.

Jovari looked at his king, his heart aching for him. "You're her mate," he said. "She will know you in her heart, even if she doesn't know you in her mind."

"I cannot bear it. If she looks at me and does not know me. What if...?" Talon winced.

"Spit it out."

"What if she sees my scars and...and recoils from me? Fears me?"

"You forget that she has *never* recoiled from you. Not even the first day she faced you."

"But that was different," Talon argued, almost petulant. "She knew how I felt about her then, that I thought her guilty of a great crime. She hated me before ever seeing me. That hate allowed her to look past...this." He waved a hand over himself.

"Talon," Jovari chided. "You know her better than any of us. You know her mind *and* her heart. What does your gut say?"

Talon's throat bobbed. His head rested against the tree behind him and he closed his eyes. At last, he said, "She is too pure, too good, too kind to run from me no matter *what* I look like."

"Exactly. Stop letting your fear manipulate you. Get some rest. Your exhaustion is clouding your judgment."

A loud exhale and then, "You're right. But you first. I'll take the first watch."

They fell silent, then. He propped his back against a tree and closed his eyes, falling asleep immediately.

Hours later, they continued their journey northwest. It was difficult, keeping out of sight, flying low enough to go unnoticed by airplanes but not too low to be spotted in the sky by humans. They relied on the pull Talon felt, the mate connection guiding them to Claire. Every so often, they tried to call out to her, mind to mind, but their nearing proximity did nothing for the barriers caging her mind, caging whatever magic allowed them to reach her.

Hours blurred together. They spoke little. Both were too exhausted to converse, too tense and worried to voice their concerns.

It was dark when at last, the familiar sight of Claire's farmhouse came into view. The lights were on, glowing like a beacon, beckoning them. They landed in a nearby corn field, just out of sight. Talon shifted then, falling to his hands and knees, gasping as he tried to take in air. Jovari could barely keep his feet. He was so exhausted, his vision darkened at the edges; he had to blink to see clearly. The only reason he didn't collapse beside Talon was because it was his duty—*his honor*—to watch his king's back.

A sense of relief settled over his shoulders. The sight before him almost didn't feel real. They'd made it, even if they were worse for wear.

Talon collected himself, then climbed to his feet. He took a few gasping breaths, then took off at a quick pace, a determined set to his shoulders. His face said everything—exactly what he intended.

A rush of panic seized Jovari. Mustering what little energy he had left, he staggered forward, grabbing Talon by the arm. Stopping him. "You cannot," he warned, hoping Talon didn't attack him for it. "If you go in there now, this will end badly."

"I don't care," Talon growled, shooting him a poisonous glare.

But the king didn't pull his arm free. "My mate is in there, Jovari. You would dare keep me from her? I didn't come all this way—"

"*Think*, Talon. She has forgotten who she is. She's probably scared, even confused. You yourself are a frightening sight, especially right now, with your wild eyes and scarred face. You cannot simply storm into her home. Her parents will call the authorities. They'll think you're just another person chasing her story. *She* might even call the authorities. You are not a king here—do not forget that."

Talon's shoulders slumped. His gaze remained fixed on the farmhouse, his chest rising and falling in heavy bursts. They studied the property from the shadows of the cornfield. "I... I just... I need to see her. To know she's safe."

Jovari exhaled. "Her bedroom window is that one." He pointed. "If you need to get sight of her, then fine. But don't you dare risk exposing yourself. Not until we have a plan of approach," he said. Talon scoffed. "I am serious. Give me your word that you won't do something reckless, or I'll do what I must to keep you from blowing this whole operation."

Talon growled. When it was evident that Jovari wouldn't back down, he snarled and said, "Fine. I won't expose myself."

Jovari nodded and released him. He kept close as Talon strode forward. They crept through the yard, locating a portion of the porch that looked sturdy. Together, they silently climbed onto the awning before finding Claire's window.

The sharp intake of Talon's breath told him enough. His king had caught sight of his queen. Despite his desperation, he held back, allowing Talon to look his fill. A shudder wracked the king's body, as if seeing his mate for the first time in weeks had unlocked something deep inside of him.

"Well?" he asked.

"She's with someone."

"What do you mean?" His panic flared again. He didn't wait for Talon to answer. Instead, he scooted closer until the two of them could share the space beneath Claire's window. He peeked over the window sill, blinking against the bright light of her room. The first thing he saw was his queen. Something unspooled in his chest, something that had been wrapped tight. She was alive and well. Unharmed. Whole. Even if her mind wasn't.

Then his eyes fell on the woman beside her. He blinked, taking in her loud pink hair and dainty features. *Pink hair?!* How was that even possible?

*"Is she a threat?"* he found himself asking.

*"It doesn't look that way,"* Talon said. *"Actually, I remember her from Claire's memories. Only, her hair was different. Blonde like Claire's, instead of pink. They're childhood friends, I believe."*

Jovari watched the scene before him. Both women were on the floor, applying a colored polish to their toenails. The pink haired woman said something and Claire's whole face lit up before she giggled. Then they both burst into fits of laughter.

*"She seems...happy,"* Talon mused, his voice laced with relief.

*"Indeed, she does."* And damn, that did something to him. Gratitude bubbled up in his chest, radiating outward. He'd seen the way his queen had looked on the news. He'd seen the hopeless desperation on her face, the confusion, the upset.

She looked like a different person compared to then, all because of this strange, pink-haired woman—

*"We need to find a way to speak with her,"* Talon was saying.

*"Her friend?"*

*"No, you dunce. Claire. Gods."*

*"Right. We need to get her alone, somewhere she won't be inclined to contact authorities when she first sees us. Then we can explain who we are, and who she is."*

*"Do you think she'll believe us?"*

*"I think if we give her the whole story, she won't have any choice."*

*"But..."*

Jovari pulled his gaze away to look at Talon. *"But what?"*

*"It's not enough, telling her. I need her to remember."* Talon's throat bobbed. Jovari reached out and squeezed his shoulder. *"I can't bear it, if she can't remember the way she feels about me. I need... I need her."*

*"We'll make her remember, Talon. You'll make her remember. We'll figure out a way. I promise."*

Except, he had no business making such a promise because there was no promise of certainty. No guarantee that she'd be free of whatever poison Kane had inflicted. So he said the words because he needed to hear them just as much as Talon. Because they both needed hope. Both needed to do whatever necessary to get her memories back. The alternative was too horrible to consider.

CHAPTER 5

# THE FOREST'S MAGIC

*Kastali Dun*

Reyr stared into the fire, sipping his wine. He should have poured himself something stronger, but it wasn't wise. This way, at least he could drink and keep his wits about him. The keep was quiet, the hour creeping well past midnight. Still, he was not in bed.

How did Talon do it for hundreds of years? Day in and day out. Balancing the cares of the kingdom in one hand, and his life in the other. He had never truly understood until now. No wonder the king had such a temper. He was impressed Talon wasn't fully insane—

*"Something's happened."* Koldis's voice interrupted his silence. Immediately, his body went on full alert, muscles tensing. *"Taylynn's just arrived with Fright. She won't tell me what's going on. Can we call a meeting?"*

*"At three o'clock in the morning?"* he demanded.

But that was the way of it, wasn't it? They'd instituted an unspoken rule, made it a point to gather together whenever anything serious required discussing, or decisions needed making. Whoever was present, at least.

44

Saffra had been gone for weeks, so the rest of them were carrying on as best they could.

*"It seems serious,"* Koldis warned him. *"And you know Taylynn isn't one to overreact."*

*"Yes, fine. Gather them."*

He pushed aside his worry—his fear. Talon and Claire had been gone *months*. His stomach ached just thinking about it. Yet, they'd expected this. Planned for it even, using him as a body-double.

His mind went back to those days after Cyrus went missing. When one month had stretched into another, and then another. When Talon had been worried sick, more temperamental than ever. He'd sent three of his own shields to search for Cyrus when he could no longer risk the uncertainty. When was *too long* long enough? When should he make the same call, to send someone after Talon and Jovari. After Claire. With Bedelth gone, there were only four of them here. He couldn't risk it.

He took a big gulp of wine and considered. Cyrus had been gone more than half a year, seven or eight months. He frowned, considering. How long had he been with Claire? A week? He swore under his breath, surging to his feet—

Koldis strode in, hand in hand with the sprite princess.

"Time is different there," he blurted, vocalizing his realization. "We never questioned it because we were too fraught over Cyrus's death. Too caught up in what was happening to Claire when we reached the capital. But he was gone for months, even if he was only in her company for days."

Koldis blinked, frowning at him. "What's this about, now?"

"Time—in Claire's world!" he cried. Koldis wasn't keeping up. He looked at Taylynn. "Did you know?"

Her brows rose. "About time? Yes."

He swore again, louder this time, then hurled his goblet into the fireplace. The wine exploded out of it, metal thudding against the logs, causing one to split. An eruption of sparks and embers followed.

"Gods, man, get yourself together." Koldis gripped his shoulder and gave him a little shake.

Reyr took a deep, steadying breath, then ran a hand through his hair, trying to pick at the snarls. It was a wonder it hadn't all fallen out. "We should have known," he scoffed. "We should have known when Talon went through the gate. Should have known it would take an age for him to return to us. I never would have agreed—"

Koldis snorted at the same time Taylynn said, "You know that is not true. You would have done whatever your king asked of you, no matter the situation."

He made a distressed sound in the back of his throat. Mostly because she was right. He would have done anything Talon asked of him.

At least Taylynn didn't berate him for being so blind. They'd had all the evidence, all the pieces right there in front of them, but they'd never truly discussed it. They might not get Talon and Claire back for many more months, if not years.

The room began spinning. "I...need to sit down," he breathed, then collapsed into his chair—Talon's chair.

The door opened and a sleepy Desaree shuffled in, Verath on her heels. Verath looked none too pleased to be pulled from his bed at this hour. Not that the drengr needed much sleep. He was probably more irritated that they'd pulled Desaree into this, more than anything.

Jocelyn followed, along with Dallin.

The sprites slept in the lower levels of the tower. They were summoned as well.

"We have a problem," Taylynn said when everyone was settled. Desaree and Jocelyn, falling into old habits, grabbed drinks for those who wanted them. It had taken Verath pulling Desaree onto his lap to settle her. He'd been unusually clingy since her near death experience. Rightfully so.

"We have a lot of problems," Verath growled, "so you're going to have to be more specific."

"It's lovely to see you too, *Verath*," Taylynn purred.

A low growl sounded from Koldis's throat, a threat and a warning, that none ought to cross his mate. Gods, they'd all been at each other's throats lately. Despite the fact that they relied on each other now more than ever, they were also quicker to bicker. Quicker to anger. Quicker to lob insults.

Every single one of them was stretched thin on patience. Him, most of all. He felt as if he might shatter at any moment, a mixture of loss and stress, fear and uncertainty.

"Forgive me," Verath said, exhaling. "Please, explain."

Taylynn took a deep breath. "It took me some time to discover it, tied up as I've been with the dragon eggs. I came as soon as I could. The magic of the forest is broken."

The room fell silent. Then—

"What do you mean, broken?!" Feowen stepped forward, frowning. "The forest doesn't *break*. That's...that doesn't even make sense."

"But it does," Taylynn said, blinking. She was calm, even now. Too calm. Too ancient. It was almost creepy. How did Koldis stand it? "The magic is tied to the king tree, and the king tree is tied to its queen—our queen. Who is no longer in this world."

Several of the spriten guards swore.

"Well, that indeed is a problem," Koldis said.

"One I've no idea how to fix," she admitted.

"Can it be fixed?" Reyr asked.

"Oh, certainly," she said, sarcastically. "It just requires the return of our queen."

Reyr scrubbed a hand over his face. "Which we discovered as of a few minutes ago could be years." His voice cracked on *years*. Several voices in the room erupted. What did he mean, *years*? So he explained what he'd only just realized about the time difference.

The sprites didn't look as shocked as the drengr, as Desaree and Jocelyn. Never mind that Bedetlh and Saffra were gone. He could only imagine what their reactions would be upon discovering this. At least they need not worry about their king and queen returning before them.

"What do we do in the meantime?" Gorded asked, stepping away from the wall where he'd been leaning. "If the forest cannot protect itself, our blessed city is also unprotected. And the stones?"

"That's my biggest concern," Taylynn mused. "We have two

options. The first, hope no one notices that the forest is currently merely a forest, and stays away. It *does* have a reputation, after all. The second? I get the stones out, and we find a different way to protect them—"

"The last time the stones left the forest, Kane tried to take them," Desaree warned.

"Kane is currently working to gather the other stones he's hidden, isn't he?" Koldis asked. "Based on Saffra's vision?"

Taylynn lifted her brows, glancing around the room. "I take it that's why Saffra and Bedelth are not here?" Koldis nodded. "Then perhaps we use this distraction to our advantage."

"I'll come with you—" Koldis said.

"You will not!" Reyr interrupted.

"You let Saffra and Bedelth go." Koldis lifted his brows in challenge.

"Because Saffra needed a mode of transportation and her mate would never allow it otherwise. *Your* mate is perfectly capable of handling herself."

"I'm going with her," Koldis said, a finality in his voice.

Reyr clenched his teeth. And *this* was why shields were not supposed to take mates. It turned them into overprotective ninnies. Not that he could blame either of them. He'd have done the same with Gemma. In fact, he'd do the same with Claire, even though she wasn't his.

Claire's cat—no longer a kitten—hopped into his lap. He absentmindedly stroked Batty's fur, reining in his frustration and worry. What difference would it make, having Koldis here or not? He still had all of Claire's guards. The thought of Kane getting the remaining two stones... No, he couldn't consider it. "What of Fright?" he asked.

"He will return to the hatching grounds. Some of the first eggs should hatch any day now."

A feminine squeal sounded. Jocelyn quickly covered her mouth, her brown skin flushing. "Sorry," she muttered. He knew all too well how badly the females of this group had wanted to be there for the initial hatching, to see the baby dragons.

His heart tightened thinking of Claire, at the thought of her missing this. Perhaps she'd get to see one of the later hatchings instead. Assuming she returned. Ever. There were still other females who hadn't yet laid eggs. Gods, he needed her here, needed Talon back. He missed them both so badly he ached. And not just because their jobs were too damned much.

"Fine," he said, rubbing his temples, trying to stave off his budding headache. "I cannot keep you here, Koldis. Do what must be done. Keep Kane from getting the stones. If we lose this kingdom before our king returns..."

For the first time, he saw a flash of worry on Taylynn's features. She caught her lower lip between her teeth. His brows pulled together. He didn't like her expression, not one bit. It was too unlike her. And that frightened him most of all.

TALON'S THRONE WAS COLD. His job, thankless. His people, demanding. Reyr had been holding court for months. Each day stretched into the next, endless, monotonous, draining. The only thing keeping him sane was his nightly flight. He'd taken up one of Talon's habits—many of his habits, really—but one that helped. Each evening he flew to Irelia island and back. He walked its shores, its ancient hatching grounds, the old ruins of a dragon clan lost to time. It helped clear his mind.

When time permitted, he sparred with Verath and Dallin. He was pleased with Dallin's progress, his mastery of the blade and other weapons. He'd taken to shadowing Verath in most of his duties and was a quick study.

A knock at his door startled him out of his thoughts. "Enter," he called. Taylynn walked in leading a dark-haired woman with blue eyes.

He frowned, looking the stranger over. Strangers weren't supposed to enter the king's tower. Not now that they were working doubly hard to ensure their secrets didn't slip. "What's this?" he demanded, tossing his quill on the desk.

"Claire's new body-double."

"I'm sorry. What?" He surged to his feet.

Taylynn laughed, the musical notes of her voice momentarily captivating. "I'm leaving with Koldis tonight, Your Majesty. This must be done before I go."

"This?! Her? You cannot possibly—"

"I absolutely can, and do."

"She could ruin us."

"I've sworn her to secrecy. I've bound her oath with magic. While I don't have Claire here to do a perfect replica, I know enough going from memory."

"This is preposterous," he cried, rounding the desk. The woman kept her eyes downturned, her expression blank. "How could you possibly think this would work? Never mind the body-double idea, but the fact that she's obviously a poor fit."

He sensed more than saw the woman flinch at his words.

"She will do fine," Taylynn lifted her chin. "Besides, this whole charade needs to work. Claire has been gone for months. You cannot explain away her absence any longer. Don't think I haven't heard that people are talking. The throne next to yours remains empty."

He hated that she was right. Hated that it felt like failing. That he couldn't do this alone anymore.

"And what? You think this—*this girl*—can simply step in and fill Claire's shoes? It's absurd. She could never. No one could. Claire is irreplaceable." He didn't miss the way the woman's cheeks flushed. Still, she kept her gaze downcast. "No. This isn't happening. Take her...home, or wherever it is that you found her."

"I can go," the woman said, her voice low. At the same time, Taylynn said, "I will do no such thing. You want this ruse to work? Then it must happen."

Gods damn it! His heart began to race. His eyes darted to the woman, assessing. She didn't even have the courage to look up at him.

"We haven't gathered to discuss it," he argued, hoping to stall. "The others won't—"

"The others have already agreed. I talked to them while you were managing court this morning."

He rocked his jaw back and forth, irritated. They were *supposed* to have meetings for this sort of thing. Decisions were made as a group. Then again, Taylynn hadn't been around when this habit began. Still, it felt as if she'd gone behind his back.

"I would advise, Your Majesty, that you do this," she said, leaving little argument in her voice. "The alternative could have catastrophic results. If Claire and Talon are gone for years—?"

He felt as though he might die if that happened.

"All right," he snapped, keeping his gaze on the woman before him, on her head of dark hair. "Fine. Do it." He pinched the bridge of his nose. "But how do you expect her to—what's her name?—to pull this off? She's nothing like Claire."

"Her *name* is Merrian. She merely needs to sit with you during court, at public dinners, be seen wandering the halls of the keep. The people of Dragonwall must see that their queen is hale."

He ground his teeth, holding back a growl. There were *so* many reasons why he didn't want to do this. None of which he wished to voice. Thus, he had no choice but to agree.

"Merrian," he said. The woman finally lifted her blue eyes to his. For a moment, he was captured by what he saw there. She might have appeared quiet and afraid, but there was fire in her gaze. Defiance too. Unlike most, she didn't shy away from the sight of Talon's face. "Do you know who I am, girl?"

Except, she wasn't a girl. Not even close. She had a woman's face and a woman's body.

"Yes, Your Majesty. I mean, that is to say, I know that you are not truly King Talon. That he is with his queen, away on business. That we must stand in for them until they return. I am sworn to secrecy. If I should try to tell any others—besides the king's inner circle—of who I am, the words will fail me."

Her voice was pleasing, though not as pleasing as Claire's. Despite the fire he'd seen in her eyes, she was fidgety and unsure of herself, twisting her fingers together as she spoke to him. She looked nothing like Claire, either, but that wouldn't matter once Taylynn worked her magic.

He let out a loud exhale. "Good."

Taylynn said, "You will need to help her with her mannerisms and behavior—"

"Desaree and Jocelyn can help with that." He waved a dismissive hand. "Or her handmaidens. I've got about six hundred missives to write,"—it was a vast exaggeration—"so unless you need anything more from me, take her and be done with it."

Taylynn eyed him. He didn't miss the irritation on her features. Likely because of the way he was dismissing her. But, he didn't care. He'd stopped caring about how his words and actions affected others weeks ago. Months ago?

It was unlike him, so unlike him. But what did they expect? Becoming someone else wasn't simply a cloak he could don and shed at will. He'd had to fully become something that wasn't him. Still, he was desperate for the day when he could abandon this role, go back to feeling like himself again.

"I'll complete the transformation, then set her up in the queen's chambers below. Feowen assured me they'd make all the arrangements to see her comfortably settled into the role."

"Good," he said, taking a seat at his desk. "I'll let him handle it, then." With that, he returned to his work without so much as a glance towards his new queen as she departed.

# CHAPTER 6
# LIVING A LIE

*Kastali Dun*

Merrian stared at herself in the mirror, touching her new face, studying her foreign features. She expelled a loud breath. In years' past, she'd never considered herself bad-looking, per se. But to wear the face of the queen? Gods, she looked positively divine.

Heat flushed her cheeks. She shouldn't think like that. It made her seem pathetic. There was nothing wrong with the way she *normally* looked, with her nearly midnight black hair and blue eyes. Her generous curves, wide hips, and gentle smile. She wasn't used to being skinny and toned. It felt...different. Not good or bad. Just different.

It was the turquoise markings though. That was the strangest bit of this. They scrolled across her skin—

A loud knock sounded before her bedroom door opened. "Forgive us, Your Majesty. But we must get started."

"Merrian," she corrected. "Or Mer, if you'd prefer."

"*Your Majesty*," the spriten woman returned, sounding only mildly exasperated. "Ayas Drollaya. We were told by our princess that we must use your titles and your disguise-name at all times."

*At all times?!* Her heart skipped a beat. "Even...even when we're alone like this?"

"Even so," the sprite woman said.

And so it began.

Would she even remember herself when this was all over? What she looked like? Who she was?

"I am Selphie Norin," the sprite woman said, pulling her from her dark thoughts. "This is Miera Balleth. We are Queen Claire's— *your*—handmaidens. Our common tongue is...improving. But, if you find our accent difficult to understand, please ask us to repeat."

"I think your accent and your common tongue is fine. I understand you well."

"Good." Selphie nodded.

Gods, they were so...ethereal. So *otherworldly*. To think, they'd be serving *her*. She'd never in all her life had someone to wait on her hand and foot. Sure, she'd been more privileged than most after discovering her magic. But this was...extreme.

"Where are you from?" Miera asked, striding forward to lay a gown across the bed.

"Oh. I... The north, initially. I trained there, mastered my magic with the mages at Northedge. I eventually made my way south. I've been living in Kastali Dun for almost ten years now."

Miera nodded. Arranging the fabric to her liking before glancing around.

"Come, we must prepare you for the evening meal." Selphie reached to remove her robe. "It will be your debut back into society."

"Wait! Tonight?!" She clutched the fabric that hid her nakedness. "Shouldn't I...practice first?"

"No need for practice," Selphie said. "Come, we are no stranger to nudity. We must dress you."

Nerves overtook her entire body. No need for practice? Shouldn't she at least get trained on the queen's mannerisms? Even the king—Lord Reyr—had said she was a sorry excuse for Claire. It had hurt more than she wanted to admit. Of course she'd never be so lucky to be *that* amazing. To be a real queen, even if the woman had started off an outsider.

Mer sighed, lifting her chin. This was her first test. She might as well act like a queen if she was going to be one for the foreseeable future. "Very well, get me dressed."

"Good!" Selphie clapped her hands together.

Admittedly, she was rather eager to try on the gown they'd brought out. It looked positively dreamy—nicer than anything she'd ever put on her body. Would she feel like a queen in it?

While there were many mages like her living in the city, selling their magical abilities to make a living, she'd never been wealthy. She could have taken up a better paying job. Bottled brews to sell at high mark-ups. Charged obscene amounts as a healer, peddling her services to the wealthy, but she'd taken a different calling. One far less glamorous.

And here she was, by the strangest turn of fate.

Her handmaidens set about preparing her for the evening meal. She sighed in delight as the silken chemise and gown slid down over her bare skin. Gooseflesh pebbled everywhere it touched. She gasped as it tightened around her waist, sucking in a breath. This gown was of the new fashion, the one Dragonwall's queen had set about making popular. It had translucent arms and showed more skin than she was used to. *But*, it was breathtaking—literally and figuratively.

They worked on her hair, next. She luxuriated in the feel of another's hands on her scalp. The feel of being pampered as her cheeks were brushed with rouge, her eyes lined with kohl. Priceless jewels were strung about her neck. It wasn't until a gold crown was placed atop her head that the room began to spin.

She was doing this—*really* doing this.

"Pick up your gaze," Lord Reyr barked, his voice low. "You keep staring at the floor like that, and you will ruin this for all of us."

She snapped her eyes upward, ignoring the flush coating her

skin. Being scolded was never pleasant. Being scolded by a king's shield? By Lord Reyr disguised as King Talon? It made her insides squirm with frustration and hurt.

She wanted to snap back at him—to tell him that she was *trying*, that she was doing all of them a favor, that she desperately needed the compensation Princess Taylynn had promised. Instead, she did what the world believed a good queen would do. She honored her husband's—her fake mate's—order.

They strode arm in arm into the grand dining hall. It was currently only half full. Benches scraped as occupants stood. Reyr didn't falter. He continued his clipped pace down the central aisle, forcing her to rush just to keep pace with him. Rather than complain, she merely clenched her teeth.

"It wouldn't hurt to nod and smile at your people," he said. "Claire never eyed them like she was ready to do murder."

She huffed under her breath. The *only* person she was inclined to murder was *him*, if he didn't stop being so rude. Was she going to say that? No. Because she didn't have the courage to. But at least she could think it. And that was satisfying. So, she did the best she could. She offered a few nods and shaky smiles.

"This is such a bad idea," he muttered as they reached the dais. Taylynn hadn't seemed to think so. She almost reminded him of this. But...what good would that do? He was determined to be against her from the start.

He led her around the table, pulling out a chair and motioning for her to sit. As he scooted her in, he leaned forward, his lips brushing her ear. A shiver raced down her arms, straight to her fingertips. He spoke the way a lover might. Anyone watching would have thought it. Except, his words weren't that of a lover's as he said, "All you need to do tonight is be silent and seen. I need not remind you what is at stake should you fail. You might think playing dress up is fun, but our lives aren't a game. Ruling a kingdom isn't a game."

Her body flushed hot. "I never said—"

But he was already taking his own seat.

This was a mistake—a huge,  colossal mistake. Was it too late to change her mind? Had Princess Taylynn already left? She glanced around but saw no sign of the sprite.

Her heart began to race, palms growing sweaty with panic.

"Hello there, *Your Majesty*," came a voice. The empty seat beside her was taken up by the newest shield in the king's retinue. Lord Dallin. The head table's other chairs quickly filled with Queen Claire's spriten guards.

"Oh, hello," she managed, trying to steady her voice as she looked at the young drengr.

"I don't believe we've officially met," he said, leaning in close to whisper in her ear. "I'm Dallin, and *you're* Merrian, but I'm not supposed to use your real name."

"Most of my friends call me Mer," she whispered back.

"Well then, *Mer*, it's nice to meet you. We can keep this our little secret, yes?"

A smile bloomed on her lips, a genuine one this time. "I don't mind if you use Mer if ever we're out of earshot of others. It might help me remember who I am."

"Then that's exactly what we'll do."

"I like you already," she decided.

"What's not to like?" he teased. His eyes flicked towards the corner of the room and she followed his gaze, spotting a couple of men taking their seats.

"Friends of yours?" she couldn't help but ask.

"Something like that." His tone was unreadable.

"Wait. Is that a…a goblin?!"

"Aye. A new emissary, recently appointed by the king. His name's Unka. And that's Mikkin, there, and Jamie with him."

As if he sensed them, Jamie lifted his gaze and locked eyes with Dallin. Whatever simmered between them was broken almost as quickly as Dallin looked away. She almost asked him about it, but decided that it was not her business.

Food was brought forth and they began eating. She glanced shyly at Reyr several times, trying to be discreet. He didn't look once at her—not until he received an obvious elbow prod from Lord Verath, who sat on his other side. The shield whispered something in the king's ear that appeared to irk him. After that, Reyr gazed in her direction a few times, whispered a few bits of information in her ear about various nobles' names that she ought to know going forward, and passed the behavior off as fond affection.

They were *supposed* to be mates who were deeply in love, after all. She almost snorted at the idea. The thought of loving him after how he'd treated her thus far? Gods, she'd rather die a spinster.

The rest of the meal, fortunately, was pleasant. She and Dallin were going to become the best of friends. He refrained from asking personal questions, in the event they were overheard by servants. Instead, he made conversation by telling her everything about his day. His training with Lord Verath. The errands they'd run. The more difficult tasks in the dungeons, meting out justice.

The rest of the evening was a blur. She returned to the king's tower, arm in arm with a silent, brooding Lord Reyr, who detached from her the moment it was acceptable. She was introduced to her queen's guard, and made it a point to memorize their names the moment they gave them. They told her little tidbits about themselves, so she memorized that information too. Then she was coerced into a meeting with the king's inner circle. Though, not without a heavy dose of backlash from the stand-in king.

"There's absolutely no reason she needs to be here," Lord Reyr growled as everyone began taking their seats. She'd been ready to disappear through the door leading down to her chambers, when Desaree and Jocelyn had cornered her, dragging her back.

"She absolutely *must* be here," Lord Verath argued. "If you expect her to stand in as queen, then she needs to know what happens around here."

"I don't *expect* her to stand in as queen," Lord Reyr all but growled. "Because *I* wasn't the one who gave her the job! I had no say whatsoever in the matter. That was all Princess Taylynn's doing."

"Not just Taylynn's," Prince Feowen said, jumping in. "It was all of us. After she suggested it, it was an obvious necessity. Obvious to *all* of us, anyway. Clearly not you. Shocking, since you're the king and all..."

"Really, it's…" Mer swallowed, trying to find her voice. "It's no trouble for me to turn in for the evening," she found herself saying. She tried to back towards the door again, only to find her arm still linked through Desaree's. "There's no need to get riled on my part. I'm happy to leave you to it. Especially since my only purpose here is to be seen and not heard." This last she said directly to Reyr, throwing his words back at him.

His expression darkened. The king's angry, scarred face was not an easy sight to behold. "You're not going anywhere," he snapped, which made no sense after the way he'd wanted to dismiss her.

"Good, then it's settled," Feowen said, grinning.

Her gaze remained locked on Reyr's. Gods, she wanted to throttle him. Instead, she clenched her jaw and let Desaree lead her to an empty place on the sofa.

Then, just so that he wouldn't have more to throw in her face, she made it a point to be seen and not heard, letting the others carry the entire conversation. This was something they did nightly, she came to realize. Meeting to go over the day's events, important matters, decisions that required attention. All this time she'd assumed the king ruled in a solitary manner, but this proved otherwise.

She found herself wondering how Queen Claire put up with it. How she managed to give so much of her time to this kingdom, especially when its king was such a pain. Then she had to correct herself, to remind herself that Reyr *wasn't* the king. That the queen was mated to the *real* king, and that they were very much in love.

It had only been a single day, and already her mind was slipping, blurring the lines between reality and whatever lie she was stuck in. She had no idea how she'd manage this for months, or even years, except that by the end of it, there might be nothing of herself left.

*Somewhere Up North*

Saffra gnawed on her lip, waiting. The cold dread of worry seeped into her bones as quickly as the chill in the cavern. The black surface of the lake left her skin crawling.

For long minutes she waited, resisting the urge to jump in. Then, finally, a ripple. She blew out a breath. Her shoulders relaxed as Bedelth's head breached the surface. "Oh, thank the gods," she muttered. He began swimming for the shore. "Anything?" she called. Her voice echoed off the cavern walls. She winced at the sound of it.

"No," he called back.

Her stomach plummeted. "You're sure?"

"I'm positive," he managed before wading out of the water. He muttered a word and the heat from his hands dried his clothing.

They had agreed he would be the one to go into the freezing water. With his dragon fire warming him from the inside out, he wouldn't succumb to its frigid temperatures the way she would. Still, it had been near torture waiting for him. Not knowing what lurked beneath the surface. Anything could have swallowed him up. Like a giant fish. Did they exist down here? Or what about snakes? The cave had those, didn't it?

She reminded herself that he was a drengr.

Her eyes darted out over the water, struggling to accept the truth. That they had been unsuccessful. Bedelth knew exactly what to look for. She'd used their connection to share images of each stone's hiding place, careful to include every detail. He knew what was waiting in the depths of this cavern's lake. Still, she couldn't help but ask, "Did you check the whole lake bed, just to be sure?"

"I checked everything, Saff. There was no sign of it. Its resting place was empty. We're too late."

Her legs wobbled and she sank down onto her bottom, onto the shale beach. They were too late. *Again.*

The first failure might have been a coincidence. After searching north and east of Zaikar's lake, they'd come up empty-handed. The green stone hadn't been there, though there'd been signs of it. She'd almost felt its power, remnants of it soaking into the land where it had rested for months and months.

"The blue stone should have been here," she whispered, biting her lip. It was impossible to ignore the sense of dread settling over her shoulders. The sense of failure. Her breaths came faster and faster until tears clouded her eyes.

"We should leave," Bedelth said, a warning. There were things lurking in this deep cavern that frightened even him. But...she hardly heard him.

"What's the point of it all," she demanded. "Why would the gods show me a vision when it comes to nothing? Maybe it was meant as a warning, not a call to action. Maybe all I've done is send us on a wild goose chase."

Her stomach knotted. Just another bad decision. Like the one she'd made that had gotten Claire kidnapped and sent back through the gate.

Would their absence cause something bad to happen in the capital? Something they wouldn't be there to stop. "Oh, gods."

"Saffra, come. We need to leave."

"What's the point?" she cried again, this time slamming her

palm down onto the shale beneath her, hardly caring that it cut into her skin.

Bedelth swore under his breath. "All right, enough of that." Before she could blink, he scooped her up and marched them out of the large cavern. She managed to regain her footing and her dignity. They walked the remainder of the way out of the tunnels. She brooded the entire way.

The contrast between the darkness in the cave and the bright sunshine was jarring. She blinked, her eyes watering. Things felt less bleak than they had moments ago.

"Do you need a minute, or are you ready to go?" Bedelth eyed her warily.

"I... Go where?"

"North, obviously. For the red stone."

She snorted. "Like it will even be there."

"Saffra," he warned. She heard the years in his voice. It made her feel young, childish. But could he blame her? They'd been traveling for weeks, always searching. Days spent studying the terrain, pinpointing iconic places in the landscape to narrow down each stone's location. They'd never had a fighting chance, had they? Kane knew exactly where the stones were because he'd put them there for safekeeping, and it had taken him no time to retrieve them. He was probably ten steps ahead of them already.

"We should just go back."

"We will not. We have a job to do, and we are here to do it."

"Claire and Talon could already be home by now."

"That does not matter to this mission. We fly north, to the ruins you saw, the edifice in the mountains."

She suppressed a shiver. They had left that one for last because it frightened her the most. An abandoned fortress deep within the northern mountains, its ramparts crumbling, its walls all but haunted. "What if we fail?"

"Then we fail." Bedelth shrugged. "At least we did all we could." She looked at him, admiring the steel in his voice. He wouldn't blame her for this, but that didn't stop her from blaming herself. As if sensing her thoughts, even though their minds were not yet permanently melded, he said, "You need to stop doing that."

"Doing what?" she snapped.

"Self-sabotaging. Taking on the weight of things that go wrong. Claire's disappearance—"

"Don't, Bedelth. Just, don't." She couldn't go there right now. She wrapped her arms around her middle, shivering against the cold.

Bedelth sighed, then pulled her against him. He held her close for several moments, resting his chin on the top of her head. The feel of him calmed her. He took her hair in his fist and gently tilted her head up to look at him. "We do the best we can and nothing less. That's how we live with ourselves. That's how we sleep at night."

Her chest fluttered, struck by the way he looked at her. The fire in his gaze. The sincerity. The *love*. Her worries disappeared, replaced by amusement. "That's not exactly how *I* sleep at night."

"No?" He lifted a brow. A blush crept up her neck. "Ah, yes. But of course. You sleep because once my fingers are finished with you, you've no energy left for anything else."

"Bedelth," she gasped, swatting at him. Her skin turned hot enough she expected steam to roll off her. He merely chuckled and stepped away, taking her hand and leading her to a safe place he could transform. He was right, they needed to finish this. Even if it ended in failure.

BEDELTH'S SCALES weren't hot enough to eliminate the frigid chill that settled deep in her bones. The fortress was exactly as she'd seen in her dreams, a dark crumbling thing, sick with rot and decay. The red stone was hidden deep within.

It had taken nearly two weeks to reach this place. It was Bedelth who'd spotted it, with his keen eyesight. She almost wished he hadn't.

He circled, looking for a safe place to land, then descended, his talons clicking on the ancient flagstones. She slid off his back and pulled her cloak tightly around her shoulders. Her body shivered anyway. Bedelth was beside her in seconds, looking out over what was once a vast courtyard. One side was a sheer drop straight off the mountain, the walls crumbling into nothing. The other was a curve, cut into the mountain's side.

"What is this place?" she breathed.

"If I had to guess? A stronghold that belonged to the ancient dragons."

"You think?" That jolted her.

"Look at the doorways, the openings. Those aren't built for humans. They're ten times the height and width. I could wander its halls in my drengr form, if I wanted."

She expelled a breath. "It might be safer if you did."

"I would, except we would have no way of communicating." He threw her a look, his brow arched.

"Oh. Right." They were not yet bonded. Months ago, she'd dreaded the idea. Now she was eager for it.

She took several steps forward, studying the doorways. Four dark yawning mouths that led into the foreboding depths of the mountain. There was no telling which they should take, so she started forward for the one closest to them. Bedelth reached for her wrist, halting her. "I go first," he warned. She would have challenged him, were it not for her racing heart.

She licked her lips, then nodded.

They entered using orbs of light, dimmed to a dull glow. It would not do to disturb the things that slept in this place. The corridor was wide enough for a fully grown drengr, larger even, to accommodate the massive dragons of old.

The air was cold enough to burn her lungs. She wrinkled her nose. It smelled like rot and decay. The walls were blackened with mold. Some dripped with moisture.

Bedelth set a slow, careful pace. The deeper they went, the more she felt the pressure of the mountain above her, around her. The corridor sloped downward, then disappeared. They reached a staircase massive enough for a dragon. Each step was several feet wide as it was tall.

Bedelth stepped off the first, dropping down with a quiet thump. He turned and lifted his arms. She regarded him, then looked down. He huffed. "I'm aware that you can jump, stubborn little mate, but there are twenty of these. Perhaps save your strength?"

"Good point." She pressed her lips between her teeth to keep from smiling.

She let him take her by the waist and lift her down. They carried on like that. Bedelth dropped to the next step. Reaching for her waist, he lifted her down. When they reached the bottom, she tilted her head back to search the top. The climb up looked daunting.

"Come along." Bedelth took her hand, giving it a reassuring squeeze before dropping it. He continued on ahead, ever the gallant knight.

The tunnel curved and dropped deeper into the mountain. They passed doorways leading elsewhere. Many into what she believed were private accommodations, massive rooms that once housed individual dragons.

They wandered for hours until it felt as though they'd descended into the very depths of the earth, deep below the mountains. The air turned hot and suffocating. She no longer huddled in her cloak, but let it trail behind her. Even Bedelth's forehead gleamed with perspiration.

The corridor opened wide, leaving them in a cavernous chamber. She gasped. Their orb lights only illuminated a small section, but she knew exactly where they were. She'd seen it in her dreams. Seeing it in real life was completely different.

The ground was made of soft sand. Her boots sank with each step. The heat radiating from it made her feet nearly uncomfortable. She barely noticed, too distracted by the sea of colorful fragments, like broken glass. Like someone had smashed thousands of vases.

"Dragon eggs," Bedelth murmured, awed. "Just like the hatching grounds at Irelia Island."

She'd never been to the island, but she had heard stories. She blinked, taking it in. Her feet became uncomfortably hot and she was forced into motion. She shed her cloak, leaving it for later. They lumbered through the sand towards the middle of the vast cavern. The crunch of egg fragments beneath their feet was unavoidable, but she couldn't help her flinch.

In her dream, she'd seen the red stone on a square plinth in the middle, protected by a glow of magic. There was the plinth now, cast in dim light. But...there was no stone upon its surface.

She didn't feel even a prickle of disappointment. She'd already known it wouldn't be here. Had already prepared herself. Still, they stopped before it. She pressed her palm to the surface. A faint buzz of magic met her skin. "It was here...not long ago." When she opened her eyes, it was to find Bedelth's gaze on her, his lips pressed into a thin line. "We failed."

"There is still hope," he said.

"Is there?"

"The stones in the forest remain protected. He will not have all five and can do nothing against us unless he does."

Her shoulders fell. "Still, it would have been a massive victory."

"I know." He reached out and brushed his fingertips over her cheek. A tear. She hadn't even realized she was crying.

The whisper of sand made them freeze. Their gaze held for an instant. Bedelth's eyes went from soft to wary. The hairs on the back of her neck lifted. They whirled, turning towards the darkened cavern. Bedelth's hand went immediately to the hilt of his sverak.

She muttered a word, sending their orbs flying high and wide.

Something moved in the shadows.

"Stay close," he warned, making her heart take off in a gallop. "Draw your blade."

She was no good with a blade—not like Claire, anyway. Her skill lay with a bow. But Bedelth had insisted she bring one, a long knife the length of her forearm. The slide of metal sounded as he drew his sverak. She did as ordered, clutching her weapon.

Another twist in the shadows made her breath catch. A soft, hissing laughter floated out over the sand. Her stomach dropped.

"He knew you would come," a voice whispered. This time, from behind. She whirled, squinting into the darkness.

"Show yourself," Bedelth commanded. The two of them stood back to back now.

More quiet laughter reached them, hissing over her skin. Her heart pounded, sending a roar of blood past her ears. The shadows moved again, this time materializing into dark figures gliding towards them.

"Oh, gods," she breathed, dread settling over her. "I thought Claire destroyed them."

"She did," Bedelth said.

The one nearest them spoke, its voice a whispered hiss, "She destroyed many of our kind—your bitch queen. But not all of us." They glided closer. "Plenty of us still live to be summoned. Now that she is gone, our master has begun again."

There were four...no, *eight*. Terrible odds against the two of them, especially when she was no help with a blade. There was no telling how many more lurked in the shadows, waiting. Bedelth muttered several words, making their orbs flare brighter. The vodar wraiths were brightly illuminated. They hissed, faltering for just a moment. A thimble of hope exploded in her chest, only to die just as quickly. The light was not enough to deter them.

"You are too late," the vodar hissed. "But our master knew you would come. He knew you were hunting the stones. He sent us to deliver a message."

"Saffra, you are the light of my life," Bedelth said, his words urgent, his voice pitched low. "You know this, yes? Of course you do."

"Bedelth, please!" Why was he saying this to her *now*?! Did he think they wouldn't make it?

"We have no choice but to fight our way out of here. Can you protect yourself with magic?"

"I..." Her lashes fluttered.

"You will not leave here alive," came another hiss.

"I can," she told Bedelth, steeling her nerves. If she was his light, then she intended to live so that he could say more things like that to her. To the vodar, she hefted her blade and said, "What's the point of delivering a message if you're just going to kill us?"

"Your death *is* the message," they hissed, then surged forward. She had barely a moment to begin chanting before dodging the nearest wraith. Her words wrapped her in a protective barrier like an invisible second skin. She dropped and rolled out of reach, continuing her incant. Light burst across the hatching grounds as Bedelth locked swords with a group of wraiths. The others fell upon her.

She fired off a handful of fireballs. Flames struck and exploded against the wraiths' invisible protective shields. She cursed under her breath, firing several more. They moved closer, forcing her back —away from Bedelth.

"Stay close!" he shouted, but it sounded too distant.

Panicking, she glanced around the cavern. Using words for wind and sand, she called up a small tornado of sand around herself, blinding them to her exact location. It didn't matter. Blades pierced the sand cloud trying to pierce her. She cried out, jumping and dodging. Slowly, she worked her way back towards where Bedelth ought to be.

The sound of their battle echoed off the walls. Metal clashing, magic sizzling, the earth rumbling. The air smelled like sulfur and melting glass.

She moved through tactics, alternating between fireballs and bursts of sand, trying to distract and even blind the wraiths. Bedelth was within reach now. He flowed like water, swinging and dodging. She'd never trained for magical combat. Not like him. He sent pulses of charged lightning  to get in close—close enough to kill each wraith. With every head that rolled, there was one fewer wraith to fight.

Sweat dripped down her skin, making her clothes stick to her body. Restricting her movements. Her muscles turned sluggish. Each incant took a little something out of her. Her breaths became wheezing gasps.

They were down to three now, between the two of them. Her magic was failing. A sword came from overhead, swiping down to cleave her in two. She lifted her own blade, managing a bone-jarring block. She cried out, whirling away and tripping. A hissing laugh sounded. She scrambled backwards on the sand. The wraith stalked towards her. It lifted its sword, swiping downwards. She cried out and rolled, felt the force of the blow graze her skin, graze the barrier she'd put in place. It flickered, but held.

Blow after blow rained down upon her, weakening her magic, then shredding it. She didn't have the time to get up. She could only roll and dodge. Her shield winked out, her magic utterly spent.

She scrambled backwards, swallowing down air, choking on it.

"He will be so pleased when I tell him of your death," the wraith hissed. Its poisoned sword came down again and she managed to kick out with her booted feet, surprising it as her foot made contact with its smoky legs. But the wraith's blade grazed her bicep. She screamed, the sound raw and jagged.

A massive blade arced through the air. The wraith's head was removed at the same instant its body disappeared. Everything fell silent. She was too shocked to move. Bedelth stood, his chest rising and falling in heavy bursts, staring down at her with wide eyes.

Gods, she'd never been so relieved to see him.

There were beads of sweat coating his bare arms, his forehead. "Battle rage looks good on you," she blurted, just before a surge of pain exploded up her arm. She screamed again, looking down at the black line that oozed blood and smoke. She had a brief moment to register what it meant. That she was about to die from a poisonous incision.

Then everything went dark.

# CHAPTER 8
# ONE CONDITION

*Battle Ground, Indiana*

Talon stepped from the cornfield and right into Claire's path. She froze, her eyes going round as she gaped at him. He froze too, caught up in her gaze like he'd been snared. The sight of her standing before him, close enough to touch, felt so *right*. He wanted to drag her into his arms, to kiss her, to bury his nose in her hair and inhale her scent. He wanted her so badly, every bone in his body ached.

It was careless to risk himself like this—he knew that. He'd caught her taking an afternoon walk, and seen the opportunity. He might not get another chance like this for days. So, he'd made his move.

Did she recognize him? After all this time spent agonizing, did she truly see him and know him? His heart pounded in his chest.

"What—?! Who...?" She took in his manner of dress, her eyes drifting down his body. She lingered on the sword currently strapped to his back. The blades sheathed in his bandolier. Something flashed over her features and her mouth opened. To scream? To shout for help?

*I'm your mate!* he wanted to cry. Instead, he held up his hands,

70

placating. "Please," he found himself saying. Was that a shiver racing through her at the sound of his voice? "I... I just want to talk. Do you recognize me?"

Her brows drew together. She rubbed her chest, right over her sternum. Her eyes narrowed, flashing dangerously. "Is this some kind of sick joke? You show up here dressed all old-fashioned because you saw me on TV and thought it would be funny to play a game?"

He couldn't help the small grin that pulled on his lips. Gods, he'd missed this side of her, the side that didn't fear him when everyone else would have cowered or stammered their way through their words. But his lips flattened almost as quickly. "I wouldn't joke about something like this. I came to bring you home—"

"I *am* home—"

"Your true home, Claire. With me, in Dragonwall."

She sucked in a sharp breath. "Dragonwall? You... You know about Dragonwall?"

"So, you do remember something." A flare of hope filled his chest and his pounding heart began to calm.

"No. I mean, I don't remember anything. But Irelia said—"

He blinked. "Irelia? Surely you don't mean *Princess Irelia*?"

Because that would be impossible.

Claire's lips parted and her head tilted. "You know her?"

"I know *of* her. Explain," he commanded. A mistake as soon as it was out of his mouth.

She drew herself up, then crossed her arms. "I don't owe you—"

The stalks behind him parted and Jovari appeared. "What our good king meant to say was that Irelia disappeared from our world a long time ago. She was presumed dead. He's merely confused as to how she could have spoken at all."

"Jovari," he warned.

Claire's eyes darted between them. "And who are you? Another supposed person from Dragonwall? How do I know this isn't some elaborate prank? Did someone tap our house and listen in on our dinner conversation last night? Is this all a joke to prove I'm some kind of—"

"This isn't a joke," both he and Jovari said in unison. Talon pinched the bridge of his nose and exhaled. "Look, there's a lot you don't remember. But I promise you, I can explain everything if you'd let me. You've been in our world for about a year, and then you were sent back here. It seems as though your memories and magic are bound somehow."

Gods, he wanted to tell her everything right this minute. That she was his mate. That they were in love. That he'd worshiped her body so thoroughly the last time they'd been in bed together, he could still remember the taste of her on his tongue—

"Okay..." she blew out a breath. "So you're not some kind of news crew looking for a story."

"Does he look like he'd be part of a news crew?" Jovari drawled.

A laugh burst from Claire's lips. "No. I guess you're right. Wait, did you... Did you say he was a king?" she asked Jovari.

"I am," Talon said, his chest puffing out.

"He is," Jovari confirmed.

"So would that make you Irelia's dad or something, since she's the princess?"

Talon laughed. He couldn't help it—the ridiculous notion. "Irelia was long before my time, Claire. She's... It's a long story. But I'll tell you, if you'd like to hear it?"

"Please say yes," Jovari added, like he couldn't take another moment of this. Couldn't take another moment of watching his poor king suffer.

Claire gnawed on her lower lip, a tell he knew for nervousness. "Maybe we should do this inside. I'd rather not stand out here in case my parents come looking for me. Come on," she added, leading them down the narrow lane that bisected the fields.

He blew out a breath and followed. Somehow this was going better *and* worse than he'd hoped. Better because she was giving him a chance to explain. Worse because he feared that her situation was critical. She couldn't remember anything of who she was.

When they reached the edge of the field, she stopped them. "Stay here while I check if the coast is clear."

"You've got to be kidding me," Jovari muttered.

"What?" she said, throwing him a grin that instantly made Talon Jealous. He wanted that warm grin on him instead. "I don't want my parents to know that I'm letting strangers into our house. They'll have a fit. At least, until I know you're not like... psychopaths or something."

Talon snorted. If this were any other circumstance, he'd be furious that she was so callously letting two unknown males into her home. They'd definitely be having a talk about this later, once she remembered. Clearly, she was too trusting.

But he was desperate to fix this, so he nodded and let her slip away.

She returned a few minutes later, informing them that her mother had already left for the doctor and would be back in a couple of hours. She guided them inside. He hungrily took everything in. This was the place she'd grown up. He'd only ever seen it in her memories. Seeing it in person was an entirely different experience.

She led them into a sitting room. He froze when he noticed the old woman lounging in an armchair, knitting needles in hand, a large spool of yarn at her feet. "So, *you're* the ones Claire just warned me about," she harrumphed, looking them over before returning her gaze to the task at hand. She appeared unconcerned but he'd caught the gleam of curiosity in her.

"You must be Irelia," he chanced.

"Heard of me, have you?"

He snorted. If ever he'd wanted to question the relationship between Claire and Irelia, it was obvious now that they were definitely related. Albeit distantly. "There are paintings in the keep," he said by way of explanation.

"Ah. Of course." She set her things down. Only now did he see the true hunger in her gaze. "My mother? Is she still alive?"

"Long since dead, as is your father. Some fifty thousand years ago, in fact." Irelia's lips parted and she blinked. "How long has it been for you in this world, Princess?"

Irelia's throat bobbed. "Two thousand years, give or take a handful."

Jovari swore. "Time moves differently here? Slower?"

"It would seem so, which explains why Cyrus was gone for so long," Talon mused.

"It also means that every day here is…" Jovari trailed off, doing a quick calculation before he said, "about a month in Dragonwall?"

It was Talon's turn to swear. They'd been gone at least seven months?! Gods!

Jovari must have sensed his sudden panic. He placed a hand on Talon's shoulder and said, "Reyr will handle things. You put him in charge because you trust him. Remember? They will manage without us."

"Reyr?" Claire said the name, blinking.

Talon perked up. "You recognize it?"

She frowned, thoughtful, then shook her head. "I thought… No…"

He exhaled, a sense of heavy pressure settling in his chest. "We cannot delay here, Claire. We must take you home. Tonight, if possible." He reached for her, forgetting for a moment as he tried to take her hand in his. To touch her, desperate for the feel of her skin against his.

She stepped out of reach and made a sound of disagreement in the back of her throat. "I'm not going *anywhere* with either of you."

"You made a choice—" Talon began, trying not to let her behavior and words wound him. None of this was her fault, after all.

"What he *means* to say, my queen," Jovari said, jumping in, "is that he cannot do this without you."

Her eyes went round. Irelia gave a bark of surprise that almost sounded pleased. Claire stuttered, "I… Did you just call me…?"

Jovari went down on one knee. "Your kingdom needs you, Your Majesty. Not just Dragonwall, but the sprites, too. You are still their queen. Until and unless you hand the crown over to Taylynn."

Claire's head began to shake in disbelief. Her eyes darted to Talon, sudden understanding blooming in her gaze. "If you're a king and I'm a queen... Are we...married?! I... *No*. This is ridiculous. None of this makes sense."

His chest caved in. Of course she couldn't fathom being married to him—bonded to him. Why would she, when she could do so much better?

*You are my mate!* he almost shouted, once again. But this time, it was shame that kept his lips sealed. The last thing he wanted was to frighten her away. No, it was better to win her over, get her home. They could figure the rest out later.

"You promised to explain everything," Jovari reminded him, coming to his feet.

"Yes, forgive me, Claire. I was getting ahead of myself. How about I start at the beginning—"

"Wait." Claire held up her hand. His lips pressed into a line. "We're not doing this without Leah."

"Leah?" Jovari frowned. "Your pink-haired friend?"

"We haven't a moment to spare," Talon said. "We're doing this now." Impatience sent heat prickling across his skin.

"No. We are doing this on *my* terms." She pulled a device from her pocket, one of the *cellular*-things humans used. Her fingers *tap-tap-tapped* across the screen. He took a long, deep breath, willing patience into his being. Finally, she looked up and said, "She's on her way. She'll be here in fifteen minutes." Then she went and sank onto one of the sofas.

Irelia seemed to sense the tension in the room. She chose that moment to make small talk, asking questions about Dragonwall, the great keep, about the rule of succession and who'd taken over after her parents. Fifteen minutes felt like an age.

The pink-haired woman finally knocked and was admitted. "You said it was an emergency," Leah whispered, eyeing the two of them with suspicion.

"It is. Thanks for coming. Looks like I might be about to figure out what is going on with my memories." Claire gave her a long hug that made him jealous all over again. He'd been on the receiving end of those hugs and knew exactly how special they were. He watched, certain that his gaze was of the devouring sort.

"Who are they?" Leah asked when they broke apart.

"We're drengr, from Dragonwall," Jovari said, stepping forward. "My name is Jovari, and this is Talon, the king of Dragonwall."

"And *I'm* apparently his queen," Claire said in a sarcastic voice that illustrated exactly what she thought of that.

Talon's stomach churned. He took a deep breath and reminded himself that she hadn't balked at *him*, hadn't run from him, hadn't been disgusted by him. Her disbelief was more to do with how absurd this appeared, rather than the fact that they were mated. So...he let it go.

"A queen, huh?" Leah looked between them, then grinned. "Fancy."

Jovari and Claire both snorted, then shared a look. Claire immediately schooled her features and dragged Leah to the sofa. "We should get this over with before my mom gets back."

"Right." He squared his shoulders. Jovari came to stand beside him as he launched into the most epic tale he'd ever told. He told her about how a dragon had fallen from the sky and into her cornfield. How she'd selflessly rescued it, only to find that it wasn't a dragon at all, but a drengr shifter named Cyrus. One of his six shields.

He relayed the details of what brought her into his kingdom, how she'd flown to the capital. How she'd been tried for murder—though he glossed over the unsavory parts, because he was too ashamed to reveal them just yet—and how she'd settled into life at the keep. He told her about Kane, and everything she'd done to fulfill the promise she'd made. From training with a sword to mastering her magic.

He revealed the details of their discovered mate bond, of how they'd danced together at the ball, of how she'd made the decision to train with the sprites. He let her see how much her leaving had hurt him, even though it had been the right thing. How her months away in the forest had been the most difficult of his life.

"Their queen tried to kill you," he explained, "you were forced to kill her and take up the spriten crown." At this, Claire sucked in a breath. Almost like she remembered. But he could tell that she didn't, not really. "Then you returned to me. We fought to regain Fort Squall, which was when you snuck off to try and save the dragons. Even after I forbade it. You've never allowed anything to stop you from doing what you feel is right."

He could tell from her attention that she was hanging on to his every word. "What happened after that?" she breathed.

"Then we returned to the capital and completed our bonding ceremony. You became mine in every way, and I became yours."

At his words, her skin flushed. He loved when she blushed. A sense of satisfaction made him warm all over.

He told her about the attack on Kastali Dun, of how they'd flown together into battle, and what had gone so wrong afterward. "And that's how you came to be here, with no memory of any of it. The potion that Kane used on you—for I'm certain that's what it was—bound you tightly. Otherwise you'd be able to hear me speaking to you, mind to mind. You'd have access to your magic, your memories, Cyrus's gift, all of it."

Silence fell. He could hear the *tick-tick-tick* of a clock somewhere in the house. His audience simply stared at him. Even Irelia appeared speechless.

"What happened to Kane?" Leah was the one to voice the question.

"He got away," Jovari said, eyeing her curiously. "Every day we spend here, close to a month passes in Dragonwall. He could have already moved against the kingdom."

"But, you said one of your shields is disguised to look like you? So if Kane doesn't know you're gone...?" Claire let the remainder of the question go unfinished.

"He wanted you gone from Dragonwall so that I'd be weakened, or tempted to go after you."

"Which is exactly what you did!" she said. "Don't you think that's a little rash, as a king? To leave your kingdom unprotected like that?"

Gods, he didn't know whether to rush to her and hug her, or fight back. Because she was right. Except, "There is no world in which I will live and rule without my queen by my side. I will not do this alone. Your kingdom needs you, Claire. *I need you.*"

Her expression softened. She scrubbed a hand over her face. "You can't just expect me to...to drop everything and go racing off to save *your* kingdom based on an elaborate story. It's a good one. I'll give you that."

"Apparently, it's *your* kingdom too," Leah teased, bumping her shoulder against Claire's.

Claire huffed. "Yeah, *apparently.*"

"Allow us to take you back," Jovari said. "Allow us to prove it to you. Once you see it, once it is confirmed, there will be no question."

"You dropped everything once before," Talon reminded her, hoping to counteract her misgivings.

"It does sound pretty cool," Leah said. "And now you know where your markings came from. You have magic. You're a queen—a real queen. Honestly, I'm surprised you're not immediately on board with this. Hell, I'd drop everything and go if someone was offering me the chance. We both know I have nothing keeping me here, and neither do you."

They shared a look, and Talon found himself holding his breath. Gods, if Claire said yes this easily, he'd give Leah whatever she wanted as a thank you.

"What about my parents?" Claire asked.

Leah shrugged. "What about them? They've got their lives here. They're happy here. Tell them that this is what you want. They can't keep you against your will. Miss A would never hold you back from doing what you wanted, and neither would your dad."

Claire heaved a sigh. "Yeah, but trying to explain this to them."

"They believed your grandmother, when she told them everything."

"No they did not. They merely tolerated it."

"I thought I did rather a decent job of convincing them," Irelia interjected, looking smug about it.

"Besides, there are a few ways to prove that this is all real," Leah said. "Have them show your parents their dragon forms. And that place where you rescued the other dragon? Surely there's some kind of evidence. A crater or something, out in the cornfield. That should be all the confirmation we need to know if they're telling the truth."

"And if they are?" Claire asked.

"Then you go," Leah said, shrugging. "I'll miss the hell out of you. You're my best friend. But I'm not selfish enough to hold you back."

Claire eyed her, and something passed over her expression. Talon had become a master at reading her face. He wasn't surprised when she said, "Okay. I'll go on one condition."

"Name it," he said. She might not know it, but he did. He would give her whatever she wanted. There wasn't even a question.

"Leah comes with me." She lifted her chin as if he might contest her on it. Leah sucked in a breath.

"And what of me?" Irelia broke the silence. "I've lived out most of my years here and wouldn't mind returning to the land I came from, if only to let my bones lie under the earth from whence I came."

Talon shared a glance with Jovari, who looked on the cusp of protesting, even if it wasn't his decision. They'd fly faster with just Claire. But he couldn't stop himself as he said, "You're both welcome to join us, if it means we can leave tonight."

Then he held his breath and waited for their answers.

CHAPTER 9

# A BRUTE OF A KING

*Battle Ground, Indiana*

Claire picked at her dinner, stealing furtive glances at the massive drengr sitting across from her. The king of Dragonwall. At *her* table. A real king, like something out of a fairytale.

Not that she could truly fathom the gravity of it. All she knew about Dragonwall was what she'd been told. First, from Irelia, and then from these strange beings. But that wasn't even the half of it. He'd claimed they were *mates*. That she was his queen.

The mere thought left her heart thudding with...what? Eagerness? Wariness? Confusion? Apprehension? So many emotions. She could hardly name them all as they jumbled together inside of her, making her insides squirm and dance.

Earlier, they'd gone to the crater, found it hidden within the cornfield, something her parents hadn't even discovered. Then, much to everyone's shock, both Talon and Jovari had proven themselves by transforming into dragons. *Real freaking dragons!*

It was only for that reason that her parents were here at the dining table. They had no choice but to believe what King Talon had claimed. Not that they were happy about it. They sat silently as

80

Talon and Jovari rehashed everything for her parents, explaining why they were taking their only daughter away. That it was unlikely she'd ever return.

Her father wore a permanent scowl. "I refuse to believe my daughter threw caution to the wind and married some hulking brute of a king just to help him rule his kingdom."

She gasped. Then her eyes shot to the king, hoping he wouldn't smash their table, roar like a dragon, or shout *"Off with his head."* Wasn't that what kings did?

Michael Evans was often firm, having once been a surgeon who held literal lives in his hands. Clearly the idea of his only daughter married off—without her father having been involved—rankled. He was making that clear.

"I would *never* hurt her," Talon all but growled, just as Jovari chuckled and muttered the word *brute* under his breath, as if he found it amusing. "She is more precious to me than life itself."

Claire blinked. There was a deep sincerity in the king's words. The thought that someone other than her family and best friend felt like that for her...she hardly knew what to make of it.

Her father only harrumphed and said, "She'd better be."

"She is." The king's voice was hard and unyielding.

Something hot slid down her insides and pooled in her abdomen. She discreetly studied his scars, the way they lined his face, the most prominent slashing diagonally from eyebrow to jawbone. What had *done* something like that? Despite them, she found him handsome in an unconventional way. Not so much because of his face, but because of the way he carried himself, his broad shoulders, his towering frame, and even the deep rumble of his voice.

Yes, admittedly, she liked his voice very much. Too much. What was wrong with her?! She hardly knew this man, no matter what he claimed. She was practically drooling over him when she ought to be wary.

Her father was right. He *was* a brute, with layers upon layers of muscle and a head of messy hair. Not to mention all the growling, like he was a vicious predator.

"Claire Bear, does this sound like something you'd do? Marry this man—this, *drengr?*" Her father tripped over the unfamiliar word. Unfamiliar to *him*, but not to her. Because when she'd spoken it earlier, something about it had felt normal.

Every eye around the table snapped in her direction. She felt her cheeks warm. If she was a queen like they claimed, shouldn't this be easier? This was the part where she ought to square her shoulders and lift her chin. The part where she gave a nice, concise, definitive answer. "I..."

"An entire kingdom witnessed the ceremony," Jovari said, coming to her rescue. "Myself included. You wore a beautiful black gown and cape. There were scales around your neck."

"Black?!" Her father's eyes bulged. "Why not...*white?*" he spluttered. It wasn't because white was the traditional color worn. Not entirely. Probably more because her mother had saved her wedding dress in case Claire might want to wear it someday. And... she had intended to.

"Because mates wear the color of their intended's scales," Jovari explained.

She exhaled. She wanted to remember, truly, she did. She tried to picture it. Her standing hand-in-hand with King Talon, dressed in an opulent black gown, gazing into his eyes. As she tried to picture it, Talon met her gaze from across the table. His silver eyes dragged her in, snaring her until she couldn't look away. Heat rushed to her cheeks. The way he was looking at her now, it looked exactly like she imagined him looking at her during their ceremony.

"I love you more than anything in the world," he murmured, holding her captive like prey caught in a predator's grasp. "There is nothing I wouldn't do to protect you, to bring you home, to keep you."

Shivers raced over her skin. His words were bold, daring, *possessive.* They were also a promise. More importantly, they felt right, even if she couldn't remember anything between them, couldn't remember the history that had created the feelings he spoke of.

Still, she knew with certainty that she was safe with him, that he meant what he said.

"She doesn't look convinced about any of this," her father huffed, because he couldn't drop it. "Frankly, neither am I."

"Michael," Alexandra murmured, reaching over and placing a hand against her husband's forearm. "Look at the way he looks at her. Do you really think...?"

Her father sighed, then rubbed a hand over his forehead. All the fight seemed to go out of him at that. That's all it was. A father fighting for his daughter, reluctant to accept that she was no longer his little girl.

"Dad, it's...it's fine," she managed. "I'm going with him. I've already agreed."

"So you've said," her father supplied. "And we aren't going to stop you."

She blinked at him. "You're...you're not?" She did not expect him to give up so easily. But she was relieved, nonetheless.

"I'm not."

"You could both come with me?" She threw a quick glance at Talon, *daring* him to deny this request. He'd already agreed to bring Leah *and* Irelia. What were two more in the grand scheme of things? Especially if it meant having her parents with her. Talon merely stared, his face completely expressionless. Was he always this difficult to read? If so, why had she ever agreed to marry someone made of stone? But he wasn't, was he? He *hadn't* been stone a few minutes ago, when he'd professed his love so easily.

Her father opened his mouth, then sealed his lips together.

"That's sweet of you to offer, honey," her mom said, throwing a nervous glance towards the drengr at the dinner table, "but our lives are here. Our friends are here. The farm is here—you know how your father loves the farm." Alexandra exhaled. "You were always destined to grow your wings and fly the nest. While we didn't have *this* in mind, we won't stop you either."

"But...what if... What if I never see you again?" She glanced at Talon again, waiting for him to supply some form of reassurance. Surely someone with the ability to turn into a dragon could find some way to keep them all together. And yet, she knew deep down that it was not meant to be.

"You will always have us in your heart," her mother said. Claire swallowed against the lump growing in her throat. "It sounds as if your destiny is so much bigger than us, anyway. Than this farm, this life, our world. Sometimes, sacrifices must be made. I suppose this is yours. And who knows what the future holds. Maybe someday you'll come back to visit."

Claire felt the warm droplet before she realized what it was, and dashed her hand across her cheek to wipe it away. But it was too late. King Talon was staring at her, scowling. His features were no longer made of stone. *Huh.* All it took was a single tear.

Alexandra cleared her throat and said more brightly than the occasion warranted, "You should all finish your food. You have a long journey ahead of you, and you'll need your strength."

Except, Claire couldn't manage to take more than a few bites. She hated that they were rushing off. That she was leaving with someone she hardly knew. She understood why. Of course she did. They'd explained the time difference. How every minute was precious. How every moment wasted could mean the fall of their kingdom. *Her kingdom?*

And yet, she couldn't help but wish there was more time with her family, more time to get to know the male who claimed to be her husband. Then again, something also told her that there'd never be enough time, no matter how much they gave her.

"I should run home and grab a few things," Leah said, breaking the silence.

Jovari looked like he might argue. It was Talon who said, "Very well. We can afford a few more minutes."

"How about some dessert, then?" Alexandra asked.

Leah rushed off, and the rest of them tucked into her mom's baking. "What did you say this was called, Alexandra?" Talon scraped his plate clean. Claire could only blink at him. At how quickly he'd inhaled it.

"Bread pudding. Would you like some more?"

"Yes, please, if you wouldn't mind?"

"I'll get it," Claire blurted, then quickly jumped to her feet. If she sat another moment at this table, her fidgeting would get the better of her. She snatched his plate and disappeared into the kitchen. She was scooping more desert from the tray when she felt a presence behind her. The hairs on the back of her neck prickled, then a shiver of awareness raced all the way down her spine.

She froze.

Hands came up on either side of her, braced against the tile countertop. Caging her in. Instead of fearful, she felt an electric thrill.

His palms were huge, fingers long and elegant. There were ropy veins that started on the backs of his hands and traveled up his forearms, then disappeared beneath the roll of his tunic sleeves. She swallowed against the rising lump in her throat.

"Claire."

His utterance, the way he said her name, sent shivers racing across her skin. His voice was a low growl next to her ear. His nose dropped to her hair, nuzzling against her as he inhaled, breathing her in. It was a primal gesture that made her insides clench with desire.

But...he was a *stranger*! She didn't know him!

"I want to touch you *everywhere*. To kiss you. To hold you."

Her mouth opened and closed like a fish out of water.

She couldn't remember a time someone had spoken to her like this. Probably because no one ever had. Or, at least, that she could remember.

"Then why don't you?" she challenged. Her words were bold. Bolder than she felt. But if he was a king, why hadn't he just done exactly whatever he wanted?

"Because you don't remember. And the last thing I want is to frighten you away."

"Oh." She was *almost* disappointed. Even if kissing him would feel as if she were kissing a complete stranger. Not that there was anything wrong with kissing strangers. To each their own.

She released the serving spoon clenched in her fingers and whirled to face him. A bad idea. It brought her face inches from his.

Her chest brushed against his. A sharp intake of breath filled her lungs. The way he looked at her made her knees weak, like she was the sun and he was a planet, desperate to throw himself into her orbit and never leave.

He lifted a hand and she watched, transfixed, as he caught a strand of her blonde hair, rubbed it between his thumb and forefinger. A breath shuddered out of her when his mouth came to her forehead; his lips were gentle, soft, pressing a kiss there in the most endearing way. The way a husband would kiss a beloved wife.

Suddenly, the idea of kissing a stranger sounded really, *really* great. As long as it was this stranger. As long as it was him.

"I think we *must* be mates," she blurted, then clamped her lips shut.

He pulled back and his mouth twitched. Amusement. She wasn't sure how she could tell, except that deep down she must have known him even if her memories didn't.

"And why is that?" he asked.

"Because the idea of letting you touch me everywhere, kiss me, hold me,"—she threw his words back at him—"sounds really *really* good right now."

Molten fire flashed in his eyes. His pupils blew wide. He lowered his head, his gaze fixed on her mouth. Her pulse ratcheted up, racing in anticipation—

"There you are. Your mother wanted to see if you needed—"

Talon went rigid, eyes still locked with hers.

"—help. Am I interrupting?" Something about the way her father said it meant he *knew* he was, and he'd done it on purpose. It was probably a good thing.

She blew out the breath she'd been holding. "Nope. No. All good here," she managed, stepping around Talon. Her cheeks flamed. She felt like she was fifteen again, getting caught with Jake in the barn.

Her father lifted his brows, then turned to Talon and said, "I'd like a word with my daughter."

Talon nodded once, his jaw clenched, then walked out. She watched him go.

"For a king, he's surprisingly restrained."

"Dad!" she hissed, double-checking the doorway, that he'd actually gone back to the dining room and couldn't hear them.

"What?" Her father shrugged. "I half-expected him to start making royal decrees, or whatever it is that kings in his world do. I'm sure he's used to getting his way."

Her mouth popped open. "Is *that* why you've been baiting him this whole evening? All that *brute* nonsense?"

Her father's grin was slow. "I wanted to see what kind of man he is."

She snorted. "Firstly, he's not even human, so he's not a man. He's a drengr male. Secondly, what if he'd just...incinerated you on the spot?!"

"Then he wouldn't be deserving of you," he said, lifting his eyebrows. She crossed her arms, glaring at him. "Marriage isn't easy, Claire Bear. It takes effort, hard work, and a great deal of patience."

"Well, he certainly had patience dealing with *you.*"

Michael Evans sighed. "You're really going through with this." It wasn't a question.

A niggling spear of doubt crept in. "You...you don't think I should?"

"I didn't say that." He came to her and rubbed her arms up and down as if she were cold. "I think...I think that whatever's going on with you, the markings, your disappearance, your missing memories, this is the answer to everything. I don't think you have a choice." He blew out a breath. "I mean, it defies everything I've ever known about the world—magic and dragons and sprites and all that. I'm a man of science, after all. You know that."

"Your brain must be exploding right now," she teased.

"Actually, it's *imploding.* But yes."

That brought a laugh to her lips. She couldn't help herself. She threw her arms around his neck and hugged him, squeezing as hard as she could.

"Apparently I saved the life of his guard," she told him, her voice muffled against his shoulder. "I don't remember it, but when he fell, he was bleeding to death and I stitched him up." Her father made a humming sound. "Looks like some of your knowledge wore off on me after all."

"Of course it did," he said, sounding proud. "I'd expect nothing less from my daughter. Nothing less from a *queen*. Wait, do parents have to say *'Your Majesty'* if it's their own kid?"

Her laugh was more of a snort. She pulled away and wiped her eyes. "I don't think so. I wouldn't want you to, anyway. It sounds too weird coming from you."

His eyes twinkled. "You'd better go and get some time with your mother. She might not look it, but as soon as you leave, she'll be a sobbing wreck."

"Thanks, Dad. For everything. You... I'm really lucky to have you as my dad."

Something flashed over his face, there and gone. It looked a lot like tenderness. "And I'm more lucky—*and proud*—than you could ever know." He cuffed her on the arm. "Now go, see to your mother."

She knew exactly why he was shooing her away. He needed time alone to process before they said their final goodbyes. Her gut wrenched but she did as he said, grabbing the second serving of bread pudding for King Talon. He was back at the table where she deposited it.

"Mom?" Her mother was smiling, soaking up whatever story Jovari was regaling her with. Apparently all the juicy details of their wedding. "Do you... Do you think you could help me pack a few things?"

Her mom blinked, then smiled. "Of course, honey. We'll leave these three to their dessert."

"I ought to grab a few things myself," Irelia said, hobbling to her feet. "Thank you for the fine dinner, Alexandra."

"It was my pleasure, grandmother."

Claire linked her arm through her mother's as they went upstairs to soak in their last moments together.

# KISSING A STRANGER

*Battle Ground, Indiana*

Claire looked over the small stack of books she'd selected. "I never thought I'd be forced to pick favorites," she said, sighing. Her mother chuckled. "I've got to decide which books I'll be content reading for the rest of my life. Reminds me of the ice breaker question people like asking. If you were stranded on a desert island, what book would you want to have with you? You know?"

"I know." Her mother offered her a soft smile. "But I'm sure they have books there, too."

"Not *these* books!"

They'd spent the last twenty minutes packing. Her Osprey backpack had gone missing—perhaps already in Dragonwall from her last trip—so she was using her mother's. How was she supposed to fit all of the most important things in her life into such a small pack? Leah was probably facing the same challenge.

She blew out a breath. "Do you think I'm making the right decision? By going?"

Her mother was silent, thoughtful. "I do."

"But why me? You're related to Irelia, too. It could have been *you* that got chosen as the return-queen."

Her mother adjusted everything in the backpack, finding a place for her books. "I think that no matter what a person believes in—the fates, gods, a creator, or otherwise—things happened this way for a reason. It was meant to be *you*. If I had gone, your father and I wouldn't have met. You wouldn't exist. That would be a travesty."

The tears she'd been trying to fight pooled in her eyes. "I just... What if I'm not a good queen? What if I can't do it?"

"Oh, honey." Her mom moved to cup her cheeks. "Do you really think that drengr male downstairs would be here if you weren't worth it? If you weren't special to him, to his kingdom?"

A tear slipped down her cheek, then another. She grasped her mother's hands against her face. "I guess you're right."

"Moms always are," Alexandra teased. She stepped away and glanced around. "Shall I pack that, too?"

Claire looked over at the armor she'd been discovered in. The outfit splashed across all the tabloids when she'd shown up at the embassy headquarters. "No. It should stay here. I'd like you to have it, to remember what I am, or remember me by, I guess."

"We have plenty to remember you by, honey. But... I'd like that." Her mother hesitated. "Well then. I think that's everything."

A knock sounded. Her heart fluttered when King Talon poked his head inside. "I thought I'd check on you."

Her mom held her gaze and softly said, "He's good for you, I think."

Heat rushed to her cheeks and she couldn't help but steal a glance at the king, who just stood there on the threshold of her bedroom. *Checking* in on her. Like he couldn't be away from her for too long. It was obvious in the way he devoured her with his gaze.

"I'll be downstairs," her mom said, giving her arm a quick squeeze. "Take as long as you need."

Talon stepped aside, giving Alexandra room to withdraw, then entered and shut the door behind him. Her heart thrashed. He was here—in her room. He seemed to feel the same surprise, because his gaze darted over everything, taking it all in. "It's different, seeing it in person after seeing it in your mind," he mused. "You really *do* have a lot of books."

"I like to read."

"I know," he huffed. The sound of it made her warm all over. He began to move through the space, taking it in. She stood frozen in the middle, a ball of nerves and anticipation. She hadn't forgotten their almost-kiss, hadn't decided if that was a good thing or not.

He stopped at a photo on her dresser. A picture of her and Leah at the county fair. They'd been sixteen at the time. They both held giant cones of fluffy cotton candy. Talon's fingers brushed the frame. "You do not wish to bring this?"

"I... No. Since Leah is coming with me, I thought I'd leave it for my parents. I don't want to change my room too much, you know? I thought they'd like it if I kept everything here. So that they can, you know, come in here and remember me if they're ever feeling lonely." Her voice cracked.

Talon was across the room in an instant, pulling her into his arms, wrapping himself around her. She breathed an *oof* sound as he swallowed her up. She should pull away. She really should. But it was impossible to resist.

Her body tensed briefly, then relaxed into him. It felt good. She felt...protected.

"I'm sorry this is so hard for you," he murmured. "When you and I discussed our union, when we discussed your choice to become queen, we spoke of this. You coming home. Coming back here was a line in the sand for me. I made it clear that I couldn't risk you to the unknown. Couldn't risk you coming back here because of all that could go wrong. I hated that you were forced to make that choice, to choose between becoming my queen and coming back to your world."

She listened, desperate to hear what he had to say, if only to help her remember. "And... I made the choice anyway, despite that? To never see my family again?"

He made a low humming noise. "It was a difficult decision, but I think deep in your heart you always knew you would choose the crown over anything."

She pulled back, frowning up at him. He didn't release her, but she could see his face better this way. The scars that covered it. "The crown, or you?"

A flash of something crossed his gaze. A look of uncertainty that he tried to hide. "Me. The crown. Both. It was a package deal."

"If I had to guess, I chose *you* and agreed to take the crown only so that I could have you."

His eyes widened.

She knew it was the truth, knew that what she said was correct. She knew herself enough to know she'd never choose a crown, never choose power for the sake of it. That there had to be a deeper reason. *He* was that reason. "I chose you, Talon, and now I'm starting to see why."

His expression crumbled. It was more emotion than she'd seen from him all day. His throat bobbed but when he opened his mouth to speak, nothing came out. Her gaze dropped to his lips. This felt like the moment they were supposed to kiss. Her stomach erupted with butterflies as he leaned down towards her—

"Oh! I... *Oh*." Leah stood in the doorway. "I just thought I'd tell you I was back and ready to go."

She expected Talon to release her, to spring away. Instead, his eyes stayed locked with hers, lips hovering inches away. "We'll be along in a moment," he said. His words felt like a command. Leah got the message loud and clear. She shut the door, leaving them alone. "Would you be terribly angry with me if I kissed you?"

A little embarrassing squeak fell from her lips.

She hadn't expected him to ask, but he was gazing at her, waiting for an answer. She almost refused—he was a *stranger* to her! But...weren't they supposed to be married? Married people kissed all the time. Even if she couldn't remember him, that didn't change what they were. Or, maybe that was just a convenient excuse to justify what she wanted. Because no, she wouldn't be angry if he kissed her, not even a little bit.

He leaned in, giving her every opportunity to pull away. She held her breath. Time stopped as his lips pressed against hers, soft but tentative. She gasped at the feel of him, the press of him, the warmth of him. The *rightness*.

When she didn't pull away, he kissed her in earnest. She responded, melting into him, moving her lips in time with his. A hand came up to cup the back of her neck, holding her there with no chance for escape. She tipped her head back and he took that as an invitation. He groaned, his tongue slipping in and roving over hers with desperate need. He kissed her like he'd been starved. Like she was the first meal he'd had in weeks. In a way, she supposed that must be true.

Her abdomen clenched. But her desire was quickly replaced by images darting behind her eyelids. She felt transported. As if she were in a different place. There was a castle by the sea. Walls of stone with arches and turrets and rich furnishings. She caught a glimpse of Talon in his throne room, staring down at her with an unreadable expression on his face. And another glimpse, holding his hands at the base of the dais, staring into his gaze—

She gasped.

Talon immediately pulled away, looking down at her. "What is it?" His drawn brows puckered the scars on his forehead.

"I..." She frowned. "I thought I saw something. Us? Memories?"

"You got your memories back?" A surprised laugh parted his lips.

Disappointment squeezed her chest and she shook her head. "No... I... Maybe some of them?"

He stared at her for a long moment. "What about Cyrus?"

"Was he the one that died?" Her head tilted.

"Yes. You don't hear him speaking to you?"

She shook her head, biting her lower lip. Talon's shoulders fell. "Whatever Kane did to you, he's got you locked up tight. You can't hear my voice in your mind, or Jovari's. You can't hear Cyrus, which means he must be locked in whatever cage that the sorcerer placed around your memories and your magic."

Fear turned her blood to ice. "What if he didn't cage it? What if he just...*took* it?"

She cut herself off from asking more, because the one question she didn't voice was the scariest. What if she never got her magic back? Never got Cyrus back? Never remembered? Would Talon still want her?

Talon's jaw clenched. "I refuse to believe that for so many reasons. Namely, Kane would have needed to extract those things from you, and there's no undoing the gift Cyrus gave you. No, Kane enchanted you, used a concoction...somehow. I was in your mind when it happened, but I was just as quickly ejected, as if a barrier was put in place."

"So...you think I will get everything back?"

"I think we already know the answer to that." A wicked smirk pulled at his lips. She hadn't see him smile, not really. But this? It made her pulse skip. "My kissing you made you remember something. Therefore, it seems the best way to fix all this is to just keep doing it."

She gasped as his mouth crashed down against hers. There was no hesitation this time. He claimed her with a possessive need she felt straight to her core. When he pulled away, they were both breathing hard.

"Anything?" he asked.

She bit her swollen bottom lip. "I... I thought I saw a forest, maybe?"

A smug look crossed the king's features. "Good. Well, then. There's hope. We've solved the issue. I'll be sure to kiss you at every available opportunity."

"Talon!" she hissed. "This isn't some kind of...of..."

"Of what?"

"I don't know. This is serious."

"Of course it is, which is why I'm being perfectly serious."

"No, you're acting all...all *smug* about it. Like you couldn't be more excited to kiss me."

"Am I *not* supposed to be excited about kissing my mate? My queen? My *wife*?"

"No, I mean—yes. That's not what I meant."

"Then what did you mean?"

"Are you always this difficult?" she snapped, irritation burning her cheeks.

"Oh, just wait until you remember how difficult you used to find me." There was a gleam in his eyes, like he couldn't wait for that. "Maybe next time I kiss you, that will be the memory you discover."

She clenched her jaw. Of course she liked kissing him, and she barely even knew him, so that was saying something. It just felt like his excitement about kissing her, about using his kisses to bring back her memories, felt like a front. Like a convenient excuse to have her. Like her lost memories were suddenly a good thing, so that he could have his mouth on her whenever he wanted.

Then again, she *did* like the idea of his mouth on her. A lot.

*...Damn it!*

Now she was all jumbled up.

"We should go." He stepped away, snatching up her backpack before holding out his hand. She hesitated. It was a simple gesture, really. Something that came from habit. She wondered how often he'd done that exact thing, how often he'd held out his hand for her. Wondered how often she'd simply stepped up to him and laced their fingers together. Except this time, she merely glared at him and marched right on by. His gruff huff followed her out of the room.

The others were downstairs. Leah had a similar backpack, which she'd slung over her shoulder. She and Jovari were glaring at one another. A curious desire to know *why* had her glancing between them. She'd have to ask Leah about it later.

Irelia had only a small bag of belongings. She stood off to the side and looked surprisingly nervous. Much like she'd looked the entire dinner, when her eyes would occasionally snap up in surprise towards one of the drengr, as if they'd said something to surprise her, when they hadn't said anything at all.

She went to her father first, lingering in his arms. They'd said everything they needed to earlier, so she merely squeezed him tight. "Be careful, kiddo. Trust your gut. You'll do fine."

"Thanks, Dad," she managed.

"You make us so proud," her mother whispered as they hugged. "I can already imagine the kind of good you're going to do in their kingdom." The words brought tears to her eyes, but she blinked them away.

"Take care of her," her father said, a stern, unforgiving note to his voice. Talon merely nodded and said, "I will."

A few more hugs were exchanged between Leah and her parents, then they were out the door, emerging into the darkness. Talon pulled her aside. "Are you open to flying with me?"

She blinked. "Why wouldn't I be?"

He hesitated. "Before we mated, the only time our minds connected was when we touched—your skin to my scales. I'm not sure if that will happen now, but if it does..."

"You mean that I might be...like...in your head?"

He nodded. "And I will be in yours. We would share thoughts, memories, everything. Perhaps it might even unlock your memories...somehow." He didn't sound all that hopeful about it.

Her stomach squirmed. Sure, they'd kissed. Yes, it was the best kiss of her life—that she could remember. But did she have the courage to grant him unlimited access to her thoughts, her memories, her life, when it felt like he was a complete and total stranger?

"I have already seen everything within you, love." His words were low, gentle.

She chewed on her lower lip. "Right. But I don't know if..." She shifted uncomfortably. The expression on Talon's face shuttered. He saw her answer before she gave it. Guilt gnawed at her. "I'm not sure I'm ready for that, regardless."

"Even if it might work? Even if it might unlock your memories?"

Her pulse raced beneath her skin. "I... I don't know if I'm ready to share my mind like that."

He gave a quick nod, his face wiped clean of emotion. He was so good at that, hiding what he felt. "Of course. I understand. Why don't you fly with Jovari then, just in case, and I'll carry the others."

"Are...are you sure?" A weight lifted from her shoulders, even though the guilt remained. She'd half expected him to protest. To beat his chest in typical male fashion and demand she fly with him, because she was his, or some such.

Only, he didn't.

He reached for her, brushing a fingertip along her cheekbone in a gentle caress. "It will be all right. When you're ready, we will fly together."

"Thank you." Her words were soft. She hoped he understood how grateful she truly was. Today had been a lot, and while it felt like she was doing him a favor by returning to his kingdom, he wasn't pushing for more. He wasn't throwing his weight around as king.

He moved away, conversing quietly with Jovari, who glanced in her direction with a look of surprise. Their discussion over, they transformed into hulking dragons. She couldn't help her gasp, even though she'd seen it earlier. Their belongings were secured to harness straps. Claire and Leah helped Irelia climb upon Talon's back first. He had to press his belly on the grass, but it was still a struggle to get her into place. Leah did a little better, settling in and tightening the leg straps for both her and Irelia.

Once they were secured, she confronted the beautiful sapphire dragon before her. Jovari was noticeably smaller than Talon, but no less mighty. She managed to climb into place on her first try. She couldn't help but wonder if the motions were ingrained within her like some kind of muscle memory. How often had she flown astride a dragon before today?

That thought made her glance over her shoulder. Her gaze lingered on Talon in his drengr form. Even in the darkness, his iridescent scales glittered with a range of colors. His large head was turned towards her, eyes fixed on her. She felt like a mouse under his gaze. Jovari shifted abruptly. She lurched, grasping at the harness to keep from falling. A tiny, surprised squeal fell from her lips. A warning growl sounded low in Talon's throat. Jovari answered it with an amused huff.

Her parents waved at them from the porch, shouting their goodbyes. There was a lurch, the press of gravity, and then they were springing skyward. She gasped, pulling in a breath as the ground fell away. Nearby, she heard both Leah and Irelia give similar cries of surprise. Then, they were flying.

# CHAPTER II
# A WITCH'S COTTAGE



Koldis stayed close to Taylynn, despite knowing the forest wouldn't swallow him whole. He'd sensed the difference the moment they had arrived. The usual foreboding magic wasn't there. Normally, the forest would warn travelers away. If they *still* ventured into its depths, it would rearrange around them to trap them, confuse them, and even drive them insane. It was a protective mechanism meant to keep people from finding the spriten cities within, particularly Esterpine.

Without its magic, their journey through the trees took days. Far longer than it would have, had the trees swept them straight to their destination. The magic, when it worked, folded space and time, drawing two places together and eliminating the path between. He'd experienced it multiple times with Claire.

"Finally," Taylynn breathed, as their path widened and the city loomed before them. Her relief at the sight of Esterpine's gate unraveled the knots in his shoulders.

"Not used to finding things the old fashioned way, huh?"

She threw him a glare that said, *very funny*, clearly uninterested in his teasing. This was a serious matter, not one to be made light of. Except, she'd been in a serious mood for days. He longed to lighten her burden.

He inhaled, breathing in the pine and floral scent of the city. They began passing glass houses tucked beneath the roots of giant trees. Everything looked so familiar, as if he'd been here just yesterday. He'd never admit that it calmed him, seeing this place again. His mate's home. The place he'd discovered their bond. It held a special home in his heart now because of that.

Sprites went about their daily lives, pausing to bow when they spotted Taylynn. They paid him curious glances. They didn't know about the bond, but they'd learn of it soon enough. He hoped there'd come a day when his presence would be as accepted as hers.

"*Ayas Loaya,*" a guard greeted as they approached the palace. "*Aahm tir nin outah barihon?*"

Koldis frowned. Once they were mated, he'd understand the language perfectly. Until then, he was forced to pick out various words. He recognized *barihon*. They were asking about their queen —Claire.

Taylynn gave an answer that made the guard nod grimly. She ascended the stairs, not bothering to wait for him. He trailed after her, feeling a little forgotten, though he didn't take it personally. He'd grown used to her ways. It was best to leave her be when she was in this state. The state of carrying the weight of her people upon her shoulders.

The queen's advisors were waiting for her. They held hushed conversations in a language he could not understand. The sprites knew something was amiss. They'd been the first to inform her of the changes within the forest. She'd been honest with them about the nature of the situation. They looked to her in their queen's absence.

It was a burden he wished he could shoulder with her—for her. It was in his nature to want to nurture and protect his mate. To muscle his way in and pick up the load she carried. Listening to Taylynn converse in Ednuar, answering questions and advising her people, he'd never felt more helpless.

He hated it, even knowing it was something he had to accept. He would—of course he would. Especially if it meant getting to keep her.

"Come along," Taylynn said nearly an hour later, once she was finished. She took his hand, looking as eager to be away as he felt.

"Where are we going?" he asked as she led him through the city.

"My home."

He faltered, then quickened his stride to walk beside her. "You don't live in the palace?"

She huffed. "Not for a long time, Koldis. I prefer to make my own way. While I have accommodations there, my true home is hidden in the forest. Though..." She frowned. "We'll have to find it the *old fashioned way,* as you put it." A smile tugged at her lips, the first he'd seen in days. He wanted to see ten more just like it—no, a thousand. Ten thousand.

Unable to stop himself, he changed the hold of their hands, twining their fingers together. Her lips parted and her eyes dilated, just from that simple act. He was pleased to see a slight flush creep up her cheeks. It wasn't for the first time that he wondered what sort of romantic encounters she'd had before he came along. He'd be a fool to believe her a virgin. Not *this* woman, this thousands of years old creature. He'd be lying if that didn't intimidate the hell out of him. More than he cared to admit, anyway. Just meant he needed to show her how proficient a partner he could be for her. Gods, he couldn't wait for that.

Several hours later, they stood before a cottage. Well, cottage was a rough word for what looked nothing like the elegant glass houses in the city. He frowned. "You...live here?"

"It's rather quaint, is it not?" Her expression beamed with happiness and pride.

"Quaint is one word for it. Looks like a witch's cottage more than anything."

"Oh, stop." She swatted his arm. "Witches are for storybooks."

"Is that so?" He pulled on her hand, dragging her to him. The feel of her body in his arms set him on fire. Before she could squirm away, he dropped his mouth to hers and kissed her. She instantly softened in his arms, kissing him back. Her tongue was tentative at first, flicking out in search of his. At the feel of it, he groaned. Her hair was thick in his fingers and he clenched it in his fist, holding her there, right where he wanted her. Gods, it was torture, having this female but not truly having her.

When they pulled apart, they were both breathless. Her accusing glare made him chuckle. "I've been wanting to do that all day, *Ayas Loaya*," he drawled. Her chuff was meant to sound like a scoff. It only made him grin wider.

"Come, let me show you my *witch's cottage*." She tugged on his arm, leading him past overgrown shrubs and vines bursting with colorful blooms. A butterfly landed in her hair and she paused to laugh, the sound mesmerizing and beautiful. He reached out with his finger and it crawled onto the tip of it. They held it between them. Taylynn whispered something and it flew off. The whole area was swarming with butterflies. Bees, too.

The wooden door of the cottage opened with just a touch. She led him inside. Glowing lights came to life. He blinked, taking everything in.

It was... It was...

Taylynn's lyrical laugh made him blink. "The look on your face is priceless, *Drengr*."

"It's not what I imagined and yet, it's exactly as it ought to be."

Her lower lip caught between her teeth. Was she being...shy? It certainly seemed so.

The cottage was more forest than anything, except, it was very obviously a place for living. He didn't know where to look first. There was an alcove of narrow shelves stacked with books. Another with bottles and vials in different colors, full of ingredients. Vines covered everything. Dried herbs hung in clusters from the beams in the rafters.

A wooden table sat in the middle of the space, covered in fragments of parchment and broken quills, empty ink bottles, and other bits and pieces. A cold hearth was across from that, with a massive cauldron for cooking or brewing.

Another alcove held a bed, heaped with pillows and linens. It was large enough for two, for him, thank the gods. The walls of the alcove had more shelves bursting with more books. Some were spilling out and all were a mess of sizes and ages. There was a wardrobe beside the alcove, its doors hanging ajar. He spotted a mix of fabrics bursting free, from gauzy and delicate to practical and durable.

A small sitting area was off to the side of the sleeping alcove with two worn but cozy arm chairs, a small sofa, and tea table. There was another small fireplace to center it.

A narrow ladder took his gaze upwards to a tiny loft. A platform, really. A shelf spanned the platform with potted plants. The floor was heaped with pillows and rugs. A place for reclining, then.

Mullioned windows let in patterns of light, half overgrown with greenery. The light danced on all the surfaces. It was utterly perfect.

"Do you like it?" Taylynn was suddenly before him, taking in his wondrous expression with a hopeful one of her own.

"I more than like it," he growled. He reached for her hips, lifting her, clearing a space and setting her on the table where he could better kiss her. He stood between her legs and ravaged her mouth, kissing without restraint. She responded eagerly. "Tell me we might stay here for a while. Just us. I want you all to myself."

She nipped at his lower lip. "We have a job to do."

"I know," he groaned. "But I'd like to test out that bed over there. Is it comfortable? Looks like it was made for me. *For us.*"

A breathy laugh escaped her lips. He loved making her laugh. Loved the sound of it. Was addicted to it.

He hadn't done much of it over the past few weeks, since they'd left the keep.

Their journey had taken them first to the hatching grounds, where the wild dragon hatchlings were due any day. They'd spent time with Fright before venturing on foot into the heart of the forest. She'd been distant over the past few weeks. Now, she seemed present. He wasn't about to waste the opportunity.

He splayed his hand over her stomach, pressing her backwards against the tabletop. A surprised breath escaped her lips. "I think before trying the bed, though, the table will do just fine." He bent over her without giving her a chance to squirm away, kissing her jaw, her neck, trailing downwards until her clothing got in the way. She laughed when he bit her through the fabric, as if to rip it in two.

They became a mess of limbs and mouths as he worked to shed everything that kept her hidden from him. He intended to taste every inch of her flesh before he let her go. Sensing his need, she didn't fight him, instead growing pliant and soft beneath his hands. Beneath his ardent lips.

Everything else disappeared when the sound of her gasps filled the cottage. His worries, their missing king and queen, the threat of Kane—all gone. There was only his mate, beautiful and breathless beneath his mouth, her hands tangling in his hair as she pulled him more firmly against her center. Only the taste of her. The desire to make her feel good.

In those moments, that was all that mattered.

Night had fallen. He'd moved them both to the bed, where they lay tangled in a mess of limbs and lips. "You've got too many clothes on," she complained, burrowing against him. The sight of her naked skin on display made him uncomfortably tight in his pants, as he had been for the past few hours.

He'd made a thousand plans in his mind for their mating, for when the time came. Pictured taking her a thousand different ways. Imagined all the sounds she'd make for him. Until then, he was forced to exercise restraint. There was plenty to do that didn't involve sealing their bond, and he intended to explore all of it. He would know her body inside and out, better than he knew his own, when the time came.

"Take them off, then," he challenged, right as the sound of a growling stomach filled the cottage. They both laughed. "Or, on second thought, let's get you some food."

She pouted, a face he never imagined a princess like her might wear. "Ignore my stomach. It can be sated in other ways."

He huffed, rolling out of bed and stalking around her living space. "Where's all the food?" he groused.

She sighed, coming up to her knees to watch him. Her eyes were wide and seductive, lips swollen from kissing. For a moment, the sight of her naked, full breasts on display, struck him dumb. He stood there, staring at her chest. His mate. *His.*

"Trap door next to the table—into the cellar."

"Huh?"

She laughed, sinking back into the blankets. "Gods, you're hopeless."

He blinked. "Trap door...right." He shook his head, clearing out the image of her there with all that skin, and found the latch on the floor.

Stairs took him into a generous cellar bursting with sacks of grain, fruits, vegetables, nuts, and even hard cheeses, all preserved by magic. The space was arranged ideally for food preparation. He found a tray and began gathering a modest meal, laying it out to be eaten with their fingers. As soon as that thought came to him, he smiled. Yes, he'd very much like to feed his hungry little mate straight from his hands.

When he returned with two goblets of wine and a heaping tray. He found Taylynn lounging in a gauzy robe. He climbed into the heap of blankets, setting the tray between them. He wasn't subtle in the way his gaze raked over her body, barely hidden beneath the shimmery fabric.

Her stomach growled again and he reached for an apple slice, lifting it to her lips. "Eat," he demanded, his voice rough, low. Her eyes darted to his in question before her mouth obediently opened. He felt the flick of her tongue against his fingers. There was something sensual about watching her chew, watching her throat bob as she swallowed.

He knew, without a shadow of a doubt, that she had never been vulnerable like this for *anyone*. Regardless of whatever lovers she'd had before him, she'd never revealed herself as she did for him. It was a prize beyond imagining.

By the time their food was gone, he was aching. There was no comfortable way to sit. He was all but ready to morph into a drengr and shred his pants. Taylynn put him out of his misery, clearing their meal away and putting her hands on him, removing his clothes and bringing him to completion in the most wicked way. He'd expected it to offer relief, but it hadn't. Instead, her deft handling of him left him hungrier than when they'd started. He suspected it would always be like that for them, even once they'd bonded.

Buried beneath the blankets, he held her close, skimming his fingers along the soft skin of her bare back, listening to the sound of her steady breaths. "We should set out first thing in the morning," she said, a lazy quality to her voice.

"Agreed." He angled his face to kiss her forehead. "Will we be successful?"

"I cannot tell. I..."

"It's all right," he soothed, pulling her more tightly against him.

Since the king tree's disappearance, her foresight had dried up. She'd been reluctant to tell him at first. This was a matter of pride for her. Losing the ability made her feel as if she no longer had anything to offer.

"What does your gut tell you?"

She nuzzled into the crook of his shoulder. "That we are too late." Her words were a gentle whisper.

He tensed. "And if he has all five?"

"Then he will surely make his next move against the kingdom."

"Have you any idea what that might be?"

She was silent for a long time. When he tilted his head to look down at her, he found her eyes already on him, something akin to despair in their depths. His stomach hardened. "He will use them to overthrow the monarchy."

His jaw flexed. "Then we can't let him get the last two. We'll set out at first light tomorrow."

"Tomorrow..." she breathed. He settled against her, listening to her breaths as they evened out. Eventually she fell asleep, but it was lost to him. So he simply held her, memorizing the feel of her body against his, until the light stretched long and the first, faint blue vestiges of dawn pricked through the windows.

# CHAPTER 12
# PELWYNN

*The Gable Forest*

Koldis couldn't help his wandering mind. Couldn't help the thoughts that replayed every moment from the night before. The feel of Taylynn's flesh beneath his fingers. The small sounds she made. The taste of her lips—

"Not long now, I think." Her voice jolted him.

"You *think*?"

"It's different when the forest isn't guiding me," she explained.

He pressed outward with his mind, feeling a collection of skittering consciousnesses. Squirrels and chipmunks, concerned about their foraging. Rabbits. Birds, too. Even the distant flicker of a unicorn.

What would it be like, he wondered, to have so few cares? He couldn't fathom it. His entire life had been spent caring about one thing or another, and those cares had only gotten worse.

"I think... Yes. Just here." Taylynn stopped at the edge of a clearing. He came up behind her, pressing close against her back. He couldn't help himself, couldn't help the shiver of eagerness that raced over his skin. Gods! He was lovesick.

At the center of the clearing there was a tree—not the king tree.

It was stunted, its trunk and limbs gnarled with age. There was a gaping hole in its center. He knew without having been told that the stones were hidden within the tree. Or, that they should be.

He took a step around Taylynn. Her hand shot out, fingers wrapping around his wrist. He froze. "Wait," she warned. "Let me check the wards."

"I thought the forest—"

"Do you want to get sliced to bits based on my assumptions?"

"For what it's worth," he said, grudgingly, "I trust your assumptions."

He trusted her wholly.

She sighed, shaking her head. Then she lifted a hand and moved forward, as if feeling the air. Her hand dropped. "As I suspected. Nothing."

"So the protective wards are all gone?" She nodded in confirmation. "But the stones?"

"Let us hope they're still safe. Stay here, I'll check."

He fidgeted, watching with his heart in his throat. She strode across the clearing and stopped at the gnarled tree. Her arm delved into the hole at its center, disappearing into its trunk, all the way to her shoulder. A small cry of relief fell from her lips.

"All good?" His own relief was palpable.

"All good," she said.

A twig snapped. His eyes darted up and his blood ran cold. From the far side of the clearing, a slithery voice said, "Excellent. I would have been most displeased."

Taylynn went rigid, her arm still hidden within the trunk of the tree. Koldis's hand went straight for the hilt of his sverak as the undergrowth parted. He blinked. Knowing what he would see still didn't prepare him for the gut-wrenching shock of it.

Kane emerged, his movements hindered. At first, Koldis couldn't tell why. Then he spotted the body Kane dragged behind him, bound and gagged.

"Kane," Taylynn hissed. She didn't move, didn't pull her arm free. Like she was afraid to. Koldis growled low in his throat, a warning.

His first thought was to protect his mate.

Taylynn's eyes settled on the prone figure Kane was dragging behind him. "Oh, gods! Pelwynn! What… What have you done to him?!" she demanded.

"I've poisoned him," Kane said, a triumphant smile spreading across his lips. "One of my own unique concoctions, I'm afraid. There *is* an antidote. Just one dose. I'll give it to you, if you hand over the stones. Otherwise I'm afraid he's minutes from death."

Poison?! Koldis glanced down at the prone figure. His stomach twisted. There was no denying Kane's words. The veins in Pelwynn's body were blackening, making his skin look marbled.

"No," Taylynn gasped, the blood draining from her face. It was clear that whoever this Pelwynn person was, he meant a great deal to the princess. Which meant he meant a great deal to Koldis, too.

His skin flushed hot with anger. This was the sorcerer who'd taken Claire from them. Who'd sent her through a portal back to her world, forcing his king to follow after. The same sorcerer responsible for killing Cyrus.

Spots prickled his vision. If Kane had the antidote, he'd be carrying it somewhere on him. Koldis could kill him and acquire it. He took a step forward, drawing his blade.

"Ah, ah ah," Kane chided, holding up a hand. A glass vial caught the light. "One step closer and I smash it."

He swore under his breath, frozen with indecision. His eyes darted to Pelwynn, dying on the ground. The sprite was ancient, his movements sluggish. Pelwynn's eyes were wide with pain.

"There now." Kane turned his attention back to Taylynn. "Retrieve the stones and toss them over."

"You think I believe you?" she spat. "That if I simply hand them over, you won't vanish with the antidote?"

"You have my word."

"The word of an asarlaí," she scoffed.

"I'll leave it right here with him," Kane said, his voice calm. "All you need to do is toss me the stones."

Pelwynn had enough strength to frantically shake his head.

Taylynn caught the movement. Her features softened, turning stricken.

Koldis swore under his breath.

Had Saffra been successful? It was impossible to know if she'd managed to capture the other three stones. But if she hadn't, handing over the remaining two would be the end of it. They'd lose everything.

"Give me a moment," Taylynn managed, showing a sort of hesitation he wasn't used to. She turned away from Kane, from Koldis, pressing her forehead against the old tree. He could picture her face, eyes shut, willing answers into existence. He could picture her indecision.

He knew what she would choose and he couldn't fault her for it. Sacrifice one sprite for an entire kingdom? It sounded mundane, and yet, even the death of one person felt like too much.

Even Pelwynn was begging her with his eyes. Begging her to make the correct decision. Shaking his head in a silent plea.

"All right." Taylynn lifted her head. "I've made my decision." She freed her arm and stepped away from the tree. There was a flash of something in her hand before it disappeared into her pocket.

"Stupid girl," Kane hissed with anger. The glass vile shattered in his palm, its contents dripping uselessly onto the ground. A sob burst from Taylynn's chest at the certainty of Pelwynn's death.

Koldis growled, "I'll kill you for—"

"Take her!" Kane commanded, issuing the order to some unknown observer.

Koldis had only time to blink before the forest erupted. He cried out in warning, sprinting to Taylynn's side. A hissing, ripping sound filled the air. His stomach plummeted. He'd heard the sound before, when he'd first come here. He knew what he was about to see. The clearing filled with bodies of roots, twisting and moving with inhuman speed. The root men. Sentinels of the forest. Only—

"What have you done?!" Taylynn cried, shock limning her features.

"It was easy to twist them to my needs, without the precious protection of your forest."

The bodies were easily eight feet tall, their faces empty and unseeing, mouths yawning open. These sentinels were caretakers of the forest. They distributed reincarnated souls from the king tree, giving new life to the spriten kingdom. Lending a sentience to so many trees.

Now they were under Kane's spell.

The closest sentinel lunged. Its body was made entirely of roots snaking over the forest floor as it moved. A hand reached for Taylynn's throat. He cried out, slicing through the air and removing the arm.

"No!" Taylynn screamed, her voice pained, as if he'd harmed something precious. Didn't she understand? The forest's sentinels were not what they'd once been.

"We don't have a choice," he shouted, slashing out again and again. He had to protect her—had to protect his mate above all others. Had to protect the stones she carried.

Taylynn simply stood gaping, as if she couldn't quite believe what was happening.

Kane had taken something precious and used it against her, relying on her disbelief to stun her. The move cost them. Taylynn shook herself and managed an angry cry, stepping backwards. She lifted her arms and began to sing.

It was too late. A sentinel came from behind and snatched her up, its roots growing, weaving about her body until she was caged. Angry fury burst from her lips.

"Do something," he shouted, slashing and hacking at the powerful sentinels.

A root twisted around her mouth, gagging her. She choked. While she could do magic without words, she was too busy gasping for air, trying to breathe. To stay alive.

Heat and pain erupted along his arm. He swore, spinning on his heel, driving his sword into the closest sentinel. Hot blood dripped down his bicep. More roots lashed out at him.

His breaths came faster, more ragged as he hacked at the roots surrounding them. One of them snaked into Taylynn's pocket, groping. Meanwhile, Kane laughed. "The magic of your people cannot harm them, Princess. They are of the forest. But keep trying. I do love the sight of your pointless struggle."

Koldis roared, surging forward with renewed determination, fighting through thick roots to get to her, but it was no use. There were too many of them. Roots crept around his feet and snaked around his legs. He struggled, trying to reach his mate. He hacked at them, muscles straining. He roared with fury.

A quick movement made him glance up. A small pouch flew through the air. Kane caught it with a deft hand. "No!" he roared, redoubling his efforts.

Kane tossed it into the air then pocketed it. "Thank you," he said, sparing a single glance for Pelwynn. "It's a shame, really. He might have lived."

Koldis roared again, his gaze darting between Taylynn's stricken face and the sorcerer who held her attention. All the while, he cut at the roots holding him in place.

A wall of water appeared, a portal. The vial that had carried it dropped to the ground, forgotten. Kane offered them a cutting smile then stepped through. Taylynn screamed in fury. The sound of it shook the trees. He caught a glimpse of cave walls through the water before the portal disappeared, taking Kane with it.

He hacked himself free, stumbling forward. "Don't... Don't kill them," Taylynn rasped, right before he beheaded the sentinel who held him hostage. "Please! I can... I can..."

Tears streamed down her face. He only just realized that with Kane gone, the sentinels had fallen still. Taylynn dropped to the ground with a thump. Before he could go to her, she was scrambling forward, crawling towards Pelwynn.

"Pelwynn," she sobbed, pulling him into her arms. "Pel?"

Koldis dropped to his knees beside her, his mind racing. "Is there any way to save him? Surely you can...?"

"I... I..." She cradled the sprite's body against hers, rocking him, smoothing his white hair from his wrinkled brow. "The poison. I... I don't know." Her eyelashes fluttered, blinking back tears. She began to sing, her voice cracking. Words poured forth in a language he hoped to one day understand. They spoke of sorrow and desperation. Their plea made tears of his own spring to his eyes. He blinked them back.

One minute stretched into two, into three. Her voice grew more frantic. Still, nothing happened. If anything, the black veins beneath the male's skin worsened. Pelwynn's glowing marks dimmed, fading. Taylynn's voice faded, falling silent as another sob wracked her body.

"Tay...lynn," Pelwynn breathed, lifting an arm. His hand shook, strained. "Do not cry for me, Princess."

"I'm sorry," she breathed. "I don't know how to save you."

"You cannot, child. I am well past that. Save your breath...for something that matters."

"I failed you. I should have... I could have... I..."

*I could have saved you,* was what she tried to say. Despite everything, Kane had gotten the stones. If she had handed them over, maybe Pelwynn would still be alive.

Koldis swallowed the bile rising in his throat. He glanced between them, helpless to do anything. He'd never seen the spriten princess reduced to tears. The sight of her sobbing, struggling for words, made his breath catch. "Tell me what to do," he begged. "How can I fix this?"

"You can't!" Her breaths caught on another sob. "Even my magic won't..."

"Stop this," Pelwynn managed, brushing a finger over her tears. His hand dropped, going limp. "I am old, child. My time was coming. We both knew this."

"But the tree," she managed. "The fruit. How will we... How will I...?"

"You won't." Pelwynn's words carried a finality that made Taylynn's expression break further. "Bury me near my cottage, will you? I'd like my body to feed the garden." A keening wail broke from Taylynn's lips. "Tell Claire that...that I am sorry I did not say goodbye. She's to have my cottage, if she'd like. And you'll care for her, won't you? See that she becomes the queen this kingdom yearns for. Be her sister and her friend. Help her with her magic, when she needs it. I…" Pelwynn's voice faltered, his eyes turning glassy. "I am proud of how she turned out, that I could do this one thing to mitigate Isabella's mistakes," he decided. "She is…strong. She will endure…even though I must…must go…" Pelwynn's eyes shifted to Koldis. A smile spread across his lips. "I'm glad you found my Taylynn. She needed someone…someone like…you. You'll care for her, yes?"

"Of course," Koldis rasped, his throat thick. "Always."

"Good. She has a wild spirit, my Taylynn, but deep down, she longs to be tamed. The two of you will do well. Yes. Yes…" His words died.

"Pelwynn, no…" Taylynn sobbed, curling over him.

"Goodbye…child," he breathed. A ragged breath followed, then Pelwynn fell still.

A scream tore through Taylynn's throat. The world around them rustled uncomfortably, sensing her grief. Chills made his skin prickle.

The sound of slithering roots made him jerk. He looked over his shoulder to see the last of the root men retreating. Kane's disappearance had given them their bodies and minds back. He wanted to destroy them, simply for existing, for costing them the stones. But…he couldn't think of that now. Couldn't think of what would happen now that Kane had the missing two. He could only hope that Saffra had been successful, because if she'd failed…

No. He wouldn't acknowledge that. Wouldn't think about Taylynn's expression the other night, when she'd told him what would happen. How the kingdom would fall.

For now, his only thought was her sorrow.

He knelt with her for a long while, rubbing circles across her back. Eventually, the world darkened and he bid her come away with him. He carried Pelwynn's body cradled in his arms, following as she guided them back the way they'd come.

They buried Pelwynn where the ancient sprite had requested, in his beautiful garden surrounded by proud trees. He hadn't known how important Pelwynn was until Taylynn explained it.

Only then did he realize the gravity of Pelwynn's death. Pelwynn had been Claire's secret tutor. The one who'd taught her how to use her sprite magic when Marquin had failed.

Now he'd never get the chance to thank him in person. He could only shovel dirt, one mound at a time, to show his gratitude. No magic was used—it didn't feel right to make this easy. With every movement, his heart cracked a little more. He pictured Claire's grief, pictured her expression when he finally told her what had happened. His queen would be heartbroken.

But even more than that, they had failed.

CHAPTER 13

# THE DINER

*Somewhere Over North America*

Jovari was on edge. His muscles tensed as the overhead chime announced their arrival. This was such a bad idea, for so many reasons. He'd tried to talk some sense into Talon, but the king wouldn't hear a word of it. What the queen wanted, the queen got. He would refuse his mate nothing.

"Be with you in a moment," a voice called from behind the counter. It was a middle-aged woman with coiled red curls.

"Sure, thanks!" Claire called. She made a show of inhaling, clinging to Leah's arm. "It smells so good!"

"I'm going to order everything on the menu," Leah said. "I could eat like, five burgers."

He shared a perplexed look with Talon, who merely shrugged and grinned. He'd never seen the king grin so much in his life—Talon was *not* a grinner. He refrained from rolling his eyes and glanced at Irelia. "What of you, Princess? Are you going to eat five burgers, too?"

They'd already explained on the walk over what a *burger* was. Meat and bread, essentially. Like most things, the names amused him. But he wasn't supposed to be amused, damn it. He was

117

supposed to be annoyed, because he'd told them that this was a bad idea. That they were wasting time. That they were risking themselves. Risking running into trouble with every human settlement they encountered. Trouble that could keep them from getting home.

Alas, none of them seemed worried.

Irelia harrumphed at him. "Stop calling me *Princess*. I stopped being that when I left Dragonwall. And no." She patted her middle. "I've got enough padding already. One will do. Or perhaps some French toast."

"Ouuu, French toast," Leah breathed. "Maybe that's what I'll get."

He scrubbed a hand over his face. Gods above, have mercy on him.

It had been Claire's idea to stop at a diner to eat, despite his best efforts. Despite the risk of being recognized. Despite everything.

He glanced at the fading light outside. It would be dark soon. It was less stressful flying at night.

Regardless, they didn't have time for stops like this. Every minute, every day, would cost them in Dragonwall. Claire had begged, though, arguing that they should all have a good meal in them before passing through the gate.

Hence, why they were here.

There were only a few patrons this evening, occupying the mix of booths and tables. Loners, most of them, though he spotted a small family of four, with two little ones. His eyes snagged on the children and he huffed, pulling his gaze away.

"Now, then." Stella—according to her name tag—appeared before them, her hands on her hips. A frown materialized as she looked them over. "Is there some kind of renaissance fair nearby I didn't hear about?"

"Oh!" Claire and Leah giggled. "No. They just...felt like playing dress up?"

Stella's gaze lingered on Claire. Recognition lit her features. A brief tense moment filled the air.

Claire swallowed. "Uhm. I'd appreciate it if you didn't, you know, say anything about who I am to anybody."

"I have no idea what you're talking about," Stella said, feigning confusion before offering a conspiratorial grin.

Claire's shoulders relaxed. "Thank you."

Stella gave a terse nod. When her gaze passed over Talon's scars, her smile turned forced and she quickly looked away. "Table for five?"

"Yes, please," Leah said. "And tell me you sell milkshakes."

"Oh, the very best, yes." Stella snatched up a stack of plastic sheets with pictures of food and led them to a large, horseshoe shaped booth. "This okay?"

"Perfect," Claire and Leah said in unison. Jovari's brows lifted and he shot Talon another look. But Talon wasn't looking anywhere other than Claire.

They squeezed into the booth.

"So, it's just me tonight," Stella explained. "Can I start you off with something to drink?" She produced a writing utensil and pad of parchment from her apron, looking expectantly at them. Claire, Leah, and Irelia fired off drink requests he'd never heard of—whatever a *Coke* was, he couldn't say—then looked expectantly at them.

"Oh. Uh. Do you have any water?"

Stella paid him a bemused look. "You want lemon with that, hun?"

"Of course not!" He shot Claire a confused glance. She pressed her lips together.

"She means, do you want a lemon sliver served with your water," Leah said, leaning in to whisper. He tensed, leaning away from her, but not before getting a whiff of her lavender perfume. He eyed her and she merely shrugged.

"I'll have what she's having," Talon said, motioning towards Claire.

"You got it. I'll have those out for you in just a minute." She walked off.

Claire shuffled the sheets of plastic to each of them. He ignored his and said, "Why don't you just order for me, my queen?"

"Oh! I can order for you," Leah piped up, practically bouncing in her seat.

"No."

"No?" A flash of hurt passed over her features.

He exhaled. "Apologies, that came out rude. I would prefer it if my queen would."

"Well," Claire said, attuned to Leah's emotions, "I think I'll delegate the job to Leah, since she so nicely volunteered."

He clenched his jaw.

"Thank you," Leah said, bumping her shoulder against Claire's. They sat in the middle of the curved booth, side by side. He sat on Leah's left, with Irelia on his left. Talon sat on Claire's right, hovering.

Stella returned, setting drinks before them. When she handed out long white things, he ignored his. The others ripped the paper free and plunked drinking straws into their cups. He took a drink of his, shocked by the ice. The others found it perfectly normal.

"Now then, what can I get you to eat?" Stella had her pad out, ready to write down their requests. He observed as each was given, things like waffles and burgers. Something called a *club sandwich*— which he was certain had nothing to do with clubs of the weapon variety. Onion rings. The list went on.

Leah ordered for him, but he ignored most of what she fired off. He didn't know what to make of her. The first time they'd spoken, just before the start of this journey, he'd pulled her aside in the foyer and tried to dissuade her from coming. "You shouldn't rush headfirst into this because of some misplaced sense of adventure. You have a life here. Tell Claire you aren't going," he had told her.

"You know nothing about my life here," she'd said, her bubbly personality morphing into anger. "If Claire wants me to come, then I'll come. Last I checked, she's queen and gets the final say."

They'd argued for a few more minutes, until Claire's mom had appeared. After that, they'd resorted to silent glares. It had been a relief when she'd flown with Talon and Irelia.

He'd apologized this morning, albeit grudgingly. Mostly because of her glaring every time they stopped. Much to his surprise, the moment he'd said he was sorry, her entire countenance towards him had changed. She'd gone from silent and simmering to friendly and smiley.

He wasn't sure which version of her he preferred.

"So..." Leah said to him, bumping his shoulder to get his attention. He exhaled, willing patience into existence. Stella had already wandered off. Claire and Talon were focused on each other, talking in hushed voices. Irelia was gazing around the diner, lost in thought. "What is it you do in Dragonwall? Like, what's your job?"

He stared at her. "My job."

"Yeah, like, what you get paid for and all that." She waved a hand.

"I'm a king's shield."

Her brow furrowed. When he caught himself lingering over her expression, he shook himself free.

"So, like, a fancy bodyguard or something?"

"Aye. A *fancy* bodyguard," he repeated, unamused.

Her eyes flicked to the blades strapped in various places about him. "That's cool."

*Cool?* He frowned. Was she being genuine or sarcastic?

"All right," he said. "What is it *you* do here? Your job?"

"Oh." Some of the light went out of her eyes. He almost regretted asking, but then he reminded himself that he really didn't care. "Well, I'm a server and a bartender at Shannon's with Claire. To pay the bills and all that. But I also volunteer at the library. It's a bit of a commute, but I like it."

His head tilted. "You're a scholar?"

"I... No." A look of confusion crossed her features. "Like, I shelve and care for books, host book clubs, stuff like that."

"I see..." he said. A pink tinge appeared on her cheeks. She looked away from him. A sliver of guilt formed in his gut. "We have a massive library in the capital," he blurted. "I'm sure you would like it. If... That is..."

"Oh!" Her expression immediately brightened. "Do you think they'd let me work there?"

"I mean, those who care for the library are castle servants who specialize—" He stopped himself and shot Talon a glance. "If you're concerned about finances, I am sure Claire will take care of you. The coffers are quite large."

"No. I mean, that's nice and all, but I'd like to make my own living wherever I land."

"I understand."

"I could always fall back on my bartending experience. That makes good tips."

"A tavern wench?! Absolutely not." Something inside him turned hot. The refusal was out before he could stop it.

"Why not?" She lifted a brow in challenge.

"Because most taverns in the city are disreputable and you're the queen's best friend. The gossip would lend itself to scandal."

It was an easy excuse, one that made the most sense.

Leah snorted. "Whatever. I'll figure it out."

"That so?"

"Listen, *dragon man*, I learned how to take care of myself a long time ago."

He snorted. It was on the tip of his tongue to inquire, but he squashed it.

Stella appeared, her arms laden with plates. She deposited them then went back for more. "Gods, woman, how much food did you order me?"

There were three plates before him alone. Between all of them, the entire table was covered.

"You look like a man with an appetite," Leah said, a purr to her voice. One moment she was glaring, the next, friendly, and now... flirting?

He huffed, ignoring her words. "I take it, that's a burger?"

It was taller than he'd expected, a bun stuffed with lettuce, tomato, and a few other things he wasn't certain about.

"Yep." Leah's lips made a popping sound.

"And what about that?"

"Fries." She reached for a red bottle and squirted a red sauce beside them. "Ketchup. For dipping." She snatched up a fry and demonstrated. He couldn't help but watch her chew, then swallow. He blinked, ripping his gaze away. Not before he noticed the playful grin that spread across her lips. Like she'd caught him staring.

He copied her actions, dipping the fry in sauce before eating it. He made a grumbling sound as he swallowed.

"Good, huh?"

"It's...acceptable."

"Oh, stop." She elbowed him in the ribs. "I'm not blind. You look like you just tasted the best thing in the *world*."

He ignored her, looking at everything else.

"That's a blueberry waffle," she said, pointing to it. "I got you an omelette, too, with bacon and cheese. There's also a side of onion rings. And if you're still hungry, you can try some of my fettuccini Alfredo."

"Feta—*what*?" He looked at her plate, brow furrowed. Noodles swimming in a white sauce. Huh.

She was already wrapping them around her fork. He looked away, tackling his own food. It was divine, albeit a little rich. Still, it was perfect for his growling stomach. He wouldn't dare admit that he was enjoying himself.

"I take it, that's French toast?" he asked Irelia. She merely hummed, eyes closed while she chewed. He was tempted to try a bite but she looked rather protective of her plate.

Talon also had a massive burger in front of him. He was enthusiastically devouring it, snatching up fries in between bites. Claire had ordered him a *club sandwich* too, which he discovered had layers of bread and other things like lettuce and bacon, all held together by thin *toothpicks*.

Claire had a stack of pancakes before her, which she'd doused in syrup. He didn't miss the way Talon snuck bites off her plate. Every so often, she sipped from the mug of light brown liquid. Talon didn't touch his—not after his first sip when he'd grimaced and quickly set it back down again.

"It's coffee," Claire said when she saw Jovari staring.

He blinked. "Is it...good?" He didn't think so, based on Talon's initial reaction.

"Would you like to try?" She handed the mug over. It was warm and smelled uniquely appealing. He took a sip and his brows shot up. Claire's expression fell. "You don't like it either, do you?"

"I..." He took another sip. "Actually, it gets better upon the second try." When he took a large gulp, she snatched it back.

Stella came over to check on them. He ordered a coffee for himself. Claire helped him prepare it with cream and sugar. Talon merely glared at him.

He ate everything Leah had ordered for him, unable to decide if he'd enjoyed the burger or waffle more. His stomach was full and content. Yet, when Claire asked for a dessert menu, he was already eager to try something else.

She and Leah ordered a spread of items. When Stella returned with them, he found many familiar sights. Pies, cakes, cobblers. The ice cream was something he'd never tasted, and he commandeered it for himself. Claire hoarded a large cupcake piled high with frosting. When she got a bit on her nose, Talon leaned in to kiss it off. Jovari pretended not to see, grumbling something about *mates*.

The door chime sounded. He looked up to see a group of men walk in, their loud voices carrying through the establishment. He stared at them, taking in their black vests and worn pants. Some had chains hanging from belts. They all had black ink tattoos covering their skin.

Stella seated them at a large booth near the door. A tickle of unease shot down his spine. "We should leave now," he warned. "We've lingered long enough."

Stella came by and dropped off their bill. Claire grabbed it and provided a stack of currency to pay for everything. Apparently she'd brought it with her for this reason, specifically.

His neck prickled. He could feel eyes on them and didn't like it.

They shuffled out of the booth and made for the door. The

voices of the newcomers quieted. Then, "What the fuck kind of costume is that supposed to be?"

They kept walking.

"Hey! I'm talking to you!" One of the men came to his feet. Their entire group smelled of stale drink. Drunk, no doubt.

"Isn't that the girl from the news?" one of the others demanded. "It is! I'd recognize that pretty face anywhere. Too bad she's a freak. Bet aliens really *did* get her." They shared a laugh.

Talon let out a low growl, his steps faltering. Hot anger clogged Jovari's throat but he pushed Talon forward. "Keep going," he snarled. "The last thing we need is to draw attention. I told you this was a bad idea."

"I can take every single one of them," Talon growled. "Let me at them."

"Yeah, and get the cops called on us," Leah squeaked, dragging Claire along.

"Fair point," Talon huffed. "But let it be known—"

"Yes, yes," Claire cried. "Let's go!" Then it was Claire dragging Talon by the arm.

They rushed from the diner and didn't stop to look back. He didn't breathe easily until they'd left the small settlement for the open fields beyond, the dark swallowing them up.

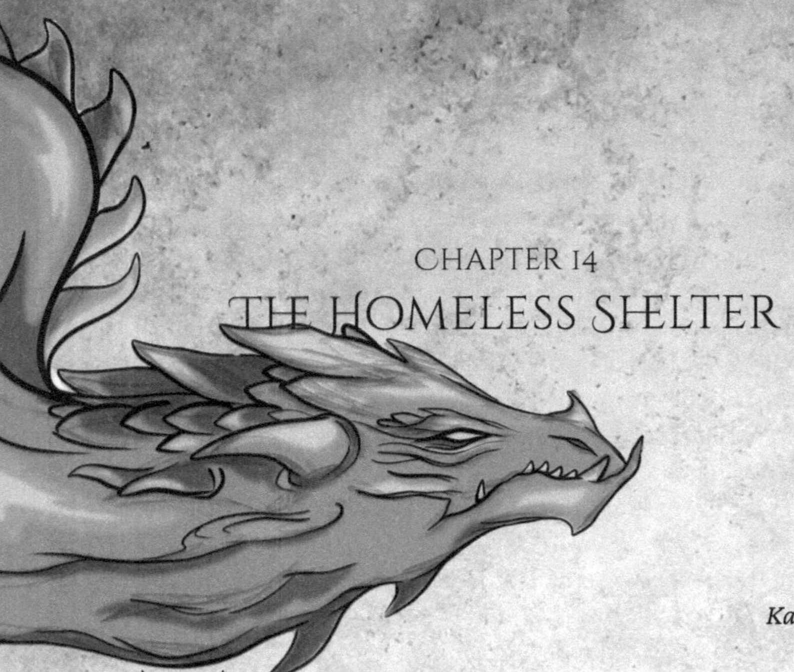

# CHAPTER 14
# THE HOMELESS SHELTER

*Kastali Dun*

Merrian cringed at the sight of her hem, stained with mud. Ordinarily, there would be no saving this gown. But nothing about her new life was ordinary. Hopefully, her spriten handmaidens had some form of magic capable of restoring it—*she'd* certainly never been proficient with cleaning cantrips of the magical variety—otherwise, she hoped it wasn't one of Claire's favorites.

The city's streets were always filthy, but especially today, after two days of rain. The sun was finally shining. She intended to take full advantage of the day. Especially since she had some free time away from her new duties as queen.

She paused, lifting her face towards the sky. She took a deep breath. The air was briny and fresh, with only a hint of mildew, and very little of the usual stench. Life in the keep was stuffy. She'd never realized how much until recently.

She sloshed through another puddle, her boots squelching in the mud. She had tried hiking up her skirts, she really had, but she'd since given up. Besides, wasn't a queen above such things?

She had fifty gowns, at least—no, even more. Surely *someone* in her position wouldn't care.

"Your Majesty," Dallin warned, a hint of exasperation in his voice. He always said it that way. Their little joke. "Are you sure you know where you're going?"

Passersby gawked, scrambling out of their way. It was impossible to go unnoticed with such an entourage. Not only was Dallin with her, but an entire regiment of spriten guards trailed in her wake.

"I know exactly where I'm going," she announced. "Follow me."

They rounded a corner, trudging deeper into the city's depths. The back alleys of Kastali Dun were a maze—one she'd memorized years ago. A nondescript door came into view. She couldn't help her smile.

Behind her, Feowen muttered something under his breath. She didn't care to listen. Instead, she knocked.

There was a pause, then the door swung open and a harried looking middle-aged woman answered. Her face had laugh lines that spoke of a hard but fulfilling life. Her hair was hidden beneath a kerchief. The woman looked at her first with annoyance, then with wide eyes as she realized who stood upon her doorstep. "Your... Your Majesty," she sputtered.

Mer ignored the pinch in her chest. It was a *very* different greeting than what she was used to from Glenna. Normally, they'd already be hugging, each trying to speak over the other as they caught up on all the latest news.

"Hello, Miss Surati." Glenna's eyes widened in surprise. Mer forged ahead. "I had a couple of hours free, and have come to assist in any way that I can."

Glenna Surati operated a shelter on the outskirts of the Pauper's District. There were a number of these establishments in this part of the city, but Glenna was one of her favorite people so she'd chosen this as her first stop of the day.

"You... But... You..." Glenna's eyes flitted between her and her entourage. "But, Your Majesty, surely..."

"I can assure you I have nothing more pressing at the moment. Please, I know you need assistance, both healing and otherwise."

Glenna cleared her throat, rubbing a hand over her collarbone. "Very well then, this is all very untoward."

"Certainly," Mer nodded, her expression serious.

"I must warn you, our house isn't…isn't fit for someone in your…position."

"Miss Surati, you forget that before I came to Dragonwall I was an outsider, and even after I arrived, I took on the role of a servant, cleaning chambers and such."

"Yes, but…but servant work in the keep is a far cry from the likes of us!" Glenna snapped, then blanched. "Forgive me, I did not mean to be so forward."

"There's nothing to forgive. Please, let's go inside. I will help with whatever I can."

"That would be most welcome." Glenna stepped aside, her expression nervous as Mer walked into the receiving room. She couldn't help but wonder if the real queen would ever come to a place like this, or if such behavior was beneath her. From what she'd learned through the others, Claire would be the first to help a woman like Glenna Surati.

Dallin and her guards followed close on her heels, filing into the parlor. She caught a flash of Feowen's expression, curious but also guarded. His eyes, like those of her other spriten guards, darted around, searching for danger. They'd find none here.

The room was dimly lit and sparsely furnished. Her guards fanned out to inspect their surroundings. A small gasp drew her attention to the doorway. Peeking out from the shadowed hallway beyond, two little faces appeared, a boy and girl. She recognized them instantly and almost called out their names. Blood filled her mouth as she chomped down on her tongue. Mer might have known them, but Claire did not.

"Tir, Nira!" Glenna snapped, going rigid with embarrassment. "You know better than to spy when we have guests."

But Tir and Nira didn't hear Glenna. They were wide-eyed, enamored by the otherworldly bodies filling the parlor. "It's all right," Mer urged, biting her bottom lip to keep from grinning. "Would you like to meet my guards?"

Nira stared, her soft brown eyes sparkling with curiosity. Tir, on the other hand, squealed with glee and rushed forward. Nira eventually followed her brother out of the shadows.

Mer was about to facilitate introductions between everyone when Feowen stepped forward instead, a wide grin on his face. He went down on one knee and said, "Well, hello little ones. What are your names?"

"Tir!"

"Nira!"

"Well, now. Those are nice names," Feowen announced, keeping his smile bright and inviting. "And how old are you?"

"Six," Tir announced.

"Both of you?" Feowen lifted a brow.

"Uh-huh." Tir nodded vigorously.

"We're twins!" Nira said proudly.

"I thought you looked like siblings," Feowen said, his expression turning serious. "Siblings must always look out for one another, yes?"

"I always take care of my sister," Tir said proudly, lifting his chin. Feowen reached out and tussled Tir's shaggy brown hair.

"No! I take care of him," Nira countered, as if jealous of the sudden attention her brother was receiving.

"Is that so?" Feowen turned his fierce regard upon the little girl. She was growing more comfortable in his presence. Several spriten guards shifted. The moment Nira was reminded of their presence, her mouth snapped closed. "Oh, don't fear them, child." Feowen took her hand in his and gave it a little squeeze. "Would you like to learn their names?"

Nira nodded.

"Me too!" Tir announced.

Feowen began making introductions.

Mer took the opportunity to pull Glenna aside. "I'm certain you must have some sick occupants? With my spriten abilities, I can do what I can to heal whomever requires it." It was a lie. She was no sprite, even if the markings on her skin fooled everyone. But she'd do her best.

"We would be most grateful, Your Majesty," Glenna said, her face flushed.

"And what of your funding? How are you getting by?"

Glenna's throat bobbed, eyes darting to the floor. "We do the best we can, Your Majesty. The supplemental funding we receive each month is put to good use."

"But it's not enough, is it?"

She already knew the answer. She and Glenna had held many long conversations on the matter. It was unlikely that the woman would admit that to the queen, though.

"I... I am grateful we get anything at all," Glenna said.

"Well, let's go over the numbers before I leave and we can determine where your deficits lie. I brought coin enough to cover necessities, with a little extra."

Glenna's lips parted in surprise. "That would be... Thank you, Your Majesty."

Glenna took her on a tour of the shelter, leading her through the large rooms packed with cots arranged in various clusters. Those who ended up here had little privacy, but a bed and a roof were better than the city streets. There were four large rooms in total, taking up space on the upper floors. The lower floor was reserved for a cookery, dining room, and sick room.

The dining room consisted of makeshift tables made from crates and stools. Glenna worked hard to make her shelter cozy. She repurposed various items, and covered the tables with repurposed fabric for tablecloths to make them look fancier. Today, she had several bouquets of dried flowers placed about, giving the room an inviting feel. Several clusters of people were gathered together sipping tea and playing cards. They all gaped at her—the queen.

Glenna's shelter was only meant to be a pass-through for those who fell on tough times, but often, people stayed for months, even years. She would never turn someone away who didn't have a home. But she did require everyone to follow certain rules, to respect each other, and to stay out of trouble while they attempted to get back on their feet.

The sick room was located at the end of the hall, across from Glenna's own private apartment. That way, she was within shouting distance should emergencies arise. With low funds, the room was little more than a cluster of cots, curtains, a sanitary station, storage shelves, and a single window, currently open to air out the stench of sickness. It wasn't great, but it was the best they could do.

Half of the beds were filled.

"It shouldn't take me long," she told Glenna. "I'm sure you have other things to oversee, so please, don't let me keep you. I'll come find you when I'm finished."

"You're sure?" Glenna twisted her fingers together.

"Positive. Thank you."

"Good. Well, then. I'll just see if your guards would like some tea, then." Glenna slipped from the room.

Dallin, Feowen, and Jeanine had followed her in here, Feowen's two admirers creeping along behind him. There was a woman scrubbing out rags in the corner. Her work stalled as she gaped at them.

"Hello," Mer said. "I'm Queen Claire."

"I know!" the woman said, breathless.

"Right. Yes. Of course." It seemed everyone knew who Claire was, even if they'd never met her.

"I'm Amelie, Your Majesty," Amelie blurted, then flushed when her eyes fell on Feowen. She couldn't blame the poor woman. He *was* beautiful to behold. Jeanine smirked, clearly aware of the effect he had on others.

"You can call me Claire. This is Dallin, Feowen and Jeanine. We're here to help." Her eyes darted around the room, taking everything in as if for the first time. "Can you tell me what ails each of them?"

"Certainly." Amelie set off to explain each patient's ailments. Once that was complete, Mer sent her off on an errand. Feowen was silent, trailing after her as she went from bed to bed, laying her hands over each person and healing whatever she could.

Some of them were too sick to comprehend what she was doing. Others were well enough to gape or even profess their undying admiration. A few were shy, and told her she ought not to trouble herself with them, as if they weren't worth her time. Those were the ones she put the most effort towards.

As was usual, the symptoms ranged. Some sicknesses were more permanent and required deeper healing. She wasn't especially powerful, but she did what she could. For the issues that were chronic or terminal, she addressed the symptoms to help ease their pain.

That was, until Feowen pulled her aside. "That man—Amelie said that he has a terminal wasting sickness?"

"In his intestines," Mer explained.

His lips pressed into a line and he nodded. "Let me try."

"You're sure?"

"Yes." Feowen stepped forward, greeting the man with a low voice. He hummed, running his hands over the man's body. It took long minutes, but eventually the prince looked up with a pleased expression. "I think I have fixed it. I'm not like other sprite healers, who specialize in this sort of thing. But..."

Mer expelled a breath. "I think whatever you did is far better than anything I could manage." There was no disguising the gratitude in her voice.

She worked with Glenna afterward, going through the shelter's numbers and handing over enough coin to get everyone in the home a new set of clothes and enough food to see them through the next two months.

Glenna was in tears by the time she left.

Glenna Surati's shelter was only the first. At the second, more of the spriten guards grew curious with her work. They offered to help with the sick. A fierce sense of pride well up inside her. Of course Claire's guards would be selfless. She shouldn't have expected anything less. She simply wasn't used to people in power noticing the needs of others beneath them.

They worked at two more shelters after that before heading back. As they made their way through the streets to the castle, Dallin escorted her. "I'm taken aback," he admitted. "I never expected you to want to help all of those people yourself."

"Happy to surprise you," she said. She was weary but satisfied by a full day of labor.

"You do this regularly? Attend to the sick and homeless?"

"I do. Though, usually I charge a small fee for my healing, if I can. I've got to feed and house myself, too. But I only charge what I need to survive. It's far less than any mage healer would charge."

"That's...admirable. The queen would approve. Not that I know her as well as the others do. Still, I don't think she realized there was such a need."

Mer found herself snorting. "Most folk are oblivious to the needs of those less fortunate. It's not usually a conscious decision. Everyone has their own busy lives. Even still, there are plenty who do nothing when the evidence is right under their noses. I would imagine that Claire simply wasn't exposed to places like the Pauper's District on a regular basis."

"No, I cannot say that she was. King Talon didn't like her wandering about, unless it was to the market."

"Understandable. Especially after what happened to her, when she was kidnapped."

"Exactly," he said. "I think when she returns, she'll like meeting you."

Mer's stomach squirmed at the thought. "Really?"

"Really."

She wasn't sure how she felt about the prospect. Nervous, to meet the true queen? Unworthy, because she wasn't all that important? Fearful, because Claire might dislike anyone trying to pose as her? Or excited, because what she was coming to learn about the queen made her want to truly know the woman? Regardless, it wouldn't be possible unless the queen returned. She hoped for all their sakes that she did.

CHAPTER 15

# IMPOSTERS

*Kastali Dun*

Merrian sat silently on her throne—Queen Claire's throne. She offered the occasional nod or murmur of greeting as courtiers came before the king to sort out matters of importance. Court was held daily, with both morning and afternoon sessions. On top of those, there were meetings with the merchant's guild, various craftsman guilds, the lower council, and so on and so forth. While she wasn't expected to attend everything, Reyr insisted on her presence for most of them.

She wondered if he was secretly trying to torture her?

"I heard you went into the city yesterday," Reyr said, looking out over the cathedral style hall. "To the Pauper's District." His words were low enough to go unheard by others. The only reason he spoke at all was because they were in the middle of a short intermission; courtiers were socializing, freely moving about the throne room.

"I did," she confirmed. "Dallin accompanied me. As did the queen's guard."

"I'm aware." A long pause, then, "Dallin informed me that you visited the homeless shelters and spent time with their sick."

134

Her jaw clenched. She had taken a liking to Dallin, but she felt almost…betrayed that he'd reported her comings and goings. It made her wonder how much he'd told Reyr.

"I wasn't aware that spending time with the sick was a sin."

"It isn't. But it could be dangerous."

"Oh? How so?"

"Your health," he grumbled. "Humans are known for their weak disposition—catching illnesses and all that. Who knows? You could pick something up and die within hours. We'll have to go through this whole business all over again." He gestured towards her crown.

A small scoff burst from her lips. "Firstly, Your Majesty, there are healers for that. I'm a queen now. I can afford even the most expensive healer, should I take ill." Unlike the poor folk in the shelters she'd visited. "Secondly, being a healer myself, it is unlikely that I will succumb to anything and die within hours—"

"What are you talking about?"

She laughed, incredulous, because he didn't know. "Princess Taylynn didn't tell you?"

"Tell me what?" Reyr's gaze remained on the courtiers, tracking their movements.

"That I'm not human. I'm a mage—a low level mage, yes. But I have magic, nonetheless. Long life. The ability to heal more quickly than a human because of my blood. I'm not going to pick up some illnesses and drop dead."

Reyr tensed beside her, his mood instantly darkening. It was obvious that he didn't like not knowing this. Perhaps if he'd taken the time to get to know her, he wouldn't feel so blindsided. "Be that as it may," he said through gritted teeth, "there are already charities set up for that sort of thing. You cannot simply drain our coffers without following the proper protocol."

Gods, now he was grasping at straws. What was it about her behavior that bothered him so much? Was it really that he was against helping the poor and destitute? Or did it have everything to do with her? Likely the latter.

She rocked her jaw side to side, irritation clouding her vision.

"Believe me, I'm well aware of the *charities* put in place by the crown. Well aware of how well they truly serve their purpose. And you need not worry, Your Majesty, the money I spent yesterday was from my own personal account. You know, the one you pay into so that I can be here, disguised as your missing queen?"

She caught a slight flush creeping up his neck. His eyes darted to her before quickly returning to the courtiers still milling around. He seemed to have nothing to say to that. Good.

Mathis, the steward appeared. The throne room was called to order, as he introduced the next person on the agenda. She wanted to listen to what they said like a good queen, but she was fuming. Her head filled with angry buzzing, like she'd stuck it into a hive of bees.

The patron was a woman. She spoke with the king for several minutes. A decision was made, though she couldn't have said what. She clenched her muscles tightly, watching as the woman walked away.

"Why do you hate me so much?" she whisper-hissed before the next patron was announced. She regretted the words the moment they were out.

A breath blew from Reyr's mouth. "Hate is a strong word. Dislike would be better."

Her mouth popped open and she quickly closed it. She knew he didn't like her. Hearing him say it shouldn't be such a surprise. "I did absolutely nothing to you. Other than being here. Taylynn asked me to take this position. Should I have refused?"

The next patron was announced and Reyr motioned them forward. "...No," he said after a long pause. His jaw was clenched. The admission had cost him.

"Then *why*?"

"I'm allowed to dislike people. There's no law that says I have to like everyone in existence."

It was the stupidest thing she'd ever heard. She wanted to tell him that, and yet she still struggled to speak her mind. The constant reminder to be seen and not heard—his words—haunted her.

What if she just...slipped away? Left. Abandoned this ungrateful male and left him to flounder on his own.

No. She needed to stop thinking that way. Taking a deep, calming breath, she attempted to focus on the court proceedings.

Try as she might, her mind kept popping back to the king beside her. He hadn't answered her question. Being allowed to dislike someone wasn't an explanation.

Was it because the spriten princess had appointed her without consulting him? Probably. And yet, as a spriten princess, Taylynn had more authority than Reyr. Being a fake king didn't grant him status over her. So technically, it had been within Taylynn's right. Besides, everyone in the inner circle had agreed that this was necessary.

Over the past month, she'd studied Reyr—who looked exactly like King Talon. How could she not? He was imposing and impossible to ignore. Unfortunately, she'd gleaned no obvious reason for his dislike.

She *did* notice that he appeared near his breaking point. He snapped at everyone—a trait the actual king supposedly possessed. He never appeared to sleep. The few times she'd come up to the main room in the king's tower, when she also couldn't sleep, he'd been there brooding. Today, he appeared on edge. Crushed, no doubt, under the weight of the kingdom.

She tried to put herself in his shoes. To see things from his perspective. His best friend, his shield-brother, and his queen were all missing. He was worried, perhaps even frightened. And here she was, a nobody, who thought she could simply step in and take Claire's place.

Gods, no wonder he disliked her.

Except, it didn't give him the right to be rude, even hurtful. If she was capable of seeing things from his perspective, then he ought to be capable of seeing them from hers. To know that she was doing this as a favor. That she was here to help, even if money was a huge motivation. It wasn't like she was a selfish, money hungry person looking to take advantage of the royals.

Her head gave a painful throb. Too much thinking. Too much stress.

She nearly burst into tears when the steward brought an end to their morning court. Especially since afternoon court had been canceled, so that the king could attend to other pressing matters. Gods, she hoped she wasn't needed—

The throne room's doors crashed open. Cries of surprise spread through the courtiers.

At first, she ignored the noise, too caught up in her frustrated emotions. Then, someone screamed.

Her breath froze in her lungs. More screams followed as people stumbled, retreating from the lone figure that strode into the hall. He was cloaked, his face hidden.

Mer's heart took off at a gallop, hands tightening on the armrests of her throne.

The guards outside the doors were no longer standing. She caught sight of their prone figures, blood pooling around them. Her stomach lurched, bile rising into her throat. A frightened squeak slipped from her lips. Several courtiers tried to slip through the doors, only to be stopped by guards in foreign livery.

She made to stand, to flee through one of the side doors, but a hand closed around her forearm.

"Don't move," Reyr ordered in a voice she'd never heard from him before.

Verath and Dallin surged protectively in front of the dais, drawing their sveraks.

"No need for that," a slithering voice called from beneath the hood. A hush fell over the throne room. A few whimpers sounded.

"Kane," Reyr growled, coming to his feet.

Bony, pale hands lifted, peeling back the hood that disguised a gaunt face. Mer couldn't stop staring at the sorcerer's blood-red eyes. Kane. It was Kane! Oh, gods! They were all going to die!

Her eyes darted towards the side door again, but her body refused to move. Deep down, she knew that if she tried to flee, Kane would strike her down with magic. Besides, she couldn't abandon the courtiers, even if her magical abilities were laughable at best.

Everyone believed she was their queen. They thought that with her, they'd be safe. That she'd use her incredible magic to defeat Kane.

Only...she couldn't.

"Good morning, *Your Majesties*. Or should I say, imposters!" Kane's accusation left the courtiers muttering. Reyr's hand jumped to his sverak. Kane clicked his tongue. "I wouldn't do that."

He shed his robe. At first, she merely gazed at him. Then she noticed his breastplate. Along the collarbone were indentations. Stones. There were four, with a fifth spot empty.

Kane lifted a hand. Within his palm, a golden stone glittered.

Reyr swore under his breath, his skin blanching. Because he wore Talon's face, his scars stood out like silver lines. His eyes flashed with fear.

"If you draw a single blade against me, this stone goes into its place, and we all know what happens when it does."

More muttering from the courtiers.

Kane barked a laugh. "Ah, of course." He turned towards the crowd. "Most of you don't even know what these are. They're dragonstones, forged by my ancestors, the ancient asarlaí. Their sole purpose was to act as a failsafe, to ensure that dragon kind never got too powerful. Only, I don't think they ever planned for what happened afterward. *Tsk tsk.* That is neither here nor there. Bring all five stones together and every being of draconic descent, be it dragon or drengr, turns back into the substance from whence they originated. Isn't that how the story goes?" Kane looked at Reyr for confirmation.

Reyr's breaths came faster and faster. "What do you want?"

Mer had to commend him for his steady voice. Hers would have broken into a high pitched squeak. In fact, she probably couldn't form words if she tried.

"The kingdom," Kane said. "What else?"

"You think I'm going to step aside and doom my people—?!"

"Your people?!" Kane laughed. Mer's skin broke out in chills.

"You aren't even their king." Courtiers glanced at each other with questions in their gaze. "Oh. But of course. They ought to know. You see, everyone," Kane said, addressing the throne room, "your lovely king and queen aren't who they claim to be—"

"Enough!" Reyr cried. His chest rose and fell in rapid pants.

"Oh. No. They ought to know. Here is how this will go. You're going to step aside while I take the throne. We'll show these lovely courtiers—soon to be my *loyal* subjects—exactly who you are. If you don't, well, I'll just turn you to stone and do it anyway. No?"

Reyr's throat bobbed. Mer's eyes darted between Reyr, the two shields at the base of the dais, and the rest of the courtiers. No one moved. Kane held the remaining stone in his hand perilously close to his chest.

Her stomach clenched painfully.

"Do it," she hissed under her breath to Reyr, begging him to surrender. "You have no other choice."

She hated the words as soon as they were out of her mouth, because it felt like giving up. Dallin and Verath glanced over at them, their expressions anguished.

Reyr's eyes darted towards hers before returning to Kane. "If I agree to step aside, what of these people? What of Dragonwall?"

Kane chuckled. "You think I'd slaughter them? Come now," he tsked. "Who would I rule if I killed them? No. Everyone will have a chance to swear themselves to me. All who are loyal will live *happily* under my new rule. I'm not a barbarian," he added, scoffing.

Mer clenched her jaw hard enough her teeth nearly cracked. It took everything in her to keep her mouth shut. To keep from arguing that point.

"Come now, surrender. You've lost. Surely you can see that."

"I have your word, then?" Reyr asked. "You'll allow them to live in exchange for loyalty?"

"As I said." Kane's expression glittered with preliminary triumph. He knew he had won. They all did. What other option was there? They couldn't doom an entire race of drengr. What would happen if the drengr turned to stone? Could it be reversed? Would they know themselves afterward if it was?

Or...was it certain death? Dead, the drengr would be useless. They needed to remain alive, so they could fight back.

"Very well." Reyr's words were heavy as a hammer blow. They settled into the silent room. Tears sprang to her eyes. She wanted to reach out and grab his hand—she might have hated him, but right now, it was them against Kane's evil. "I will surrender the throne."

"And your...*shields*?"

Dallin took a step forward, as if to attack. Verath's hand shot out, wrapping around the young drengr's forearm. "We surrender," Verath said. He dragged Dallin aside, leaving the way to the throne free.

"Good. Then, as a last matter of business—" Kane's hand flashed. Two guards came forward in foreign livery. It took her a moment to realize they were Osheans. She only knew because she'd seen so many dead ones after combing the battlefield outside the city's walls.

The guards walked up to the dais and presented two vials.

"Those are for you," Kane explained. "Drink them."

"That wasn't part of our agreement," Reyr bit out.

"You are not in any position to argue. I could kill you right here on the spot. Instead, I have other plans for you. So, drink up, that way your beloved kingdom knows you've been lying to them."

She and Reyr exchanged a glance.

"And if I refuse?" Reyr asked, lifting his chin.

Kane waved his hand again, flashing the stone. "Then you know what will happen. It's good insurance, is it not? Bring all five stones into contact and you cease to be a problem for me."

Reyr's jaw ticked. "Fine," he bit out. The guards climbed the dais stairs and handed them each a small vial. She had no idea what was in it, only that whatever happened next wouldn't be pretty.

"Now, do as I say," Kane hissed.

Popping the cork, she lifted the vial to her lips and drank.

# CHAPTER 16

# LOSING THE KINGDOM

*Kastali Dun*

Reyr ignored his pounding heart, the warning blaring in his mind, and tipped the vial into his mouth, swallowing down the contents in one gulp. The concoction burned all the way down, its flavor acidic. He recognized the taste: hints of dragon's bane and something else. He shuddered. His skin broke out in a sweat and his body began trembling.

Verath, who'd kept a steady stream of communication with him, went silent.

A muted gasp sounded beside him. He jerked his head to the side, abandoning his own discomfort. His imposter queen looked exactly like he felt. Her eyes were wide and unseeing. He reached out, taking her arm just as her body sagged. Then her facial features began to change, her hair darkened, and she shrank several inches.

His body was changing, too.

He distantly registered gasps from the courtiers. Registered that Dallin and Verath were also handed similar vials. Registered that they also drank them.

What choice did they have?

He blinked as the discomfort faded. Claire's lookalike was no longer standing before him. Instead, Merrian gaped up at him. He wanted to ask if she was all right, but Kane was already speaking.

"So you see," he told the crowd. "They are not your rulers after all. Your rulers are *gone*. King Talon abandoned you. He isn't even in this world anymore."

Cries of surprise echoed through the hall.

Reyr's skin heated with anger. "He's only gone because you—"

"Ah-ah-ah. I'm king now. I get to decide who speaks and what truths are told. Oh, and I'll be taking that." Before Reyr could react, Kane muttered a few words under his breath, an incantation. The heavy crown upon his brow flew into Kane's free hand. His other hand still held the glittering golden dragonstone.

If only he could grab it from the sorcerer—

"Guards!" Kane's voice rang out. "Seize them! Toss them in the dungeons."

"Aren't you going to kill us?" he scoffed. He would have preferred it. At least dead, he wouldn't have to face this failure.

As if reading his mind, Kane said, "I want you to watch me rule in place of your precious king. If he returns, I'll enjoy witnessing the moment he realizes that you lost him his kingdom."

It took every bit of Reyr's control to remain in place. He wanted to surge forward and attack. Wanted to plunge his blade through the sorcerer's chest. Even at the risk of damning all of dragon kind.

But the sorcerer would never allow him to get close.

A set of guards in Oshean livery marched forward. He eyed them with distaste. It confirmed Talon's prior suspicions that Kane was working with Oshea.

Merrian cried out as they were taken. "Don't hurt her," he growled at her guards. They ignored him, wrenching her arms behind her back, clapping her in shackles. He was vaguely aware of them doing the same to him.

Merrian's blue eyes flashed with fear, her chest rising and falling in rapid bursts. He hadn't ever seen her like this—so terrified she could barely breathe—and it did something to him.

"It will be all right," he told her in a low voice. It was all he could think to say, even though it was a lie. Nothing about their situation would be all right.

Kane had succeeded. Their worst fears had come to life. It was stupid to hope that Bedelth and Saffra might beat him to the stones; he couldn't bear to think about that—about what Kane had done if he'd intercepted them. Or Koldis and Taylynn, for that matter. But they were alive. He knew in his heart that his brothers were alive. He would have felt their deaths. Which meant they'd failed. Kane had the stones and he was helpless to do anything about it.

They were dragged away, Dallin and Verath behind him.

"One more thing before you go," Kane added. "If you try to escape your guards, or if you do not stay where I put you, I'll turn you to stone." He flashed the golden dragonstone again in warning. "I gain nothing by keeping you and your kind alive. I'm only doing it out of the kindness of my heart."

Reyr scoffed. "Right. *Kindness.*"

What a farce.

Kane's pale face turned splotched with anger. "This kingdom never belonged to you, *Drengr.* It belonged to the asarlaí. Your kind only took it. So yes, I'm taking it back. Enjoy your cell."

With that, the sorcerer strode to the dais. Reyr caught a glimpse of him ascending the stairs before the guards dragged him away. Just before they passed through the doors, he heard Kane's next command issued to the Oshean guards. "Bring everyone within the keep to the throne room. Immediately. Use force if you must. It's time to learn where their loyalties lie."

Reyr's stomach squirmed with dread. There were too many people loyal to the crown—so loyal that they might choose death over life. He didn't want that. He'd rather they pretend to serve Kane. Every death would be his fault.

Cries sounded throughout the castle as people were dragged from their chambers. Servants pulled from their duties. He watched as nearby guards escorted a huddle of people towards the throne room. Gods, Kane had made quick work of his takeover.

There were no Oshean ships in the port, which meant he'd been lying in wait, plotting in secret.

"Can't we...do something?!" Dallin hissed. They were nearly to the dungeons. Once they went in, they wouldn't come out.

"Do something?" Verath snorted. "And risk the ruination of our kind?"

"What if he's bluffing?"

"He's not bluffing," Reyr said.

"Quiet! All of you!" one of the guards snapped, shoving him forward with more force than necessary.

Merrian walked beside him, her head held high. Despite her posture, he didn't miss the fear in her blue eyes.

He caught a flash of movement in his periphery. Pale skin and luminescent markings. Prince Feowen. The sight made his shoulders instantly relax. The prince motioned with a finger to his lips, then slipped into the shadows.

Thank the gods Claire's spriten guards hadn't been in the throne room. From the looks of it, they might be safe. He could only hope they escaped before Kane combed the castle, looking for them.

He wasn't sure how thorough the sorcerer would be. Was the city also taken? Would there be Oshean guards at the city walls, denying entry and exit to those passing through? What would happen to Kastali Dun's citizens?

Darkness swallowed them up as they descended into the depths of the keep. The dungeons were a maze of tunnels. The guards that normally occupied the guard room had been disposed of. They lay prone on the ground, their throats cut. He swallowed, looking away.

They were taken to their respective cells.

"Enjoy your new home," one of the guards sneered, unlocking his shackles and then Merrian's before pushing them through a door.

"Get your hands off me!" Merrian hissed. She stumbled, tripping and falling to her knees before the door slammed shut behind them.

He heard another clang before silence descended. It was heavy and oppressive. Then, there was the only sound of their ragged breaths, his and Merrian's. The darkness was absolute.

Out of habit, he muttered a cantrip to create an orb of light but nothing happened. "Godsdamn it!" he swore, pulling at the shackles around his wrists.

"What's the matter?" Merrian asked, standing.

"There was dragon's bane in the brew he forced on us."

Merrian let out a colorful string of curses. He blinked, taken aback. He'd never heard her lose her composure. "It prohibits the use of magic," she realized.

"Exactly." While he could see in the dark, he doubted she could. "Are you..." He cleared his throat and tried again. "Are you all right? Are you hurt?"

There was a long silence. "...No."

He expelled a breath. "Good." He walked across the room and slid down the wall, coming to sit on the floor. He closed his eyes. Perhaps he could sleep and forget any of this had happened.

"What... What do we do now?"

His eyes flew open. "Are you serious?"

"Obviously."

"Gods above, woman. I don't know. Sing lullabies? Braid each other's hair? Waste away in this cell? Take your pick."

"There's no need to be rude."

"Rude?! The kingdom of Dragonwall has just fallen to a sorcerer and you're worried about me being rude?!"

She tutted, then walked over to the opposite end of the cell, sinking down onto the floor like he'd done. He waited for her to say something else. To snap back. Claire would have. Instead, she just ignored him. And maybe that was worse.

In the crushing silence, his chest caved in. He had failed. Months upon months of work, and it came to nothing. He'd lost them the kingdom.

Talon had trusted him with this.

He felt numb.

None of this seemed real.

Maybe it wasn't.

~

Reyr opened his eyes. He was greeted by a familiar darkness. Everything came rushing back. He dragged a hand over his face.

"You're awake."

He blinked, registering Merrian's voice.

Several days had passed, but he didn't know how many, exactly. It was impossible to tell in a place like this. Impossible to track time in the darkness.

"Is your telepathy back?"

He blinked. His mind was fuzzy and sluggish as he tried to reach out to Verath, to Dallin, to anyone, but nothing happened. "No."

Kane kept him plied with a constant supply of dragon's bane concoctions. If he didn't drink them, the threat was always the same. Annihilation of dragon kind.

Part of him was tempted to test the sorcerer's claim. To see how far he could push Kane before he brought the stone into contact with the others. If only to end this.

Merrian didn't answer. He wasn't surprised. She'd taken to ignoring him. Besides the occasional question, she kept to the opposite end of their small cell, as far away from him as possible. There were cells enough beneath the keep that Kane could have separated them, but he had a feeling the sorcerer had paired them up on purpose. If only to make everything worse.

Instead of suffering in silence, he was forced to suffer with an audience.

It was just as bad, if not worse for her. There was no privacy. They were forced to use the bucket in the far corner, which got dumped once a day. While he didn't particularly care about such things at his age, she was younger and had balked, holding out for as long as possible before she could no longer ignore her body's functions. He didn't tell her that the drengr could see in the dark— not that he'd watched her empty her bowels.

At least her not knowing this little fact gave her the illusion of privacy.

Not for the first time he wondered how old she was.

Her words came back to him—that she was a mage. She might have looked twenty-something, but she could have been a hundred and he wouldn't know. Mages lived long lives. The more powerful, the longer they lived. Marcel was hundreds of years old. Saffra would live to be hundreds of years old—until she completed her bond with Bedelth, after which she'd share his lifespan.

A clang sounded. He jerked, then came to his feet. The sound wasn't unusual, so he already knew what to expect when the small pass-through opened and a tray of food slid in. The pass-through closed with a clang.

He eyed the tray. A spread of boiled meat, bread, roasted carrots, and fruit. There was a pitcher of water. It was barely enough for two. At least it was edible. He'd half expected starvation, or to be served some form of inedible mush. Many of the prisoners were given rations of pottage. Kane was flexing this supposed *kindness* he'd mentioned, probably congratulating himself over it. Such a kind and just ruler. He was forced to withhold a snort.

He pictured the gaunt sorcerer sitting on Talon's throne, a smug expression on his face as he went about ruling Dragonwall.

That was the worst of it, though. Not knowing the truth of what was happening. All he had to go on were Kane's words. It sent his mind spiraling every time he thought about it.

A light flared, an orb, brought into existence by Marrian's muttered words. Kane didn't know that she was a mage, so he hadn't bothered to take her magic. It didn't surprise him that the sorcerer had underestimated her, assuming her to be some expendable human.

He plucked up a bit of food, quickly swallowing it down, then took the rest to Merrian. "Not half bad."

She only huffed, snatching the tray and scarfing down the rest. If she noticed that he was purposefully eating less than usual just so that she could have a full serving, she made no comment. Gods, what would happen when he went without hunting? How long could a drengr go without feeding that urge? Would the dragon in him go insane?

What a thought! Perhaps he'd become a little more like Talon. He'd already gotten half-there over the past several months.

He went back to his spot opposite Merrian and leaned his head against the wall. All he could do was sit and think.

And think.

And think.

And think...

It was a blessing when he managed to doze. At least then his mind softened so that he might temporarily forget how bad this was. How horribly he'd failed.

The guards came with another dose of dragon's bane. He'd swallowed three now. No, perhaps four. He was losing count.

It never tasted quite as harrowing as the initial concoction, the one that had also reversed the sprite's magic for his disguise. Whatever Kane had concocted had been powerful.

They didn't simply drop off the vial and disappear, either. They stayed to make sure he took it. He knew what would happen if he didn't. The threat was always the same.

He sensed something was different this time when they stepped into the room. Merrian cowered in the corner, her posture wary. They never paid her much attention, but that didn't stop him from putting himself between them.

"The king has a message for you," one of the guards said.

It illustrated his desperation, the way he latched onto those words. He was hungry for whatever scraps of information he could get.

"Oaths from all the courtiers have been sworn. Rewards granted to those especially loyal. The leaders of each fort are on their way to swear their troth today. Invitations have been sent to the sprites and dwargs. All those who fail to appear will be considered traitors."

"Kane is delusional if he thinks—"

The guard's fist shot out, connecting with his stomach. He

keeled over, the wind and words knocked out of him. His movements had grown sluggish thanks to the dragon's bane.

"You *will* respect his majesty with proper use of titles when you speak about him."

Reyr spit on the ground beside the guard's foot. "Maybe I'll return that blow, see how far *King Kane* lets me go before he makes good on his threat. Hmm? I doubt he'll destroy my kind if I break your nose."

The guard took a step back, finally wary as he said, "His Majesty fully expects the dwargs and sprites to refuse. He's hoping for war." Then he retreated from the room, an empty vial in hand, and slammed the cell door.

CHAPTER 17

# REACHING ESTERPINE

*Northern Wilderness*

Bedelth's chest heaved. Each breath seared the insides of his lungs. He strained, ignoring the pinpricks of light swallowing up his vision. He had stopped feeling the pain in his shoulder joints hours ago, numb to it. He couldn't feel his forearms either, even though they were still in the same position, still cradling the beloved body of his mate. He'd wrapped her in her cloak to keep her warm.

A sharp pain splintered down his wing joints and he cried out, forced to drop in altitude.

No. Just a little longer. He could see the trees on the horizon. See the sea of green stretched out across his vision. Five more wing beats, he told himself. Just five more. Then he would stop.

Five beats later, he promised himself five more. And so on and so forth.

His thoughts were fragmented. A mix of guilt and pain and fear. Fear so immense he couldn't think straight.

He'd gotten to Saffra's wound in time, using magic to keep the poison from spreading. Still, a good part of the skin surrounding it was already blackened. The sight brought too much pain to the surface. Reminded him of how Cyrus had suffered. How he'd died.

Just five more beats.

Another debilitating cramp seized his wings. Oh, gods. For a moment, they stopped beating all together. Then he was plummeting towards the earth. A new panic took hold.

Ignoring the searing scream of his muscles, he forced his wings to flare out at the last moment, catching the wind before they gave out entirely. It was enough to slow him, but not enough to save them.

A roar burst from his jaws. He curled his body around his beloved mate, crashing to the ground at a dangerous speed. He rolled, keeping Saffra protected within the cocoon of his body. The earth shook with the impact, dirt and debris flying as he carved a crater into the land. Then he just lay there, his giant draconic chest heaving.

He blinked once. Twice. Feeling the clear inner membrane beneath his eyelids stick to his dry eyes. Then, he scrambled into motion, unfurling his body to check on his love. Safe—she was safe and unscathed. Her eyes darted frantically beneath her lids. She didn't wake, and that's how he knew it was bad. She hadn't opened her eyes for more than a full day.

When he'd departed the ancient hatching grounds, leaving the foreboding mountains behind, he'd kept her cradled against his body. She had drifted in and out of consciousness, remaining mostly unconscious for long spans of time, but never this long. Setting her gently onto the ground, he lifted on his hind legs and stretched.

Spasms wracked his body, seizing control. His muscles gave out and he immediately collapsed beside her. He considered transforming, carrying her in his arms and walking, but he didn't even have the energy for that. When had he taken his last break? He couldn't remember—hadn't even slept for three days.

His vision darkened, then faded entirely.

~

A RAGGED SCREAM tore his eyes open. He surged up into a standing position, talons digging furrows in the dirt. Saffra was writhing on the ground, her body contorting. He dropped his snout to her, brushing his forked tongue gently over her fevered skin. Her cries turned to pained whimpers. Just a little longer, he wanted to say. He almost transformed, just so that he could speak aloud to her, but resisted the urge. It would waste too much energy—too much of his magic needed to keep her poison from spreading. No, he had to keep going.

"Bedelth…" she managed, her eyes still squeezed shut. She knew he was there. Could sense him. That would have to be enough.

The moment he reached for her, she gave another cry. He pressed his snout to her cheek and was immediately engulfed in her mind. The pain seized his breath. He didn't breathe for several long seconds.

Then he did what he'd done before. He took her pain and funneled it into himself as best he could. Her whimpering stopped. He was careful to keep contact as he picked her up, cradling her body against him, keeping her face pressed to his scales. It was the only way. He couldn't bear it otherwise. Couldn't bear her suffering when all of this was his fault.

He deserved the pain.

She was his mate and he'd failed to protect her. His hind legs sprang from the ground. His muscles protested as he stretched his wings. The pain only mixed with what he already felt. Moments later, he was airborne.

Hours passed in a haze. The forest grew closer until the trees rose up like a wall. He was already descending, prepared to trek blindly into the forest's depths, even knowing the risk. But then he spotted it, right where it ought to be. Riltar Outpost.

He'd drawn the map in his mind. All those hours spent racing south. Hoping beyond hope that he judged his direction correctly.

He plummeted towards the forest outpost, letting out a warning roar. A plea for help. Several sprites emerged from the outpost building. He set his mate gently on the ground before transforming.

"Drengr, what brings you...?" Their eyes darted towards the figure on the ground.

"Your mate?" One of the sprites asked.

There were three. Two females and a male.

"I need... I need to get her to Esterpine." The sprites exchanged a look—one he couldn't read. "Please. She's been poisoned. I need a guide."

"What is your name?"

"Bedelth. I am—"

"Ah. Yes. A shield." They exchanged another look and then, "You may fly her there yourself."

He blinked, then blinked again. "We only tell you this because of who you are. The forest is unprotected—its magic is gone. You may fly directly over it, south-west from here. You ought to see the sky-gazing platforms in the canopy. From there, you may descend into the city."

He didn't question the *how* of it. He merely nodded, thanked them, and transformed again, wasting precious magic. A few moments later, he was gathering Saffra into his arms. Her unconscious form pliant in his arms.

He sprang into the air and took off over the trees.

There was supposed to be magic here, intended to keep dragons from flying overhead. That magic acted like a wall, stopping all those who might pass through. Only, it didn't stop him.

He followed the sprites' instructions, keeping his eyes peeled for the sight of the sky-platforms. Hours passed. The sea of trees beneath him felt endless. Every second, Saffra was closer to death. Every second, he risked losing her forever.

Gods. He never should have taken this mission with her. It had been for naught. And all that had come of it was this. He'd only just won her to him, only just earned her love, and now he was going to lose her.

His heart cleaved in two, the thought crippling in its devastation.

No. He wouldn't lose her. He couldn't. Just a little further.

He spied the platforms, letting out a joyous roar as he descended. He draped Saffra's body gently onto the wooden planks, then back-winged to get some height before transforming. Sweat beaded his brow. His muscles strained as he picked her up again, finding the stairs, carefully navigating them.

His heel slipped and he cursed, slowing down.

He went around and around, sinking deeper into the forest's depths, until the city materialized below him. He spied the crystal palace in the distance through the trees, gleaming like an ice sculpture.

"Help!" he shouted as soon as his feet hit the ground. He took off sprinting in the direction of the palace. "Help! Someone, please! We need help!" He was not above begging.

His cries brought spriten onlookers as they emerged from glass houses and the forest beyond. They wore confused expressions, though surely they recognized him. This wasn't his first time here.

A male stepped into his path, halting him. "What is the matter?"

"She needs healing. She's been injured—poison. The vodar." He could barely form words, his breaths labored. The crowd murmured. Then it parted.

What he saw next made him fall to his knees with relief; he held Saffra against him, a sob of relief tearing from his chest.

"Bedelth?" Taylynn's gentle voice was filled with concern. Her eyes darted to the form he was curled protectively around. Then another body stepped out from behind her.

"Koldis?!" he gasped.

Koldis glanced between him and Saffra, then his face paled and he rushed forward at the same time as Taylynn.

"Save her," he begged of them, imploring the sprite princess. "Save her, please. I'll do anything."

"Come, bring her to me," Taylynn said, her expression stoic and unreadable. Koldis grabbed his elbow and lifted him to his feet. Together, they rushed through the city.

~

Bedelth watched as Saffra's eyes fluttered before they finally opened. Her hand was cradled in his. It tightened, clutching him before it relaxed again.

"Bedelth?" Her eyes locked onto him. Emotions flashed across her gaze. First, confusion, then relief.

"I'm here," he murmured, leaning in and brushing her cheek with the backs of his fingers.

"Water," she croaked.

He reached for the cup at her bedside, helping position her so she might drink. She took a few tentative sips, then drained the entire thing, sighing before falling back against the pillows.

"Where... Where am I?" Her eyes darted around their surroundings.

"In the kingdom of the Sprites. Esterpine."

His mate's lips parted. "This is Esterpine?" Her keen gaze took everything in anew. They were in a glass house, one of the guest houses within the city. The same that Claire had stayed in during her first visit here. Ironic really, that Claire had recovered from her wound in the same place Saffra now did.

He hummed, then brushed his fingertips over her face. "How do you feel?" he asked, glancing down at her bare arm. The sight of it made him flinch—not because of how it looked but because of what it reminded him of.

She noticed his reaction and frowned, looking down. "Oh."

"Forgive me," he croaked. "I... I failed you."

"Bedelth, no—"

There came an impatient knock on the door. They both froze. Before he could speak, it swung open and Koldis rushed in, his eyes wide with shock.

Bedelth surged to his feet. Somehow he knew. "No."

Koldis's throat bobbed. "The news just arrived."

"No," he said again. A finality in his voice. As if that could change what had happened.

"What's... What's going on?" Saffra managed.

Koldis's gaze finally snapped to her. She was sitting now, pushing the blankets away from her legs. "Don't stand up," Bedelth barked, sounding more forceful than intended. She needed to rest. Her body had been through too much.

"Someone needs to tell me what's going on right now, or I'm going to lose it," she demanded. "You both look as if someone died."

"Reyr?" Bedelth asked. "Dallin? Verath?"

"We don't know yet." Koldis looked dazed. "But I don't think... We would know, wouldn't we?"

Bedelth gave a jerk of a nod. Yes. They would feel it—surely.

"Enough!" Saffra snapped.

"Forgive me," Bedelth said again, scrubbing a hand over his face. His nose tingled. Was he going to cry? Good gods. If ever there was a time, this would be it.

"The capital has fallen," Koldis said.

"What?" Saffra's breathless cry filled the silence. She sank back onto the bed. "No it can't... The stones. He still needs the other two."

"He got them," Bedelth managed. He sank back into his chair just before his legs gave out. "We... You were sleeping, but Koldis and Taylynn, they..."

"We failed." Koldis lifted his chin, squaring his shoulders to accept the blame for what had happened. "Taylynn and I found the stones and let them slip right through our fingers. I don't think either of us expected Kane to show up like he did, to use her weakness against her. The sentinels..." Koldis shook his head, like he couldn't say another word.

Bedelth already knew the whole story. Saffra had been unconscious for two days. It was plenty of time to discover what had happened. All the while, Saffra had been in a deep, healing sleep. The sprites had done everything they could to purge the poison from her body. He wasn't as good as Koldis when it came to healing. Hence, the blackened flesh around her arm. They'd almost considered removing it entirely, but her hand was still usable, even if a good part of her bicep was now completely dead flesh.

They'd enchanted it, turning it into a hard, bark like substance. No blood flowed in that region, though it did flow through a portion of her arm, down through her forearm and hand. She would feel nothing if cut there again, but it would allow her to keep her arm, the shape of it anyway, and she could wear long sleeves to cover it so that no one knew of its existence.

He hoped she would cover it. If only to avoid the reminder of how he'd failed to protect her. Of how this was *his* fault. Would she blame him? If she did, he deserved it.

"So, it's over then?" Saffra's voice was weak. "That's... That's it?"

"It's not over," Koldis growled. "I'll fly there myself and end him—"

Saffra's burst of laughter was deranged. "You? End him? Please, Koldis!"

"I will not just sit here and—"

"The only person who has any chance of ending him is Claire," she cried. "And if she can't, we're all doomed. Except, she's gone! All because I fell for Kane's stupid ploy—"

"Enough!" Bedelth roared. Gods, he was so tired of her blaming herself for that. Not that he was in any position to judge. He certainly took the lion's share of the blame now. "Where is Taylynn?"

"If you're counting on her to come up with some miraculous solution, think again," Koldis growled. "My mate isn't everyone's problem-solver."

Bedelth recognized the defensiveness in Koldis's tone. Hot shame coated the inside of his throat. He slumped back. "Forgive me. I didn't mean... I only wished to know if she had any recommendations on how we might proceed. I certainly doubt she condones sweeping in and confronting the sorcerer who now holds all our lives in the balance."

Koldis stalked across the room and plopped down on the sofa. "She doesn't," he muttered. "When I told her my intentions, she told me that she had more important things to do than listen to my stupidity and stalked off, adding that I could come and find her when I pull my head out of my rear end."

Saffra's laugh was genuine this time. "Sage advice."

Koldis huffed and a small corner of his lips tugged up before his expression turned grim again.

"What do we do, then?" Bedelth voiced the question they were all struggling with.

"If Claire is the only one who can fix this, then we are probably stuck waiting for her."

"I'm tired of assuming our queen is responsible for fixing all our problems. She has enough on her shoulders as it is," Koldis said, irritated.

"She chose this," Saffra reminded them. "She made the promise. Irresponsible or not, she spoke the words that made her fate our reality. Like it or not, she's the one who must end him or the promise might end her in return. Our job is to make it as easy for her as possible."

"She's not even here," Bedelth huffed.

Koldis sat up straighter. "But she will be, won't she? When Talon and Jovari bring her back? I was with Jovari the first time. He knows where the gate is nearest to Claire's home. I assume that's the one he will use to return. Which means..."

"They'll travel through the Kengr gate," Bedelth and Saffra said in unison, before looking at each other.

Bedelth huffed. "By being here in Esterpine, we'll be directly in their path."

"Then, let's make sure we have a plan once they reach us." Koldis stood. He walked over to the bed and bent, kissing Saffra on the forehead. Bedelth blinked. Were it any other male outside of their circle, he would have seen red. But this was his brother. All he felt was warm affection for Koldis and his gentle gesture.

"I'm glad you're feeling better, Saffra," Koldis said. "And don't worry about the arm. I think it looks fearsome." Then he offered her a grin and left, quietly closing the door behind him.

# CHAPTER 18

# SWEARING AN OATH

*Kastali Dun*

Tamara's breaths were shallow as they made their way into the quiet streets of Kastali Dun. The difference in the capital was stark. She saw few people roaming the streets, shutters locked tight. A heaviness permeated the air, the dread nearly tangible.

Flying over the city was no longer permitted. The drengr were required to enter through the gates like everyone else. Byron kept a tight hold of her hand, leading her through one of the poorer districts. The people of Fort Squall trailed behind them, drengr and riders alike.

They'd been summoned. Ignoring it would have meant the end of dragon kind.

"I think I'm going to be sick," Byron muttered. She squeezed his hand offering gentle reassurance.

"Your father would want you to do this," she whispered. "Reyr would want you to do this."

"Then why does it feel like I am betraying them?"

"You are protecting the drengr race. There is no betrayal in that." If only believing her words was as easy as speaking them.

The thought of swearing fealty to Kane was abhorrent. It made her feel as sick to her stomach as he felt.

The clatter of hooves and wheels made them stop and step aside. A large, barred wagon came into view, heading towards the docks. The sight of it, stuffed full of people, made ice slide through her veins. It was flanked by soldiers on horseback wearing Oshean livery. "Stand back," they ordered, turning sneers upon them. She and Byron stepped further out of the way.

She stared in shock as the wagon trundled by. It was massive, a cage more than anything, with people stuffed together like livestock. "Please," a woman cried, reaching for her, her face stained with tears. "I have children."

She took a step forward, only to be pulled back by Byron. *"Careful,"* he warned, glancing towards the Oshean guards. *"We have no power here."*

Confusion warred with fear.

A man on horseback trotted somewhat behind, his gaze greedy and pleased. His clothes were different from the fashions worn in Dragonwall. An Oshean merchant, perhaps?

"You there," Byron said, grabbing the man's attention. "Who are those people? Where are you taking them?"

The man turned to scoff at them. "What's it to you, *Drengr*?" His words were heavily accented. Byron's gaze was hard, unrelenting. The man huffed and said, "Suppose there's no harm in telling you. They're bound for the slavers. Criminals and such."

"The... The slavers?" she cried. Her heart began to race. He couldn't just—

"Don't you know, girl?" The man was quick to grin. The sight made her muscles lock up. "Slavery's legal, now. I paid a pretty steely to buy them from the city's jail. Criminals don't deserve freedom."

"And what about after all the criminals are sold? When there aren't any left?" Byron spat.

The man fussed with his sleeve, unconcerned. "There are always people eager to break the law." With that, he trotted off, catching up to the carriage.

"We have to do something," Fierran said from behind them.

"There is nothing we can do—for now." Storm clouds brewed in Byron's gaze. "We must do as we were ordered or risk the lives of our kind. But I will look into it. Now come, all of you."

THE THRONE ROOM had changed since the days of King Talon and Queen Claire. Every beautiful stained glass window had been shattered and replaced with depictions of the asarlaí. Black flags and Oshean livery decorated the rafters. A heavy presence of guards kept conversation to a dull murmur. It made tears spring to her eyes, to see it so diminished.

For weeks, rumors spread regarding the absence of Claire and Talon. Byron had learned the truth of it months ago, but he'd sworn to Reyr that he would keep it a secret. They remained silent as the members of their fort grappled with confusion in the wake of Kane's ascent to power. Why would their monarchs disappear? Why would they abandon them to a fate such as this?

The real reason was almost worse than the speculation over it. It kept her up at night, sick with worry. Had the king found his mate? Had he gotten trapped in Claire's world? Why else would he be gone for so many months?

Maybe it was better this way. Tucked away in her world, Claire was safe from the monster who now sat before them.

"Come forward," Kane ordered. He lounged lazily on his throne, a hand fisted around the fifth dragon stone.

She shot Byron a glance. His jaw was set. He led her to the base of the dais where they were commanded to kneel and swear allegiance to the worst sort of person in the kingdom. Her gaze darted towards the guards on either side, standing proudly in their Oshean livery. It didn't feel real—none of it felt real. This was a fever dream, surely. It wasn't happening.

*"Deep breaths, love."* Byron's voice steadied her.

He went first, speaking the words of Kane's oath. "I, Byron the Blue, leader of Fort Squall, do so swear my loyalty to King Kane, to be true and faithful, to obey the law which he sets. To uphold order as befits his will. If I fail to keep my oath, my life is forfeit."

She repeated the words in turn. They tasted sour on her lips. The magic was binding. She felt it wrap around her heart, pulling tightly, chaining her. They might be only words, but from this day forward, they could not act directly against their new king.

One by one, each drengr and rider spoke the same words. She glanced around the room. Courtiers stood off to the side, watching with defeated expressions. They had sworn oaths the day Kane ascended to power.

Fort Squall wasn't the first to pledge. Fort Lin had been summoned a week prior. Fort Edge would be here next week. Kane was careful to plan it accordingly, to keep the forts separated. He forbade them from visiting Fort Kastali whilst here. They were allowed to spend one night in the city, then they were expected to be on their way—

"We will not swear an oath." Dagen and Sandra stood before the dais, their shoulders back, chins lifted. Her stomach squirmed at the sight. Byron swore under his breath. "I understand why my comrades must," Dagen said, "but we cannot."

*"Dagen, don't do this,"* Bryon warned. *"They're just words. Your heart is what truly matters—"*

"Dagen," Fierran growled in warning from beside them. Dagen and Sandra were two of the oldest remaining members of the fort. They'd nearly won the vote as fort leaders. She almost envied them. She wasn't brave enough to choose death over life. Not if it meant serving someone like Kane.

*"It isn't brave, it's foolish,"* Byron pointed out to her.

"We would rather die than serve a tyrant," Dagen hissed, eyes locked on Kane. He ignored the pleas of his other fort members.

"Then die, you shall." Kane motioned and two guards stepped forward. "On your knees."

Her eyes widened as both Dagen and Sandra complied.

"No!" she whispered. This couldn't be happening. Surely they would change their minds and swear an oath. "No!"

Byron gripped her hand to keep her from rushing forward, from throwing herself in front of the people she was supposed to protect.

The Oshean guards stepped up behind them.

"Final chance," Kane taunted. "It makes no difference to me whether you live or die. But your comrades seem to prefer you to live."

"Dagen!" Byron warned. "I command you—"

"Get on with it, then," the aging drengr growled. Sandra reached for his hand. Were it not for the slight tremor in the way she latched on to him, she would have appeared unfazed.

Tamara stifled a sob.

"Very well. I condemn you both to death. You will not receive a drengr's mourning. Your fellow comrades will not take to the skies to sing their song, nor will you be put to the flames. This I command. You may die." He gestured.

Swords lifted, glinting in the torchlight. She sucked in a breath. They were dark metal—ice metal.

*"Look away, love,"* Bryon demanded. *"Now."*

*"I—I can't."*

Blades cut through the air simultaneously. There was a sickening squelch as they met sinew and bone, slicing cleanly through. Sandra's head was the first to fall, blood spurting from her severed neck. Then Dagen's followed, the light gone from his eyes. Only then did she squeeze her own eyes shut. A single tear rolled down her cheek. She could not cry—not here. Not when she needed to remain strong for her people.

The turmoil in Byron's mind slammed into her, nearly knocking her off her feet. She steadied her thoughts, then opened her eyes. Oshean guards dragged the bodies away like this was some normal occurrence. How dare Kane deprive them of a proper burial?!

Byron fought the urge to shed his skin, to morph into a drengr and keen into the open sky.

The others fought it too.

Oaths were given by those who remained. She thanked the gods that no one else opposed the tyrant sitting on Talon's throne.

She couldn't afford to witness another death today. Fort Squall had already lost too much.

~

Master Arden's office was cluttered with ledgers, parchment, broken quills, and the like, all stacked precariously on crates piled three and four high. The cabinet behind his desk held a shelf of liquor bottles, mostly empty. Tamara took it in while Byron introduced himself, allowing the dock master to pour him a drink. She politely declined.

Arden himself was an older man, in his late forties or perhaps, early fifties. His skin showed signs of working outdoors, long hours spent in the sun. But he had kind eyes that crinkled. Not that he smiled much. None of them had much reason to.

Her stomach hadn't stopped churning all day.

"Now, what can I do for you, Lord Byron?" He eyed them warily, as if simply being in the same room might get him into trouble. It was expected, given the climate. Drengr were no longer regarded as they once were. Kane was too quick to punish those suspected of treason, and the drengr were the most likely culprits for inciting it.

"I'm looking to get in touch with a certain merchant captain," Byron asked. "Goes by the name of Bennett. I'm told you might know when he was last here, or where he might be off to?"

"What's this about?" Arden's eyes narrowed.

"He and my father were good...acquaintances. I had hoped to catch up with him, is all. I'm only in town for the night, and wondered if he was here..."

Arden blew out a breath. "Things here have been dangerous, Lord Byron. I'm hardly master of my own port. Whatever your business with Bennett, I cannot let it come back to me. I got my wife and children to watch for, see."

"I have no interest in putting your family at risk. I simply wish to catch up with the man, is all. I swore an oath to the new king. I can't very well break it without his knowing."

"True. True. Very well then, I'll check." Arden flipped open a massive book on his desk, thumbing through the handwritten pages of his ledger. "Well, looks like you're in luck. Bennett arrived four days ago. Dropped off and picked up some new cargo. He is set to depart in the morning. You might just catch him."

Bryon hid his relief behind a masked expression. "Any idea where he might be staying?"

Arden huffed. "Where all the other sailors stay. Somewhere along the row here."

A fist banged on the door. "Arden, you're needed on dock twelve. One of the Oshean vessels are claiming—"

"Give me a moment," Arden roared, making Tamara jump. To them, he added, "Never a moment of peace. Well then, I think I must be off to sort things. A word of caution, while you're in this part of the city. It's the only area that doesn't have a curfew. But you should still be careful, nonetheless."

Byron thanked the man before they rushed away, in search of the famed captain of the *Lady Faith*. The row of taverns and inns along the massive port were bustling. Each tavern was full of sailors from around Dragonwall and beyond. She saw Osheans walking freely and fought the urge to lash out at them.

They entered the nearest tavern, *Belly Up*. It was a wash of stale ale, sweaty bodies, and raucous laughter. Sailors didn't much care about politics. Clearly the change in rulers hadn't affected their mood.

"How will we find him?" Tamara managed, taking in the numerous bodies.

"You there," Byron reached for a serving girl, bringing her to a stop. "I'm looking for a fellow by the name of Captain Bennett. Know where I might find him?"

"What business does a drengr have with a ship's captain?" She eyed him warily.

"Just an old friend," Byron said, producing a silver. He slipped it into her palm.

Her brows lifted. "Well, he does like to frequent *Nag's Head* when he's here. But I haven't seen him in months."

"*Nag's Head*," he repeated.

"That's down the row a ways," she gestured, pocketing his silver.

They made their way down the row. Bennett wasn't at the *Nag's Head*, but one of the barmaids, a woman named Morita, was confident they'd find him at the *Brickyard Inn*, Marcy's place on Port Right Lane, one street over. "I feel as if we're chasing geese," Tamara muttered, noticing the darkening sky.

The common room at the *Brickyard Inn* was a contrast to all the taverns they'd passed. It was quiet and comfortable. Patrons sat clustered on sofas, sipping tea. She glanced around, then felt a burst of recognition as Byron found what he was looking for.

"Can I help you, sir?" A young woman stepped forward. "Will you be wanting a room?"

"Just here to see a friend, thanks." Byron slipped her a silver and she took the hint, scurrying away.

Byron strode forward towards a group clustered near the window. It was obvious they were sailors. What surprised her was their subdued behavior and muted voices. Her eyes caught on a woman within the group, hair shorn. She was uncommonly pretty.

"Captain Bennett?" Byron asked. The group quieted.

The ship captain looked them over and huffed. "Well, well, well." He glanced at the others and said, "Leave us. You too, Cat." The female huffed, paying him an irritated glare before striding upstairs. "Have a seat."

Byron pulled Tamara down next to him, keeping a firm hold of her hand. "I'm not sure if you know who we are."

"I know exactly who you are," Bennett said, leaning back. "What I don't know is why you sought me out." Tamara stared at his hair, fascinated. She hadn't known any sailors. She'd been raised in a lord's household. Her parents never allowed her near anyone or anything they deemed *unsuitable*.

"Wondered if you could tell me about something I saw earlier." Byron recounted their experience with the prisoner's wagon, asking Bennett for whatever details he might have.

"Oshea thrives on slavery," Bennett explained. "It's been

around since the dawn of their empire. They see our kingdom as an opportunity. Kane has legalized the export of slaves as part of his contract with the Oshean empire."

"He was taking mothers," Tamara spat. "How can he get away with that?"

"Same way tyrants get away with anything else? He claims that only charged criminals are available for export. But anyone can be charged with anything, if you catch my drift."

"We catch it, all right." Byron's expression was murderous.

"Question is, what are you drengr folk willing to do about it?" Bennett leaned forward, a challenge in his gaze.

Byron rubbed a hand over his face. He suddenly looked so, *so* tired. It was a wonder they hadn't crumbled beneath their leadership roles.

There wasn't a whole lot they could do without acting out against the new king, without putting their oath and thus, all of dragon kind at risk. But she felt the spark of something in Byron's mind. Felt the rush of adrenaline as he leaned forward and said, "I think I have an idea."

When she got a hint of what that idea was, she grinned for the first time in days.

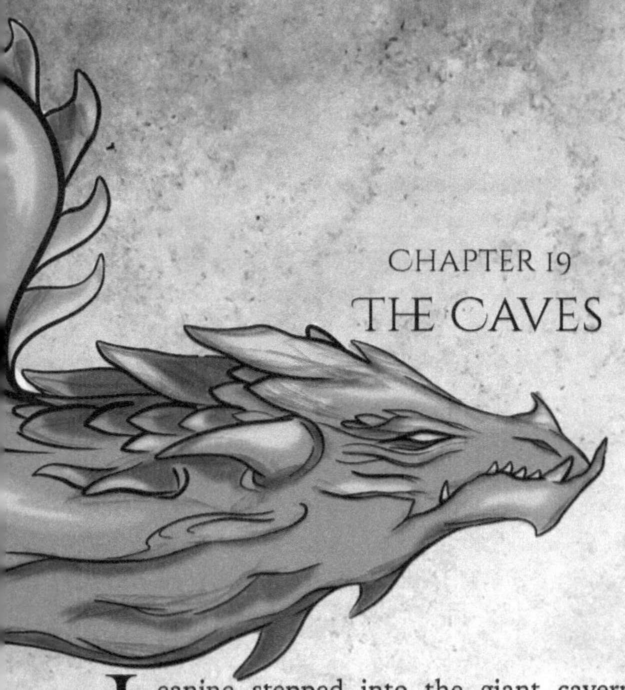

CHAPTER 19

# THE CAVES

*Kastali Dun*

Jeanine stepped into the giant cavern, arms laden with supplies. Tess had packed two baskets brimming with food and other critical necessities. The space was a flurry of activity. Cots were set along the perimeter, scattered around the stalagmites jutting up from the floor. Makeshift dining tables had been erected out of crates and boxes. Even a latrine area was cordoned off, with curtains to offer a bit of privacy.

The central command area was located near the southern end of the cavern. Her eyes darted there, immediately finding Prince Feowen. *Her* prince. She took a deep breath, trying to calm her fluttering heart. He stood over a map outlining all known tunnels and passageways beneath the keep. Several sprites stood beside him, along with a handful of castle guards.

There were a few servants wandering about, helping others get settled in. She spotted Desaree laboring over a cook fire, spoon in hand. She rushed towards her, setting down the supplies. "It hardly looks the same as when I left it," she admitted, impressed.

"Welcome to the resistance," Des said, doing an admirable job of hiding her emotions.

169

Des had cried herself to sleep these past few nights. She'd done a good job at hiding it, but Jeanine had heard her. Had crept over and wrapped Desaree in her arms, holding her and rocking her. The first few nights there'd only been a few cots, left over from the time spent brewing poison for the fight against the dragons.

They'd made do until it was safe to speak with Tess. While the head woman had been forced to swear allegiance to Kane—it was that, or death—she'd risked her life by helping them in secret. The keep was crawling with Oshean guards. Anyone caught showing disloyalty was punished. Brutally.

"What news?" Desaree asked, looking hopeful.

"I'd rather not repeat myself, so finish up here and we'll go report to command. Where's Jocelyn?"

"I'm here." Jocelyn appeared, a bowl in hand. She dumped the contents into the simmering pot of stew. They were now forced to do their own cooking.

Desaree set her spoon into its holder and together they walked across the cavern. Feowen glanced up, did a double take, then smiled. Her stomach flipped. Even with everything going on, he could still fluster her with his attention.

"Jeanine," he said, straightening. "You're back."

Three of Claire's spriten guards, Aithlin Naeris, Filvro Holowyn, and Rahlif Dorvyre stood with him. The others were unaccounted for at the moment, probably mapping out more of the secret passages. The castle guards standing at Feowen's side were Eloi Ruybal, Fio Lima, and Lucas Cirvino. She'd only met them two days ago.

"How did it go?" Feowen asked, striding around the table. He leaned in to brush a gentle kiss over her forehead. His gesture made her flush. She glanced at the others. If the sprites disapproved of their prince's decision to love a human, they made no sign of it.

"Better and worse than expected," she answered. "No one spotted me, so there's that. Tess said that everyone she's spoken to in secret is still loyal to King Talon and Queen Claire. No surprise there. They're all hiding it as best they can, to stay alive. Those who aren't..."

Her mind flashed to what she'd seen earlier. The bodies. She pushed the image away.

"What happened?" Feowen sensed her discomfort. He'd grown better at reading her. It wasn't a surprise, given how close they'd become. What they shared.

"There was another uprising," she explained. "A group of commoners who acted out against Kane in the name of Queen Claire."

Feowen swore under his breath. "We already warned everyone in the city. They should at least *pretend* to be loyal. Their lives depend on it."

The entire city was itching for a fight. No one wanted to remain under Kane's rule. They were forced to bide their time or suffer the consequences.

"Those poor souls," Jocelyn whispered, stricken.

"I saw the bodies myself," she added. "Strung from the keep's walls for everyone in the city to see. He wasn't gentle with their deaths." Bile crawled up her throat at the memory. She pushed it down again.

"Something tells me that isn't all."

"It's not." She took a deep breath. "Three more Oshean ships have arrived, several asarlaí included—they call themselves *wielders*. Turns out we didn't kill everyone in that battle."

"That's no surprise. It would have been too risky to send everything at us," Feowen mused. "They probably only sent a portion of their armies and sorcerers."

"Kane has promised them portions of land around Dragonwall," she said, "so long as he rules the majority of it. There's all kinds of talk, of instituting new rules for magic. Naturally, you can guess who those rules will favor."

"The people with magic," Desaree answered for them.

"Exactly," Jeanine said.

"That explains why Oshea helped Kane in the first place." Feowen looked disgusted. "Who knows what he promised. I'm sure we're only seeing a small part of what is to come. What else?"

"He's hunting everyone known for being loyal to Claire and Talon. All of their closest friends and guards. Us, basically."

She'd be lying if she said the news hadn't made her sweat. Any moment, someone might discover where they were hiding. They took extreme measures to ensure no one got caught in the passages, but it was only a matter of time.

"Well, that's not exactly a surprise," Feowen mused.

"He's forced the kingdom's mages into helping. He's using their magic to try and locate us."

Feowen swore again, louder this time.

"Marcel refused," she said, swallowing. "So he...he..." She trailed off.

"Dead?"

"Dead," she said, exhaling. "I only heard about that from Tess."

"What?!" Desaree and Jocelyn gasped. While Jeanine hadn't known the Grand Mage, the others had.

"Six days," Feowen muttered. "Six days and we haven't caught a break."

"Well, we haven't been discovered," Jeanine offered, almost scoffing. "That's got to count for something—"

A surprised shout cut her short. There came a commotion near the edge of the cavern. Claire's three other spriten guards came rushing towards them. Their expressions left her heart racing with hope.

"We found it!" Jassin Orythra said, the first to speak. "We found a tunnel that leads directly into a single cell in the dungeons."

"Gods above!" Desaree's cry sounded. Jeanine turned just in time to catch Desaree before she collapsed to her knees in relief.

"It's just here," Gorded Cawyn announced, striding over to the map. He took up a quill and began sketching a new path. "We searched for hours. We were not expecting to emerge into a cell. It was locked, of course. Nothing a little of our magic can't open. But we dared not. Not just yet. In case we might be spotted."

"You found them," Jocelyn breathed, an expression of relief on her features.

This was huge! After all, that's what they had been doing these past days—among other things. Looking for Reyr and his imposter queen Merrian. Looking for Dallin and Verath.

When it came to the secret passageways, Desaree and Saffra had the most knowledge of any of them. Using resources they pilfered while sneaking about the keep, they'd parsed together a massive map outlining everything they already knew or discovered. It was slow going, as Feowen only allowed certain people out into the passages. It was a risk, getting caught.

"What's all the commotion?" came a new voice.

Mikkin appeared, trailed by Jamie, Berbik, and Unka.

Jeanine had grown familiar with the four of them these past few months. Berbik had decided to stay in the capital to act on behalf of the dwargs, while Unka had been named an official ambassador for the goblins. It still took a great deal of getting used to on her part. The first few times she'd seen Unka, she'd itched to slit his throat. His people were responsible for her village. For the deaths of so many. The death of her father.

But...he was on her side, apparently. Mistrust him as she might, she trusted the king's decision. Even if it was a struggle.

Jocelyn quickly brought Mikkin up to speed on everything while the sprites poured over the new addition to the map. Mikkin had played an active role in the war against Kane, gathering the dwargs together to support King Talon's cause. He'd spent time in Shadowkeep's dungeons. Not many could boast of such. He had a good reason for it all, having lost his entire family to the wild dragons acting under Kane's orders.

"Now that we know where Verath and the others are," Des said, interrupting the group. "We need to make contact with them. To make sure they are all right."

Jocelyn slipped her hand into Desaree's, lending her support. "They're alive. They're okay."

"I know they're alive," Desaree said. "But we don't know what state they're in. We need to find a way to help them."

"We will," Feowen said. "I stand by my word. Getting to them is our highest priority. Jassin, Gorded, gather whatever supplies necessary. We leave in five minutes." Desaree stepped forward, but before she could speak, Feowen added, "Sprites only for this mission." He threw an apologetic look towards Jeanine. "It's too dangerous. We might need magic to avoid discovery and we cannot risk that. However, if... If you would like us to deliver a message, Desaree, now would be the time to formulate one."

Desaree looked as if she might protest, but logic won out. She nodded.

"Verath is strong," Jocelyn murmured. "He will be okay."

Desaree could only swallow and nod again.

The king's shields were alive. They knew that much. Kane loved public spectacles. He would have made a grand one if he'd killed Talon's most beloved guards. No, they were still locked in the dungeons. But in what condition?

Everyone scattered. Desaree went to quickly write a letter, Jocelyn to help her. Feowen stepped up beside Jeanine, lifting her chin for a brief kiss. "Any sign of Claire's spriten staff?" he asked, pulling back to look at her.

He'd sent her on a secret mission. None of them had seen the queen's spriten staff. In the chaos after Kane had appeared, while they fled into the tunnels, they'd tried to take it with them, knowing how valuable, how important it was. Under no circumstances could Kane get his hands on it. Only, it hadn't been propped against the wall. For months and months, it had sat untouched, as if waiting for her to return.

"No." Jeanine's shoulders dropped. "I searched everywhere. It's like it just *vanished*. I can... I can go back and look again."

"No. You took enough of a risk already, sneaking into the king's tower."

"I made sure Kane was away at court. It's not like he keeps guards in there."

"Even still." Feowen stroked a strand of hair away from her face, tucking it behind her ear. "I can't risk you like that. I trust that your search was thorough. That staff..." He huffed. "I think it has a mind of its own. For all we know it knows it's in danger and simply disappeared."

"We'd know if Kane found it."

"We would." He leaned in, letting his lips linger on her forehead. "You did well today. Get some rest, yes?"

She nodded, giving him another kiss, sharing his air as they breathed against each other.

Feowen was every inch the prince. She'd watched him step into the role of authority the moment things had gone south. From getting them to safety, to taking control in the caves, he was their new ruler until they got their shields back. Until they got King Talon and Queen Claire back.

"Be safe," she murmured, pressing her hand against his beating heart. She couldn't bear the thought of him getting caught by Kane. Of what the sorcerer might do.

"I will. When I return, let's sneak off together, yes?" His eyes sparked with mischief. Her insides squirmed in delight. She nodded and he grinned.

There was another flurry of activity as the new search party gathered what they would need. Supplies, food, perhaps even medicine for Dallin, Merrian, Reyr, and Verath. Who knew what state they'd be in.

Then, they departed.

She drifted over to Mikkin and his posse as they made their way back towards the center of the cavern, to where the strange mausoleum existed. "Any luck?" she asked.

Berbik had already taken a seat, the same seat he'd occupied for days, to stare at it. He merely grunted. "Thoughts take time," was what he'd said the first time she'd asked. It had been a surprise to them all, when he'd made the announcement, that the mausoleum was of dwargen make, that it had a style and cut of stone only dwargs were capable of. That his people had likely been contracted to build it long ago. He'd known all that just from looking at it.

What he didn't know was how to open it. But he'd assured them there was a way. "Our people are crafty. There will be a switch or lever somewhere, hidden, like a puzzle. I just need to riddle it out."

All she could do was take a seat next to him and wait. Wait for him to think of a way to open it. Wait for her lover to return from his mission locating the shields in the dungeons. Wait for her queen to return. Wait for their lives to return to what they should be.

Taking a deep breath, she did exactly that.

# CHAPTER 20
## SURPRISE VISITOR

*Kastali Dun*

Merrian shivered, curling in on herself. The winter months were not kind to those living in the dungeons. She tugged her threadbare blanket tighter about her shoulders.

"Here—" Reyr draped the other over her. He must have seen her shivering. She'd refused it the last time he'd offered, mostly out of spite. Now she was too cold to even form words. She kept her gaze averted, even though she wanted to snap at him, to shove off his offering and ignore it. How *dare* he show any kindness towards her?! After how he'd treated her.

She was only in this mess because of him—because of his inner circle. She'd agreed to stand in as their imposter queen. There'd been nothing in the fine print about living as a prisoner. Then again, it was her fault for not considering the risks.

She'd believed the queen to be untouchable. Believed that the king's guards would be hellbent on protecting her, that no harm would ever come. Well, she'd been wrong.

About all of it.

Her thoughts jumped to Glenna Surati and some of the other

shelter caretakers. What was happening now that the king was deposed, now that a tyrant sat on the throne? Would he still shell out funds for those in need? Or would he tear down every bit of infrastructure meant to help, dooming Dragonwall's citizens?

"Where are you from, originally?" Reyr's voice pulled her from her thoughts. "Here? Or, did you come from somewhere else before?" She didn't answer. "Still giving me the silent treatment, I see."

She clenched her jaw. Part of her wanted to tell him to shut up. The other part, the part that wasn't petty, decided to stay quiet.

"I'm not from Kastali Dun myself," he said. She exhaled, shutting her eyes and leaning her head back against the stones. Maybe if she couldn't see him, she could tune him out better. "I spent most of my younger days in Fort Squall. My parents were fort leaders there. Didn't come to Kastali Dun until King Talon made me his shield. After... After Gemma died."

Her eyes twitched beneath her lids. She fought the urge to open them and look at him, if only to see his expression. Who was Gemma? Never mind, she didn't care.

"It was..." He exhaled. "Gemma was my mate. Losing her broke something inside me."

Okay, maybe she did care then. Just a little. Just a touch.

"I didn't want to go to the capital—after it happened, I mean. I wanted to slink off and lick my wounds. Maybe leave the kingdom altogether. Truthfully, I just wanted to die."

Her eyes snapped open. The pain in his expression made her heart squeeze involuntarily.

"Talon convinced me to swear an oath instead." A scoffing laugh fell from his lips. "I thought it might help me forget. Maybe even help me heal. Serving a greater purpose than myself—all that."

"Did it?" The words were out before she could stop them.

"Yes. And no. Gemma was half of my soul. She took that half with her when she died. But...it got easier. Hundreds of years passed. Sometimes I'd feel guilty. A whole day might go by where I didn't think of her. Then I'd go to bed angry for being so selfish. For having gotten wrapped up enough to forget her, even if for a little bit."

Mer's chest caved in. "I'm sorry," she found herself saying. "That you lost her. That you were forced to carry on all these years without her."

He huffed. "I don't deserve your apology."

She lifted a shoulder to shrug.

"What about you?" he asked.

This time, she didn't ignore him. "What about me?"

"Where are you from?" he tried again.

She exhaled. "Up north. I was born in a village not far from Northedge, actually. I was sent to the big city to train when my family discovered that I had magic." He made a humming sound so she continued. "I spent ten years training with other mages. I never showed much promise. Not like my classmates. Simple cantrips, if I was lucky. But I did seem to have an affinity for healing—though not the kind of healing skilled mages possess. Pain relief, mostly, cuts, bruises, the easier maladies and sicknesses. I couldn't fix the rotting illnesses."

She pressed her lips together and fell quiet. She'd said more than she had intended. Reyr didn't deserve to know anything about her. He'd never wanted to before. He must have been truly bored to ask in the first place. It wasn't like there was anything better to do.

"And your family?"

She scoffed. "Dead."

"I... I'm sorry." There was a long silence. "What happened?"

She studied him. There was genuine concern lining his features. Gods, she hated looking at him. He was a direct opposite to King Talon in every way. At least before, King Talon's scars made him difficult on the eyes. Now, he was the handsomest thing she'd ever seen. It made her want to despise him even more.

Only, she'd never despised anyone. No, that wasn't true. She hated a certain *type* of people.

"Mages," she said. Reyr's brows pulled together. "My parents and siblings got sick. I didn't know. I was still in the midst of my training, living in the city of Northedge with the other students. They got sick and asked for medical help, but didn't have the funds for a mage healer. The standard healers couldn't do anything for them. It was an infection, an extremely contagious one. It killed several families in my village."

She gritted her teeth, trying not to allow the old, hot anger to bubble up inside her. She'd gotten good at suppressing it over the years, over the decades.

"I'm sorry," Reyr said again. He hesitated, opening and closing his mouth like he wanted to add something more. Then he fell silent.

"Why do you hate me so much?" she found herself asking. It was the question she'd posed the day they'd lost the kingdom. A question that had eaten away at her since the moment they met. Maybe now, he'd finally give her a real answer.

Reyr scoffed. "I already told you, I don't hate you."

"Right. You merely *dislike* me."

He lifted a hand to pinch the bridge of his nose, then exhaled, his hand dropping to his side. "I fell in love with her, you know. The queen. Claire. When she came to our kingdom as an outsider. Before she was anyone. Before she and Talon fell in love. How ridiculous is that? I betrayed my mate bond by falling in love with her, only to realize that my king also loved her. And worse still, I kept things from my king, secrets, her secrets, when I was honor bound to serve him."

Mer frowned, uncertain where this was going.

"I left, naturally, but getting over her wasn't easy."

"Did you? Get over her, I mean?"

He closed his eyes, letting his head fall against the wall. For a while, she thought he might not answer. "Yes and no. I still love her, I will always love her. But she belongs to another, and I have finally moved past being *in love* with her. I would still give my life for her in a heartbeat, but I no longer imagine what it would be like to—" He made an angry scoffing sound.

"To kiss her? To hold her and make love to her?"

"Yes. That. I feel guilty for ever having thought about it. She's my queen. She's mated to my king. And I love them both dearly."

There was a long silence and then, "What does this have to do with disliking me?"

He sighed. "I have been through a lot of extreme emotions when it comes to Claire. I always wanted to hate her for what she did to me, but I couldn't. I could never."

"So instead, you chose to hate someone who merely looked like her," Mer said. Suddenly, his behavior made a lot more sense.

"I miss her—miss *them*. Gods, I miss them so much," he admitted, running a hand over his face. "Seeing you when you looked exactly like her, but knowing that you *weren't* her, knowing that I couldn't hug you and be happy that you had returned, knowing that she could be hurt, or worse..." He trailed off. "Seeing her face was the constant reminder that she wasn't here. It has been...difficult."

Mer exhaled, her shoulders falling. "I thought you disliked me because I wasn't good enough to be her."

"No," he said emphatically. "I might have said something along the lines, but that was never really why. Do you... Do you understand now?"

"I do."

"Please, forgive me." His gaze was earnest, and she saw something in the depths of his eyes. A lurking desperation. He really *did* want her forgiveness.

"I... I don't know if I can just—"

"I understand," he said, cutting her off. "I'm not asking for it right at this moment, but perhaps in time."

"Perhaps in time," she confirmed.

There was a click. They both froze. She immediately snuffed out the mage light, plunging them into darkness.

Not a moment too soon.

The door to their cell swung open. The last person she ever expected stood in the doorway.

"Feowen?!" she breathed.

"Well hello there, Merrian. Glad to see you alive."

She surged to her feet, covering the distance between them as Feowen and two of her spriten guards—no, *Claire's* spriten guards—swept into the cell. Reyr was also on his feet. She threw her arms around Feowen, caring little that he wasn't really her guard. That he was a spriten prince and she was a nobody. Friends were allowed to hug, weren't they? He was still her friend, wasn't he? Even if she was no longer the imposter queen?

"You came for us," she breathed against his shoulder before embarrassment got the better of her and she backed away.

"In a sense," he said, setting a pile of supplies on the ground. He turned to Reyr. "Good to see you looking like yourself again. Here—" Reyr flinched but didn't move. Feowen's hands swept over his head while he hummed something under his breath.

Reyr gasped. Blinked. Then said, "You—how did you do that?"

Feowen only chuckled. "It won't be permanent. Kane will send his lackeys back to dose you with more dragon's bane. Until then, I suggest you make the most of your telepathy. We're cut off, so we've no way to get into contact with the fort's drengr."

Reyr's eyes took on a faraway look before he gasped. "Karanth says they've sworn allegiance to Kane, but they're alive and unharmed. For now."

"Karanth? For Kastali's leader?"

"Yes." Reyr's eyes went unfocused again. "Karanth said all the forts were required to swear oaths to Kane. That those who didn't were put to death. We lost..." He gasped, his chest tightening. "We lost six pairs."

Feowen winced, nodding. "Anyone who wished to stay alive was forced to. Don't hold it against them—"

"I don't. I'd rather our people live." Reyr exhaled. Mer watched the tension leave his shoulders.

"When Kane arrived, a number of us snuck off and didn't get caught." Feowen shot a wink at Merrian. "We've already formed a resistance...of sorts."

Merrian perked up. "Jeanine, too?"

"Yes. She's safe. Pretty miffed that she didn't get to come along."

"What of the others? Verath? Dallin?" Reyr stepped forward. "I can't seem to reach them."

"You are our first stop." Feowen grinned. "We'll drop by their cells on the way out, so that you can have a little time to speak with them before you're dosed again." Feowen exhaled. "I wish I could get you out of here—"

"You can't," Reyr interrupted. "Kane made it clear that if we try to escape, if we move against him in any way, he will find ways to punish our people."

"Or turn you to stone," Feowen added.

"Or that, yes." Reyr rubbed his temples. Mer watched him. He'd transformed back into a ruler in minutes. His shoulders were straight, his chin raised. "Tell me of your efforts. You mentioned a resistance."

"Ah. Yes. That." Feowen grinned.

Mer listened with wide eyes as Feowen relayed everything that had happened since Kane's arrival. There was a cave below the keep that no one knew about. It was being used to hide Claire's spriten guards, along with a number of people they managed to get out. From there, they were exploring the passages, looking for one that led beneath the city as a way out.

"It took us ages to find the one that brought us here," Feowen explained. "We came immediately, knowing you would need us."

"What's the plan?" Mer found herself asking. "How do we get our kingdom back?"

Feowen massaged his temples. "We've toyed with a few ideas. But it seems that anything we try will result in one outcome. The annihilation of dragon kind."

"Unless we can get the stones," Mer said.

"Unless, that," Feowen agreed. "Though, Dragonwall's people seem to have other ideas in mind?"

"Like what?" Reyr demanded.

Feowen sighed. "They've been making things difficult. There have been several uprisings, protests throughout the city. Unfortunately, anything drastic results in the deaths of whomever was behind it. Bodies strung from the castle walls, that sort of thing."

Merrian winced, bile rising in her throat.

"We've tried to spread the word—warned everyone to stand down—but they won't have it. The people have a mind of their own."

Reyr rubbed the back of his neck. "Gods," he swore under his breath. "This is all falling apart."

"We thought about contacting my sister. But even if she sends an army of sprites, Kane will probably demand they turn around and go home, or turn you all to stone as the alternative."

"Then it's hopeless," Reyr muttered.

"I still think we should try to steal the stones," Mer said.

"He wears them every day in a breastplate on his chest." Feowen leaned against the cell's wall. "All but the one, which never leaves his hand. Like he's waiting to use it. Lording it over us."

Jassin's head popped into view. "We are out of time, my prince."

Feowen exhaled. "Keep those supplies hidden. If you have any requests, we'll be by again in a few days. We dare not risk discovery."

"Yes, yes of course." Reyr nodded.

Feowen reached out, taking Reyr's forearm, then pulled him into an embrace, thumping him on the back. "Take care of yourselves. We'll figure something out."

Mer watched the exchange, a lump rising in her throat. *Would* they figure something out? Or would they be stuck here forever?

# CHAPTER 21
## A FUTURE

*The Kengr Gate*

Leah's thighs ached. No, scratch that. Her entire *body* ached. She was from rural Indiana and no stranger to riding horseback for hours on end. She'd grown up around horses, even competing in dressage. That was before everything had fallen apart. Her old life felt like eons ago, like it belonged to someone else, someone she hardly knew anymore.

Flying on the back of a dragon wasn't like riding a horse. The motions were different. They were more magnificent but also far more uncomfortable. You couldn't simply stop your dragon and hop off for a break. Landing took time. Getting on and off took strength. Being in the sky was cold and empty, even though it was thrilling. Her skin was wind-chapped and sunburned, despite the sunscreen she applied in vigorous amounts. And she was always thirsty, her throat always dry.

They took infrequent breaks, just enough to relieve themselves, or catch a few stolen hours of sleep. She was exhausted, both mentally and physically. So, when they finally descended towards the gate that would take them into Dragonwall, she nearly wept with relief.

Jovari had been their guide. He'd come this way before with Claire, the first time she'd traveled to his kingdom. Despite what Leah had witnessed so far, her mind wanted to deny it. Her best friend had lived an entire life in another world. Dragons existed. Magic was real.

They were somewhere in the Canadian wilderness. An entire day had sailed by without a single sign of civilization. Soon, she'd leave her life behind and start a new one. Something about that had her heart pounding with equal parts of fear and excitement.

The gate was deep in the forest. They'd landed at the nearest clearing, then muddled their way through the dense growth. "Before we pass through, I'd like a word alone with Leah," Jovari surprised everyone by saying. "You lot go on ahead. Give us a few moments."

Her hackles raised. She knew immediately what this was about. She wasn't sure why he was wasting his time. Her answer wasn't going to change.

Claire gave her a questioning look. "Go on," she said, reassuring her. "I'll be right along."

Irelia eyed the gate, her shoulders set, then walked through. Leah blinked, staring at the point where she'd disappeared. Talon offered Claire his hand. They shared a look before walking through.

Leah blinked again, then turned towards Jovari. They were alone. "I know what you're about to say."

He crossed his arms, eyeing her. "I'm not going to dissuade you from coming."

"You're not?"

"No." His admission sounded more like a scoff.

"But you want to, don't you?" He blew out a breath, looking up at the canopy of trees. "Yeah, I thought so. Go ahead, then. Tell me how dangerous it is. Tell me that I ought to stay behind."

"You think I would have you stay behind and leave you here all alone?" He gestured at the wilderness.

"I could find my way home just fine." She lifted her chin. It was a lie. She knew very little about survival. And so far from civilization, she'd be lucky to last a couple of days. Assuming a bear didn't eat her first. Or a moose didn't trample her. Or…whatever else.

"I'm sure you could," he said, looking her up and down, his eyes burning a path over her body. Her skin flushed. Shockingly, there wasn't any sarcasm in his voice. He honestly believed she'd make it out here alone if she had to.

Damn it!

Why did he have to be so infuriatingly handsome? With his auburn hair and perfect cheekbones and warm eyes. It didn't help that he stood a full head and a half taller than her. Didn't help that he was corded with muscle. It especially didn't help that whenever he turned into a drengr, he was the most beautiful shade of sapphire blue she'd ever seen.

"Fine. Then why are we having this conversation?"

"*Because,* I want to make sure you're okay with this." Now he just sounded exasperated. "It's not too late. I can turn around and fly you home if you ask it of me."

"Oh, *my*—!" She cut herself off. "So you *are* trying to dissuade me?!"

"No. I'm offering you an out—if you've changed your mind. If you want it."

She sniffed. "I haven't—changed my mind, that is." He gave a rough nod, his gaze never leaving hers. "In case you didn't know, I have nothing here. My parents are dead. I have no siblings. My aunt is a bitch. Her husband and kids are even worse. Claire is my best friend. No—my *sister.* Her parents were my second parents. She's the only family I have left, and now, she is on the other side of that…" She waved a hand toward the gate. "So no, I'm *not* leaving her."

Even if she was scared. As if she'd ever admit that to him.

"Very well. That's good, because you need to be brave for what we're walking into."

"I can be perfectly brave." She pulled her shoulders back.

"Then let's not waste another minute."

"You're the one wasting time, dragon man." There wasn't any rancor in her voice. Perhaps because she was mildly touched by his thoughtfulness. Unless this was all a disguised attempt to keep her here. She really didn't know.

Jovari snorted and offered his hand. She stared at it. When he didn't drop it, she reached out and took it. His skin was warm, his palm firm against hers. She ignored the way her heart jumped at the contact. He pulled her forward, stopping just before they passed through the markers. "Ready?"

Her heart lifted into her throat. She was no stranger to stressful situations. No stranger to fear, either. She nodded and took a step forward.

They passed into the unknown together.

There was only darkness. The cold pressed in around her. Her heart skipped irregularly, beating in a fit of starts and stops. Jovari was no longer with her, and that scared her more than she cared to admit. She opened her mouth to call for him—

The nothingness disappeared. She was greeted by a dark sky lit with stars. She gawked. It had been late afternoon just moments ago. The change was jarring.

"There you are." King Talon's voice rang out into the night. She looked up to find him eyeing them. She dropped Jovari's hand like it had burned her, hiding hers behind her back.

Claire was seated in the grass, arms braced behind her, gazing up at the night sky. She looked comfortable, like she'd been here a while. Irelia sat beside her in much the same position.

Jovari scrubbed a hand over his face. "Finally," he muttered, glancing around. He was more relaxed than he had been moments ago. She barely knew him, and yet she could tell that being back in his own world put him more at ease.

Talon walked over and squeezed his shoulder. "Good to be back, hmm?"

"Indeed. Claire? Has she—did it—?"

"No. I already asked. Nothing so far."

Jovari's shoulders dropped, as if he'd been counting on a miracle and was vastly disappointed. They'd all hoped that passing through the gate would somehow free Claire's memories and magic.

*Magic.* She let the concept invade her mind. A small seed of longing burst in her chest, roots shooting outward to coil around her heart. How often had she wished for magic? A way to save her dying dad? A way to bring her mom back? A way to fix everything?

She let it go, glancing around to take in her surroundings. "Are those...?"

"Mountains, yes." Jovari's voice sounded right beside her. When had he crowded in so close?

"They're...tall."

"Taller than anything I saw in your world, yes." He sounded proud of that. She could only snort. She went to Claire, taking a seat in the grass beside her. Their shoulders brushed and Claire gave a soft smile.

"What's going on between you two?" her bestie asked.

"Not sure what—"

"Oh, come on. I'm not blind. There's...tension and whatnot."

Leah snorted while Irelia merely chuckled. "I already told you before. Nothing's going on. He just wanted to make sure I was okay with coming to Dragonwall. He offered to take me back if I wasn't."

"And...are you?" Claire's gaze was a weight. "I realize I didn't exactly give you much choice."

"Where you go, I go." She bumped their shoulders. "I missed out last time. If you hadn't come back..." Her throat closed up.

Claire's features softened. "But I did come back."

She didn't want to think about the alternative. What it would've been like to live without the only person she really loved. To watch Claire's parents grieve as the years passed. To grieve with them. To wonder and never know where she'd gone or if she was alive.

"Now that we're back," King Talon announced, we don't have to rush. Time passes normally here.

Claire snorted, craning her head back to see him. "Or maybe time passes normally in *my* world, and it's just fast here."

The king pressed his lips together and *smartly* didn't argue.

"What our king is *trying* to say," Jovari cut in, "is that we don't need to sacrifice comfort for speed. It's dark out. We can make camp and rest here if you'd like?" He looked between the three of them.

Irelia harrumphed. "These old bones hurt no matter what we do, so it makes no difference to me."

Claire shot a look towards the gate. A shudder went through her. Talon immediately sensed it. "What's wrong, *mih cralla?*"

Leah had heard the endearment before; she didn't know what it meant.

"I... I don't know. I don't like that thing."

Leah frowned, looking towards the onyx pillars. Besides their obvious use, they looked rather harmless. Still, she came to Claire's aid and said, "Maybe we can fly a little further and make camp elsewhere?"

That's exactly what they did.

An hour later, Jovari and Talon descended. The landscape was vast and open. Prairie lands as far as the eye could see. There wasn't any firewood, but it was warm enough to go without a fire. They set out bedrolls in a row and went straight to sleep.

IT WAS STILL DARK when her eyelids fluttered open. The night air was filled with the drone of chirping insects. She lifted her head. Claire was on her left, softly snoring. Talon was on Claire's other side. She half expected to find them spooning. Instead, Talon was wide awake, gazing adoringly at his sleeping mate.

The sight made something painful twist in her chest. What would it be like to have that kind of love? To have someone adore her so much, they traveled across worlds to find her?

She met Talon's gaze. He gave her a small nod of acknowledgment. A snoring-snort shattered the quiet. Irelia was sleeping on her right. She grumbled and flopped over.

Jovari's bedroll was empty.

Leah caught sight of his silhouette in the distance, keeping watch. He must have traded shifts with Talon. That was probably what had woken her.

She clumsily got to her feet, barefoot, stepping carefully through the dirt and tall grasses to meet him.

He glanced over at her approach, then turned back towards the open land beyond.

"You should sleep while you can." His voice was low and rich. She liked the sound of it, even if he did annoy her sometimes. It wasn't fair that everything about him was...pleasant.

"I'm awake now." She shrugged. "I can keep watch if you'd like to get some sleep. You're the one doing the flying."

He grunted but didn't retreat. They gazed silently out at the horizon. Jovari broke the silence and said, "What happened to your parents? You mentioned that they were dead." She flinched. "Apologies—"

"No. It's...fine. I don't mind talking about it, you just caught me off guard is all. My mom died when I was nine—head on collision. A driver fell asleep at the wheel and drifted into her lane. She was coming home after a twelve hour shift. It wrecked my dad. He was never the same. He got sick when I was sixteen. Colon cancer. I'm not sure if you know what that is? Anyway, it's super aggressive. He fought it as long as he could but...he died three months before my eighteenth birthday."

Her throat closed up. Even though it was the same toneless, robotic speech she'd made countless times, it never got easier. Jovari swore under his breath. "That's awful, Leah. I'm sorry." She lifted a shoulder—an automatic response she'd grown accustomed to giving. "So before, when you said you learned how to take care of yourself, you weren't lying."

"Unfortunately not. My dad became a single parent. When my mom passed—she was a nurse—our income was cut in half. Dad had a landscaping business, so he doubled his working hours to make up for it. We both gave up luxuries we'd grown accustomed to. There was some life insurance money, but my dad put it away for my college fund. In the end, I ended up clearing it out to pay his medical bills. I... I never got to go to college."

The darkness hid the flush that crept up her neck. The embarrassment. Seeing many of her classmates go off to earn degrees while she continued to wait tables.

Jovari made a humming noise. "I learned from Claire that attending college is common in your society?"

"It is. If you want a decent wage. College, or at least a trade school, is necessary. Is that not the case here?"

"It's not. Our ways are very...different."

"I figured as much."

"Higher pursuits of education do not exist here," he explained. "Scholars are patrons of the library. Elsewise, people of trades receive training during their apprenticeships."

"That's kind of a relief," she admitted. "I've always felt like such a failure, not attending college when many of my peers did. But here it's the norm."

"Young adults are expected to begin work or apprenticeships around fourteen or fifteen, depending on the kind of family they come from. Working class, obviously. Those of nobility on the other hand do not need to work."

"What does—did—Claire think about all that?"

"About how our society functions?" She nodded. "As you might guess, it took time for her to adjust, but there are things she disagrees with. Things she wants, and even plans to change. Especially where women are concerned."

A soft smile touched her lips. "I'm not surprised. What about... Does she have friends? Or just you and the king?"

"Oh, she's done a fine job making friends."

For as long as she could remember, she'd been Claire's best friend. But what if now, Claire had found someone to replace her? A little kernel of uncertainty took root in her chest, but she stopped it from spreading. "What are they like?"

"You'll love them," he said, his voice warm with promise. "Desaree was her first, I think. She's now her lady in waiting. Desaree is involved with Verath."

"Verath?"

"One of the king's shields—like me."

"Oh." That made her perk up. "A fancy guard."

"Yes," he chuckled. "A fancy guard."

She had wondered if the king's shields took lovers. Mostly because she couldn't help it when she looked at Jovari. Even if she ignored the budding feelings in her chest.

"Then there's Saffra," he continued. "She's the king's prophetess—his seer. She foresees events, past, present, and future, when the gods will it." Leah's lips parted. "You will like her, too."

"She sounds...important."

"Very. Then there's Jocelyn. She's Saffra's handmaiden. And there's also Jeanine—one of Claire's guards. Plus others in Claire's guard, along with her spriten handmaidens. I think even Princess Taylynn could be considered a friend, even though they are distant cousins."

"Wait, Claire has a queen's guard?" Her words were whisper-shrieked.

"Indeed." Jovari's mouth twitched.

"Wow." She glanced over her shoulder at Claire's sleeping form. "It sounds like...like she has everything."

Her words came out choked. She was happy for her bestie. She really was. But, it also reminded her of how wrong everything had gone in her own life. Claire had always had stability, a good family, a college education. Had always had a bright future ahead of her.

She wanted that too, so, *so* badly.

She lifted her chin. This was a chance at a new life. She wouldn't squander it.

"I'll let you take over watch, since you offered," Jovari said, sensing the change in her mood. Perhaps he realized that she wanted to be alone. "Wake me if you spot anything concerning."

She swallowed, nodding. That he trusted her enough to sleep wasn't lost on her. "Thank you," she said, for more reasons than one. Their eyes met in the darkness, holding for a brief moment. He understood and nodded, then walked off.

She turned her gaze back towards the wilderness. Towards Dragonwall. Towards her future, and took up watch.

CHAPTER 22

# MESSAGE FROM THE KING TREE

*Northern Wilderness*

Talon tried to ignore the dip of his stomach as he led Claire away from their camp. They'd flown all day, resting several times to stretch and see to their needs. It felt good to step away and simply *walk*, especially with her at his side.

It was almost cruel, being near her all day and yet, being deprived of her. She had made her discomfort clear, that she wasn't ready to fly with him. He tried not to take it personally. Especially when going without her touch, even for the period of a day, frayed his mood.

The prairie was alight with the sounds of insects, its grass high enough to skim his thighs.

Gods, it was good to be back in Dragonwall. He'd felt a weight lift the moment he set foot on the other side of that gate. It didn't feel like home, per se, but close.

Claire walked with her shoulders back, her chin lifted. She looked every bit the queen, with a backdrop of stars above them. "It's beautiful here," she breathed. "I almost didn't want to believe this existed. Despite everything, your story, your proof. It's really... real."

"Seeing the truth always makes it easier."

She hummed in agreement.

"This was our tradition, you know." He couldn't help himself in bringing it up, hoping to trigger her memories. He took her hand and draped it around his elbow. He craved contact, looking for any excuse to touch her, even if it was the brush of a knuckle here or the trail of a fingertip there. "You and I took walks every day. It was one of my conditions for forgiveness, after you risked your life to fight the vodar." His lips twitched, fighting against a smile. Gods, she'd never been good at following rules. "One hundred walks together to get to know each other better. That was before you touched my scales."

"Before we became mated," she said, her expression thoughtful as she puzzled things out.

"Yes. Although after we discovered our bond, we often preferred flying together instead."

Her eyes darted to his and away again. She cleared her throat. "I admit, it's difficult—piecing together the bits and pieces of our lives."

"I know." He hated that she was forced to take this beautiful thing between them and force it to make sense. It had never made sense to him. He had never quite understood how he could be so lucky to have earned her. Perhaps this was only a bump in the road. This challenge between them. Perhaps they would be better for it. Stronger. Perhaps their love would only bloom deeper.

"So…" she said, filling the silence. "Am I the only one who thinks something is going on between Leah and Jovari?"

His steps faltered. "Something is going on between Leah and Jovari?"

"Yeah. Haven't you noticed?" She watched him, gauging his reaction.

He kept his face unreadable. How had he been so blind? The last thing he wanted was to appear oblivious. Not when it was his job as king to be perceptive.

To be fair, he didn't notice much beyond Claire these days. A mixture of fear over losing her and relief over finding her had turned him into something unrecognizable. He spent nearly all his waking moments either thinking about how to help her, or gazing wistfully at her.

Claire huffed. "Well, there's all this tension between them. Jovari tried to keep her from coming with us, you know. He wouldn't have done that unless he felt very strongly towards her. Do your shields make it a point of striking up romances?"

He rubbed a hand over his face. "You have no idea…"

He'd have to pay better attention from now on. The last thing he needed was Jovari, the kingdom's biggest flirt, engaging in some dalliance with his mate's best friend. When he inevitably broke her heart, that would only make things tense between everyone. "I'll have a talk with him."

Claire merely shrugged. "They're both adults."

"Even still…"

"So…" she said again. Probably because he was terrible at filling the silences between them. Before, it had been easy. While she wasn't a different person, it still felt unknown and frightening, this thing between them. "I haven't had any more of my memories resurface. I thought…"

He frowned, glancing down at her. Inevitably, his eyes fell to her lips. "Were you expecting them to come back?"

"Well." Her bottom lip caught between her teeth. "I guess I was expecting…something."

Oh. *Oh*! For all that he'd teased her about kissing her, this was their first time alone since the start of their journey. There hadn't been time before. A low growl rose in his chest. Her eyes widened at the sound. He didn't give her time to pull away. Instead, he grabbed her face and brought their lips together.

*Mate* his brain screamed. *Mate*!!

She melted against him, returning his kiss with a hunger he hadn't expected. Then again, perhaps she'd spent the past few days replaying their first kiss in her mind. He had. Over and over and over. But that wasn't the only thing he replayed. The night of their bonding was unforgettable. He could enjoy those memories while she couldn't. Not until she got them back.

As if the fates could hear him, she gasped and pulled away, her eyes wide. "*Oh*. Oh, my god."

Even in the darkness, he saw the hot flush of her skin. It wasn't from their kiss. "What did you see?" he rasped.

"I...we...our mating ceremony. Did you really...you started calling me *mih cralla*. After we..." She cleared her throat, rubbing the back of her neck. Despite not having access to her mind, *mih cralla* wasn't an endearment he'd forgotten. He'd simply been waiting for her to ask about it.

A delighted laugh burst from her lips. "Did you really tell me you would willingly worship me on your knees?"

"Yes," he growled. "I will gladly do so now, if you'll let me."

She squealed as he pulled her against him and captured her mouth again. He bent over her, forcing her back to arch, holding her as he ravaged her mouth. He took and took, delving deep with his tongue, willing her to remember more.

They were breathless as he pulled away, their chests rising and falling in tandem. His hips pressed against hers and he groaned, the sensation of her sending sparks shooting up from the base of his back. Gods, she felt like heaven against him. "Fly with me tomorrow," he breathed. "Please." His voice all but cracked on that last word.

He wasn't someone who begged. Not unless it was his queen he was begging to. "Please—"

*Thunk.*

Claire's soft intake of breath made him freeze. He whirled in the direction of her gaze, expecting to find danger. Instead, he balked.

"Did that just...fall out of the sky?" She gazed at the thing that had appeared. His mouth opened several times but he couldn't quite form words. "It's so pretty." Before he could stop her, she bent over and lifted the spriten staff into her hands. The moment she touched it, her eyes widened. "Is this...mine?"

His heart took off at a gallop. This was it—the moment she'd regain her memories. The moment he'd get her back. Surely whatever magic the staff held would fix everything.

"Your memories," he breathed. "Your magic. It's back?"

"I..." She frowned. "No. It just...called to me. Somehow I knew. Is it really mine? But, where did it come from?" She looked up, as if some answer would come from the sky. It was cloudless. There was nothing there.

"The king tree," he said, trying to ignore the sinking feeling in his stomach. "It must have sent it to you, somehow. But yes. It's really yours. I left it in the castle for safekeeping before coming to find you."

She held the staff, turning it over. "It's... I think it's trying to tell me something." He held his breath. "It wants me to come."

"Is that what it's saying?" He knew that the king tree had often spoken to her, using the staff as a conduit.

"No. There aren't any words. Maybe the spell—or whatever is binding me—is keeping that from happening. But there's a feeling, like an emotion? I don't know. I can't quite... I need to go somewhere. The forest. There's something in the forest that will help me."

He exhaled. It felt like all his worry fled with his breath. "The king tree. Of course. I bet it can heal you."

"You think?"

"Why not? I was already planning to take us through the forest on our way back to Kastali Dun. I had hoped that the sprites might be able to do something—counteract Kane's magic somehow."

"Oh. That's...that's good then. Now we have even more reason to go."

THE FOLLOWING MORNING, Talon didn't bring up his offer. Claire would either choose to fly with him or not. He prepared himself for disappointment, but that didn't make it any easier when she climbed onto Jovari's back.

"*I'm sorry,*" Jovari said, the thought quiet in his mind. "*She just needs time.*"

"*I am aware.*"

*"So, the staff? What do you think it means?"*

He fell into the therapeutic motion of flight. Each beat of his wings was soothing. Below, the landscape was a blur of spring colors, the snow freshly melted. *"It means that the king tree cannot get through to her after what Kane did."* Talon tried to hide his fury over the thought. Kane's magic was so powerful, the binding blocked even the highest power in the world. *"I think the tree sent the staff to get her attention. Or mine. I'm not sure which."*

*"So, Esterpine, then?"*

*"Esterpine."* They were still a couple of days from reaching the trees. But the sight of them appeared on the horizon later that afternoon. Little smudges of green, just discernible to his keen gaze. Claire wouldn't be able to see it for some time yet. When she did, would she feel the connection?

Would she remember?

They landed for a short break. He kept a careful watch on Jovari. The females went off on their own in search of privacy. Once they were airborne again, he said, *"Is something going on between you and Leah?"*

Jovari sent him a mental snort. *"No."*

*"Good. Keep it that way."*

*"As if I had planned otherwise."* Jovari scoffed. *"Have you ever seen me get serious over a woman?"*

*"No, and that's the problem."*

There was a long silence and then, *"There is nothing between us."*

And yet, even if Jovari couldn't sense the lie in his words, it was there.

*"Make sure it stays that way,"* Talon all but growled in warning.

*"Is that a command, my king?"*

He exhaled a plume of smoke. *"Yes. If you must take it as such. We all know you leave a trail of broken hearts wherever you go."*

*"Can you blame me?"* Jovari teased, though he didn't miss the narrowly disguised hurt in his voice.

Talon almost apologized, then stopped himself.

*"Fine,"* Jovari begrudgingly said at last. *"Message received loud and clear. I'll spare her my wiles and let her keep her heart."*

*"Thank you."*

*"Where's this coming from, anyway?"* When he didn't answer, Jovari added, *"Did she say something about me? Oh, did she tell Claire something? What was it?"*

*"You sound far too curious. Which reinforces my suspicions."*

*"Forgive me if I like to know when others talk about me."*

*"She didn't say anything."* His admission probably dashed Jovari's hopes. *"Claire only thought there was something between the two of you and casually mentioned it."*

*"Ah."* There was a long beat of silence and then, *"Our queen has nothing to worry about. I have absolutely no interest in the pink-haired human. I merely tolerate her presence because she is Claire's friend."*

They fell quiet after that.

Jovari was the youngest of them—or he had been, until Dallin—but he was still a shield. He'd given his word and that carried weight. Talon would just have to trust that he'd keep it.

# CHAPTER 23

# THE MISSING CUTLERY

*Kastali Dun*

Mikkin shared a furtive glance with Jamie. A sheen of sweat covered the lad's forehead. "Relax," he muttered under his breath. "If they were going to figure us out, they would have by now."

Jamie blew out a breath, shifting to get comfortable on the long bench they shared with a number of other patrons. Nobility, mostly. The great hall was surprisingly full. Kane wanted to play king, and he couldn't do that with an empty castle.

Mikkin spotted plenty of familiar faces. Everyone here had sworn oaths of fealty to their new ruler. Not that they'd been given a choice. It was that, or death. He and Jamie were the only imposters in the room. But if their tablemates recognized them or recalled their absence during the oath ceremony, they didn't comment on it.

He adjusted his sleeve before taking a sip of water.

The mood in the great hall was dismal at best. Patrons kept their voices low, if they spoke at all. It didn't stop the gossip from spreading through whispers.

"…the line was out the door," the man beside him was saying. "At least a hundred. All for the same complaint."

"But surely they aren't *all* missing," said the woman across from him.

Mikkin cleared his throat, keeping his voice low. "Did something happen?"

"Oh, you haven't heard?" The man beside him looked him over, but there wasn't any suspicion in his gaze. That didn't mean he could be trusted. Any one of these people could turn him over to Kane for a bit of favor. Just because they didn't like their new king, didn't mean they wouldn't lick his boots.

"Apparently this morning, every single wheel in the city went missing."

Mikkin's forehead furrowed. "You mean, like…"

"Wagon wheels, cart wheels, carriage wheels, you name it. Lord Murry—you know Lord Murry, don't you?"

"I know Lord Murry," Mikkin said. He sat on the lower council.

"Right. Well, Lord Murry had a standing appointment with the merchant guild. His Majesty put him in charge of drafting up their new charters. Anyway, he went to leave his town house, and come to find out, his carriage was out of commission. All the wheels—gone."

Mikkin furrowed his brow, feigning shock. A few missing wheels didn't sound all that worrisome. But since his tablemate expected outrage…

"Come to find out, wasn't just him," the man whisper-hissed. "It was everyone else, too. No one can travel in or out of the city unless they're on foot or horseback. None of the market wares could be carted to the market. Had to close the whole thing down."

"That's unfortunate." He rubbed his jaw, contemplating. It seemed an odd occurrence. That it should be city-wide reeked of mischief.

"Didn't hurt the bigger merchants any," the man continued. "They've got storefronts so they don't rely on carting their goods about. But everyone else suffered."

"You think it was the resistance?" Jamie asked, leaning around to whisper his question.

The man's face paled. "Sure hope not. No one knows for certain, though, do they? Only rumors. Anyway, everyone that lost a wheel came to lodge a formal thievery complaint with the steward. They all want compensation. Don't think a single one of them will get so much as a steely—"

Silence fell.

Mikkin looked up in time to see their new king silhouetted in the hall's doorway. He suppressed a shudder. The entire room came to its feet. He ground his teeth and did the same.

His entire purpose of being here was to spy. He and Jamie were dressed in fine clothes, pretending to be cousins of Lord Glover. Lord Glover was the only member on the lower council privy to this entire charade. He knew a group of them had gotten away. That they were now in hiding, though he didn't know where. Having people on the inside allowed them to come and go more easily within the keep without attracting attention.

Kane surveyed his court, red eyes tracing over faces. Mikkin's left hand clenched into a fist. Beside him, Jamie shifted, keeping his eyes downcast.

He could almost feel Kane looking at him. Would the sorcerer recognize him? Months ago, he'd been a prisoner in Shadowkeep. He looked different now. He'd shaved and trimmed his hair. He was no longer covered in grime. Besides, fine clothing went a long way to transform a person.

The room seemed to exhale when Kane strode to the head table. It was empty of course, save for a single place setting. He eyed Kane's attire. The breastplate was firmly in place. Four out of five stone slots were filled. Given that Kane's left hand was fisted, he assumed the fifth dragonstone was with him.

Only when Kane rounded the table and took his seat did the rest of the hall follow suit. A few minutes later, side doors opened and servants swept in. The silence was suffocating.

Normally, this would be a happy time. A time for idle chit-chat. Stories swapped. Drinks filled to overflowing.

Instead, a cloud of fear pressed in around them, sucking the life out of the hall.

Platters of food were carefully deposited. He reached for the one nearest him then paused. Others were likewise glancing around in confusion. He hadn't noticed anything amiss at first. But now—

A chair scraped. Worried gasps filled the hall. Kane surged to his feet, forcing every patron to stand with him. "You there!" Kane barked, pointing at a fleeing servant. The servant froze. An older man with a neatly trimmed beard.

"Yes, Your—Your Majesty."

"Where are all the serving spoons? Where is all the cutlery?!"

"I... Forgive me, Your Majesty, but there isn't any."

Even from the far side of the hall, Mikkin noticed the way Kane's jaw twitched with irritation. "What do you mean, there *isn't any?*"

The entire hall seemed to hold its breath. Everywhere he looked, wide eyes stared in shock, waiting for Kane to order the servant's death, or better yet, kill the man himself.

"This...this evening, we..." The servant fell to his knees, prostrating himself on the floor. "Forgive me, Your Majesty. We looked, but it's all gone. It disappeared this afternoon. We checked everywhere. Even...even the storage rooms."

The silence stretched on. Then, "Bring me the head woman."

Mikkin's heart stuttered. Tess. Was she the person behind this? Surely not.

"What's going on?!" Jamie whispered.

"If I knew, lad, I'd tell you."

"Is this some kind of...of prank?! Who would do such a thing?!"

"Again," Mikkin said, "if I knew, I'd tell you."

The servant scurried from the room, bowing every few steps like that might save him. Kane remained standing, everyone did. It made it harder to see around the heads. He was taller than most, so he had a clearer view. Some people pressed up onto their toes to see better.

Tess strode into the hall, her kirtle billowing, head held high.

Mikkin swallowed the acid lifting in his throat. His people needed her, relied on her for supplies down in the caves. He braced himself, knowing that he might be forced to witness her death.

"You summoned me, Your Majesty?" She gave a grand bow.

"What is the meaning of this?! Where is all the cutlery?"

"It is as Seth said, Your Majesty. This evening, we discovered it missing—"

"I should kill you where you stand!" Kane seethed. "If you discovered it missing, then why have you served dinner? How are we to eat, if we cannot—?"

"You informed me just last week, that if meals are not served on time, you'd have my head. I am only following orders, Your Majesty."

Mikkin's grip on the edge of the table tightened. He half expected Tess's head to roll here and now for the way she'd spoken to Kane. That woman must have had a death wish. Admiration welled in his chest. She had courage in spades.

"This should have been brought to my attention. Immediately."

"I apologize, Your Majesty." Tess gave a bow. "You are right. In the future, when things of this nature happen, I will be sure to inform you."

Kane's lips curled with fury, baring his teeth. Mikkin's eyes darted towards the nearest servant's entrance. It wasn't far. Perhaps he could get Jamie out…

"I assume you are looking for the culprit?"

"Of course. I plan to interview every single servant in the keep."

"Good. I want whoever is responsible found and brought to me. In the meantime, everyone may starve. No one eats until punishment is meted. Have dinner delivered to my quarters."

"Your… Your Majesty. You cannot—"

"I can! If my subjects think such behavior is funny, then everyone will suffer the consequences. Shut the cookery down. No one eats. Not in their rooms, not in the hall. Nowhere. Perhaps that will motivate our miscreant to come forward."

"What of all this food, Your Majesty." Tess waved towards the overflowing platters covering the tables.

"Throw it out. Feed it to the pigs. I don't care. No one in this keep gets so much as a bite—" Kane's eyes darted to one of the courtiers near the head table. The young man held a bread roll in his hand. He had just taken a covert bite. He stopped mid-chew, then quickly swallowed, his throat bobbing.

"Guards," Kane shouted. Several Oshean guards stepped from the shadows. It seemed Kane didn't trust any of the old castle guards. "Bring that man to me."

The man flung the roll onto the table, then took a quick step back. It was too late. The guards advanced on him. He turned on his heel to run down the aisle. Two more guards stepped into his path. They grabbed the young man and dragged him to the head table. His body was entirely supported as his feet dragged over each of the steps.

He began sobbing, babbling apologies.

"All of you—sit. Witness what happens when you disobey my orders."

The entire room sat as one.

Kane remained standing. He muttered something, a cantrip, and the man's discarded roll soared through the air. It landed in Kane's free hand. The guards pushed the man to his knees. His body shook.

"Since you were so hungry. Here. Eat." Kane shoved the roll in the man's mouth, down his throat. He began to choke, struggling, pulling against the guards' hold.

"Look away, lad," Mikkin said into Jamie's ear.

Jamie was pale, shaking with anger. "I'm not a child."

"Yes, but you don't have to watch this."

"I imagine I'll see worse before this is all over."

The man on the dais continued to choke. Mikkin couldn't see his face, thank the gods. His body thrashed, but the guards held tight. Eventually, he fell still. The guards released him and his body crumpled to the ground. He lay unmoving. Dead by suffocation.

Kane nudged the body with his foot, pushing it until it rolled face up, eyes wide with shock, staring unseeing at the ceiling. Mikkin swallowed back the acid rising in his throat.

Kane surveyed everyone. "Anyone else care to test my patience? No? Good. If I discover *anyone* flouting my decree, you will suffer the same fate."

Kane turned to Tess. "No one eats," he reiterated.

Her face was pale. "As...as you command, Your Majesty."

"Good. Clean this up." He waved a hand over the hall.

Tess backed away, then spoke to one of the servants lurking in the shadows. Moments later, servants rushed in, carrying away the fragrant platters of food. The guards lifted the dead body and dragged it from the room.

Mikkin was no longer hungry.

"I'll never look at bread the same," Jamie whispered under his breath, clutching his stomach.

Kane waited until everything was cleared away, until the body was gone, then strode from the hall. The rest of them stayed seated in silence for a long time after that.

# CHAPTER 24
## THE FOREST WAKES

*Esterpine*

Koldis woke to a gasp. Not *his* gasp, though. Taylynn was sitting upright in bed. For a moment, he could only stare at her, blinking lazily. Her shimmery, translucent gown had slipped, the left strap leaving her shoulder bare.

His mouth watered. He wanted to lean in and kiss her skin, taste her, but her wide eyes startled him. She stared blankly at the opposite wall of their sleeping nook. "What's the matter, little witch?" He leaned in, brushing a lock of her hair behind her ear.

She blinked, coming back to herself, then turned to him. "The forest. It's...awake."

His stomach pitched as the realization sank in. He sprang from the bed, suddenly wide awake. His body was ready to move, to do something in response to the news. "They're back? She's back?!"

Taylynn exhaled, looking far more calm than he felt. "Back in our world, yes." A faint smile tugged at her lips as she witnessed his distress. Then, with feigned exaggeration, she flopped onto her back, nestled among the pillows and blankets.

"How can you just lay there? We need to tell the others.

Bedelth. Saffra. We need to finish making preparations. We need—"

"Yes, yes, by all means," she groaned. "I'm going back to sleep. Someone kept me up half the night." She turned on her side, dragging a pillow to her chest to cuddle it. Suddenly, he was very, *very* jealous of that pillow. Perhaps telling the others could wait. But... no, it couldn't. He had too many questions and so much energy all of a sudden. The need to move, to act, gripped him.

It was time to take back their kingdom.

"Is Claire—did she come through the Kengr Gate like we anticipated?"

"Hmm?" Taylynn's hooded eyelids were already fluttering.

"Gods, woman." He bounded to the bed and ripped the pillow away, lowering himself into the cradle of her thighs. "You can't just drop that kind of information on me then go back to sleep. I need details."

She blinked up at him, then offered a slow, lazy smile, like a cat who'd just caught a mouse. He didn't like being the mouse, so he growled. But...it was such a sweet smile. He brushed a kiss against the corner of her lips.

"There is not much to tell, really." She ran her fingers through his hair. "I can feel it. The forest has woken up. The king tree's focus is back in our world once more, which means so is the queen." She closed her eyes and sighed. "I guess that means I really ought to rise. I am certain the king tree will wish to speak with me."

Oh how the tables had turned. Now *he* was the one who wanted to keep her stuck in bed. The feel of her against him, soft curves against his hard muscles, was divine. He pressed his hips against hers. A whoosh of breath left her lips, tickling his skin.

He kissed her once, twice, savoring the feel of her mouth, then pulled back. "She's really back," he said, blinking. "After nearly a year."

"Indeed." Taylynn trailed her fingers over his cheek, along his jaw. "You really ought to tell the others. They will be beside themselves with joy. Plus, if you wouldn't mind speaking with Tasar. He will want to know."

"Can you not meet with him?"

"King tree, remember?"

He exhaled, pressing his forehead into her neck. "Fine. Fine. Just let me savor you a moment longer." He'd had weeks upon weeks to do exactly that. Every moment had been equal parts torturous and wonderful. He had a feeling that once Claire reached them, there would be no time left for savoring. That this was going to be a race to the finish line, to see things through. The final stand. But...after that?

He kissed down the column of her neck, hesitating at her clavicle, then flicked his tongue against her skin like a serpent, tasting her. She hummed with delight. Flattening his tongue, he licked a trail over her skin, up, up, up, until he reached her chin. "Mine," he breathed. The primal, animalistic side of him, the dragon lurking beneath his skin, took great pleasure in reminding her that she was his, and that he was hers.

"I shall never forget it," she breathed, before guiding his face to hers. Capturing his lips with hers. Their kiss was languid and exploratory. There wasn't time to be hungry—not this time.

Eventually, he dragged himself away to get ready for the day. They parted ways on the outskirts of Esterpine. She gave him no definite answer as to when she'd return. Now that the forest was truly alive again, he worried there'd be long stretches between seeing her. She had a reputation for disappearing.

He dragged a hand through his hair in frustration.

It was on the tip of his tongue to ask her—no, *beg* her—not to stay away for long, but he stopped himself. She was a creature of the forest, beautiful and unfettered. Asking her to be something other than herself would be a travesty. So he put his selfishness aside and trekked into the city.

Bedelth and Saffra were still sleeping when he reached them—presumably sleeping, anyway. He had to pound on their door repeatedly until he heard sounds from within. The toppling of something. A thud as it landed on the floor. A muttered curse that followed. Footsteps. Then Bedelth was at the door, glaring. "Is there a reason you have interrupted my mate's sleep?" His voice was a lethal growl.

"Gods! Do I sound like that when I get protective?"

Bedelth only blinked, then relaxed his shoulders. "I think you're probably worse."

Koldis chuckled. "Fair. And yes, I've news. Let me in."

They assembled in the small sitting room.

Saffra had tears streaming down her face as he told her the news. She leapt into Bedelths arms and buried her face in his chest. "I thought... I thought she might never...return." Her words were managed between gasps. Of everyone, Saffra had taken Claire's disappearance hard. He only knew because Bedelth had confided in him of the guilt she felt. It was absurd, of course, to think it was her fault. Kane had done what he'd done and no one was to blame for it. But that's how guilt could be. It wasn't always rational or practical.

TASAR WAS AN UNUSUAL SPRITE. His dark hair was threaded with silver, likely intentional. Sprites were immortal and didn't age— except in rare cases like Pelwynn—but they did enjoy manipulating their appearance to suit their needs. Tasar's hair made him look older, wiser. Only his eyes made him look ancient, though. The rest of him was flawless.

They were of the same height, though where he was layered with muscle Tasar was lean. Didn't matter, though, because Tasar outmatched his strength. They'd crossed blades several times after his arrival. The spymaster bested him every time.

But what made Tasar truly unusual was his paranoia. Like others of his profession, he used magic to disguise his spriten markings, making it impossible to know how many he had. It looked like he had none, but without magic, he'd have died a long time ago.

Tasar had a nervous twitch. It was unpredictable. He would

still, his head darting to one side, as if he could hear things no one else could, then his body would twitch in response, and then he'd carry on as if nothing had happened. His eyes were never settled, always in motion, as if he expected an enemy to jump out of the foliage. And he insisted on preparing his own food, even brought it with him whenever they gathered for meals.

Koldis met the spymaster at the training grounds, calling him aside to take a walk.

"You must be here to tell me of the queen's return," Tasar said.

"Why am I not surprised that you already know?"

"You know what I am, Lord Koldis. What I do. You shouldn't be." Tasar clasped his hands behind his back. He stilled suddenly, head jerking to the left, eyes darting in the same direction. "Yes. The forest is finally waking up."

Koldis shuddered. Tasar gave him the creeps sometimes. All the time, really.

Tasar carried on. "If the queen has traveled through the Kengr Gate, as suspected, she should reach us in a matter of days. She will be eager to visit Esterpine."

"Yes, that is our hope," Koldis said.

"Not a hope. It is fact."

"Right. Are your *Delles* ready?"

"Oh. We are always ready, Drengr." The smile Tasar offered gave him chills. "We've been ready since the princess summoned us."

Tasar wasn't just any spymaster, he was the leader of *Thorios Delles Briahaad*, which roughly translated to *Eastern Ghost Unit*. Or, *Ghosts* for short. He wasn't sure where they'd gotten their name, but it fit. They were something akin to a mix between spies and assassins. Though, their services hadn't been much used since the age of the dragons. That didn't mean they stopped training. Nor did they stop watching.

This was the first time the *Delles* had been called upon in any formal capacity.

"Have you any news of the capital?" Koldis asked.

"Oh, yes. Always." Tasar hesitated. "There have been several rebel movements. Attempts to rile Kane. Small things like missing cutlery and livestock running amuck. Several days past, all the Oshean guard uniforms went missing."

"Someone is pulling pranks?"

"From the looks of it."

Koldis swore under his breath. That was a sure way to get killed under Kane's reign. "I assume you know who."

"Oh, I do, yes, but Kane is having quite the time identifying the culprit. He can't just kill all of his subjects. The rebels meet in seedy taverns after dark, plot ways to irritate the king, treat it like some kind of game. It has only gotten worse since..."

"Since what?"

"Since the king demanded to know exactly what was going on. Now he is kept informed of all the little mundane things his subjects do to rebel. It keeps him quite busy."

Koldis snorted. "I bet he's regretting his desire to rule already."

"Perhaps."

Their path branched and they went left, looping around the outskirts of Esterpine. It was Koldis's turn to hesitate. He caught the thoughts of several fleeing critters. The creatures sensed that there was a predator in their midst. He was forced to listen to their frightful mutterings. But he pushed their disjointed thoughts from his mind, focusing on Tasar.

"Perhaps he will be too distracted for what comes next," Koldis mused. He could only hope. "Can you depart in the morning?"

"We are ready to serve our queen, Lord Koldis."

"Good. We are counting on you."

"It will be done."

They parted ways. He suppressed a shiver as Tasar walked away, glad he was on their side.

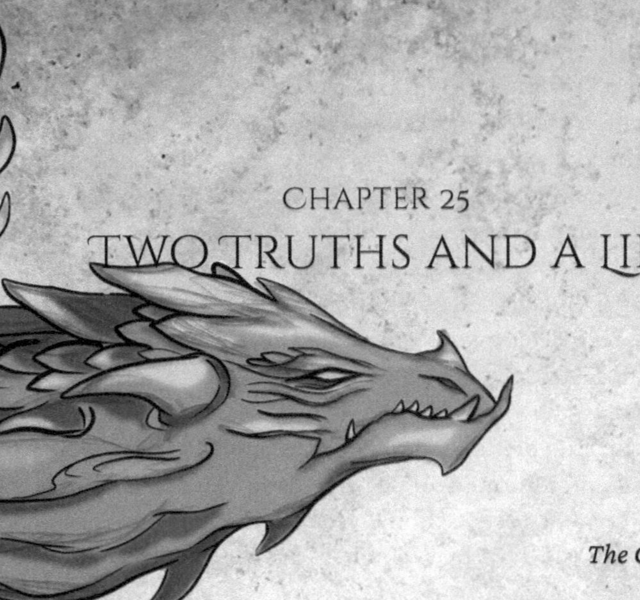



# CHAPTER 25

# TWO TRUTHS AND A LIE

*The Gable Forest*

Jovari descended towards the wall of looming trees. A strange feeling settled over him. He'd been in this situation before. *"We are here, my queen."* He said the words, even though she wouldn't hear him. He'd been doing it a lot lately. Talking to Claire while they flew, keeping her mind company even if she couldn't hear him. A part of him hoped that eventually, she'd respond.

*"It isn't too late to head east, to the outpost,"* Jovari said to Talon as the ground rushed up to meet them. *"We could follow the tree line."*

*"That would be another day or two. We don't need guides."*

*"Very well."*

They landed. He waited for Claire to dismount and untie her things before transforming. His gaze darted towards Leah—a habit he couldn't seem to break. She took hold of Irelia's elbow, helping the older woman find her feet. Irelia's movements were stiff, her muscles tight from disuse. Leah's eyes met his and held before she led the old woman away. He watched them for several heartbeats before turning.

Only to find Talon watching him. Damn it. He lifted a shoulder before walking towards Claire. "Okay, my queen?"

"Yes. Fine. I..." She stood staring at the forest. Her hand lifted, fingers grazing the skin at the base of her neck absentmindedly.

"You had much the same reaction when you saw it for the first time."

She blew out a breath. "Yes. I can feel it calling to me."

"Then we ought not linger."

"But..." She bit her bottom lip.

Talon strode over, brushing a lock of hair from her face. "All right, *mih cralla*?"

"What if we get lost? Or, I mean, if I get us lost?"

"We won't get lost," Jovari assured her. "You had no problem finding Esterpine the first time."

"Yes, but that was before the sorcerer cursed me."

"You are not cursed." Talon's voice held a hint of frustration. This wasn't the first time he'd said these words. "You are simply bound. We will free you, I swear it. We will find a way."

She exhaled.

"Perhaps the way lies ahead," Jovari suggested, sweeping his arm forward, "in there."

"I hope so..." Claire's throat bobbed. He hated seeing his queen so uncertain. So worried.

It was such a stark contrast to the woman he'd come to know. That broke his heart. Seeing her changed like this—seeing what Kane had turned her into. A woman hesitant and unsure of herself.

They took some time to rest before setting out with Claire in the lead. He and Talon took up the rear of the procession. "Remember how unsettling this place used to be for us?"

Talon snorted. "It still is."

"Oh, come now, you have to admit it isn't as bad as the first time." Still, he rested his hand on the pommel of his sverak.

Talon huffed, shaking his head. "Fine. You're right. It's not as bad, especially having her with us. You know, I've never been here with her."

"Do you think the sprites can do it? Heal her?"

"I will beg them on my knees, if I must."

"Taylynn, perhaps?"

"If she is here. Yes."

The trees were large, towering over them. They grew tighter the further they walked. Eventually, daylight disappeared, to be replaced by the effervescent glow of blueish green. His gaze was in constant motion, searching for threats in between stealing glances at Leah. He liked witnessing her wonder. Her eyes were wide, taking in the world around her. "Look at those little light-things," she whispered, pointing to the undergrowth. "They're like fireflies."

"They're beautiful," Claire breathed.

They walked arm in arm, Irelia trailing behind them.

Claire kept her staff in hand. He still couldn't believe it had appeared out of thin air. A good sign as any that this was where they were meant to go.

They occasionally stopped to rest.

A path seemed to open for them. He could only hope it was a direct shot to Esterpine. Their positions fluctuated. Eventually, Talon walked up front with Claire, and he found himself in the back with Leah. Irelia took the middle position. He was impressed that the old woman could keep up. Though, he was certain that Talon's frequent insistence on resting was so that she could catch her breath.

"You seem tense, dragon man." Leah's voice had him focusing on her.

"Because I am."

"Why?"

He exhaled. "You should probably help Irelia in case she needs extra support."

"I'm fine, *dragon man*," Irelia called over her shoulder, taking up Leah's nickname.

"Do you not want my company?" Leah's expression fell. "I can go—"

"No, no." His hand darted out to wrap around her elbow,

keeping her beside him. "I apologize. You're right. I'm tense. It's the forest."

He didn't tell her the real reason. That Talon had warned him away from her. Talon's warning didn't mean they couldn't walk or chat together. The problem was, she was already becoming a distraction. Getting to know her more would only make matters worse.

He slowed his pace to match hers, which put a little more distance between them and Irelia. Talon was still conversing with Claire. At least he wouldn't notice.

"Why does the forest make you uneasy?" Leah stole a glance at him.

"It's a drengr thing," he found himself explaining. "The sprites have always been at odds with those of dragon kind. Things have improved over the last year or so, naturally." He gestured towards Claire. "But the forest has never been friendly towards outsiders. I guess you could say that it will take time to adjust to this new world we live in."

She hummed. "Well, I'll just have to do my best to keep your mind off it."

Her grin made his heart skip. Yes. No. No, that was the worst idea. He cleared his throat—

"Let's play a game."

"A... A game?" He glanced sidelong at her.

"Yeah, to pass the time. Two truths and a lie. You ever played it?"

"Uhm..." He frowned. She wanted to play *a game*?!

"I'll go first. I will tell you three things about myself. Two of them will be true, but one of them will be a lie. You will have to guess which one is the lie. If you do, you win."

He opened his mouth to decline, then swiftly closed it. "What do I get if I win?"

"Well..." She appeared to think it over. "The winner gets a favor of their choosing, to ask at any time."

He snorted. "No. I don't trust that you won't ask me to do something outlandish."

"Afraid you won't win?"

"I didn't say that." He frowned.

"Fine, then let's have a go. Three rounds. The one with the most points wins. I'll even go first, show you how it's done."

He exhaled, rubbing a hand over his face. Around them, the trees grew denser. He kept his ears pricked for sounds that might be out of place. "Fine. Let's play."

She grinned. He had a sudden feeling he was going to regret this.

"Okay. Here we go." She appeared to think for several moments, then said, "My favorite color is pink. I once had a horse named Neigh Neigh. When I was young, I wanted to be a nurse when I grew up."

"And I have to guess which of those is false?"

"Yup." She offered him a mischievous grin.

He frowned, mulling it over. "The horse. You did not have a horse named Neigh Neigh."

She laughed. "I did! I really did. Great name, right?"

"It's a ridiculous name," he muttered, but found himself grinning. "But, wait. So then, you didn't want to be a nurse?"

"No, I did. My favorite color isn't pink."

"But, your hair." He scowled, studying her. He was sure it had been a true statement.

"They were out of lavender hair dye. My favorite color is purple. So, I win that round."

He huffed. "Tell me about this horse of yours. Whatever possessed you to name it that."

"Ah-ah-ah. That's not how this game works. Your turn."

He lifted his brows. "Fine. I was fourteen when I fledged. I am not a fan of sweets. I enjoy reading."

"Well, I saw you eating ice cream at the diner so...must be the first one."

"Nope. I really am not a fan of sweets. I merely tolerated it because I've never had something like that before."

"So...you hate reading?"

"I do. I really do. You couldn't pay me to sit down and read a book."

"You're joking." Her jaw dropped. "What's wrong with reading? Have you always been like that?"

"Ah-ah-ah," he chided, throwing her words back at her. "That's not how this game works."

"Ugh, really?" She rolled her eyes.

"You started it," he groused.

"Fine. We both lost. Next round." She seemed to grow more serious. She was quiet longer this time. "I have trouble sleeping at night. I've only been in love once. And, it's my fault my mom died."

His steps faltered. He stared at her, completely forgetting about the forest. It had to be the last one. Her mom had died in a car accident. She'd already admitted that. Which meant, she'd been in love. Something hot exploded in his chest. She was so...young. He didn't like the idea.

"The last one," he blurted.

"Nope. That one is true. It's the second one. I've never been in love."

He stopped walking. "That's... You can't cheat."

She stopped too. "I'm not cheating. I picked a hard one to ensure that I win."

"But your mom—"

"My mom died because of me."

His lips parted. "Leah... You cannot possibly believe that. You said your mom died in a head-on collision—from a car accident." She lifted a shoulder. "So why would you think it's your fault."

She started walking again. "It's your turn, Jovari."

He watched her back for several heartbeats, then started walking again. "I don't want to play anymore," he decided.

"That's not how this works. We had an agreement. It's your turn."

"Fine." He ground his teeth together. "My parents are still alive and I care for them deeply. I've never been in love. And... I have trust issues." He wasn't sure why he'd blurted the last part, except that it was the truth.

She appeared to think it over for a bit, then, "You *have* been in love, haven't you. It's the second one."

He was quiet for several moments. "Once."

"What happened to her?"

"You win this round. Point to you. Your turn. Final round."

She sighed. When she next spoke, her voice was barely above a whisper. "After my father died, I tried to kill myself. I collect teaspoons and have over one hundred. I don't celebrate my birthday."

His blood ran cold. He gripped her arm, stopping her. This wasn't a game anymore and he wasn't having fun. "You shouldn't joke about such things," he said, his voice low and serious.

"You think I'm joking?"

The thought of her trying to kill herself—his stomach roiled. Bile rose in his throat and he swallowed it down. Surely it wasn't true—couldn't be. She seemed so sure of herself. He never would have—no, it couldn't be true. Moreover, why should he care if it was? He wasn't allowed to get attached to her. She was Claire's friend—nothing more.

"I don't believe it," he said at last. "It's the first one that's a lie."

"Wrong," she said, her gaze a challenge. "I don't collect teaspoons, but my mom did. Loved them. And she did have over one hundred."

She pulled her arm free and marched away, shouting over her shoulder that it was his turn. Damn her.

He caught up. "Fine. You want to get serious. Let's get serious. I was a fool for thinking love lasted forever. I once ate someone's pet grazer. And...I'm so glad I met you."

Her steps faltered. He studied her, watching as her cheeks flushed. Suddenly, he knew he had to backtrack, to lie. "Well, anyone would be glad to have met me, so it must be the second one. You really ate someone's pet grazer?"

"Yes," he lied. "Point to you. Looks like you won two to nothing. Guess I'll owe you a favor." Part of him kind of liked the idea. He was curious to see what she'd ask for. But most of him just felt emotionally drained. This was not a fun game.

"Yay! Go me!" She grinned and skipped away—as if she'd never dropped serious information on him—to link arms with Irelia.

He exhaled. He'd intended to alienate her with that last one. He'd never eaten anyone's pet grazer. The truth was, he really *did* wish he'd never met her. Especially now after what she'd just revealed. He tightened his hand into a fist and continued at a slower pace.

How in the name of the gods was he supposed to stay away from her now?

The hours slipped by. He found it harder than ever to keep his eyes off her. She'd given him so many questions and had refused to elaborate. It's like she'd done it on purpose. Now he was forced to wonder about everything.

Eventually, the foliage changed, and their path opened up. He caught sight of a statue, disguised with ivy. He'd seen it before, hadn't he? Esterpine must be close.

"Did you see that?" Leah asked, pointing to another, drawing Irelia's gaze in that direction.

Several figures materialized in the gloom. At first, he thought they might be sprites. Talon froze, forcing Claire to stop beside him. The rest of them piled up behind them. A moment later, there was a feminine cry. One of the figures detached and rushed forward, straight for Claire. It wasn't until she was close that he realized who it was. Saffra threw herself at Claire, wrapping her up in her arms. Claire stiffened, but didn't push her away.

"Oh, gods. You're here. You're actually here! I had a vision this morning that we would meet here, so I brought the others." Saffra was weeping. Smiling. Holding Claire at arm's length to study her.

He looked up to find Koldis and Bedelth. They wore serious expressions. Not joy, as he'd expected. Instead, he sensed dread. That could only mean one thing. Something was very, very wrong.

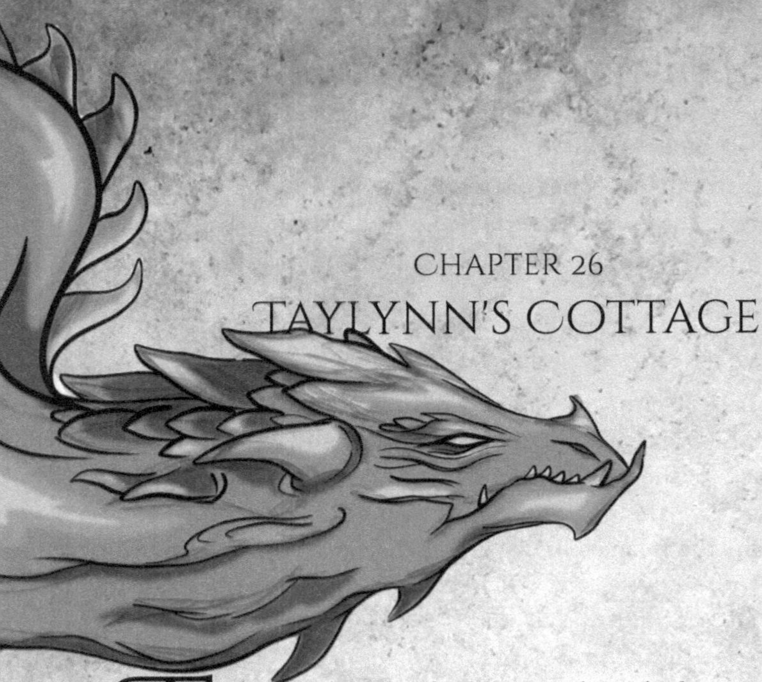

# CHAPTER 26
# TAYLYNN'S COTTAGE

*Esterpine*

Talon studied his shields. Somehow, he knew. His stomach turned rock hard. Something was wrong. "What is it?" he barked right as Claire said, "I'm sorry, but do I know you?"

Saffra dropped her arms and took a surprised step back, frowning. "Do you...do you *know* me?" Something flashed across the seer's face. Too late, did he remember what had happened to Saffra's fiance, Commander Daxton. This wasn't the first time Saffra had been forgotten. That would definitely open old wounds.

He stepped forward to explain, "Kane has her trapped under a spell. She can't remember anything from her life here. Not...not even me."

Saffra blinked, then glanced behind her at Bedelth and Koldis. "But..."

"Why are you here?" Talon demanded. "In the forest. What's wrong?"

This time, Koldis stepped forward. "It's... It's the throne..."

"No." He took a step back. The comforting feel of Jovari's palm squeezed his shoulder. He shrugged it off. "Tell me it isn't true."

"We lost the kingdom," Bedelth said, scrubbing a hand over his face, his features etched in sorrow.

"No," he repeated, shaking his head. It couldn't be real. There was no way. He'd...he'd taken measures to avoid this. Dragonwall couldn't fall. Kane couldn't have his throne.

Claire looked alarmed, glancing between everyone. "Are you... his other shields?"

"You truly don't remember us?" Koldis looked hurt, but Talon didn't care about that right now. All he could think of was Bedelth's news.

"How?" he demanded. "Tell me how it happened? What... Is Reyr—?"

"Alive. They're alive, as far as we know."

He blew out a breath. There was that, at least. He wasn't sure how he'd handle Reyr's death. Any of their deaths. He would have completely lost it, here and now. Even still, he felt the tether on his control begin to fray. "How long have we been gone?"

"Nearly a year." A clear, musical voice rang out. A moment later, Taylynn appeared. Both Claire and Leah gaped at her. "Welcome back, my queen."

"Taylynn," Koldis said, moving towards his mate. He bent to kiss her forehead, the greeting affectionate.

It had been a long while since Talon had lost control. His skin itched, his scales threatening to break free. "Someone better tell me how that piece of filth sorcerer is sitting on my throne. Now!" His words were a low growl.

"Peace, Your Majesty. Let us go somewhere we can speak privately. My cottage is just this way."

He nearly refused, but Claire threw him an alarmed look, as if sensing that he was seconds from changing. He blew out a breath. "Yes, all right. Lead the way."

"Good." Taylynn set off, Koldis beside her. The rest of them followed.

He did not wish to frighten his mate. This would give him a moment to collect himself. A warm hand took hold of his. He jerked at the surprising contact, then looked down. Claire twined their fingers together. Warmth exploded in his chest. It was the first time she'd initiated contact since their reunion. "Are you... okay?"

He took a deep breath. "I'm not sure. But...better now that I'm touching you."

"Does it calm you? My touch?"

"More than you would believe," he admitted.

She captured her lip between her teeth, like this pleased her. "Then I won't let you go, Talon. Come on."

Gods, hearing her say that...

Hearing his name on her lips...

She pulled him along, keeping pace with the others. They'd spent the entire walk to Esterpine chatting about inconsequential things. She told him stories about her childhood—some of which he was already familiar with, but he let her because he liked listening to her talk—while he told her stories of the time they'd spent together. She loved the forest. He could see it on her face every time she caught sight of something beautiful.

Even her marks seemed to glow brighter under the foliage.

They emerged into a clearing that housed an overgrown garden. At first, all he saw was foliage, until the shape of a cottage took form. "Come," Taylynn said, motioning them to the door.

He blinked, then caught Koldis's eye. *"She lives here?"* he asked. *"Why not the palace?"*

*"She doesn't like the palace. This is home for her. Be respectful."*

Talon lifted his brows. Since when did his shields offer reprimands in the form of warnings? He exhaled. They must have grown bolder in his absence, or forgotten what it was like to have a king around.

"Oh, it's so quaint," Leah squealed after walking over the threshold. "How cute! You really live here?"

He didn't hear Taylynn's reply from inside.

"Well, *mih cralla*? After you."

Claire grinned, pulling him along behind her. He was the last to enter.

"Wasn't...?" Koldis scowled. "Wasn't the table smaller the other day? Actually..." Koldis glanced around, confusion written in his expression.

"I couldn't very well host six people besides myself in that small space," Taylynn teased, throwing him a fond look. "It's enchanted to fit whomever it needs to fit. And since we have a king in our presence, well!"

Koldis snorted.

They took seats around the table while Koldis disappeared into a cellar. He returned with a tray of food. Jovari threw him an amused look, to see him play the role of servant. But they were all starving, so they didn't complain.

Taylynn's gaze finally lingered over Irelia. Slowly, her smile widened. "The tree warned me that you were with them, *sarihon*."

Irelia groaned, leaning back in her chair. "Am I supposed to know what that means?"

"It means *princess*."

Irelia snorted. "I'm no princess, girl."

Taylynn giggled—actually giggled, covering her mouth and all —before straightening. "You are Isabella's daughter. Her sister— my grandmother—was your aunt. My mother, who is now dead, was your cousin. That makes you a princess and technically, it gives you the right to claim the throne, if you wish it."

"Are you barking mad, girl. I came here to live out my remaining days, not be some kind of queen."

Taylynn hummed, though she shared a look with Koldis before turning back to the woman. "How old are you?"

Irelia shrugged, "Two thousand years, give or take."

"Ah, but of course. Here you'd be some fifty thousand had you remained within the forest. I knew someone else that old..." Her expression fell.

"This is all fine and great," Talon bit out, tired of waiting, "but you promised answers."

"Talon," Claire chided, squeezing his hand. She hadn't dropped it, so both of them had been eating one-handed.

"Yes, yes, the kingdom has fallen," Taylynn tsked. "We did everything we could to keep that from happening. I cannot say exactly how it fell, as none of us in this room was actually there. But I can explain the events leading up to its fall. From there, we only have the information provided by my spymaster."

"Go on," he said.

She launched into an explanation, the others filling in little details while he listened. It all started with Saffra's vision of Kane retrieving the stones. Panicked, she had set out with Bedelth to find them, in hopes of reaching them before the sorcerer. Not long after, Taylynn discovered that the forest had lost its magic. The stones hiding within were vulnerable. With Reyr's permission, they set out for Esterpine, but not before ensuring that the kingdom would see its queen alive and well. She'd enchanted a low level mage, someone trustworthy, to look like Claire so that Reyr might go on ruling without trouble.

"We—Koldis and I—went to retrieve the stones, but Kane was waiting for us," Taylynn explained. "He...he caught me off guard. He used my own forest against me. I..." At this, Taylynn faltered. He'd never seen her look upset, and certainly not guilty. "I failed you all. I wasn't strong enough."

It was Claire who spoke. "You can't blame yourself. If *you* were the one destined to defeat Kane, then it wouldn't be *my* destiny."

Saffra frowned. "I thought you said she couldn't—"

"I've already told her everything," he explained. "Or, as much as I could."

Saffra nodded.

"What happened next?" he demanded, squeezing Claire's hand.

"Kane took the stones and Pelwynn..."

"Claire's tutor," Koldis added. "The one who taught her sprite magic."

"I know who Pelwynn is," Talon said. He'd seen the sprite in Claire's mind before.

"He... Kane killed him," Taylynn finished.

Claire looked between them, aghast. Not because she could remember Pelwynn but because Kane had killed someone they knew.

"He wanted you to have his cottage, Claire," Koldis said. "It was one of his last requests."

Claire's throat bobbed. "I wish I could remember him."

"You will, love." Talon kissed her forehead. "When you get your memories back."

"Not long after that, Bedelth appeared with Saffra," Taylynn added.

"We failed to collect a single stone." Bedelth picked up the narrative. "Saffra had seen visions of each stone's location as Kane reclaimed them. But it took us longer to find each location than it took him to retrieve them. At the final location—"

"Darknest," Taylynn butted in.

"—he had wraiths waiting for us. It was a trap. Saffra nearly died."

Talon jerked, turning towards Saffra. "You are all right?"

"I... I'm fine now. But if it wasn't for Bedelth, I might not have survived."

Something about her words had Bedelth's jaw clenching. Talon thought he could guess why. "We were outmatched," Bedelth said. "She suffered a wound."

"I thought Claire destroyed the vodar." Jovari frowned.

"The ones Kane initially summoned, yes." Taylynn picked at a bit of fruit on the platter. "It seems he's summoned more. The vodar are keepers of hell, or, the place you drengr call undirfold. Their numbers are significant. Kane only summoned a portion of them. You defeated those he summoned. It would have weakened him and taken him time to regain the strength to summon more."

"Well, he did." Bedelth's mood was dark. "And one almost took my mate from me."

"So," Talon said, getting them back on track. "You brought Saffra here?"

"Yes. I knew the sprites had healed Claire's wound. I did what I could to contain the magic. Not as good a job as Koldis, I'm afraid." Koldis sat up a little straighter. "She..." Bedelth's throat bobbed.

"I lost a portion of my arm. Well, lost implies it's been amputated. It's still here, it's just…" Saffra rubbed her bicep, hidden beneath the fabric of her long sleeved tunic. "Dead."

Talon exhaled. It could have been worse, much worse.

"Two days later," Koldis continued, "intel arrived. The capital has fallen. Kane swept in and claimed the throne, imprisoning Reyr and Merrian—Claire's body-double. We've got spies there now, working to make ready for our arrival. We've been waiting for your return. Waiting to reclaim what is rightfully yours."

"And how do you expect us to do that?" Talon said, rubbing a hand over his chin.

"I…" Taylynn swallowed. "I think I have an idea."

Everyone perked up at that. They had all learned by now, when Taylynn talked, they listened. So,

they talked strategy for another hour until Claire began yawning.

Gods, he'd never been so exhausted in all his life. He felt numb. The news had wrecked him.

"My mate needs sleep," he said at last.

"She should stay here tonight," Taylynn said. "Tomorrow, we will figure out what is to be done about her memories. Her magic."

"Is there a cure?" Claire asked, perking up.

"If there is a cure to be had, the king tree will know. Until then, it is best we not advertise to our people that you do not know them. You are their queen. Though they will support you no matter what, showing weakness is not ideal. We must find a way to avoid that."

"And how do you propose we do that?" Talon demanded.

"I'm sure we can come up with something. A quest, perhaps, as an excuse to keep her out of sight." Taylynn appeared thoughtful, then added, "You will find an ample number of sleeping arrangements in the loft. I hope you don't mind bunking together."

"As long as I get to rest, I don't mind at all," Irelia grumbled. She'd been unusually quiet, absorbing everything with curious eyes. She seemed more relaxed now—now that they'd reached the forest. He couldn't help but wonder if it was the same reason Claire often felt more at home amongst the trees. Irelia was half sprite, after all.

"Good." Taylynn brightened. "And there is an outdoor bathing pool just behind my cottage. You will find everything you need there. Help yourself. Get clean. Koldis will have more food prepared before you turn in for the night, as I'm sure you'll be hungry again. I, however, must return to the city for a short time. I will be back later." She swept from the cottage before they could stop her.

"Well, you heard my mate, hop to." Koldis stood. "My queen, a bath?"

"Oh, yes please!" Claire's expression brightened.

Talon growled. "I'll take her. She can bathe first. The rest of you can wait."

"As if we would have it any other way," Bedelth teased, watching Talon lead Claire from the cottage. Talon grabbed her pack on the way out.

They found the small bathing pool exactly where Taylynn said it would be. "It's... Wow!" Claire pressed her hands to her chest in wonder.

Calling it a bathing pool was an understatement. The stone pool was decorated with vines and flowers, and a small water feature fed into it, creating a waterfall ideal for wetting one's hair. The small stream that fed into it babbled. There was a shelf, stacked with towels and soaps.

"It looks like you have all that you need," he said, studying the space. "Just call if you need me." He turned to leave but Claire's hand shot out, wrapping around his wrist. The contact sent a welcome jolt through him.

"You... You don't want to join me? Don't you want to get clean?"

He all but choked. "My queen—"

"I mean, it's just bathing isn't it? Isn't that something we did together before—?"

He ran a hand through his hair. "Claire..."

"I don't mind if you see me naked." The corner of her mouth pulled up. The look was pure mischief. She looked so much like her old self. It took every ounce of control he possessed to decline the offer. He leaned in to whisper, "*Mih cralla*, if I see you naked, I will have you pinned against the wall of the pool in seconds, screaming my name. There will be no escape for you. After everything that has happened, my self control is hanging by a thread. Are you ready for that?"

He felt her shiver against him. The slight gasp that fell from her lips was almost a moan. "I..."

When he took a step back, her skin was flushed. He loved the sight of it. "I thought not. I'll be out front. Call if you need anything."

With that, he cursed himself for being so proper and left.

# CHAPTER 27
# UNEXPECTED VISITOR

*Kastali Dun*

Jeanine and Feowen emerged through a hidden door and into a shadowed alley. Tall buildings loomed on either side. The door closed behind them, the sound muffled. She pulled her hood into place as Feowen did the same. They hesitated, searching for movement. Besides the noise of the city beyond, everything around them was silent. She exhaled, her shoulders relaxing.

"I still can't believe we found it," she murmured. It had taken months of exploration, but they'd finally mapped every single passage leading into and out of the keep. This was one of two leading directly into the city, right into the Pauper's District, putting them closest to the public market. The other let out into a nondescript neighborhood of tall homes in a working class part of the city, more centrally located.

Feowen merely grunted.

She reached into her pocket, removing a list they'd drafted earlier. Her eyes swept over the contents. With tensions high, it was becoming more difficult to intercept Tess for what they needed. Now that they had a way into the city without having to leave through the keep, they could come and go more freely.

The market had only just reopened a week ago, and already they'd visited it twice. They had nearly thirty people living with them down in the cave now. That was a lot of mouths to feed.

Feowen's warm palm landed on her back. "Come," he said, giving her a gentle push forward.

She folded the list and tucked it away. They paused at the mouth of the alley, checking the street beyond, mostly for guards. There were more and more Oshean guards every day. Ships arrived from across the sea and guards came with them.

They stepped out into the open and they made their way to the market, traveling at a leisurely pace. There were other passersby out and about in the late afternoon, making it easy to blend in with the crowd. The market came into view.

Feowen hesitated, reaching for the hilt of his blade beneath his cloak. "What is it?" she breathed, immediately bracing. Tall buildings along the docks cast long shadows over everything. A group of guards stood fifty paces ahead, monitoring the crowd. That didn't appear to be what Feowen was looking at.

"I..." His eyes darted around. "I have the strange sense that we're being watched." The muscles in her shoulders bunched tight. "Keep going. Don't act as if anything is amiss."

They passed the Oshean guards, keeping close to the small group of shoppers ahead of them, then slipped into the densely packed aisles between stalls. She removed the handful of cloth sacks from beneath her cloak. They slipped into an apothecary stall. The tent flaps were pinned open to let in some light and a fire burned in a nearby basin, casting everything in a warm glow.

The tent was blessedly empty, save for the merchant inside, who greeted them with clipped words, her eyes darting to the shadows beneath their cloaks. "We need these items." Jeanine kept her voice low. She handed over her list and the woman began reading it over.

"I got everything but rilu grass and bitter clove, you'll have to try the tent down the way for that," she said, handing it back. Then she set about gathering up ingredients. At the counter, they placed them into one of the bags, then handed over a stack of coins and hurried on their way.

The tent down the way did not, in fact, have what they needed, so they went to two more before collecting both items. They stopped for a bag of vegetables, then made their way to the butcher's section for meat, which was wrapped in cloth and placed into a third bag.

"Hungry?" Feowen asked as they passed an area selling cooked food. Her mouth watered at the heavenly aromas. Because they were rationing, the question was unnecessary. She was always hungry these days.

"Come on." Feowen guided her towards one of the stalls where they purchased skewers of meat and vegetables. He didn't eat meat, so she saved those for herself. And since he carried all their bags, she took immense pleasure in popping bits of charred veggies into his mouth as they walked.

Back in the cave, they had absolutely no privacy, forced to rely on stolen moments like this, sneaking into dark tunnels to share a few impassioned kisses. Even those were rare, with Feowen's duties being what they were. He hardly had a spare moment. She'd all but begged him for this outing into the city.

"Delicious," he growled, as she placed a chunk of perfectly seared vegetable into his mouth. His teeth purposefully grazed her finger as she pulled away, sending a rush of heat straight to her belly. Their eyes connected beneath their hoods and she caught a glimmer of amusement.

"Are we still being watched?" she asked. They continued on through the market.

"Yes."

"Should we be worried?"

"I am not...certain."

Feowen was always alert by nature. But he didn't appear overly concerned. That had to be a good sign.

"Shouldn't we try to lose whoever it is? I assume they're following us."

"They are," he confirmed.

How he knew, she could not say. It wasn't as if he was stealing glances over his shoulder. But, he was a sprite, and far be it from her to question their abilities.

By the time they slipped out of the market, the sun was at the horizon, casting the land into shadow. She sighed forlornly. "I wish we could stay out longer."

"Indeed."

There was a curfew in place. Anyone out two hours past dark would be punished. Already, others were making their way out of the market as well. It created a steady stream of bodies to hide among.

They retraced their footsteps back to the alley. The further from the market they went, the more things around them quieted. She could have sworn she heard footsteps behind them, but when she glanced over her shoulder, there was nothing.

At one point, Feowen chuckled.

"What?" she snapped, keeping her voice low.

"He's not going to let you see him, so you may as well not bother. You'll just get a pinch in your neck from contorting it like that."

"He? Wait…so you know who is following us?"

"I think I have an idea, yes."

"And you've known this whole time?" Perhaps that's why he hadn't seemed too worried.

"Not the whole time, no. But I have my suspicions now."

"And we're leading them right to the alley?" Her pulse sped up.

"If it is who I think it is, then everything will be fine. If I am wrong and it is someone dangerous, I'll simply kill them."

A quiet chuckle sounded somewhere behind them, making her falter. Whoever it was, they had heard his threat and thought it was amusing. Well!

Feowen rounded the corner, slipping deep into the alley before setting his bags on the ground and spinning around. He had his hand on the hilt of his blade, but kept his hood up. She did the same, ready to draw her weapon.

Several moments passed in tense silence, then a shadow materialized, as if detaching from the walls. It stalked closer, slowing. A low, musical voice said, "Took me weeks to track you down, Prince." Then, a hand went up and their stalker's hood was removed. She found herself staring into an unusual face. A face that could only belong to a sprite, with its angular features, bright eyes, and pointed ears. But it wasn't a sprite she knew.

"Well, well, well." Feowen relaxed, lowering his own hood and stepping forward before pulling the male into a one armed embrace. "I thought you had others doing your dirty work, Tasar?"

The male chuckled. "Not for something this important? Who's the girl?"

"Ahh." Feowen grinned, glancing her way. She lowered her hood, gazing warily at the stranger. "This is Jeanine. She's..." He hesitated, thinking something over, then said, "Mine. She's mine."

A rush of shock followed by searing heat stole through her. She opened her mouth to greet Tasar, but only a squeak emerged. Feowen found this amusing and chuckled. Her cheeks flushed red. But what had he expected, saying something like that to a stranger?! Claiming her.

Tasar quickly disregarded her. "I take it you got somewhere quiet we can talk? I bring news."

"Indeed I do. Come." Feowen reached for their goods, hoisting the bags up, before leading them to the secret door.

Tasar took up the rear as they proceeded into the passages. If the male was surprised, he showed no sign, quietly walking behind them. She had a million questions. Why did Feowen trust this male? Who was he? Had he come from Esterpine because he was obviously a sprite? What news did he carry? Something that might help them overthrow Kane?

It was on the tip of her tongue to ask, but she didn't want to with Tasar there. So, they walked in silence. It took nearly an hour to navigate the twisting turns before they emerged into the familiar cave they'd called home these past months. The only word out of Tasar's mouth was, "Interesting," as he surveyed it.

Something told her it would take a lot to impress this male.

"This way," Feowen said, leading them down through the clusters of stalagmites. He passed their bags off to one of the attendants at the cookfires. She shot a quick smile at Desaree and Jocelyn before motioning with her head. They quickly rushed off, likely to collect Selphie and Miera, so that whatever this was wouldn't have to be repeated multiple times.

Feowen led them to the command table at the back of the cave. They'd attracted enough attention that when they arrived, the remainder of the queen's guard and inner circle had assembled with them. She and Feowen discarded their cloaks, tossing them over nearby chairs.

"This is Tasar," Feowen said, introducing him to the others. She studied their faces, their brief expressions of surprise. A few appeared to already know him.

"What brings you here, Spymaster?" Aithlin asked. "Not that I am unhappy to see you."

"Ahh, Aithlin. It is always a pleasure to look upon your face." She snorted, rolling her eyes. Aithlin was beautiful and Jeanine had once harbored a bit of jealousy about it. Now that she felt more secure in Feowen's affections, she only regarded Aithlin with warmth. "There is still a place among my ranks if you ever decide to join us," Tasar added, entirely sincere.

"I already have my calling, as you can see."

"Your ranks?" Jeanine found herself asking.

"Tasar leads *Thorios Delles Briahaad*," Feowen explained. "The Eastern Ghost Unit. A unit of operatives that function as spies and assassins."

Her lips parted in shock. She'd lived in Esterpine for some time and had never heard of such a thing. When she looked at Tasar again, a shiver of unease passed down her spine. He was obviously not a male to be trifled with.

"Indeed." Tasar confirmed, as if reading her mind and answering her thoughts. Then he hesitated, jerked his head to the right, as if he'd heard something, and froze. She immediately tensed, expecting something to jump out at them. But the spymaster merely brushed off his reaction, turning back to the rest of them. "I come with news. The queen has returned."

"What?!" Gasps rang out through their group.

"You are certain?" Feowen said, stepping forward. Excitement danced in his eyes.

"Absolutely. Your sister and her mate sent me here—that Koldis fellow. I quite like him, actually. Sensible for a drengr, I think—"

"Get to the point," Feowen growled.

"The queen has returned to Dragonwall. We are to make ready for her return to the capital. She has reached Esterpine and will eventually come here. Have you a way she might enter the city undetected?" At this, Tasar glanced around the cave then lifted his brows in challenge. He already knew, clearly.

"There is a passage that leads directly into and out of the city," Jassin said. "As well as one that leads to the fort. We can bring her here directly without attracting notice."

"What does it matter if she comes here?" Eylon asked, placing her hands on her hips. "The sorcerer has all five stones. If we make a move against him—if our queen makes any move against him—he will simply turn the drengr to stone. The queen's mate is a drengr, you know."

At this, Tasar only grinned. It was the kind of grin that spoke of secret knowledge. Something they didn't already know.

Jeanine's heart beat a little harder. Excitement coursed through her. Was it finally time to take back the kingdom?

"Here is what we are going to do," the spymaster said before taking a sip of something from his own flask. Then he shed his cloak and took a seat at their table. "We are going to help the rulers of Dragonwall reclaim their kingdom."

Several whoops sounded. She couldn't help her grin. They got straight to work.

CHAPTER 28

# A FAIRYTALE

*Esterpine*

Leah felt Jovari's presence before she saw him. She wasn't sure how, only that she had an inexplicable awareness of him whenever he was near. Like now.

She was flat on her back, a bed of moss cushioning her body, gazing up at the canopy above. Birds swooped about, building nests and flirting. They weren't like the birds she was used to. These were bright and colorful, similar to the tropical birds she'd seen on nature documentaries, only, even more beautiful.

She'd been here for hours, just killing time. Thinking, mostly, about how things had turned out. Being in Dragonwall was a lot to digest, but being here on the outskirts of Esterpine felt like a dream. She needed time to process.

"There you are."

Chills spread over her skin but she ignored them. She couldn't afford to develop feelings for Jovari. Perhaps if it was someone else she might let herself, but something about him, *specifically*, terrified her. If she fell in love with him—which she undoubtedly would if she allowed it, because it would be too easy with him—

then he'd break her heart. She couldn't afford that. She'd suffered too many losses already and didn't intend for another.

"Here I am," she said blandly.

A shadow fell over her. Jovari stared down at her, his hands on his hips, before sinking to the ground beside her. "They've only been gone a few hours and I'm already anxious," he muttered.

"Claire and Talon?"

"No, the sun and the moon, gods woman. Yes, Claire and Talon."

She shrugged, but realized it didn't show from the position she was in. A position she didn't like to be in, with how he was looming over her, even sitting. She pushed herself up, bringing them eye level.

Claire and Talon had left on a supposed quest-thingy earlier this morning, though she knew it was in search of the king tree, which was, apparently, a magical tree that governed the world. Normally Claire would have gone alone for something like this— according to Taylynn—but Talon refused to let her out of his sight. He was quite dangerously adamant about it. So they'd set off and would be gone for who could say how long. A day? Two?

"Do you think the tree will heal her?" she found herself asking.

"It better," Jovari practically growled. He exhaled and scrubbed a hand over his face. While he appeared as perfect as ever—stupid magical creatures with their stupid magical healing abilities and their stupid long lives—his expression made him look stressed and tired. It was different from the usual *devil-may-care* look he often displayed.

"Jovari... Are you okay?"

"Me?"

"Yes, you."

"Why wouldn't I be?" He sounded almost defensive.

She sighed. "Everything has been focused on Claire and the kingdom, on what has happened, on getting her home to her people. Understandably so. But the rest of us are important too. You're important too. So yes, are *you* okay?"

"I... No, Leah, I'm not okay." He wasn't looking at her, instead, he was focused on something far away.

She reached out, trailing her fingers down the side of his jaw, then quickly retracted her hand, cursing herself. His eyes darted to hers, sharpening. "Sorry... I..."

"It's all right," he said, his voice soft. She didn't like the way he was looking at her, like he was digging into her with his gaze, like he was trying to find every hidden secret she carried, everything that made up who she was.

"I should..." She was going to say *go*, but couldn't quite bring herself to do it. Silence fell.

"The other day," he said, startling her. "When you said that your mother died because of you, what did you mean?"

She went rigid. "I should go." This time it was easy to say.

"No." His hand shot out, fingers wrapping around her forearm. "Stay."

"I shouldn't have said anything." She exhaled, cursing her carelessness. "It was just a game. Forget about it, all right?"

"Oh I don't think so. We're going to talk about this."

"Why do you care?" she snapped. "You didn't even want me coming on this trip, if I recall. You can't suddenly care—"

"I've cared for a while," he admitted. "And you can't go and mention something like that, then expect me to ignore it. Now, tell me what happened."

Her breaths came faster. She really, *really* didn't want to talk about this. Not with him. Not with anyone. Even Claire didn't know. Yet, she couldn't pull her gaze from his, from the intensity in his eyes.

It was like he'd frozen her in place with magic. Wait, maybe he had. Was that possible?

"Well?"

She blinked. "What?"

His mouth pulled up at the corner. "You were about to tell me why you feel guilty over your mother's death."

"Oh. Right." She blinked again, tearing her eyes from his. When she next spoke, her voice felt like someone else's. Far away and detached. "When I was younger, I used to do dressage—it's a competition show with horses. Not important. Anyway, I had an event coming up. My mom was my biggest supporter. She always went to my events, even painting signs with my name and all that. This one was really important so I needed her there, but the hospital had scheduled her to work a shift." She hesitated, clenching her jaw. "I begged her to come. When that wasn't enough, I guilt-tripped her, telling her I'd lose if she didn't, that I wouldn't forgive her, all that. So... So she switched shifts with one of her coworkers. If she'd keep her shift, she wouldn't have been driving home when..." A breath whooshed out of her. She forced herself to say it out loud for the first time in her life. "She wouldn't have been on the road when that driver fell asleep at the wheel. She wouldn't have gotten into the accident and died. I was so selfish."

Jovari's lips parted. "Leah, you can't—"

"No. Stop." Her throat felt thick, making it difficult to swallow. "I know what you're going to say. It's why I've never bothered telling anyone the details. You'll say it's not my fault, but it is. If I hadn't made her change her shift, she wouldn't have been on the road at that exact moment." Jovari's jaw clenched. He looked like he wanted to say more, to argue. "There is nothing you can say that will change my mind. And don't you dare feed me some bull shit about how if she was meant to die, then changing her shift wouldn't have mattered, because trust me, I've already been through every possible thought on the matter."

"I wasn't going to," he said at last, his voice low, concerned.

Her shoulders relaxed. "Good."

"But, Leah, that's a lot of guilt to carry around for anyone, especially one so young as you. And you've been carrying it for so long." She lifted a shoulder to shrug. "What about the driver? Do they not play into it? They are the one who fell asleep at the wheel. If they had stayed awake, your mom would still be alive. And what of your mom, who loved you so much that she made the choice to switch her shift so that she could be there to support you?"

She blew out a breath. Yes, maybe it was irrational—what she felt. But that didn't stop the way her thoughts needled her. Still, Jovari's words sank in deep.

"The only one to blame here is the driver," he said at last. "But I cannot force you to let go of your guilt, only you can do that."

"Right." She picked at the moss beneath her.

"What about your dad?" he asked.

"What about him?"

"You said he died, that you..." He grappled with the next words. "That you tried to kill yourself after his death."

She deflated. "Is this some kind of *question-Leah-exposé* you've got going?" He stared at her. "Fine. I guess it's my fault for opening up about that. Yes—I wasn't in a good place. The guilt from my mom's death and then when my dad died from cancer, it just..." She trailed off, trying to find her voice. "It was hard. I'd given up on college because of it, and then in the end, he still died, and there was nothing I could have done to change that."

She glanced at him and their eyes locked together. Jovari said, "I misjudged you—terribly so."

"What do you mean?" She seemed to lean in towards him, desperate to hear what he'd say.

"I didn't want you coming to Dragonwall initially. I thought you were a silly girl seeking adventure. I was wrong. You're strong —so strong, to have been through all that. There's nothing silly about you."

"I can be silly," she teased, because the moment between them had suddenly become too heavy.

The corners of his mouth twitched. Their eyes remained locked. He was so close, she felt his breath fan over her cheek. Her heart took off at a gallop. He was looking at her like...like... Was he going to kiss her?! He was! He was going to kiss her!

"What about your parents?" she blurted. He startled, then jerked back.

"My...oh. They're..."

"You said that you had a good relationship with them?"

A soft smile touched his lips. She couldn't stop staring at it. "I do. I love them. They can be a bit much sometimes, being an only child and all. My mother likes to fuss. But, they're good people."

"That's good—"

There was a rustling. Bedelth appeared. "Ah. There you are." He stared at Jovari. "Koldis and I are going to meet up at the sparring grounds. You up for it? I bet you've grown rusty in your time away." Jovari shot a glance in her direction, like he was asking for permission. She lifted a shoulder. It's not like she was his keeper.

"You're welcome to tag along," Bedelth added, looking at her. "Saffra will be there."

She hesitated and then, "All right. Let's do it."

Jovari jumped to his feet then reached for her. She took his hand, ignoring the way the feel of his warm skin made her stomach flutter. He held on a moment longer than necessary before dropping it. She swore she felt his thumb graze the back of her knuckles. Or maybe that was just her imagination.

"Would you like a tour of the city first?" Bedelth asked. She managed a nod. It was hard to keep her head on straight around Jovari, but harder still with more of the king's shields about. Two of them in the same place at once was almost too much. They were all so…so…gorgeous and drool-worthy and downright befuddling. It didn't matter that Bedelth and Koldis were taken. She still felt heat rising in her cheeks anytime they paid her attention. What would it be like in the same room with all six of them? She'd probably be reduced to a babbling idiot.

Fortunately, she was soon distracted by the spriten city. There were glass houses fitted into the roots of massive trees, nothing like Taylynn's little cottage. Staircases that wound around tree trunks, disappearing up into the canopy. Paths that were lined with statues. She could only blink and gape at everything.

"This here is the gathering area," Bedelth explained as she took in the large communal space with low tables. It was surrounded by trees and garlands of vines and florals.

"It's beautiful."

"Wait until you see the crystal palace." She felt a pressure against her lower back as Jovari led her away. She tried to ignore the feel of his hand there, but it was impossible.

"Oh. My. God," she managed as a giant palace loomed before her. Like its namesake, it was made entirely of crystal, even the stairs that led to its main entrance. "Claire is the queen of this? She... She lives here?"

"Not permanently," Jovari explained. "But she did for a time. Technically, her seat of rulership is in Kastali Dun, the Dragonwall capital south of here. But seeing as she's also the spriten queen, this is hers."

A deranged laugh burst from her chest. It was unbelievable. That her friend—the girl she'd known since they were children—was the queen of all this. It was like Claire was living in a fairytale and she... Well, she was not. Nothing about her life had ever been even remotely fairytale-esque.

She swallowed, pushing those thoughts aside.

"I'd give you a tour of the inside," Bedelth said, "but Koldis is already waiting for us. Besides, something tells me you'd rather see it with Claire by your side?"

"I... Yes, I would." She turned away from the massive palace, indicating for Bedelth to lead the way.

"Are you okay?" Jovari asked in a low voice.

"It's a lot to take in," she said.

"That wasn't what I meant. You had a look on your face."

"It was nothing."

"Tell me," he urged.

"It's just..." She blew out a breath. "I'm trying not to feel sorry for myself. Sounds pathetic, I know. I guess I'm just wondering if I'll ever get my own fairytale. Honestly, I don't even need it to be of fairytale proportions. I just... Is it too much to want a little bit of happiness? A bit of something just for me?"

He stopped her, reaching for her wrist, circling it with his fingers. Her pulse took off, thundering beneath her skin. Surely he could feel it. "It's not too much, no. You deserve all that and more, Leah." She swallowed, wondering if he was right. Did she deserve that? After what had happened to her mom? "This is your chance at a new life. Being here in our world. Something tells me good things will come for you."

"I hope," she found herself saying. He brushed his thumb over her pulse and her breath caught—

"Hey, you two coming or what?" Bedelth called.

A small laugh bubbled up in her chest. She shared a grin with Jovari before he released her. Maybe he was right. Maybe good things *would* finally come, even if there were times when she didn't feel like she deserved it.

They reached the sparring grounds. If she thought being around the king's shields was difficult, being around a bunch of scantily clad spriten warriors was even more challenging. "Be still my heart," she breathed.

"What was that?" Jovari asked, grinning.

"Nothing," she squeaked. They shared a look, because he *had* to know what this was doing to her. Was she really that distracted by all the flesh on display? Okay yes, she was. She had eyes, after all.

"Over here," Bedelth called to them. She followed Jovari over to an area they'd claimed and took the open seat on the bench beside Saffra.

"Hello again," Saffra said, offering her a shy smile.

"Hi," she breathed, feeling a little shy in return.

"It's a lot to take in, isn't it?"

"Yeah, it really is."

She and Saffra shared a knowing look.

Watching the sprites trade blows, listening to the ethereal sounds of their weapons, transfixed her. But all of that was nothing compared to the sight of Jovari shedding his shirt before taking up a stance against Koldis. Bedelth stood off to the side and played mediator.

She stared at the sight of Jovari's muscles on display, corded and thick, flexing as he began to spar with Koldis. Saffra nudged her shoulder and whispered, "You've got a little drool, just there."

"Oh, stop," she teased, feeling immediately more comfortable around the prophetess.

"Don't worry, I'll probably start drooling too as soon as Bedelth sheds his shirt."

She pressed her lips between her teeth to keep from laughing, but not before brushing a finger over the corner of her mouth just to be sure there wasn't any drool there. Jovari was truly spectacular. In that moment, she realized something with absolute clarity. It would be impossible, no matter how hard she tried, to ignore her deepening feelings for him. She was in so much trouble.

# CHAPTER 29

# THE KING TREE'S ANSWER

*The Gable Forest*

Claire tugged Talon along by the hand, savoring the feel of his skin against her palm. The forest felt like home in a way she'd never imagined. They'd set out earlier that morning in search of the king tree, relying on the magic of the forest to guide them. It was a bit like wandering around blindfolded while someone pulled her along on a leash.

"Are you okay?" she asked, stealing glances back at him.

"Fine," he bit out. Today, he was dressed in a dark green sleeveless tunic and black pants. There were weapons strapped across his chest and a sword lashed to his back, the pommel visible just behind his head. The sight of his heavily corded arms was distracting.

She exhaled. "I guess that was a stupid question. I just mean, how are you holding up in light of everything?" The news of losing his kingdom had hit him hard, even though he tried to hide it. Just that morning, he'd nearly exploded when Taylynn suggested she venture into the forest alone.

"Like I said, I'm fine. There's nothing I can do about it at the moment. So let's just focus on the matter at hand."

"Do you blame me?" she couldn't help but ask.

"What?" He forced her to stop, spinning her around to face him.

"Do you blame me?" she repeated. "This wouldn't have happened if I hadn't...if you hadn't had to come get me." Her stomach had been squirming with guilt ever since Taylynn and the others had delivered the news.

"Stop." His eyes flashed with anger, and for the first time since meeting him all those days ago, the anger was directed at her. She took a step back, but he didn't release her hand. He quickly schooled his expression. "I don't blame you, Claire." His voice was softer this time. "It angers me that you would think it of me, that you would even ask it of me."

Her shoulders dropped. "I'm sorry—I just... It's hard not to think I'm at fault—"

"Gods above!" he swore. "This is no time to point fingers or place blame. Our kingdom has been stolen. If any blame must be placed it is with me, for letting matters come to this long before you were ever a part of my life. Or with Kane, who is the one usurping the throne."

"Okay. I... I just wanted to check." Her voice came out small.

He studied her, then let out a breath. More calmly, he said, "If I am quiet and moody, it is because I am focused on ways to reclaim the kingdom. Certainly not because I am upset with you in any way."

"But it's my fault we're here. It's my fault—"

"Stop!" he snarled. She caught a flash of black racing along his skin. Dragon scales. Her breath caught as he jerked her towards him. He grasped the back of her neck and stole a furious kiss, releasing her almost as quickly. She didn't even get to kiss him back. She stumbled a step at the abruptness of it.

"We are here to undo what Kane has done, and we won't leave until we do. None of it is your fault. I'm not angry with you, beyond the anger I feel at you suggesting that I might hold you responsible for any of this." He took a deep breath, squaring his shoulders and wiping his face clean of emotion. "Now let's continue, yes?"

She swallowed, then nodded.

Several hours passed in tense silence. She thought over everything he said and began to relax. He didn't blame her, so she needed to let go of whatever guilt she felt. The most productive thing she could do was focus on fixing herself, freeing her mind from Kane's clutches.

Her belly swooped.

The sense of something imminent welled up inside her. She didn't know how to explain it, but they were getting close. Her left hand clenched tightly around the spriten staff. It urged her on.

Closer...

Closer...

Closer...

There! The trees opened up around them until she stood gaping at the largest tree she'd ever seen. Talon's hand squeezed hers. When she stole a glance at him, it was to find him staring wide-eyed at the sight before them. That was better—*much* better—than the anger she'd seen.

"Unbelievable..." he muttered.

The breath she'd been holding whooshed from her chest.

The king tree was nestled in a glade, a small pool at its base with water that trickled away from it into the forest beyond. Its thick limbs were laden with golden fruit that reminded her of mangos. She could smell the sweet scent of them in the air, making her salivate. She dropped Talon's hand. Her fingers twitched, tempted to reach for one of the fruits. The staff burned hot in her hand, nearly scalding her.

She blinked. "What now?"

"Well, perhaps you ought to touch it?" Talon suggested, sounding almost bemused. She threw him a look, only to find him staring intently at the tree.

"All right. Let me see." She moved forward. The staff seemed to like the idea. It pulsed between warm and cold in her hand as if agreeing. She rounded the small pool, hopping over the babbling brook and the many roots surrounding it. She stopped at the base of the tree. Its bark was cool to the touch.

*"At last."*

She gasped, jerking away before replacing her hand. The voice in her mind was ancient and powerful. "Are you the king tree?" she asked aloud.

*"Indeed. And you are the queen—returned to us at last."*

"I... But I don't have any recollection of being the queen. Something happened and I can't remember anything."

*"Yes. Your mind is tightly bound."*

If she weren't so relieved, she might have been shocked by the fact that a tree was talking to her in her head. But she was so desperate to undo whatever was wrong with her that she didn't question it. If this tree could fix her, who was she to judge?

"Can you help me?" she asked. "The others seem to think you can fix this?" Hope welled in her chest as the silence stretched on. She knew very little about this sentient being, only that it was powerful. The sprites revered it, as if it were a god. Surely, if anything or anyone could fix her, it was this magical being.

*"I cannot undo what the sorcerer has done,"* it said. Just like that, her stomach plummeted and her hopes fell. *"Only you can do that."*

"Me?!" She balked, trying to hide her irritation. "But I've tried. I—"

*"You must look inside yourself and confront the magic head on,"* the tree explained, cutting her off.

"How do I do that?" she begged.

A long silence and then, *"There is a woman in Ashvale. Find her."*

"Who?"

A single name was whispered on the breeze, over and over. *Lixiss. Lixiss. Lixiss.*

"What do I do when I find her?" she demanded, growing desperate. She could feel the tree's awareness pulling away.

*She will know,* the breeze seemed to say, but no more words came. She wanted to beat her fists upon the tree's trunk in frustration. She didn't know where Ashvale was. Didn't know how to get there, or who this Lixiss person was.

"Well?" Talon appeared beside her, running his palm down her back. The feel of him immediately calmed her.

She took a deep breath, and held it in to the count of three, preparing to give him the bad news. "The tree can't help me." Talon's expression didn't change, but something unreadable flashed in his gaze. "You wouldn't happen to know where Ashvale is, would you?"

His brows lifted, a hint of confusion there. "It's here, in the forest."

"Is it?"

"Yes, why?"

"The tree told me I need to go there, to find someone named Lixiss. I think she might be able to help me."

The light in Talon's eyes brightened. "Then that's exactly where we'll go."

HOURS PASSED. The only thing that signified their progress through the forest were their footsteps. The path, the foliage, and even the trees looked unchanged. "I can see why people go mad in here."

Talon merely grunted in answer. He hadn't been much of a conversationalist.

It was nearly dark and they'd need to stop soon. Her legs should have ached, but she wasn't human. Still, she *was* tired.

"I don't even know if I'm going in the right direction," she said.

"The forest will guide you. Gods, now I sound like Princess Taylynn."

She pressed her lips together to keep from smiling at his obvious irritation.

They hadn't had much time alone since departing for Dragonwall. The occasional walk here and there, a few stolen kisses. That was before the bad news. Before everything had gone to shit. Now she wasn't sure how to act around him, given his brooding, it was like walking on eggshells. Besides his abrupt kiss earlier, they'd hardly touched.

Taylynn had warned them that quests like this could take days, even weeks. Normally, when a sprite embarked upon a quest they brought nothing with them, but the princess had advised Talon to prepare for an extended journey. He shouldered a pack filled with travel rations.

"We should stop for the night," he said, as if reading her mind.

"Where? There's nowhere to rest." The narrow path was bordered by dense foliage.

"Let's keep an eye out."

Not long after, a small glade appeared. It was as if the forest knew exactly what they needed. It was almost creepy.

"This will do." Talon dropped his pack. There were fluffy beds of moss, downed logs for sitting, and plenty of overgrowth for privacy. She took a few minutes for herself before returning.

Talon made himself comfortable, sorting through their belongings. She joined him, sitting cross-legged. She watched him as they ate in silence.

"You're staring," he said, catching her eye.

"I like looking at you." The admission made her skin warm. Something flashed in his gaze. His scars were brutal, but they were also unique, and she often found herself tracing the paths of them. Memorizing them.

His throat bobbed. "Why? And if you say it's because I'm handsome, I'll laugh. We both know my face is scarred beyond repair."

She lifted a shoulder. "I still think you're handsome despite the scars."

He scoffed, but there wasn't any anger in the sound. "Always so stubborn."

She grinned, finishing the remains of her ration before getting to her feet. She headed towards the babbling brook several paces away. Talon followed. The water was crisp and cool, deeply quenching her thirst.

She stood, wiping her mouth on the back of her hand, then said without turning to face him, "I like to look at you because I want to memorize your face. There's a gap in my mind where nearly a year should live, a year filled with memories, many of you and I. Now I'm just trying to fill that gap with your face. I want to look my fill, and yet no matter how much I look at you, it will never be enough."

"Enough for what?"

"Enough for me to want to *stop* looking." Because the reality was, she didn't know him and she couldn't get enough of him.

She heard his rough exhale. It took everything in her not to turn around and gauge his reaction. Mostly because then he'd see hers. He'd see how nervous she was to admit something like this. She hardly knew him and yet, it felt as though he held part of her soul.

Darkness crept in and the forest was alive with glowing insects. Most were yellow, but she caught flashes of blue and green, a few pinks, and even a deep purple as it disappeared into the foliage. They reminded her of fireflies

"When I was a kid," she said, "I used to catch fireflies in a jar to put on my bedside table." She walked towards a cluster of flashing pink insects near the edge of the glade. She reached out to catch one on her palm. It had delicate wings and looked like a moth, though its furry body glowed in the darkness. It tickled her palm, walking across her skin before taking flight.

She giggled.

A rough growl came from just behind her. "I love that sound."

"What sound?" she breathed. A sense of anticipation stole over her.

"The sound of your laughter." Rough hands grasped her waist, turning her to face him.

Their eyes caught as he backed her up. She came to rest against the trunk of a tree. Her breath caught.

Talon's hands on her waist were heavy and warm against the thin fabric of her shirt. She gazed up at him, her lips parted. "Do you want to know why I enjoy looking at you?" he asked.

She blinked. "Oh. Uhm. Yes."

"When I look at you I see a future I never thought I would have. Endless possibilities for happiness and joy. But mostly, I see hope."

"Talon..." she breathed.

She didn't know who kissed whom, only that suddenly their lips were melded and she was devouring the taste of him. His tongue was possessive, exploring her mouth, sending sparks shooting down her spine. Was it any wonder she'd fallen in love with this male once already? Certainly not, because she was falling in love with him again.

He nipped at her bottom lip, sending hot lashes of desire straight to her core. A groan lifted from her throat. Her hands found his hair, fingers knotting in the tufts. He hoisted her up and her legs wrapped around his hips. His lips traced a hot trail from her jaw down her throat, nipping and sucking.

"Talon," she whispered.

When he pressed against her, he was hard in all the right places, making her cry out in delight. His hips ground against hers, turning her into a desperate, thoughtless creature. It didn't matter that she couldn't remember everything about the two of them. Didn't matter that all she had were stolen glimpses scattered within the confines of her mind. She wanted him, and if she let this keep going, he'd claim her completely.

Was she ready for that?

A sudden thought came to mind and she gasped. "Talon—Talon stop."

"What is it?" He immediately stopped and found her gaze.

"When we were married, mated, whatever, did we...did we use protection?" His brows knitted together at her question. "Like a condom or something? Something to prevent pregnancy?"

His frown deepened. "Of course not."

Her lips parted. "Oh. Oh, no..."

"What is it?" He kept her pressed to the tree, using his body to pin her in place. He lifted a hand, stroking her cheek with the backs of his fingers. It had only been a couple of weeks and she wasn't late with her period...was she?

Regardless—

"If we do this right now, there's a chance I could get pregnant."

Fire flared in his eyes. A low, possessive growl rumbled in his chest. He looked downright eager at the prospect as he stole her lips again and kissed her roughly.

"Talon—wait!" She pushed his face away.

"I fail to see what the problem is?" A huff of his breath tickled her skin. "You are my wife, my queen, and I would love nothing more than to put a child in your belly. An heir. In fact, we ought to try over and over until it takes, and even after just to be sure."

It sounded primitive and possessive, and yet, her core clenched with desire. "You want children with me."

"Child. Singular. And gods, yes."

"What do you mean, singular?"

Did he only want one? She'd never really given it much thought, but she liked the idea of at least two so they'd be siblings. She had been an only child and had wished for someone to grow up alongside her.

"The drengr only ever have one child. It's been that way since the dawn of our race. A curse from Isabella."

"What?!" she gasped, shock and confusion rocking through her.

"No one really understands it," he was saying, running his hands over her body like he didn't want to lose the heat of the moment. He cupped her left breast, feeling the weight of it. She stifled a groan. "It's just the way things have always been. It's why it can take decades, even centuries for a pair to conceive. My parents tried for nearly three hundred years before having me."

"What?!" she gasped again.

His lips found her neck, burning a trail down to her collarbone. He was clearly a lot less interested in this conversation than her.

"Talon—" She caught his face, bringing it level with hers. "Hasn't someone tried to do something about it? To undo the curse?"

"No. How could they? It probably can't be undone, anyway."

She opened her mouth, then closed it. She refused to believe that. But there was no use fretting over it now. He clearly had no interest in the direction the conversation had taken. Besides, she had more pressing things to worry about than breaking curses, like the persistent male who continued to stare at her like he was starved. She was the feast he wanted to consume.

"I want to wait," she decided at last. She'd already lost the heat of the moment anyway.

He froze, then continued to nip at the lobe of her ear. "All right," he said at last, but didn't stop.

"Talon," she laughed, then repeated his name for good measure. She liked saying his name, truth be told. Liked the sound of it on her tongue. The way it rolled off so easily. "If you keep doing that, my self control is going to snap."

"Perfect. That's the point," he drawled.

"No. Come on. Let's get some sleep." She pushed him away, her body screaming with anger at the loss of contact. As much as she wanted to rush into sex with him, something told her she'd be glad she waited, just a little longer, because making love to him with her memories intact would feel far more victorious.

"I'll let you cuddle with me while we sleep," she taunted, "if you promise to behave."

"All right," he rasped.

They found a soft place in the moss to curl up together. His arms felt so right as they wrapped around her, pulling her against him to be the little spoon. She sighed with contentment, thinking over their discussion. As she drifted off, she couldn't help but wonder if despite the difficulty getting pregnant for mated pairs, if she might already be carrying their child, and in truth, she really didn't know how to feel about that.

# CHAPTER 30
## SPIDERS IN THE FOREST

*Ashvale*

Claire took in the sight of Ashvale, enamored by the cottages spanning the main thoroughfare. They reminded her of Taylynn's. Only, these were less over-grown. She hadn't yet been inside the city of Esterpine—Taylynn wanted to wait for her to regain her memories first—so this was the first spriten settlement she'd set eyes on.

It had taken two days to get here. Two days in Talon's brooding company. She'd quickly learned that the best way to halt his mood in its tracks was to surprise him with kisses. She'd done so at many opportunities. But that also came with its own challenges, because he had a way of pushing her towards the point of no return, and she wasn't ready to give her body to him. Yet.

"I don't even know where to start," she mused, setting off down the main thoroughfare. Sprites were out and about, some in their yards tending to gardens, others out for a stroll. At first, no one noticed them. Then, a gasp sounded and a female sprite rushed over. "My queen," she cried, loud enough for everyone to hear.

Others stopped, turning to gaze at her. Within moments, she

was the center of attention. Sprites gathered around her, echoing their surprise. Talon moved in close, as if worried they'd harm her. His hand squeezed hers.

"I am looking for a female named Lixiss," she said. "And possibly...a place to stay."

"But, you already have a home here," one of them answered, while another said, "I can take you to Lixiss." Suddenly they were all talking at once, offering up information and making it impossible to follow.

She looked at the spriten female who'd first recognized her. Perhaps they'd met? She didn't want to ask, for fear of revealing the loss of her memories. "If you are willing, can you act as our guide?"

"Yes, of course." The spriten female looked over the gathered crowd. "Back to your own business, all of you!"

The crowd dissipated.

"This way," the female beckoned.

"What is your name?" Talon asked, saving her from having to do so.

"Neiah, Your Majesty. It is an honor to meet our queen's mate. I did not know you would be here—none of us did, else we might have prepared a feast in your honor. But that is no matter, as I am sure we can whip something up tonight."

It was on the tip of her tongue to refuse, but Talon beat her to it. "Do not trouble yourselves on our account, Neiah. We have other matters that will keep us busy tonight."

"Very well. Now, here we are. The royal cottage. This is where you stayed the last time you visited Ashvale."

"Yes, of course. I remember now," she lied.

"I can also take you to Lixiss if you are ready."

"Thank you," Talon said. "We would like to go at once."

Lixiss's cottage sat at the edge of the city's settlement. The female in question greeted her warmly, sending Neiah on her way. Her cottage was cluttered with books, crates, and other nicknacks stacked precariously. Everything looked like a single breath from toppling over.

They gathered in the kitchen around a central table. "I assume you are here for the drink of enlightenment again?" Lixiss asked, curious.

"Actually, I am not sure." If the king tree felt it safe to trust Lixiss, then she would. She told the sprite of her missing memories, of the way her magic had been cut off after Kane had done something to her. Lixiss listened in silence, bustling about her kitchen as she placed ingredients into a pot, humming here and there. When she finished, Lixiss set a cup in front of her and Talon, each filled to the brim with dark liquid. It let off a repugnant scent that had her wrinkling her nose.

"You want us to drink this? It smells foul."

"And it is. But you need to free your mind, do you not?"

"And what about Talon?"

"I should think it obvious. He is your mate. The two of you are connected, even if your mind is locked up tight. He will do this with you."

She shot Talon a look. He merely shrugged, his expression unreadable. She didn't want to drag him into this if she didn't have to.

"Are you sure—?"

"I am positive," Lixiss said, cutting her off.

"What will happen once we drink it?"

"That is for you to discover. I cannot say what the confines of your mind hold."

"I mean, will we crumble to the floor in deep sleep? Do we need to get comfortable somewhere?"

"Oh." Lixiss waved a hand. "No. There is fine."

Claire lifted her brows but didn't argue further. Instead, she reached for Talon. He took her hand, his eyes studying hers. "Ready, *mih cralla*?"

"I guess this is it," she managed, lifting the cup. He did the same. Together they drank.

She didn't breathe, doing her best to ignore the taste of the thick liquid as it slogged down her throat. Her stomach heaved. She tightened her muscles, continuing to drink. She managed to finish the cup, slamming it down on the table as she gagged. She waited for the sound of Talon's cup but it never came. She blinked—

She was in the forest. She staggered backwards a step, surprised. "Easy," Talon murmured, catching her stumble.

She whirled to find him beside her. "You're with me. I thought it would put us to sleep or something. But it looks like we've been teleported into the forest."

"It would seem so," he said, frowning. His eyes were in constant motion, taking in their surroundings.

"What are we supposed to do?" He remained silent. "Maybe we should just walk?"

"All right." He tugged on her hand and they set off. Several steps later, the forest began to change. It grew darker. The trees, once green and lush, began to rot. The sounds of birds and insects disappeared until an eery silence set in.

Her brows pulled together. "I don't understand. Is something wrong?"

Talon blinked, slowing their pace. "When you last came here, the forest was sick. But you vanquished the sickness when you killed Jade."

"Maybe it's sick again?"

Even with Talon beside her, she grew uneasy. They pressed on. The dead trees grew more grotesque with each step, curving and twisting. They reminded her of snarled words spoken out of hatred. Like someone wanted to say mean things and tear her down.

A *click-click-clicking* sound made her freeze.

"Did you hear that?" Her heart rate doubled. It reminded her of scuttling. Of insects.

Talon cocked his head to listen, hesitated, then shook his head.

Several steps later, she heard it again. Chills spread down her skin. A flash of movement made her breath hitch. She gazed into the darkness.

"What is it?" Talon asked, his voice hushed.

"I thought I saw... I don't know. Something is out there." She squinted against the gloaming.

There! She caught it again. A dark shape, low to the ground—

"Oh my—!" she cried, all but throwing herself at Talon. A giant spider disappeared into the shadows. "There are spiders here. Giant spiders. I can't—we should go back."

"Take a deep breath," Talon said, his voice low and urgent.

"Did you see it?"

"I did."

"Aren't you...?" She was going to ask if he was afraid, but then she remembered who and what he was. He could probably squash the spider in his dragon form with little effort. She was being silly. She cleared her throat. "Let's keep going."

"Good." Talon indicated for her to lead the way.

Several minutes passed, punctuated by the same scuttling sound. Sometimes it came from her left, then her right. Sometimes it was behind them, then in front of them. She got the feeling there wasn't just one spider, but many.

Was this what her other quests had been like, when she'd earned her spriten marks? Had she been forced to go out into the forest and battle spiders and other little beasties? If so, she must have been braver than she was now, to do it all alone.

That thought made her feel like a fraud. How was she supposed to be queen of the sprites, queen of Dragonwall, if things like this frightened her? She clenched her teeth and pushed aside her misgivings.

Their surroundings brightened. "Is it getting lighter outside?"

"I don't think so," Talon said softly.

She squinted. It wasn't the forest, she realized. Far ahead, something white loomed, taking up her entire field of vision. Beside her, a glimmer caught her gaze. She hesitated, looking at it. "Spider webs." She shuddered. It made sense, given all the scuttling.

Her stomach hardened into a tight ball. They were walking into a spider den, and she wasn't sure that was wise. Yet, she couldn't turn back now.

The webs grew denser, blocking off areas along their path,

forcing them to go alternate routes. Their progress slowed. "This would be easier if I had a way to—"

Her words stopped short as a sword appeared in her hand. It had spriten markings down the length of the blade. She frowned. *That* was strange. Had she been holding it the entire time?

She hacked at the tangle of sticky webs before her. They resisted at first, then gave way. A few got tangled on her hand and she hissed in disgust.

"Hold still," Talon said, helping her remove them.

There was a sword in his hand now, too. One of the swords carried by the drengr. She glanced at the black stone decorating its pommel, then looked away.

"What do we do when we get there?" She pointed at the wall of webs in the distance.

"I think we will know when we get there," he answered.

The white she'd seen in the distance was indeed a dense area of webs, wrapping around trees so tightly she couldn't see beyond. They had reached a dead end. Behind them, another spider scuttled, but when she turned it disappeared from sight. So far, none of the spiders had attacked. That had to be a good sign, right?

"What do we do now? Should we go back?"

Talon frowned, looking over the wall of webs. It traversed the forest top to bottom, left to right. They couldn't go around. Nor could they go up and over. "I think we must go through."

She saw a shadow move behind the web and jumped backwards, crying out in surprise. Then, another shadow moved, and another.

They weren't spiders, they were too large to be spiders. She placed her hand against the sticky barrier and a deep sense of recognition slammed into her. There was something on the other side, something important, and she needed to get to it, to free it.

"I think... Talon, I think those are my memories on the other side. My magic."

He looked thoughtful, placing his hand next to hers. "Yes," he said at last. Then he glanced at the sword in his hand. "But something tells me this won't be easy."

"What do you mean?" She lifted her sword, about to hack away at the dense barrier, when Talon's free hand wrapped around her wrist. "Just a moment," he warned.

"Do you have a better idea?"

He released her wrist. "No."

"Then let's free my memories." She lifted her sword again and swung it at the webbed barrier. The moment it struck the sticky membrane, a scream tore through the world. She wasn't sure where it had come from. The next instant, the sound of scuttling surrounded them.

"Watch out!" Talon cried.

She glanced over her shoulder, eyes wide with fear.

Scuttling towards them was an army of giant spiders. She had only a moment to take a breath before the spiders were on them. She swung out with her blade, hacking at legs. Talon did the same, moving with ease as he put himself in front of her.

"Take down the web!" he shouted, trying to distract the spiders.

Her breaths came faster. While she had never been deathly afraid of spiders, she certainly didn't *like* them. Seeing a mass of scuttling bodies all trying to get to her made it nearly impossible to think.

"Claire!" Talon cried again. "Hurry! I cannot hold them forever!"

She began hacking at the web, cutting through the sticky strands. Yet, every time she destroyed one, another seemed to appear in its place. Sweat dotted her forehead.

"It's not working!" she cried.

"Keep trying," he shouted. She spared him a glance, only to find a mound of spiders accruing around him. Bile surged into her throat, stinging. She turned her attention back to the task at hand. She needed something more powerful. Something that could destroy the webs once and for all.

If only she had her magic! Then she could *abracadabra!* them away, or some such. Hopefully.

She hacked and hacked, moving faster to try and get the upper hand, trying to carve a gap in the webs before they grew back.

Talon cried out. She spun around. "What happened?" she shouted.

"One of them bit me." He sounded surprised by this.

She gasped, noticing the red mark near his shoulder. Fear spread through her, numbing her thoughts. If he died here, trying to free her mind? It would be her fault.

Whirling, she channeled all her strength into hacking at the webs. A small hole began to appear, she hacked faster to keep the webs from growing back. Then, without thinking, she shoved her hand through the hole into the empty space beyond.

Something velvety caressed her skin. A memory slammed into her. It was a small black kitten, napping on her lap while she caressed its soft ears. Another memory crashed into her a moment later, but she was too distracted by the sight of webs growing around her arm to view it. She tugged, but her arm was stuck. The webs continued to knit, spreading over her shoulder, and then across her chest.

It was swallowing her whole! She screamed.

"Claire!" Talon cried out for her.

She turned to see him stagger to his knees before forcing himself back up. More red welts littered his body, poking holes through his tunic where he'd been bitten. He continued to fight, trying to keep the spiders from getting to her.

She needed to save him. She needed to destroy them. She needed—

"Fire!" she hissed, flexing her fingers on the other side of the barrier. Her arm was tingling, as if the circulation had been cut off. It probably had, as the hole in the barrier shrank around her bicep, trapping her further.

"I need fire!" she cried again, flexing her fingers, as if coaxing it to her.

Suddenly, a memory slammed into her. It was riddled with green flames and words from another language. It burrowed into her bones, twining with her mind. It was exactly what she'd needed. She began to sing, letting the words free. It was a song she'd sung before, a song that had saved her more than once—according to this memory.

Her voice grew steadier.

Talon felled another spider, barely holding himself up. Webs crept up her neck. If they reached her mouth, would they silence her song? Would they pry her lips open and descend down her throat?

She continued to sing, the words wrapping around them. A loud cracking sound pressed against her eardrums. Then, the wall before her erupted into green flames. She flinched, only to find that the heat of it didn't burn her. The tension on her arm loosened. She jerked free, then whirled. Talon had fallen to the ground. She had just enough time to lunge for the spider as it sank its fangs into his chest, right where his heart resided. She shoved her blade through its glittering eyes, moving in a way she never imagined she could. The fire spread, racing away from where the wall of webs had once been, engulfing spider after spider, the dead bodies and the live.

She gasped, dropping to Talon's side, shaking him. His eyes fluttered open. "Did you do it?"

"I... I don't know. The fire."

"Your sprite fire," he said, closing his eyes. A soft smile spread across his lips. Then, a moment later, he disappeared. She screamed as her hands fell through empty air.

When she next blinked, the forest had disappeared and she was sitting in a room, a kitchen. She blinked again, gasping. Talon was sitting beside her, his eyes open and fixed on her, a pained expression on his face. It was so intense, she could feel it inside of her as if it were her own.

"You're alive!" she gasped, throwing her arms around him, kissing him. The force of her body sent both of them backwards, until they were splayed on the floor. He grunted and his pain flared. She felt it inside her.

All she could think was, *oh, gods, he's alive*. She'd thought... She'd thought she'd lost him. The mere idea opened a chasm inside her chest. Because she loved him. She loved him *so much*!

But, it would take more than spider bites to bring him down. Wait, was that her thought, or his? If it was his...

His thoughts were in her head. She felt him there, his presence, his awareness, his—

"Oh, gods!" she breathed, pulling away from his lips, looking deep into his silver eyes. "I remember. I remember everything!"

He only smiled, brushing a lock of hair behind her ear, like he'd known all along that she would eventually conquer this. Then he groaned again, his pain flaring. Her eyes widened, sweeping over his body. When she spotted the bite near his neck and noticed how pale and clammy his skin looked, her blood turned cold. If she didn't do something, the poisonous bites would kill him.

CHAPTER 31

# A NEW TRADITION

*Ashvale*

Talon felt as though his insides were on fire, but it had been worth it. Every spider bite was worth the sight of his mate's magic and memories returned. The brush of her mind against his. The love filling the depths of her gaze.

He was only vaguely aware of his feet as he lost feeling in them. Numbness traveled inwards from his extremities. He wanted to lift his hand, to brush his fingers against Claire's soft skin, to push her hair back from her face to better see her, but he couldn't lift his arm.

Her eyes turned frantic, looking him over. The panic seeped from her mind and into his. He should have been more concerned; perhaps he was dying as a result of the poison. Yet, he couldn't seem to summon anything beyond joy at seeing his mate returned to him.

"Talon," she breathed, pulling at his clothes, then swearing when she saw more of the bites. In her mind, the bites had ripped through his tunic, his pants. Here, in the real world, they were hidden beneath the fabric, but they were no less present. The spiders must have been carrying Kane's poison, whatever he'd

268

used to chain her. Yet, his memories were intact. Perhaps it was manifesting differently because he'd been bitten.

He couldn't seem to summon the energy to worry about it. She would make it right. His mate would fix this.

"But, I don't know how!" she said. He blinked, struggling to focus on her words. He stared at her face. Her eyes were the only thing he wanted to lose himself in. He could forget about everything else.

His only disappointment was that he no longer had the strength to hug her, to wrap her in his arms. Gods, he didn't even have the strength to feel alarmed as tears began pouring down her cheeks.

A string of choked words fell from her lips. He should have known what they meant, but even his ears had stopped working. Her body glowed. Her lips continued to move and he lost himself in the cadence of her voice, rising and falling as her hands swept over him. He began to feel again—warmth in all the places her skin touched him.

A sigh of relief fell from his lips. The feel of her against him, even while he was in pain, was bliss. The pain began to fade. Moment by moment, his mind sharpened. His arms and legs prickled, as if stabbed by thousands of needles. Then—

He surged into a seated position, dragging Claire into his arms. She sprawled across his lap, then rearranged herself until she was straddling his hips, her hands roving his face. "It worked," she breathed. "It worked—"

He captured her mouth, tasting the salt of her tears on her lips as he claimed her. *"Mine,"* he told her. *"You are mine."*

*"Yours,"* she repeated against his mind, caressing his tongue with hers. He groaned.

"Well then, it appears my concoction worked." Lixiss's voice interrupted them. He'd forgotten about the spriten female. Claire broke away, a slow smile spreading across her lips. Their eyes held a moment longer before she detached herself and stood.

"Shalaya, Lixiss. Aya sahha mik." *Thank you, Lixiss. You saved me.*

"Oh, you saved yourself, Your Majesty. I only gave you the means to do it," Lixiss answered in turn.

Talon exhaled. Now that their minds were linked again, he could understand the spriten language in its entirety, not just the few words he'd memorized on his own.

"Still, I owe you a debt." Claire's gratitude filled the shared space of their minds.

"As do I," he found himself saying to Lixiss. "For helping return my mate to me."

"Oh, it was nothing," Lixiss said, waving a hand. "I serve the tree."

"Very well," Claire said, gathering herself. "If you ever need anything—anything at all—please, ask."

"I have all that I could possibly need—and more. The forest provides. But I will keep that in mind. Thank you, Your Majesty. Now, not to be rude, but I was in the middle of a very riveting book before you arrived."

"Oh!" Claire huffed, pressing a hand over her mouth, amusement dancing in her thoughts. "Right. Of course. We will be on our way."

With that, she grabbed his wrist and led him out onto the street. Across the street, a sprite toiled in a garden. Next door, another sat rocking in a chair. It took everything in him not to grab his queen and kiss her silly. As soon as the thought materialized, so did Claire's amusement. Gods, he'd missed sharing her mind.

He allowed her to lead them down the thoroughfare, filling her mind with all manner of wicked thoughts. Thoughts about what he wanted to do to her. About how he planned to worship her.

She led him to the royal cottage. It unlocked for her, sensing her blood, and he found himself in a cozy entryway. Claire removed her shoes, placing them on a set of shelves beside the door. He followed her lead. She waved a hand and all the sconces came to life with glowing sprite magic—something akin to fire.

He looked around, taking it in.

"Cozy, isn't it?"

"Yes." The entire space was made of wood, intricately carved, with archways leading into other rooms, and a main staircase that led to the upper floors. He'd explore later. For now—

Claire squealed as he pulled her into his arms, hooking his hands around her thighs as he hoisted her up. Her legs circled his waist as he slammed her against the door. He was none too gentle about it, either.

His lips were on hers, tongue delving into the depths of her mouth. Gods, she tasted like sunlight and happiness. Like everything that was good in this world. His breaths grew stilted and his pants were suddenly too tight. He wasn't going to take her against the door—or maybe he would. His mind was too muddled and her scattered thoughts only further muddled it.

"The bedroom—upstairs," she managed.

"Don't think I'll make it that far," he insisted, speaking against her lips.

He carried her to a sitting area, releasing her only briefly. They shed their clothes in a flurry of motion, tunics and pants tossed aside, scattering the floor. His baldric of weapons was flung somewhere behind the sofa. His sword, near the entryway. Their stockings were lost under the end table.

He sat and tugged her down onto his lap, straddling him. The feel of her heat against him drove him to the brink. He groaned, digging his fingers into her lush hips, relishing in the feel of her skin beneath his palms.

Her fingers tangled in his hair as she claimed his mouth, nipping at his lips, then moving on to the edge of his jaw. Their breaths came faster. His hand slipped between her legs, seeking her out. He swore. "You're ready for me." If he didn't have her now, right this second, he'd die.

There would be time to savor her later. He'd spend the whole afternoon, evening, and night showing her exactly how much he'd missed her. For now—

She cried out as he sheathed himself in one smooth motion. Her head fell back, thick hair cascading behind her. He watched her, mesmerized, as she began to move. His eyes fell to her breasts and he captured a nipple between his lips. She cried out, pressing him to her.

"Claire," he breathed, his breath fanning her skin. "Claire."

Her name became a chant, filling the air between them, interspersed with the sweet sounds she made. Their movements were chaotic and hungry. It wasn't an elegant dance, but one born of desperation, meant to bridge their time apart.

He feasted on the sight of her. Her eyes glazed with lust. Her expression filled with pleasure—pleasure only he could give. Her sensual curves.

"You are my undoing," he growled. "There is no world in which I wouldn't follow you. There is no place you could go that I wouldn't find you. You are mine."

She tightened around him. "Oh, gods!"

"Tell me."

"Yours," she gasped. "I'm—yours."

"That's right." He rocked her possessively against him. Her eyes went wide. "I love you, *mih cralla*. I love you so godsdamned much."

"Talon!" she cried. Her body detonated, the markings on her skin exploding into light. He whispered her name, following her over the edge, pulling her against him as he rode out each wave of pleasure with her.

Their movements slowed, and he buried his face in her hair, pressing gentle kisses to her head. Her muscles went limp and she leaned against him. For a long time, they just breathed.

When she pulled back, their eyes met. "What are we going to do?" she whispered, fear creeping in to her voice.

He knew exactly what she meant. Now that her memories were back, now that she was truly a queen again, she was processing the severity of their situation. The fact that their kingdom had fallen.

"Well, first, I plan to lay you across the dining table there, and feast on you—"

"Talon!" She swatted at him. "That's not what I—"

"Then, I'll take you upstairs to bed. We'll spend the afternoon making love, although I can't promise I'll be gentle. Eventually I might let you eat and drink. After that? Well, we'll worry about the kingdom tomorrow."

In truth, he was worrying about it now. More than worrying. He hadn't been able to think clearly since discovering what had happened. But it was easier to quiet his concerns with Claire in his arms, tucked away in this quaint little cottage. He could almost forget there was a disaster waiting for them just outside the forest.

They'd confront that later.

He spent the next several hours delivering on his every promise, until the taste of her and the feel of her saturated his very being. They lay entwined in a large bed upstairs. He combed his fingers through her hair, relishing the silky feel of it against his skin, savoring the press of her face against his chest.

She liked to listen to his heartbeat. It calmed her.

"I can't believe you didn't like coffee," she blurted. His fingers froze in her hair before continuing. She was thinking back over the days after they reconnected, picturing everything in a new light. "I would die for a cup of coffee right now with cream and sugar."

"I wouldn't," he grumbled. "That stuff was awful. Like drinking dirt."

"Talon—"

"Argh!" he cried, jerking beneath her. "Did you just *pinch* me?!"

"No," she lied. She did it again.

"You little miscreant," he growled, snatching her wrists and flipping their positions so that her hands were pinned above her head and he rested in the cradle of her thighs. "If you don't behave, I will have to punish you."

"Oh?" Something dark and hungry filled her mind. She bucked her hips, sending hot desire shooting up the base of his spine.

His smile turned wicked. "You would like that, wouldn't you?"

"No," she lied, her voice breathy.

"Oh, I think you would," he purred, "very much."

"Okay, maybe a little." She began to struggle, with every intention of pinching him again, just so he'd make good on his promise. She *wanted* him to punish her. The hard length of him was growing painful at the thought of taking her over his knee—

A loud gurgling sound broke through her giggles.

"Gods, woman," he swore. "Was that your stomach?" He glanced down at her bare tummy covered in glowing markings, trying not to linger on her breasts.

"Maybe." She refused to admit it outright.

He sighed. "I'm failing miserably as your mate. The last thing you ingested was that gods-awful potion."

"The only thing I'm hungry for is you," she challenged.

"Oh, I don't think so mate of mine." It was in her mind to protest. He sensed every word she was about to say. Before she could say any of them, he yanked her up by her pinned wrists and said, "Time for some food."

"No!" she protested, struggling half-heartedly.

"No? You dare defy your king?"

"I dare!"

"Then you will see what happens—"

She squealed as he hauled her over his shoulder. He smacked her right buttock hard enough to leave a mark. She cried out, wiggling against him to get free. He wasn't having it. This close, he could smell her arousal after what he'd just done. She liked it. He swore under his breath and carried her downstairs.

"Now, there's got to be some food around here somewhere." At his words, her thoughts went to the cellar where there was enough bespelled food to feed an army. "But of course," he mused. He set her on her feet.

She contemplated the space before bustling around to collect ingredients. "I hope breakfast is okay," she said, setting everything out.

"I'll eat anything," he murmured, distracted by the sight of her naked body, which sent his thoughts veering off in a wicked direction.

"Stop distracting me," she scolded.

He chuckled. "What can I help with?"

She delegated, and soon the room was filled with the rich scent of pancakes, sautéed mushrooms and onions, and scrambled eggs. They worked seamlessly, picking up tasks where the other left off on. Each time she crossed his path, her fingers trailed over his bare torso, sending shivers  across his skin. When he reached around her to grab the plate of pancakes, he leaned in and kissed the side of her neck, making her breath hitch.

The table was set, and they sat down across from each other to eat. Her eyes raked over his naked chest before settling on her plate with a happy sigh. His skin heated, but not in the way it would have were she anyone else. He'd never felt such perfect comfort in his own skin. Usually, he was the first to insist on being fully clothed, to hide his scars from prying eyes.

"Your scars never frightened me," she told him, licking her syrup-sticky fingers clean. He ignored the carafe waiting beside his pancakes and watched her in fascination, wanting to snatch her fingers into *his* mouth, instead.

A cruel smile spread across her face. She knew exactly what she was doing . His eyes darted down, to the sight of her hardening nipples.

"You know," he mused, "I think we need to make it a tradition to come to this cottage at least once a year. Just us. I rather like having a space all to ourselves. I think I'll impose a new rule while we're here. No clothing whatsoever once we pass the threshold."

Her eyes blazed with fire. "Well, it is my cottage, and I do like that rule."

He rubbed his thumb over his lower lip, watching lazily as she ran her pointer finger through the syrup oozing on her plate. He caught her hand before she had the chance to lift it, and leaned in to suck her finger clean. A low, breathy moan fell from her lips.

He pulled away. "Eat your food, then I'm taking you back upstairs."

"You're one to talk," she challenged. "You haven't even poured syrup on your pancakes yet. I'm already ahead of you." With that, she set about devouring the feast in front of her.

They ate in amicable silence. Somehow, she managed to finish first. He loved the feel of her attention as he cleaned his plate. He'd never liked others staring at him, but with her, he was hungry for it. He wanted to be the *only* person she ever looked at; a new royal decree might do the trick—written solely for her.

Too bad he couldn't do such a thing for the rest of his people, to keep their eyes off of him.

"I could heal them, you know." Her voice broke into his thoughts. He froze. "Your scars, I mean. You said that the mages were never able to heal them because of the dark magic of the Kalds. But with sprite magic, I'm ninety-nine point nine percent sure I can heal them."

He stared at her in shock. When he next opened his mouth, nothing came out. A flurry of emotions passed through him. Yearning, fear, excitement.

"Only if you want," she amended, lifting her shoulder as if it were a small offering.

He was about to say yes. Emphatically yes! To fall to his knees at her feet and beg her, but something made him hesitate. When he tried to search her mind, he found walls barring his entry. Walls that had not been there moments ago. "You like my scars," he hedged.

"I like you either way," she said.

"All right, then. What would *you* have me do?"

"I would have you make this decision entirely on your own, without my interference."

"What's the point of a mate if they don't help with decisions," he grumbled.

"Talon, this has to be your decision."

He scrubbed a hand over his face, thinking it over. He recalled what he'd looked like before. Longing filled his chest. Then he thought of what he looked like now, of the way Claire gazed at him with so much love, as if the scars didn't even exist.

"It means a great deal to me—your offer. But I decline."

Her eyes lit with surprise and something else. Approval. Respect. "You're sure?"

He swallowed. "I think so, yes."

"Well, if you ever change your mind… I'm not exactly going anywhere."

He chuckled. "Noted."

He knew his answer wouldn't change. It was easy to want what *could have been.* But he wanted the *here and now* even more. A world where his mate ruled by his side and loved him for exactly who and what he was. He wasn't the man he'd been before his scars, not anymore.

When the barriers barring her mind dropped away, he saw that he'd made the right decision.

He stood and rounded the table, scooping her up. They had the rest of this night together before reality came crashing down around them. He had every intention of making the most of it, starting with that spanking she'd earned.

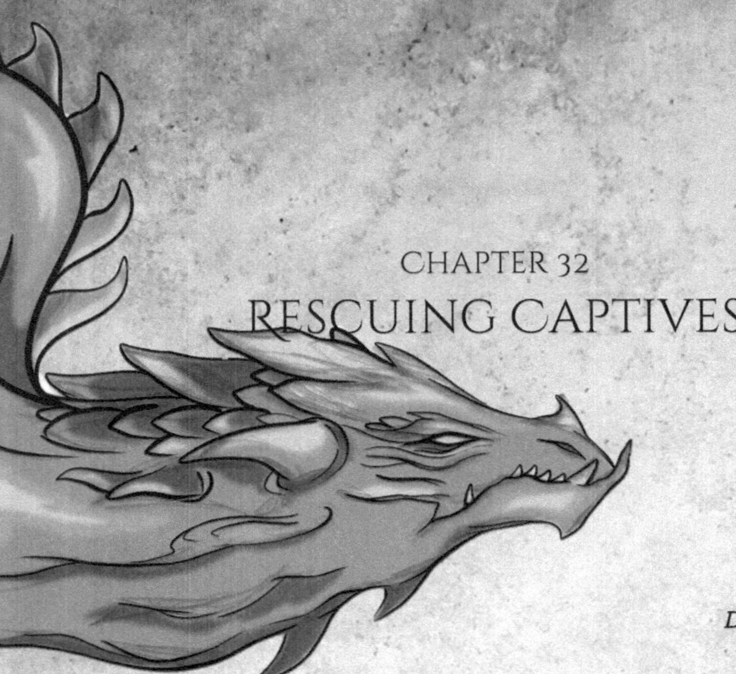

# CHAPTER 32
# RESCUING CAPTIVES

*Dragonfire Sea*

Bennett watched as the sea swallowed up the last of the Oshean slave vessel. Flotsam bobbed in the choppy waters, the only evidence that a battle had occurred. Two other vessels flanked the *Lady Faith*, awaiting his orders. "Let's move out," he called. The deck erupted into a flurry of shouts and activity. The drengr standing beside him conveyed his message to the other ships. Sails unfurled and the deck beneath his feet lurched as Jonah turned them back towards land.

Cries quieted as their rescued captives were ushered below deck to safety. He caught sight of Cat rushing between his injured men, escorting Emmon, all but holding him upright. She glanced up. Their eyes met and held. She'd been magnificent today; he couldn't wait to tell her that.

He didn't have the exact count yet, but they'd managed to rescue some one hundred captives bound for Oshea. New slaves to fuel the Oshean Empire's market, taken from city jails, ripped from their families. He wasn't stupid. He knew they weren't truly criminals—mostly. Kane found any excuse to lock more and more people up. To justify exporting them. With him in power, the Osheans now had their pick of Dragonwall's citizens.

Tris appeared on deck a few minutes later, saluting him.

"How are they?" he asked.

"They're getting settled, but definitely relived. Most are from Galadhal—Kastali Dun and its nearby towns."

"Good, get an exact headcount. Find out if they have family or friends they can return to. People who will shelter them. If not, we'll take them to Fort Squall and hand them off to Byron. The last thing I want is Kane getting wind of what we're doing."

Everything might fall apart if that happened. Kane had too much leverage. If he found out that there were drengr helping to free the slaves bound for Oshea, it would be over. The drengr had sworn an oath, and magic kept them from breaking it, but out here on the open ocean, they were no longer in Dragonwall. Oaths to the king didn't apply here. It was a gray area they'd worked around. Still, he couldn't risk Kane discovering it, but neither could he allow the Osheans to make off with Dragonwall's people. That would condemn them to a fate worse than death.

"I'll see to it at once, Captain." Tris bobbed his head and stepped away, retreating.

"Shall I have the others do the same?" The drengr beside him asked.

"Yes, thank you. I'll go check on our injured. See if there were any injuries on the other ships."

"Our drengr will see to them."

"Good. If not, I can send Cat over."

"No need, Captain."

Bennett retreated. His eyes adjusted to the dim light of the hallway as he made his way to Cat's healing room. He found her treating Emmon's battle wounds. She gave no greeting as he entered, quietly shutting the door behind him. This had become routine for them. After each battle, he crept into her quarters to watch her work magic. She'd already healed most of the injured above deck in the midst of battle. Only those who were severely wounded were brought down for more extensive treatment.

Emmon groaned. Several arrows stuck from his leg and shoulder. A massive gash along his torso had just been closed. It looked angry and pink. A dagger protruded just above his hip.

"Captain?" he managed through clenched teeth.

"Damn it, Emmon. Can't figure out if you're a shit fighter or you like putting yourself in more danger than necessary."

"We both know—gods above!" Emmon's face went green as Cat plucked one of the arrows free and immediately fed magic into the wound. "I did what I had to do," he finished, panting.

"Well! Maybe take one less arrow next time, eh?" He lifted his brows. "Cat's magic only goes so far, and you can't use it all for yourself."

"I didn't—argh!" Another arrow was free. Cat made quick work of each wound while he distracted Emmon from the pain with tough love.

"How are... How are the captives?" Emmon spoke through clenched teeth.

"Captives no more," he said. "You did good. I'm sure some will be looking to thank you once you're fit to walk the hold."

Emmon had been one of the first aboard the Oshean slave vessel. One of the first to break inside the hold where the captives were kept. That kind of bravery did not go unnoticed.

"There. All done," Cat said, moving away to wash her hands. Herbs floated on the bowl's surface. She dried her hands on a small towel then tossed Emmon his shirt. "Go visit our new guests. Find out if they have any ailments. I'll see to their needs once you've compiled a list."

Emmon opened his mouth to protest—

"Consider it punishment for being so careless," she all but purred. Her expression brokered no argument. In the past eight months, she'd managed to secure herself in the pecking order among the ship's residents. None dared cross her. Except, perhaps, himself.

Emmon scurried out the door. In the silence that followed, he watched as Cat tidied her area. She didn't look up at him once.

Her hair had grown into a shag. She kept it that length, styling it effortlessly so that it swept about her head in a halo of brown. He loved the feel of it between his fingers, when he had her pinned beneath him in his bed. He'd asked if she ever planned to grow it longer and she'd merely shrugged. Short hair was easier on a ship, and she was already so pleasing to the eye, that it only accentuated her features.

"You were impressive today," he said at last.

"And this surprises you?" She continued to work, measuring out ingredients for whatever medicine she was concocting.

"Always so difficult," he chuckled.

"You say that as if you would have it any other way."

"As much as I like your wicked mouth, there are times I prefer your submission."

She finally looked up, a challenge in her gaze. "And what times might those be, Captain?"

"When I've got you in my—"

"You're bleeding!" Her eyes fixed on his bicep.

Damn it. He'd all but forgotten about the wound. A pool of red now stained his tunic. "It's nothing, a shallow flesh wound is all." She scoffed and hurried forward. The furrow between her brow had him backtracking and a slow smile spread across his lips. "On second thought, you'd better fix it. Could be lethal."

She reached for his tunic before throwing him a glare. He was all too happy to remove it for her. Instead of the desired effect, she ignored his torso and focused solely on the knife wound. She made a tsking noise, prodding at it. He didn't dare flinch.

"You're right, nothing serious." She tossed his tunic at his face and backed away.

His lips parted. "You're not going to heal—?"

"Like you said, my magic only goes so far." The look on her face was downright evil.

He growled, stalking forward. She stood her ground, so he was forced to take her by the waist and back her up until her back was flush to the wall. "Surely you have but a drop to spare for me."

"Hmm. No, I don't think I do. But I'd be happy to stitch it closed for you. Might hurt a bit. I could give you some salve for the—"

His mouth cut off the remainder of her words. He pressed his tongue between her lips and groaned at the salty taste of her. She struggled against him, making half-hearted attempts to push him away in the game she played. He caught her jaw in his fingers, holding her in place. The moment the fight went out of her, she relaxed into him, kissing him back.

Gods, she made him feral.

A fist pounded on the door. "Beggin' your pardon, Cat, there's a few captives needing healer's attention."

"I'll... Just a moment." Cat's voice was breathy. She tried to push him away but he only pinned her more firmly, relishing in the feel of her hips pressed against his. It had been far too many days since he'd had her in his bed.

"You make me insane," he growled. "You know that?"

"Oh, do I?"

"Why won't you just move into my cabin already?" He'd asked her more than once, and she always refused.

"Sorry, but I'm a free woman. Not interested in shackling myself, not even to my ship's captain."

He made a frustrated sound in the back of his throat. "Everyone already knows what we get up to. It's not as if you're quiet—"

This time *she* cut him off, capturing his lips in a punishing kiss. When she pulled away, he saw the answer on her face. He just couldn't understand why she was so against it.

"I have work to do, Captain. Looks like you'll have to stitch that minor flesh wound on your own, or get someone to do it for you. It's not going to be me." With that, she ducked away and began gathering supplies.

He was left panting, frozen in place as she slipped out of the room, closing the door behind her. He growled and slammed his palm on the wall. What more did he need to do? Some kind of grand gesture? She was all but his, wasn't she? It sure seemed so when she was writhing beneath him most nights. And yet, she refused.

He stalked from the room in search of a distraction.

HE WAS half asleep when he felt the bed dip beside him. His eyes flew open. He was about to reach for his weapon when the smell of herbs washed over him and he relaxed. He rolled over and snaked an arm around the warm body that settled in beside him.

He nuzzled against her and froze. "What's wrong?" His voice was gruff from sleep.

"Nothing. I'm tired. Can we just sleep?"

"You never want to sleep when you're in my bed, and you're trembling like a leaf. Tell me what happened."

There was a long silence. When she next spoke, her voice was void of emotion. "One of the rescued captives didn't make it."

He stiffened. "How is that possible?"

"I think he suffered from something serious. When Emmon took note of all who needed healer's attention, he did not speak up or volunteer any information."

"Who?"

"An older man by the name of Gregory. No one really knew him."

He swore under his breath.

"I should have noticed something earlier. When I went around helping the others, he stayed secluded in the shadows—a hammock in the corner. No one said anything and I—"

"Do not blame yourself."

"Why shouldn't I? It is my job as—"

"Enough." His voice was whip-sharp.

She didn't speak again.

He blew out a breath, wrapping his arms more tightly around her. She wore a simple night shift and he could feel the chill of her skin. "Kitty Cat, this was out of your control. You are not omnipotent. They had the chance to come forward and chose to hide in the shadows. Even if it wasn't done on purpose, it still isn't your fault."

He felt her exhale against him. "Whatever. Let's just sleep."

He chewed on the inside of his cheek. He contemplated his next words, arguing with himself. Her breaths had evened out by the time he said, "I had a cabin boy, once. Gruff lad. Found him on the streets. Didn't really have a need for him, but took pity on his circumstances. Offered him a job. He was with us for three years. Became a favorite of the crew."

"What happened?" She turned so that her body faced him. He pulled her closer, tangling their legs together.

"I made a reckless decision, not so different from the one I made recently. To sail into a storm for the sake of saving time rather than go around. He was thrown overboard. Didn't even have time to react before the waves swept him away. Couldn't have gone after him even if we'd wanted to."

"Oh."

"Took to drinking more after that. Wasn't my first loss—mind. I'd lost others, a few here and there. But I'd only been a captain for five years by then, and I'd never lost a young lad. Never took another on afterward, either. Spent a few months wondering what I could have done different. Maybe I should have left him on the streets. Maybe I should have sailed around the storm and missed the delivery deadline. Lost pay is better than a lost life. Maybe I should have tied him to a damn post knowing he'd disobey my order and come out on deck to help. A lot of maybes in there."

"In the end, you did the best you could," she finished for him.

"You see where I'm going with this."

"Yes. Yes. All right."

"It's a casualty of the trade, I'm afraid. Instead, I think about the life I gave him. He was happy. We had good times."

"What was his name?"

"Corvy. Was a name he picked for himself, I guess. Didn't ever know his parents. Lived on the streets, starving all his life. Found him when he was nine."

There was a long silence and then, "Did you ever have any children?"

A surprised huff left his chest. "None that I know of. I try to be pretty careful."

"Would you claim responsibility for them, if anyone ever told you you were a father?"

A chill spiked its way through his blood. "Wouldn't lie, the thought scares the salt right out of me. But I'm honorable enough. I'd make sure the child was cared for. What are you getting at, Cat? You told me you were drinking the contraceptive tea."

"And I am. Was... Was just wondering."

He made a humming noise. "And... would you ever consider settling down, having a child?"

"Gods above, woman."

"I'm just wondering. Not like I'm ripping your teeth out or some such." She poked him in the chest.

He stroked a hand through her short hair, considering. "Never planned to have children. But if you're asking for you, then yes, I'll give you one if you want one. Anyone else can sod off."

"You sure know how to make a gal feel special."

"As long as it's this girl, that's all I care about. Now tell me true, is this all hypothetical or you really want children?"

"Mostly hypothetical. But... I could see myself wanting a child or two somewhere down the line. Far down the line, I mean. And I think if I did, I might want it to be with you."

Heat coiled in his chest. He'd never wanted children. The appeal was nonexistent. Yet, suddenly he liked her suggestion. "Make me a promise, then. If you ever decide to mother a child, keep me in mind as the father."

A small laugh burst from her chest. "Noted. Now, I'd like a little sleep, please."

"You sure about that?" He ran a hand down her thigh. All this talk about making babies had hardened him. When he leaned in to kiss her, she accepted the kiss, but kept it short.

"I'm sure. I don't think I have it in me to be intimate tonight. Not after earlier."

"Understood." Sometimes the simple act of holding someone close went a lot further than the act of making love.

He repositioned her in his arms, curling his body around hers and pressing her close. She had stopped trembling. He waited until her breaths evened out, until he was certain that she was sleeping, then kissed her temple. Only then did he allow sleep to claim him, too.

# CHAPTER 33

# A MISTAKE

*Esterpine*

Jovari hid his smile at the flash of pink when he caught sight of it. He hesitated, giving Leah a few moments to slip out of view before striding down the corridor. He paused outside the doorway, peeking inside. An art gallery.

She moved through the room, pausing before several paintings, oblivious to his presence.

He silently slipped inside, coming to a stop an arm's length behind her. "You're not hiding, are you?"

She gasped, whirling around, hand clutched to her chest. "Jovari! Don't—don't sneak up on me like that." He huffed, enjoying the look of surprise lighting her features. "And... I'm not hiding."

"No?" He glanced around the deserted room. "This is the third time you've snuck off to explore the inner workings of the palace."

"You've been following me?" Her incredulous expression shifted to annoyance.

"Why not? Had to make sure you didn't get lost."

"I'm not lost! Just...exploring."

His brows lifted. "Your best friend returned two days ago and you spend your time sneaking about the palace?"

Leah's expression shuttered. "That's because she's busy. She's got a lot to catch up on and I... I don't want to distract her."

She made an admirable effort to disguise the wobble in her voice. "Ah. How selfless of you."

"Exactly." She lifted her chin.

It had been a relief, seeing Claire return with her magic and memories intact. Even more so, seeing Talon's joy at having his queen back. The king was still grim, but every time his eyes landed on his mate, hope sparked in his gaze.

Jovari pretended to drop the subject, turning to admire the painting before them. It was of a desert landscape. Somewhere in Austar, probably. He walked closer for a better look, hyper aware of Leah's eyes on his every movement. He liked that, having her attention on him and only him.

"It's amazing how a place so bleak and desolate can hold so much beauty," he murmured, taking in the color of the sand, the shades of paint used on the sunset splashed across the sky. He turned abruptly, pinning Leah with his gaze. "She was looking for you earlier, you know." Leah's lips parted. "What is the real reason you're avoiding her?"

"I'm not—"

"Don't lie, Leah. You and I are far past that, don't you think?"

She blew out a breath. "Claire has her memories back—she has all this." Leah gestured towards the palace walls, doing her best to disguise the flash of emotions in her expression. "She doesn't need me. I'll just—get in the way."

"Leah." He took a step towards her, then stopped. "No matter what she has, she will always need friends, people to support her in her endeavors."

"I... I know that." This time the wobble in her voice was more apparent. "It's just... It's hard, you know?"

"Explain." His voice was a rough demand.

"Seeing her live her life reminds me of where I'm falling short. What I've failed to accomplish. I'm twenty-two, Jovari. What do I have to show for myself?" A dark laugh burst from her lips. "Isn't that selfish? I can't handle being around my best friend because I can't take the reminder of how she has so much and I have...nothing. She's my *best friend*! I love her more than anything in the world. No one is happier than me that she freed herself from Kane's magic—well, Talon is probably happier, since he's her mate—and yet, here I am moping about how pathetic my life is. I'm supposed to be selflessly supporting her—"

"Stop." He cut the distance between them and took her face in his hands, framing it, forcing her gaze to his. Her eyes glittered with unshed tears. "Enough, Leah. That's enough."

Her rough swallow was audible.

"You are setting impossible standards for yourself." His growl was angry—for her. Angry that life had made her feel this way. "You have faced things no one should ever face. Yet, you came away stronger. You think you don't have anything to show for yourself, but you do. You have a resilience others can only dream of. No one should go through what you did—*no one*."

Her breaths came faster. She listened to each word with wide, watery eyes.

"We do not get to choose the circumstances littering our pasts, but we do get to choose what we take with us into the future. Yes?"

She managed a rough nod even though he still held her face captive. A single tear broke free, sliding down her cheek. Gods, he wanted to brush it away with his lips. Instead, he used his thumb.

"You're right," she managed, voice rough. "I know it's not a competition."

"It's not," he said. "It never will be. But even if it was, you have already won. At least, in my heart you have." His arms dropped to his sides. Because if he didn't let go of her, it would be too easy to give in to the temptation of her.

"Jovari..." Her eyes darted to his lips, making heat drop straight into his abdomen. He felt frozen in the moment. Perhaps that's why he didn't move when she went up on her toes and brushed her soft lips against his. Once, twice, three times...

Her tongue flicked out, tracing the seam of his lips. He groaned, his restraint snapping like a dry twig. He grabbed hold of her shoulders, dragging her against him. He kissed her back, melding their lips together. It was a long time coming, and he should have anticipated this happening.

The feel of her mouth on his was intoxicating. There was only her, the warmth of her body against his, the wetness of her mouth, the sound of her heavy breaths. He forgot about everything, the problems surrounding their kingdom, his promise to Talon, even his own reasons for never letting himself get close to another female.

He forgot about those things...until he didn't.

Reality came crashing down mid-kiss. He wrenched himself away, his breaths labored, putting space between them. Hurt flashed across her features, making him feel like the worst kind of male.

"This... We... I..." He ran a hand through his hair, fingers tangling in it. "We can't do this," he settled on, unable to formulate the reason why.

Leah's skin flushed a darker shade of red. He'd embarrassed her and he hated himself for it. He wanted to tell her that it was the best kiss he'd ever had, wanted to tell her that if things were different, he would kiss her again, over and over, until they forgot their names.

Leah cleared her throat. "You're right. I... It's my fault. I shouldn't have kissed you." Something in his chest twisted when she said that. "I got caught up in the moment and...just forget it, yeah? It was a mistake."

His breath whooshed from his chest. A mistake. Why did that hurt so much?

They were words he deserved to hear.

He could only stare as he tried to gather the broken fragments of his thoughts. Part of him wanted to rush forward, desperate to drag her back into his arms. The rational part of him knew he could never do that.

"I should go and find Claire," she blurted, giving him one last chance to say something. "Since she was looking for me." When he didn't respond, she turned and rushed away. He'd never felt so alone in all his life.

IT WAS FOR THE BEST. That's what he told himself throughout the day. What he told himself as they sat down to dinner that evening.

It was an intimate affair. Claire had spent much of her time meeting with her spriten advisors. She'd pushed the matter of abdication, only to be refused. Taylynn wasn't ready. There'd been heated words exchanged, of which Jovari had only heard about second hand. He could still feel the tension radiating between the cousins.

This was their first gathering, just the eight of them. Claire sat at the head of the table, with Talon on her right and Taylynn on her left. The others had filled in around them. Koldis sat beside Taylynn, and Bedelth with Saffra.

He and Leah were the odd ones out—the only unmated coupling. He tried and failed to catch her eye. She hadn't looked at him once.

Was that it, then? Their budding friendship destroyed with one little kiss? He hated the idea, but perhaps it really was for the best.

Irelia had refused the invitation to dinner—mostly out of anger. Someone—probably Taylynn—had thrown her name into the hat as a potential ruler. She'd kept to herself these past few days, spending more and more time alone in the forest. He wondered if she intended to seek out the king tree, sooner than later. While she wasn't full sprite, she had enough blood to give her body back to the land.

Saffra leaned in and whispered something that made Leah giggle. His jaw clenched. She looked perfectly normal, as if their kiss earlier hadn't happened.

*I shouldn't have kissed you.*

*I got caught up in the moment.*

*Just forget it.*

*It was a mistake.*

He'd be lying if he said he hadn't revisited those words multiple times already, and each time they hurt worse than before. *He* was the heartbreaker. The one skilled at using words like those to end things before they started. How many lovers had he dismissed in a similar manner?

It wasn't supposed to hurt this much.

"If we travel south, it will give Claire time to revisit her mage magic," Taylynn was saying. He hardly heard the discussion, too lost in his own brooding.

"Does that mean we'll visit the hatching grounds?" Saffra asked.

"The hatching grounds?" Leah breathed. "You mean, the baby dragons?" Her entire face lit up.

He may as well have been staring directly at the sun, for all it hurt to look at her. Yet, he couldn't look away. He'd never once made her expression transform like that. Now he wondered what he'd be willing to sacrifice to have her look at him in that exact way. *Stupid, baby dragons.*

"They're not pets," he scoffed.

Leah's smile dropped, and he immediately regretted his words. But at least she was looking at him now. Even if he was the one responsible for dashing her happy mood.

"Oh, don't be a spoil sport, Jovari." Claire paid him a stern glare.

"Forgive me, my queen. You are right. I am sure they will adore your fussing."

"Exactly." Claire beamed. "Maybe with enough love and affection, they won't grow up to be bloodthirsty little beasts."

"Right." Talon snorted under his breath.

"What was that?" Claire looked at her mate, daring him to repeat himself.

"Nothing," he said, lifting his goblet to take a drink. Except, Claire was in his mind, so it didn't matter if he tried to hide it, she would know.

*Mates.* He almost rolled his eyes. He was surrounded by lovesick fools.

Then again, his own situation wasn't much better. He tried again to catch Leah's eye. She was staring at the king and queen, her expression closed off. The only thing that gave her away was the way she clenched her fork.

He recalled her words from earlier, the way she had opened up to him. Gods, it infuriated him that she was grappling with feelings of inadequacy. Didn't she see how strong she was? How resilient? How brave? He saw all that, and more.

He saw the sacrifices she'd made.

He'd said what he said, but he couldn't fault her for feeling as she did. Especially when she looked at Claire and saw a queen, happily mated. Sure, Claire's life wasn't perfect. She'd had her fair share of struggle and heartbreak. The weight of an entire kingdom on her shoulders.

But still.

Leah was hurting, and he'd gone and kissed her—well, she'd kissed him, but he'd kissed her back, encouraged it, no less. Then he'd pulled away when she was already struggling. It was a low blow. No wonder she'd said what she had. He deserved to hurt.

"There are a few things I'd like to do before we depart," Claire was saying. "I'd like to visit Pelwynn's grave, for one. I also need to seek council with the king tree."

Leah went back to pushing things around on her plate. He watched her, willing her to look up at him. She didn't.

She was freezing him out and it cut him, deeply.

But it was for the best—better this way. Talon had been right. Nothing would come of it if he pursued her. It would only make things more complicated between everyone in their group. Besides, he'd loved a human woman once, and look where that had gotten him. It wasn't a mistake he was willing to repeat. Ever.

Chairs scraped, and everyone was getting to their feet. He glanced up, surprised, then quickly did the same. Somehow he'd managed to pass an entire dinner, hardly aware of any of it.

His heart rushed as he rounded the table, hoping to catch Leah. To say—he didn't know what. Something. An apology, perhaps.

But as he reached her, she scurried off, arm in arm with Saffra. He blinked, and then they were gone.

Bedelth caught his eye and grinned, clapping him on the shoulder. "Looks like we'll be headed back home before we know it," he said.

"What? Oh. Right. Yes."

Bedelth frowned. "You okay?"

"Fine."

Bedelth's eyes narrowed. Then he huffed. "Don't tell me. You've got your sights on a certain pink-haired female that just scurried off, dragging my mate along with her. What's that all about?"

"Nothing," he snapped, then exhaled. "Sorry. It's not something I wish to talk about."

He didn't expect Bedelth to understand. Whatever growing pains he and Saffra had experienced, well, they were mates, so it had all worked out in the end hadn't it? It wasn't like his shield brother would understand.

"Well, I'm here if you decide to talk about it." Bedelth nudged him. "Until then, I found the entrance to the palace's cellar earlier, and it's filled with sprite wine. I bet the queen doesn't even know it exists. How about we go nab a couple of bottles right out from under her nose? We can grab Koldis and Talon and have ourselves some bonding time."

He was about to protest. Surely Koldis and Talon would much rather enjoy the company of their mates? Even Bedelth. Only, how long had it been since they'd had time together, just the males? Suddenly, it sounded like the best idea in the world, and exactly what he needed.

He growled with delight, which Bedelth took as a yes. Just like old times. The two of them snuck off to raid the queen's private collection.

# CHAPTER 34
# SAYING GOODBYE

*Esterpine*

Claire pawed at her cheeks, sniffling. Talon had offered to accompany her to Pelwynn's, but she'd insisted on doing this alone. She needed this time to process his loss. Despite Talon's physical absence, he was always with her, even now, as she suffered; he was a warm presence against her mind, offering comfort from afar.

Pelwynn's grave was beautiful, covered with a vining plant that grew around the statue of a phoenix and bloomed with jasmine blossoms. The inscription beneath his name read, 'Beloved friend and teacher.' That's exactly what he'd been for her, until Kane had taken him from this world.

He'd never call her *elam* again. He'd never bark orders at her in his typical crotchety manner. He'd never—

"Are you all right?" The sound of Irelia's voice brought her to her feet. The older woman came to stand beside her, staring at the statue.

She sniffed, trying to compose herself. "I'm...no. I'm not. I never got to say a proper goodbye, you know. I always thought I'd see him again. That we'd spend more time together after Kane. Long afternoons in his garden, just…sitting, until he was ready. It was always his plan to seek out the king tree eventually, but Kane stole that from him."

"You cared for him a great deal?"

"Yes." Her throat was thick with tears. "He was my teacher. He taught me—so much."

"Then I am sorry for your loss." Irelia reached for her hand, a tentative offering.

She took hold and squeezed. "How did you find me?"

"The forest, I think. It guided me to you." Irelia regarded Pelwynn's grave. "Taylynn informed me that Pelwynn knew my mother."

"Yes." The confirmation was a whisper. "He felt guilty. It's why he lingered for so long. Most sprites tire of life and seek out the king tree. Not him. He waited—for me. Can you believe it? Now I wish… I wish I would have stayed longer. Spent a little more time with him. If I had known—" A sob clawed its way up her throat.

"There now," Irelia murmured. "Death is unpredictable and inescapable. You cannot linger over the what ifs. It will destroy you. Besides, something tells me Pelwynn wouldn't want you filled with regret over him."

"I know." She swiped at her tears. "Can you believe he left everything to me? His cottage—all this." She waved a hand to encompass their surroundings. "An entire lifetime of himself, just for me. I never realized he cared for me that…that much."

"That was kind of him. He must have known how you would miss him. That this would help you feel closer to him."

"Yeah." She blew out a breath. "Want to see it? I can give you a tour."

"I would love that." Irelia squeezed her hand before dropping it.

She hadn't spent much time with her great-great-great—lots of greats—grandmother. The opportunity to be alone had been scarce. It felt good to have her here. Irelia understood loss better than most. She'd watched her family grow and multiply over the long years of her life. Had seen her offspring and relatives age and die, all while continuing to exist.

She pointed at the dummy near the edge of the garden, still standing after all this time. "This is where I first started working with a bow—to teach me to control my mind, for my magic. And this was where Pelwynn liked sitting, at this bench. He loved his garden. If he wasn't basking in it, he was pulling weeds and nurturing his plants."

They walked towards the cottage's entrance.

It was strange, seeing everything now that her memories had returned. She blinked at a familiar plot of earth, where she'd found Pelwynn gardening before she'd left. She could still see him there, toiling away with his hands instead of his magic. She hesitated before reaching for the door handle.

It swung inward on silent hinges. She stood on the threshold, frozen. Everything was exactly as she remembered it, not an item out of place. Her chest squeezed. Another sob rose in her throat.

There was a gentle pat on her shoulder. "We don't have to go in if you're not ready," Irelia murmured.

"No. I... I need to do this." She stepped inside, inhaling. It smelled the same. Felt the same.

Irelia quietly shut the door behind them.

She walked across the room towards one of Pelwynn's cluttered shelves, brushing her fingers over his nicknacks. He loved collecting things. Nostalgia washed over her. The day she'd met him was still fresh in her mind. It made her heart ache.

There was a bowl on the table, emptied, with a spoon resting inside it, like he'd just finished breakfast and had stepped out for a moment. Like he would return. Like he might walk through the door at any moment and ask her how her training was progressing.

Gods, she missed him so, *so* much.

She sank into his favorite armchair and sighed. Irelia took the one beside her. They were quiet for a while.

"I'm glad I got to see this place, where you perfected your magic," Irelia murmured. "It is an incredible accomplishment, how far you have come. You were meant for all of this."

"I'm glad, too. Gods, I wish you could have met him, though. The two of you—" A laugh burst from her lips. "You would have been such great friends." A tear slipped down her cheek at the thought of Irelia never knowing Pelwynn.

"Yes, we would have," Irelia agreed, looking around the cottage. "Though, his lack of organization would have driven me up the wall."

They both laughed.

"Have you decided what you're going to do with yourself?" she asked. "You could return to Kastali Dun with us, if you want."

It would be a chance for them to get to know each other better. It wasn't every day that long lost grandmothers appeared, especially ones with the unique past Irelia carried. Moreover, the capital was the place of her birth. What would it be like seeing it again?

Irelia exhaled. "When I left, I never intended to return."

"Why *did* you leave?" She'd always wondered what had driven Irelia to pass through the gate beneath the keep. It was a question she'd forgotten about after her memories were bound. It resurfaced now.

Irelia's eyes locked with hers. She saw the indecision in her expression. "The voices—in my head. When my magic matured. It started when I reached womanhood."

"Voices?" She frowned. Then her eyes widened. "You mean the drengr? You can hear them too? Why didn't—why didn't you say anything? That's why you left?"

"I was afraid," Irelia said. "Young and afraid. I had no idea what they were. They would come and go. I thought I was going mad. It wasn't until your mate showed up with Jovari that I figured it out, when I heard them having silent conversations about you—about all of us. Two thousand years, give or take, and I never knew. When I heard them talking, I realized what it is. But yes, when I was a child it was frightening."

She thought back to the first time she'd heard the king's shields, right after Cyrus had died. The only reason she'd known what she was hearing was because they'd been talking about her. It allowed her to quickly connect the dots. What might she have thought otherwise? Would she have known they belonged to the drengr? Would she have believed she was going crazy, too?

"I can hear them too, did you know?"

Irelia's lips parted. "No. I did not."

"And your mother, Isabella. She also had the ability to communicate with the drengr. Though, I don't think she could hear them when they didn't want to be heard. It's how she was able to talk to Vigilance—Eymar—your father. Gods, that's so weird. Your father was the first king! I don't think it really hit me until just now, saying it out loud." Generations of drengr kings had come and gone, and hers had been the first.

"Maybe it was something to do with the combination of blood," she wondered aloud. "Drengr and sprite blood. It made it so you could hear all of them unwillingly. Isabella could converse with them when she wanted to. But for you, it was involuntary, just like it is for me."

Irelia hummed. She appeared thoughtful.

"You can control it, you know. Shut them out. Reyr taught me how. I could teach you, so that when we reach the capital—"

"I will not be returning to the capital." Irelia gave an abrupt shake of her head.

"Oh." She tried to ignore the hollowness forming in her chest.

"But I will take you up on your offer—to teach me to control the ability. It will come in handy when I meet the hatchlings."

"The hatchlings?" Her eyes widened, then her mouth formed into an *oh* as understanding hit her.

"Taylynn said I would be perfect to help raise them—after I refused her offer to claim my blood inheritance. I didn't understand at first, but after some thinking, I believe she knows of my ability."

"You'll be able to hear the juvenile dragons as they speak, to know what they're talking about, if they're in trouble, or if they need anything. Taylynn's right! You'd be perfect."

Irelia chuckled. "You really think so?"

"Basically a dragon grandmother? Yes!"

The hollowness in her chest filled. Not only would it give Irelia a purpose, it would keep her from seeking out the king tree just yet. She wanted more time with her. Hopefully when this was all over, they'd get that time.

"I saved them, you know. The pregnant mothers."

"Oh? That sounds like a story worth telling."

"I suppose it is." She explained what had happened when she'd snuck away from Talon's tent in the wee hours of the morning and faced the wild dragons alone. Talon had been so angry with her. He hadn't seen things the way she did. Hadn't cared if all the dragons went extinct.

"I'm glad you kept that from happening," Irelia admitted. "When I was a child, dragons still existed in the world. They weren't all bad, you know."

A lump formed in her throat. "I know."

Sprites gathered from all over the city to celebrate her final night in Esterpine. The beautiful clearing where they took their meals glowed with light and rang with music as musicians strummed instruments. Sprites ate and drank in merriment, while some danced and others lounged.

Talon and Koldis engaged in a hushed conversation near the edge of the gathering. A quick peek into his mind told her they were discussing their upcoming journey. A hint of amusement hummed along their shared connection, Talon acknowledging her prying. Their eyes met and held from across the clearing. The sight of her in her red gown, the majority of her markings on full display, filled him with possessive hunger.

"The sooner I can get you out of that abomination of a gown, the better," he'd growled against the shell of her ear mere hours ago. She knew exactly what would happen when he accomplished *that*.

The corner of his mouth twitched. *"Thinking impure thoughts, mate?"*

*"No!"* She wiped her mind clean.

*"Liar."* His voice was like sensual claws scraping down her spine, sending shivers across her skin—

*"Ayas Drollaya."* Aolis Marquin saved her from answering. She broke eye contact with Talon and whirled towards him. Their mental connection remained, and she soaked in the low chuckle that he directed to her.

"Lord Marquin. It is a pleasure, as always."

*"Ana guiaha utah mikah." The pleasure is mine.* "I wished to inquire about my daughter," he continued in *Ednuar*. "Is she to your liking?"

"Quite. Elyon is a wonderful addition to my queen's guard." Aolis beamed. "She's a fierce warrior and I already miss her presence by my side."

"Indeed. Then, I'm sure you will do everything in your power to ensure that she is safe when you return to reclaim the capital." Beneath his brazen demand, there was a hint of worry. It was the only reason she forgave his impertinence.

She exhaled. "I will, but I will also remind you that Elyon, like the rest of my guards, knew what she was signing up for when she took the position. I have the utmost confidence that she will do a fine job taking care of herself." She spotted Leah across the clearing and added, "Now, if you will excuse me, my lord."

"Of course. *Shalaya, Ayas Drollaya.*"

She extricated herself and made a beeline for Leah before anyone else could stop her. She'd already been at her queenly duties for the better part of two hours and her patience was thinning.

"Gods, I think I might go mad if I hear another wish for my kingdom's safe return," she quietly groused, pulling her friend aside. A metal laugh raked gentle claws against her mind as Talon told her exactly what he thought of that. He'd been king for more than two hundred years. These sorts of public gatherings were old news for him.

"We could always sneak away," Leah said. Her eyes darted across the clearing, then quickly away, but not before she spotted Jovari lurking with his arms crossed and irritation covering his face.

"Okay, what's going on with you two?" She pulled Leah into a slow walk, keeping to the edge of the gathering, so as not to be overheard.

"What do you mean?"

"You've been purposefully avoiding a certain king's shield? Not to mention he hardly looks anywhere but you."

"Fine. He asked me to dance. I refused."

"That's all, is it?" She felt Talon perk up, splitting his attention to listen. *"Stay out of this,"* she warned, giving him a mental shove. He begrudgingly complied.

"Well, fine, if you must know, I might have kissed him the other day."

"What?!" she whisper-shrieked. "You did not!"

"I might have."

She sucked in a breath and poked Leah's arm. "Well? Was it any good?"

"It doesn't matter."

"Oh, come on! Everyone knows he has a reputation. Surely that means he's a good kisser."

"Yes, about that reputation." Leah scoffed.

"I take it you regret kissing him?"

"You have no idea." They passed by a group of sprites laughing and drinking their spriten wine before picking up the conversation again.

"I want all the details."

Leah exhaled. "There's not much to it, really. I was... Well, Jovari was being really sweet. Saying all these nice things—"

"Because he's a schmoozer."

Leah opened her mouth, then frowned. "I don't think it was

that. We were having a deep conversation. He just… He said something heartfelt, not something to get into my pants.”

“Okay.” She knew Jovari had a genuinely kind heart, even if he often hid it behind a teasing smile.

“Anyway, I don’t know what came over me. I just suddenly needed to kiss him, so I did. It’s like I couldn’t help myself. But then he had to go and ruin it by making it very clear that he didn’t want to be kissing me. I tried to play it off, but the damage was done.”

“Don’t get me wrong, I adore Jovari—as a shield. But you should know, he is known as one of the kingdom’s biggest flirts. I’ve heard plenty about his reputation at court.”

“And you think he sees me as a potential conquest?”

“Not necessarily.” Claire blew out a breath. “Do you like him?”

“No!” She answered too quickly.

“Leah, you know you’re my best friend, which means I know when you’re lying.”

“Fine. Maybe it’s… I don’t know. Infatuation, or something. I’m sure it will pass. I don’t want to make things awkward, you know?”

“I think it’s too late for that.” Claire glanced over and caught Jovari watching them. She lifted her brows in warning and he quickly looked away. “Want me to talk to him?”

“Ohmigodno!”

She laughed. “All right. I’ll leave you two to sort things out on your own. But, Leah, I’m here if you want to talk. I know Talon told him to stay away from you and all but—”

“Wait, what?!” Leah practically shrieked, attracting the attention of several nearby sprites. More quietly, she said, “He did *what*?”

*“Claire…”* Talon’s voice was a warning in her mind.

*“I told you to butt out of this,”* she admonished, giving him another mental shove, even though she couldn’t block him without putting more effort into it, which she didn’t want to do.

“I saw it in his mind. He gave Jovari a talking to, early on. He was worried Jovari would break your heart, so he told him to stay away from you.”

Leah’s face heated. She threw a glare in Talon’s direction. The king was staring at them with a disgruntled expression, which he quickly smoothed into nothing a moment later.

"That wasn't his business," Leah hissed.

*"Actually, what my shield does is very much my business,"* Talon growled into her mind. She offered a mental snarl in response. Nosy mate.

"Actually, I hate to tell you this, but it is his business." She absolutely hated being forced to take Talon's side over her best friend's, but Talon was right. "Jovari belongs to the king. He made an oath that binds him for life. The king has every right to exercise his will on the matter. For what it's worth, he was trying to protect you, not hurt you."

Leah blew out a breath. "You're right. I... Like I said before, it doesn't matter." She absentmindedly brushed her fingertips over her lips. Almost as if she could still feel Jovari's lips there.

Claire could see what she wasn't saying—Talon could see it too, plain as day. Leah cared about Jovari far more than she ought to. Telling the shield to stay away from her romantically hadn't prevented what was happening here. Knowing that only stoked the king's ire.

Claire was aware of him stalking over towards Jovari.

*"Talon,"* she warned. *"Please don't. Leah kissed Jovari. He did not break his word to you."*

*"He kissed her back,"* he growled.

*"You don't know that. You weren't there. Drop it, please."*

Talon's pace slowed. When he reached his shield, he clapped him on the shoulder and took up a stance beside him. She sent him a silent thanks before turning her full attention back to Leah.

"Well, you know the best way to move on from a guy?" She reached for a sprite carrying a tray of goblets filled with spriten wine. "Find a new one." She grabbed two goblets, passing one to Leah. "There are plenty of handsome males here tonight. Let's find one for you to dance with."

Leah's expression brightened. She took her goblet, clinked it against Claire's, and they drank. It only took minutes before she found a handsome young male eager to take her pink-haired friend up on a dance. She couldn't help her smirk as she watched them twirl about, which only grew wider as Talon appeared beside her and encouraged her to sneak away with him for the night. With one final glance in Jovari's direction, taking note of his monumental scowl, she slipped away and allowed her mate to make good on his promises about her gown.

# CHAPTER 35
## THE HATCHLINGS

*The Gable Forest*

Leah kept her gaze resolutely fixed on Claire's back, watching as her friend practiced magic. Talon walked beside her, lowering his head to quietly offer advice. Taylynn and Koldis took the lead, escorting their group south, towards the caves that had once housed the Forest Clan long ago.

Now, they housed a group of female dragons who'd given birth to clutches of eggs. They were going to see baby dragons! It was enough to distract her from a certain male drengr she'd spent way too much time ruminating over.

"Is there anything you miss about your home world?" Saffra pulled her from her thoughts. They walked side-by-side, following the forest path Taylynn set. Behind them, Bedelth and Jovari took up the rear.

"Oh, tons! That's not to say I regret leaving, but I miss having access to my own private bathroom. And showers, whenever I want them. Mostly, though, I miss processed foods." She groaned, thinking about her guilty pleasure. "I have a bit of an Oreo obsession."

"What's an oreo?" Saffra's head tilted.

She sighed, the sound wistful. "It's this wonderful cookie thing. It's got cream filling sandwiched between two chocolate wafers. When you dip them in milk..." She exhaled. "Perfection."

Saffra made a humming sound. "I'll have to take your word for it."

"Trust me, you'd love them. They even come in different flavors. I always bought the seasonal ones, too. It was the one thing I splurged on whenever I went to the grocery store."

"I see. What about Claire? Does *she* know about your obsession?"

"Oh, she knows!" Leah pressed her lips together to keep from laughing. "One year, she bought me an entire box of Oreo packs for Christmas. It was supposed to be a joke—a gag gift. But in reality, it was one of the best gifts I've ever received. I had Oreos for like... months."

Saffra laughed. "That sounds exactly like something Claire would do."

They both fell quiet. The forest was beautiful, filled with the sound of insects while brightly colored birds swooped about. It made sense that Claire loved it so much.

"You know," Saffra said after a few minutes, "you're going to make a great addition to our friends group."

Leah's chest squeezed. She hated to admit how hopeful she sounded when she said, "You mean that?"

"I do." Saffra's smile was genuine. "It will be nice for Claire to have someone from her past life by her side. The others will love you too."

"Thank you," she breathed, trying to ignore the way her eyes watered—

"Let's rest here," Taylynn called from the front of their group, bringing everyone to a stop. They fanned out around a small clearing. It looked no different from the other clearings they'd used along their journey. If she hadn't known any better, she'd think they were going in circles. No one else protested, so she assumed this was normal. It was their third day, and they were supposed to reach the hatching grounds by the evening.

Claire appeared beside her, hooking an arm around her neck. "Doing okay?"

"Yes, and you? How are your magic lessons going?"

Claire shrugged. "Okay I guess, as much as I hate mage magic. Talon is a patient teacher—not that he'd be patient with anyone else. I think the mate bond has something to do with it."

"I heard that," Talon called from the other side of the clearing.

Claire's laugh was breathy. She seemed happy, despite the pressure resting on her shoulders. There wasn't much time for her to practice before they left the forest. Apparently, she needed to find balance with both mage and sprite magic, according to some prophecy Saffra had made. Only then would she succeed in taking on Kane.

"Oh, look, Jovari is glaring at you again."

"What?" Leah jerked her gaze across the clearing, but Jovari was deep in conversation with Koldis.

"Hah. Made you look." Leah pinched her side. "Oww!" Claire pinched her back, until they were engaged in an all-out pinching war, something they hadn't done in a while. Soon enough, they were squealing and chasing each other around.

Talon caught on. He snatched Claire into his arms and offered a fake protective growl. Leah held up her hands. "Fine, fine. She's all yours."

"Oh, put me down." Claire's voice was filled with mirth as she swatted at her mate until he set her back on her feet.

Leah took a seat on the ground beside Saffra, who offered her a parcel of food wrapped in cloth. They'd packed rations, which consisted of bread, cheese, nuts, and dried fruit that almost tasted like candy. The drengr grumbled about it plenty, but she didn't mind.

She was overly aware of Jovari as he took a seat next to Koldis and Taylynn. It seemed everyone had noticed the lengths they'd gone to to avoid each other, even if they pretended otherwise. Jovari looked up and their eyes met. Her face heated. She offered him her best emotionless expression before looking away, feigning interest in Saffra's conversation with Bedelth.

"How much longer will it take for us to reach the capital—after we leave the forest?" she found herself asking. In other words, how long before they might reach the capital so that she could put space between herself and a certain drengr.

"Oh." Saffra looked thoughtful, taking the subject change in stride.

"Four to five days if we make good time," Bedelth answered for her. "Depends on the wind and how often…"

She didn't hear the rest of Bedelth's explanation as realization hit her. She glanced around. Everyone here was paired off. Claire with Talon. Saffra with Bedelth. Taylynn with Koldis. Panic welled in her chest. When it came time to fly south, she'd be stuck flying with Jovari, which meant she'd have to be close to him, she'd have to touch his scales, feel the warmth of him beneath her thighs.

"Oh no…" she breathed.

"Everything all right?" Saffra nudged her.

"Fine," she squeaked. "Just fine."

But it was not fine—not even a little bit.

THEY REACHED the cave at dusk. The forest around them had changed. Gone were the ethereal qualities she'd grown used to. It looked altogether ordinary, as a forest ought, with several types of trees, tall ferns, and long shadows that created patches of blackness.

"This is no longer spriten territory," Taylynn had explained once they crossed an invisible barrier, leading them through the trees to a series of rocky openings.

"Woah," she breathed, her mouth going slack. Claire appeared beside her and snatched her hand. Their fingers twined together in anticipation.

"Exciting, isn't it?" Claire breathed.

They stood before one of three massive openings. "Definitely large enough to fit a dragon," Leah said aloud.

"Large enough to fit several," Claire agreed.

Saffra appeared on Leah's other side, offering them a grin. The others pressed in around them for a better look.

A scraping sound made them freeze. A small rock tumbled toward them, disrupting the quiet, then a massive shape appeared, silhouetted in the opening. Leah squealed, but quickly recovered.

A chuckle sounded behind her. She glanced over her shoulder. Jovari. She threw him a vicious glare that silenced him before turning back to the dragon that emerged.

"Fright," Taylynn said by way of greeting. She stepped forward, brushing her hand down the dragon's forearm. Fright hummed but Koldis emitted a low growl. Taylynn snorted, throwing her mate a fond look that also carried a warning to behave. There was a long silence, then, "He says two clutches have hatched, and the third is due any day. The other two females should give birth soon."

More shadows shifted, and two spriten females appeared in the cave's opening. They greeted Claire and Taylynn with bows of deference, introducing themselves as Ayla and Nushala. "The hatchlings are doing well," Nushala informed them. "There is much game to be had in this part of the forest and surrounding lands. Their caretaker feeds them well."

Fright hummed, standing a little taller.

"Is that so?" Taylynn looked pleased.

"Good boy," Koldis praised, his voice dripping with sarcasm, which brought a snarl of warning from Fright's jaws.

"Both of you—enough," Taylynn snapped, irritation getting the better of her. Leah knew little about the white dragon, but clearly there was some tension between Fright and Koldis. "Fright, lead the way," Taylynn commanded. "We will rest here a few days before continuing on."

The cave wasn't what she had expected. Instead of dark and damp, its walls had been smoothed out, with alcoves that acted as rooms. They descended deeper into its depths. Giant murals had been painted onto the stone, depicting dragons of various colors, some in flight, some hunting, others lounging in the forest or basking in the sun.

"It's...beautiful," she breathed, squeezing Claire's hand.

"This place was once home to an entire clan," Taylynn explained. The massive corridor opened into a large, hollowed out cavern. She gasped at the sheer size of it. How could something so large possibly fit beneath the earth?

In style, it reminded her of the crystal palace. They were somewhere near the top, but the wide ledge—wide enough to fit dragon bodies—spiraled around and around to the very bottom, where a giant hatching ground sat.

The shapes far below were mere specks of color. She knew with certainty that when they got closer, she'd see little dragons as they played off to the side. Giddy excitement bubbled up inside her. They weren't pets—she knew that. Yet, she couldn't *wait* to pick one up and cuddle it. Could she? Would they allow it?

A rush of air buffeted them before a massive blue dragon rose to greet them. She gasped. This one had scales a little lighter than Jovari's. She was a female—all the dragons living here were, except for Fright. Even with her wings outstretched, she could soar comfortably around the interior of the cavern. The female paid them a glance and a warble of greeting before settling on the ledge opposite them. A moment later, she disappeared into a massive chamber beyond.

"That's Despair," Ayla explained. "Her clutch is the first that hatched. The hatchlings are below. She takes excellent care of them."

"Where did she go?" Saffra asked.

"To her private lodgings. She probably needs space. Mothering nine hatchlings is a great deal of work."

"They don't...nurse or anything?" Leah found herself asking.

Much to her relief, no one laughed at her question. "No," Ayla said. "They eat meat upon coming out of the shell—and let me tell you, they are voracious when they emerge." The spriten female crinkled her nose but did well to hide her disgust. "Their mother is responsible for teaching them how to eat, to walk, how to work their wings, etcetera. It is why we did not kill the mothers upon delivery of their clutches."

Leah gasped. "You were going to kill them?"

Claire exhaled, sharing a pointed look with Talon. "It's a hot topic of debate, but no."

Talon looked as if he wanted to disagree, but smartly kept his lips pressed together.

"The mothers are in exile," Taylynn said. "They have agreed that they will not stray far from the cavern. They have held true to their vow. Besides, where would they go? Their clan is gone. There is no one left for them but their hatchlings and each other."

"Let's go down," Claire said.

It took an hour to reach the bottom. By then, her feet were aching. The pain was immediately forgotten the moment she set eyes on the small shapes of color darting about.

She gasped.

Claire was less dignified. She squealed before rushing forward, only to stop abruptly. "Can we...? Would they allow it?"

The nearby shape of a mother loomed over the hatchlings, observing their play. Her scales were almost pink in color. Leah couldn't help but glance between the mother and young hatchlings, similar to cats in size. There had to be at least twenty. Nine from Despair. The rest must have belonged to the mother on guard-duty.

"That's Histeria," Ayla murmured beside her. "She's a bit protective, but she will not stop you if you'd like to say hello. Be warned, they are extremely curious creatures. Let them sniff your palm first. If they decide you aren't a threat, they'll allow you to pet them or even pick them up."

The males hung back while the rest of them darted forward, eager.

The little dragons on the edge spotted them first and began chortling with curiosity. She held her hand out as several rushed over. Word spread in the form of chirps and warbles, until they were swarmed by the little ones. Snouts were pressed against her palm. Beside her, Claire and Saffra giggled. Even Taylynn wore a soft smile, reaching down to scratch the eye ridges of a hatchling nearest her before sweeping it up into her arms.

They were all sorts of colors, like a veritable rainbow dancing around their feet. She reached for a small green that had finished sniffing her palm and lifted it into her arms. It warbled in excitement before reaching out with its small talons and snatching fistfuls of her tunic. It clung to her and she giggled, scratching its eye ridges as Taylynn had, before finding other places that left it humming with pleasure.

"They're extra itchy at this stage," Nushala explained. She held a small purple dragon that squirmed in her arms before tugging on her hair. "They grow so quickly that their scales get stretched to catch up with their frame."

Little talons pawed at her legs and she looked down. Some of the other hatchlings were trying to climb her. They looked up at her with eager eyes. They wanted to be held. Her heart was close to bursting at the sight.

A choked laugh split the air.

When she glanced over, Claire was sitting cross-legged as a swarm of hatchlings gathered around her, each vying for attention, mostly scratches. They pushed their hatch mates out of the way to get closer. "Are you guys going to come help, or what?" Claire called to the others. The males all stood off to the side, observing. Her order brought them forward. Soon, even Talon was grinning, a little red dragon in his arms.

Fright made a humming noise before stepping into the cluster of hatchlings. Immediately, the little things shrieked with excitement and began climbing him as he plopped down on his belly. He merely hummed in annoyance, but something told her he was only doing that for show. His fierce regard tracked each little hatchling with... Was that pride?

"He likes to act like it's insufferable," Taylynn explained, appearing beside her, looking at Fright with an amused expression. "But I think he secretly enjoys being a father figure to them."

"Do they have names?" she wondered.

"Not yet," Taylynn confirmed.

"The mothers will name them at a naming ceremony," Ayla said, holding a small bronze colored dragon, "as is customary for their culture. That usually happens about a full moon cycle after hatching."

"Oh." Leah stroked the dragon in her arms, looking down at it with growing fondness. They weren't pets, but she couldn't help but wish she might bring it with them to the capital. "Why wait? Wouldn't it be easier if they had names now?"

"Because dragons name their offspring after characteristics," Ayla explained. "It helps that they know a little of the hatchling's tendencies before they choose a name for it. Once a hatchling has its name, it will no longer be a hatchling but a juvenile. It will remain so until it reaches mating age. Usually fifteen to twenty years."

"Huh. What kind of names do they pick?"

"Usually descriptors range from positive to negative, from happy to sad. Fright is an example of a fearsome name. Though he has changed from his namesake. Envy, Pride, Fury, Rage, Spite, Torment, might be some negative namesakes. Vigilance was the first drengr king. His was a positive name. Others like Astonishment, Delight, Gladness, Triumph could be positive namesakes as well. Each name tends to influence the dragon into behaving similar to what it's called. The magic of it makes it hard for a dragon to turn away from what they become."

"Huh. I see."

"Those of the Ice Clan often chose darker names," Ayla continued. "But I think Fright will push them away from such a trend, at least for *these* little ones. They will be the dawn of a new clan. One that isn't bloodthirsty. Perhaps names likened to aspiration and hope will help usher in a new way of life."

"That would be good," she found herself saying. She hated the idea of these cute creatures becoming bloodthirsty and destructive. They seemed so innocent. "So, it's all about nurture in this case? Not nature?"

"Some would argue otherwise," Claire said, joining the conversation as she stroked an orange that had climbed into her lap. "But I believe that dragons become what they are encouraged to become. Not all dragons in the days of old were bad. Vigilance and his friends, for example. Some believe it is impossible to change their nature, but these hatchlings are going to prove the world wrong. Aren't you?" She lifted the orange until she nuzzled its face, as if it were a furry puppy, then began speaking to it in gibberish.

"Would you like to see the eggs?" Ayla asked, looking at her.

"Oh, yes!" she breathed. The others looked just as eager.

"Come." Ayla began to lead them away. "But leave the hatchlings. They are still too clumsy. Craving would have a fit if she saw them stamping around her clutch."

They bid goodbye to the little creatures before traipsing after Ayla and Nushala onto a sea of warm sand. It was littered with colorful shell fragments that sparkled up at them. The heat seeping through her feet was delightful after days of walking. It helped to ease the ache. She had half a mind to simply take a seat here in the sand and soak her sore muscles.

Craving was a deep purple color, her scales almost black. She was curled off to the side of a clutch of some twenty eggs. An eyelid peeled open as she regarded them, wariness in her gaze.

"It's the largest clutch, yet. She is very proud—don't get too close," Nushala warned. "Their maternal instincts over unhatched eggs are much more aggressive. Until they hatch, she will guard them day and night."

"Does the color of the egg dictate the color of the dragon inside?" Leah found herself asking.

"It does," Nushala confirmed.

They stood off to the side and watched as Craving got to her feet, shook the sand from her scales, then went around to each egg, nosing it into a different position."

"She rotates them every hour or so, to ensure that they stay warm and that the baby inside gets to rest in different positions."

"It's so...cute," she couldn't help saying aloud. Craving must have heard because she gave a harumph, throwing her a glare before sauntering back over to her resting place. "Cute in a very dignified way, of course!" she amended. But Craving had already closed both eyes. If she had to guess, the protective mother was only pretending to sleep and was very aware of every person standing near her eggs.

"When will they hatch?" Saffra asked, her voice laced with longing. They only planned to stay a few days before moving on.

"Any day now," Ayla said. "You might just get to see it."

Hope burst in her chest. Time was of the essence. Claire and Talon had a throne to reclaim. Yet, she couldn't help wanting to stay as long as it took, to see the hatchlings break free of their shells. Perhaps they would get lucky. Judging by Claire's expression, her best friend felt exactly the same.

# CHAPTER 36

# JOVARI'S STORY

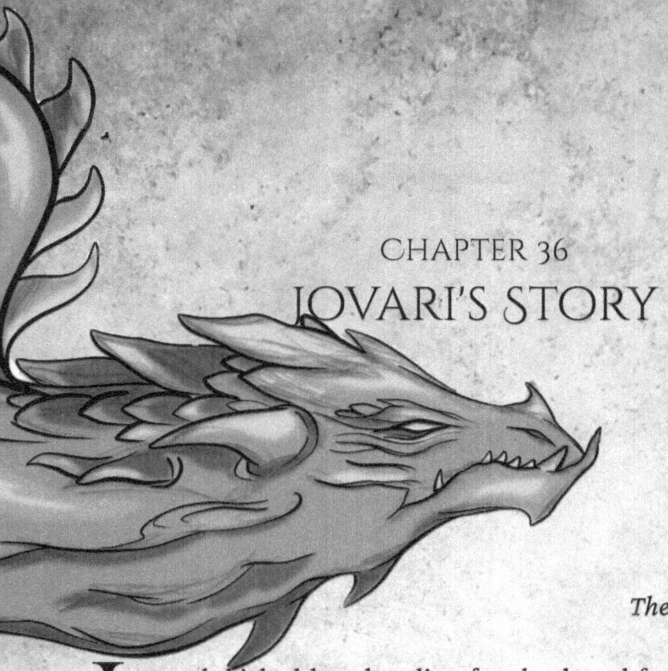

*The Gable Mountains*

Leah kicked her dangling feet back and forth, taking in the giant cavern below. It was hard to believe a place like this existed. Twelve levels below, the hatchlings were mere specks of color, darting about as they gathered around Fright's fresh kill. She could just make out the eggs warming in the sand, guarded by their protective mother.

A flash of movement on the walkway drew her gaze towards Claire and Talon. They emerged hand-in-hand from the room they'd claimed two levels above the hatching ground. With the sheer number of living spaces, there'd been enough for everyone to claim a small cavern to themselves. Naturally, everyone had paired up, except for her and Jovari, who'd each taken separate accommodations.

Accommodations was putting it mildly. The rooms had belonged to dragons long ago, which meant they were sparse in creature comforts. Hers had a stone crater sized perfectly for a curled up dragon body—a bed, no doubt—and nothing else, unless you counted the bones, which she'd promptly cleared out.

They'd stuck to the bottom most levels to remain close.

Anything higher was a hike none of them wanted. Especially since they spent most of their time on the ground floor. It was used mostly for the hatchlings and hatching ground, however they took their meals there, and used it for a gathering place.

"You shouldn't wander off in a place like this." She tensed at the sound of Jovari's voice. Of course he'd found her. Not that she was hiding. She bit her tongue to keep from responding. "Still freezing me out, I see."

"No idea what you're talking about." She kept her tone even and disinterested.

He sank down beside her, dropping his feet over the ledge. A series of high pitched screeches sounded below. She caught sight of a cluster of hatchlings as they argued over a strip of meat. Fright stood by and watched, but didn't step in. There were frequent squabbles like these to establish the pecking order.

"I'm still struggling to wrap my head around it." Jovari followed her gaze.

"What, baby dragons?" When he didn't offer a confirmation, she said, "Not sure why. You yourself can turn into a dragon. If anyone should be surprised, it's me."

"For thousands upon thousands of years, dragons were extinct—or so we believed. When a mated pair has a child, it's born human. Males don't fledge until puberty. Seeing a baby dragon is wholly foreign." He made a fair point. Still, she pressed her lips together, uninterested in carrying on a conversation, let alone spending time in his company. When the silence stretched on too long, he sighed and said, "We shouldn't let one kiss destroy our friendship." She scoffed, trying not to look at him. If she did, her resolve might crumble. "It was wrong of me to kiss you back. I enjoyed it, for what it's worth. But... I just..."

She stole a glance at him, finally giving in. His brows were pulled tight, forming a small wrinkle above his nose. She fought the urge to smooth it with her thumb.

"Look, I don't do attachments. It wouldn't be fair to lead you on. I'm sorry I didn't make that clearer before you...before you honored me with your lips."

She snorted. "As far as rejections go, I think that's the most elegant one I've ever received."

He was right, she was being unfair about this. They'd developed a friendship leading up to the kiss. Yes, she'd felt an underlying attraction the whole time and that had partially spurred things along. Still, it hurt a little, the idea that she would never have him.

"Why don't you do attachments, if you don't mind my asking? Something tells me it's not the whole shield thing."

He'd admitted to being in love once. She hadn't forgotten that glaring detail. Nor the irrational jealousy that had taken root in the pit of her stomach.

He was quiet for a bit. "I suppose you could say I learned the hard way. It was a long time ago."

"How long is long for a drengr?"

He chuckled. "Not long by drengr standards, since I'm still young. About a hundred years, shortly before I joined Talon's ranks as a shield."

"What happened?" She kept her tone soft.

Below them, the hatchlings had finally finished their meal and were contentedly curling up in heaps of tangled limbs and wings for a nap. She couldn't help her smile at the sight.

"I told you I fell in love."

"Yes, you mentioned something about that."

"She was human. I'll spare you the details—"

"Oh, but I love details. Very detail oriented, me."

He huffed. "I do not doubt it. Fine. I courted her. I lived at Fort Edge and she was a farm girl on the outskirts of Northedge. Uncommonly pretty—I know that sounds shallow, but that's what first caught my attention. I was young—*very* young—and thinking with my—" He cleared his throat. "Anyway, I'd been out flying and caught sight of her stretched out on a picnic blanket, napping. She'd admitted that she was skirting her duties, hiding from her mother. I quickly found so much more to love about her than just her looks. She was shy and reserved to those who didn't know her, but once she was comfortable, she had a way of making a person feel special, like the center of her world."

The irrational jealousy was back. She tamped it down, hoping it didn't show in her expression. "What went wrong?"

"Well, we weren't mates. We'd fantasize about it, though. She'd already touched my scales just so that we could be sure. We both fought to hide our disappointment. She wanted to leave me, but I assured her that it didn't change how I felt about her. That we could still be together without a bond. I could still love her fiercely —if anything, more fiercely—because I didn't need a bond to choose her for myself. We tried to make it work. Or at least, I thought we were doing an admirable job of it."

He blew out a breath, bracing his arms behind him so that he could lean back and look up at the cavern's ceiling. His eyes took on a far away look. "Unmated pairs can't conceive children. She was human, but I wasn't thinking about that. I was only thinking about the love we shared and what I could offer her. Turns out, she wanted a family and security more than love. She...she left me. Received a marriage offer from a gentleman in the city. She didn't love him—I know she didn't."

A flash of pain stole over his features. He was recalling the memory as if it had just happened. Without thinking, she reached for his hand and gave it a squeeze. He sat upright and latched on, squeezing back.

"I'm sorry," she whispered.

He released her hand, his expression clearing, then shrugged. "Humans age. They carry instincts just like drengr. The instinct to build a family, to create a circle of security and familiarity." He shrugged. "I didn't wait for a mate after that. I couldn't bear to spend another day in the place we'd fallen in love. I left for the south, joined up with King Talon."

"What was her name?" she found herself asking.

"It doesn't matter." His voice was bitter. "She's been dead for a handful of decades now."

"What was her name, Jovari?"

"Oralyn. Ora—for short."

She swallowed. "Thank you for telling me. It helps me to understand you better—understand why you don't do attachments. You're protecting yourself from experiencing that kind of hurt again."

"I could have married her." He kicked a foot out, letting it swing. "We could have adopted children. There's no law against a drengr doing something like that, though it is encouraged that we take mates. Doesn't matter anymore anyway, because I'm a shield. I can't marry."

She saw an apology lurking in the depths of his gaze. It sent a pang through her chest.

She'd felt many kinds of longing in her life. Longing for a mother who had died far too soon. For a father to be healthy. For a life that felt stolen from her. Now, she felt a different kind of longing. A longing for someone who was inches away, and yet, so far out of reach. A longing for someone she wanted so badly, but couldn't have.

Her eyes welled with tears. She quickly turned away, hiding her face. If Jovari noticed, he was polite about it. He cleared his throat and said, "Please don't alienate me, Leah. I can't stand you freezing me out anymore."

She took a deep, calming breath, blinking back the blur of tears, bringing the cave into focus. It was unfair to punish him, especially when she was the one who'd kissed him. Even more unfair of her to take her feelings out on him. It wasn't like he'd forced her to fall for him.

Her breaths faltered. Was that what this was? Had she really fallen for him?

Her chest squeezed. Surely she wasn't *in love*. No, of course not. She knew better than to be so careless. Especially after losing both her parents.

Still, she felt *something* beyond friendship.

"Leah?" He bumped her shoulder with his. "What do you say? Friends?"

"I can try but..."

"But what?" There was a playful tug on her hair, forcing her to turn back to him.

"I hear you're a bit of a ladies man," she explained. She tried to make it sound like a joke but it fell flat. He blew out a breath, rubbing a hand over his face. Something akin to shame crossed his features, there and gone. It made sense, why he was the way he was, especially after what he'd been through. She couldn't imagine what it would be like. He'd fallen in love, offering Ora everything in his power to give. In the end, she'd chosen someone else because of the one thing he *couldn't* give her.

Regardless, it didn't change how she felt.

"Can I be honest with you?" she asked.

"Always."

"I have feelings for you, Jovari. It just sort of...happened. Something tells me you also might have feelings for me, despite—" She gestured to encompass everything he'd told her. "It might be a little hard to be your friend and not have you, but it would be especially hard to be your friend and see you with other women."

"You won't," he assured her.

Even the mere idea of him flirting made her blood boil. She didn't have the heart to insist that he refrain from his urges altogether. They weren't anything. He didn't owe her that, nor did he make any promise of the sort. But at least knowing she wouldn't have to see him with anyone else helped ease the ache in her chest.

"Thank you."

"So, friends?" He offered her his hand. When she went to reach for it, he grasped her forearm instead. She'd seen this greeting among the drengr. She clenched his in return. They held still for a moment, their eyes locked, so much passing between them.

Was it better to have him as a friend than nothing at all? Or would it be harder?

A shrill warble echoed through the cave. She dropped his arm and they both looked down. Jovari chuckled, then shot to his feet, reaching for her.

"What's happening?" She let him pull her to her feet.

"The eggs." He grinned. "Koldis just informed me that one has started to rock."

"They're hatching?" she breathed.

"I think so. Come, let's hurry."

They left their tense conversation behind, racing down the wide passage leading to the bottom floor. Giant rooms lined the walls as they went lower, flashing by the faster they ran. She'd only explored a few of them, mostly out of boredom.

Claire had been busy the past two days, working hard to master her mage magic. While the hatchlings were the best form of entertainment, they were also exhausting. Hence, why she'd escaped to the upper levels of the cave.

They were the last to arrive. Everyone was gathered a safe distance from the clutch of eggs. Craving's deep purple body was hovering, watching closely as several of the eggs gently rocked from side to side.

The two spriten females stood at the front of their small group, next to a brownish heap. Bile rose in her throat when she saw what it was. "Is that—"

"Dead rats," Koldis explained, coming to stand on Jovari's other side. "Craving spent hours combing the cave's corridors this morning. Rats are perfectly sized for a baby dragon's first meal. Since they're too young to hunt the first several weeks after hatching, their food is presented to them. I'm told they come out of the shell *ravenous*. They might even take your arm off if you try to touch them."

Bedelth chuckled. He stood off to the side with Saffra. "You sure you ladies still want to witness a hatching?"

"Wouldn't miss it for the world," Claire breathed. She stood hand in hand with Talon, eyes fixed on the colorful shells. A splitting crack brought silence. Then another. The fragments of a pearlescent blue shell exploded upward and the first baby dragon crawled free.

# CHAPTER 37
# SUMMONING MAGIC

*The Gable Mountains*

Talon felt a burst of emotion swell in his chest, drowning out the anxiety that had plagued him for days. Beside him, Claire sucked in a breath. The emotion belonged to her, but they were so entwined, that it became his, too. It was hard to feel anything but wonder and love for the little creatures emerging from their shells. Even as they blindly squawked and clawed their way across the sand searching for food.

Craving was there, tossing rats to each of them. The green that emerged snatched its prize and ripped it to shreds before devouring it, making a bloodied mess. He preferred a cleaner approach to death, but it was young.

Then again, if he ever got his hands on Kane, he'd do exactly the same thing. Preferably with more blood. And some screaming too. Yes, he wanted to hear Kane scream, even beg—

"Oh, look at that little lavender one," Leah cooed beside them, pulling him from his dark thoughts. "That one is my new favorite, obviously."

"Because it's your favorite color?" Jovari quipped.

He shot his shield a glare that Jovari didn't notice; he was too busy looking between Leah and the newly emerged creature. His nostrils flared in irritation as he thought back to the conversation they'd shared. Leah and Jovari had been dancing around each other for days. He'd been furious about their shared kiss. Jovari had disobeyed a direct order. So what if Leah was the one who had initiated it? This awkwardness was exactly what he'd feared. Only, now it seemed they had put it behind them. Perhaps because he had warned Jovari that if he didn't fix things between them, there would be consequences. He didn't need Claire's best friend dying of a broken heart.

He'd never had to impose such a rule with Verath and Desaree. Verath wasn't prone to dalliances. Unlike Jovari, he trusted Verath with Desaree's heart. Not to mention, Verath was hundreds of years older and certainly more mature.

"Can I adopt it?" He blinked, coming back to himself. Leah had scooped up the lavender hatchling, oblivious to its bloodied snout and dead rat breath. It cooed as she scratched the ridges around its little baby spikes on the top of its head.

Claire laughed, the sound reminding him of dust motes dancing in light. His body flushed, turning molten. He couldn't help but stare at his mate, watching her take everything in with delight. He'd take the sight of her over baby hatchlings any day. Then again, he'd take the sight of her spread out beneath him, crying his name, over literally anything.

She shot him a look that said she knew *exactly* what he was thinking. Her eyebrow lifted in warning. *"We talked about this."*

*"I'm allowed to have thoughts about my mate,"* he half grumbled.

*"Yes, but not while we're in the middle of important, historic moments."*

*"Bringing you to completion upon my tongue is an important, historic moment."*

*"Gods, Talon."* Their eyes were locked, and he reveled in the sight of the heat that rose to her cheeks. He made it worse by sending her an image of exactly what she'd looked like last night, squirming beneath him. She swore and looked away, trying to distract herself with the sight of the hatchlings.

He huffed, satisfied. Getting her back, restoring her memories and magic, had taken an immense weight off his chest. Especially when he was already drowning in anxiety and guilt. So what if he used every possible opportunity between them to distract himself from the crushing fear that followed him everywhere?

He'd done the one thing no king before him had. He'd lost his kingdom. He'd failed.

Claire's head whipped around, her expression anxious. She glanced between him and the others, then blurted— "We're...uh...I need to practice, to get back to my mage magic." No one appeared to have heard her; they were all so wrapped up in the excitement of the hatchlings.

They didn't notice when she dragged him away. They certainly didn't have any idea of what she intended when she pulled him into their shared chamber and fell to her knees, making quick work of the ties on his pants before taking him. It was her way of distracting him from his dark thoughts. Gods, he didn't deserve her.

He deserved to feel every bit of his failure. To hurt. To suffer—

He sucked in a breath as pleasure zinged up his spine. Then, the only thing he knew was the feel of her hot mouth on him.

"Say it with more dominance," he corrected, watching Claire work another cantrip. They had eventually done what they'd promised, settled down to practice her mage magic. Only after thoroughly getting lost in each other. "Here, like this."

He commanded the staff on the other side of the chamber to fly into his waiting palm. It landed with a snick as it smacked against his flesh. His mate only glared.

"You're getting better, I promise. Much better. Summoning is one of the hardest forms of mage magic. Once you master it, everything else will come easier, I promise."

Claire blew out a breath, rustling the hair that had come loose around her face.

"Try again." He replaced the staff.

*"Do you have a minute?"* Koldis's voice sounded in his mind. Claire heard it and looked up.

*"What is it?"*

*"Taylynn has news. Come and meet us."* Koldis sent him a projection. They were standing in the mouth of the cavern, looking out over the forest.

"Go," Claire said. "I'll keep practicing."

He hesitated, knowing she would be fine, that she needed to work the summoning magic on her own. Wrapping his hand around the back of her neck, he held her in place to steal a kiss, lingering over her lips, enjoying the faint traces of himself on her tongue. A low growl built in his throat.

She pulled back, smirking. "Go, or you'll never pull yourself away."

He huffed. "Careful, mate. I don't take well to commands in the bedroom."

"And what, you're going to toss me onto the bedding and—?"

She squealed as he lifted her into his arms and kissed her again, effectively silencing her mouth. He could think of much better things to do with it anyway. She huffed a breath against him before he set her on her feet.

"I'll be back for you later," he promised, letting her know exactly what he would do. "In the meantime, you'd better master that summoning magic perfectly. I'll be testing you on it, so no slacking."

"Yes, sir," she taunted, her eyes flashing with hunger, even after they'd spent hours tangled up in each other.

When he finally emerged into the cavern's opening, Koldis smirked. "Get lost?"

"Something like that." Two of the three had mates now, so it wasn't like they didn't know. "Lots of passages and rooms. It's a big place to get lost in, you know?"

"Right." Koldis snorted.

The four of them stood at the mouth of the cave overlooking the forest, which sloped down around them. The entrance was located at the midpoint of a hill, which allowed the forest to hide it. But the view was still impressive.

"So? What did you call me out here for?" He looked around. "Where's Taylynn?"

"Off doing whatever sprite princesses do." Bedelth huffed, which earned him a mock glare from Koldis.

"One of Tasar's spies found us—"

"The operative you sent to the capital?" They hadn't gone into great detail about the male who headed the *delles*, a mysterious spriten unit of spies and assassins. But he'd heard enough when first learning about the fate of his precious city.

"Yes. He sent a message. They've found an entrance into the capital from outside the city walls."

He swore under his breath. While it would work in their favor, he didn't like the idea that someone could get in and out of the city without traveling past the guards manning the entry and exit points. The walls were there for a reason.

"Never thought I'd be forced to enter my own city like a miscreant," he said.

"None of us did." Bedelth's expression was somber.

"There are passages below that will take us straight to the cave beneath the keep. From there, we can reunite with our operatives within the city."

He rubbed a hand over his face, trying not to let the gravity of what came next sweep him under. They'd spent plenty of time scheming and planning. At the end of the day, it didn't matter how they took the kingdom back. It wouldn't fix the damage Kane had already done. The lives lost. The people he'd hurt.

Bedelth must have sensed his thoughts because he said, "Forgive us, Your Majesty. Had we not left, perhaps this wouldn't have happened. We truly thought going after the stones was the best course of action."

"I don't blame you," he said at last, even though he was tempted. It was easier to rail at them, to explode with anger and pin this on someone other than himself. He'd done that before, plenty.

Claire's presence surged in his mind. He could feel her quickly shuffling through the conversation. A wave of calm washed over him.

He'd blamed her, once. Cyrus's death had been unbearable. It had been easier to take his anger out on her.

*"You aren't the same as you were then,"* she reminded him.

He wanted to argue. To tell her he was no better then than he was now. Except, perhaps she was right. Her presence steadied him. He didn't lose his temper as often, especially not when she was with him as she was now.

*"You're supposed to be practicing,"* he teased, trying to lighten the mood.

*"I am."* She sent him a projection that showed a successful summoning. Her staff flew across their quarters and right into her hand.

Pride swelled in his chest. There was nothing his mate couldn't conquer, so long as she put her mind to it. Even the things that were seemingly too difficult, she'd managed to overcome.

*"Only because I had you to help."*

*"I am confident you would shine bright even without my help."*

"Gods, surely we won't be that lovesick with our mates," Koldis was saying.

He blinked, realizing he'd missed an entire chunk of conversation. "I have a feeling you'll be worse," he growled. Then, "Claire's mage magic is progressing. We ought to move forward with our plans. There's not much more training I can give her."

"You wish to leave sooner than later?" Bedelth's gaze was calculating. "If we depart tomorrow, we can reach Kastali Dun in four days, perhaps five, since we will need to stop for the ladies."

"They can sleep while we fly," he said. "It isn't as if we need to arrive rested. We won't be going straight into battle."

"The sooner we fix this, the better. If our queen is ready, then we ought to depart," Koldis agreed. "There are eight of us. We can fly fast and make good time."

Jovari stiffened. "I suppose I'll be flying with Leah."

"If you can manage to keep your hands to yourself," he huffed. "What is going on with you two? Did you smooth things over?"

"To a point." Jovari shrugged. "Don't fret. You don't have to worry about me toying with her and breaking her heart. We agreed to be friends, nothing else. No more awkward moments and all that." He kept his voice even, but he failed to hide the bitterness lurking in his eyes. It was surprising, given that Jovari had never been interested in more than bedding and forgetting the partners in his past.

"Thank the gods for that," Koldis muttered. Jovari all but snarled, rounding on Koldis, who held up his hands. "Just saying. Things have been tense between you two and it's been bleeding into everything else."

Jovari lunged—

"Enough, both of you." He pinched the bridge of his nose. Jovari and Koldis glared at each other. They had always been prone to bickering. Yes, they were best friends. Yes, they spent an inordinate amount of time together, but that also meant they easily went for each other's throats, too. "Claire flies with me from now on." He imparted Jovari with a knowing look. He didn't hold it against him, but it had been extremely difficult to see his mate fly with another when she could have flown with him. Now that she had her mind and magic back, she had no excuse to avoid him.

A rush of warmth filled him at the thought of flying with her. She returned it, sending a mental caress that had him dying to return to her. She was just as excited.

He cleared his throat. "That leaves Leah with you, Jovari. Be honorable about it, and don't make it into something it's not. Friends is acceptable, lovers is not. Saffra will fly with Bedelth. Taylynn with Koldis. We should make good time."

The others gave their consent.

"We leave at dawn."

Without another word, he retreated into the darkness of the entrance, striding purposefully down the corridor leading to the giant cavern. His mate had conquered summoning magic in his absence, and he had every intention of rewarding her in the best way possible.

CHAPTER 38

# A MISSIVE

*Kastali Dun*

Merrian heard the snick just as a folded sheet of parchment appeared from beneath the door. Reyr startled awake, blinking. He looked dazed but didn't notice what had woken him. She hesitated before rushing to retrieve the message. With a single cantrip, her mage light flared to read the contents. A gasp fell from her lips.

"Read it aloud, won't you?" Her gaze jumped to Reyr. He didn't bother to get up. After months, she found him sleeping more frequently. It was easy to become depressed in a place like this. With everything weighing on him, she understood.

Reading the note word for word, she said, "The king and queen have returned to Dragonwall." Ryer sucked in a breath. "Too dangerous to visit in person. Will send word when we know more. Feowen." She crushed the note in her fist, clinging to it like a lifeline.

Reyr stood. "Let me see that."

He read it over, his eyes darting across the short missive several times. His breath came faster and faster. She spotted a sheen of

332

moisture in the reflection of his eyes when they caught in the mage light.

"This is good, right?" she asked, then wanted to kick herself for failing to think of something better to say. "Now that they're back, they can fix this."

Reyr was still breathing hard. He clenched the note and began to pace. At last, he went to the wall and slid down it.

"Reyr?"

He put his head in his hands. She couldn't blame him for being overwhelmed. His shoulders began to shake. Was he...laughing?

"Reyr?" she asked again, concerned. A strangled sound wrenched from him. No, he wasn't laughing. She rushed to him, crouching beside him.

"Oh, gods," she breathed. "It's all right." But it wasn't.

He began to sob in earnest as she pulled him into her arms. In that moment, she forgot everything she'd ever disliked about him. After so many months together, he had mended some of his transgressions in the form of apologies, but she'd never truly forgiven him. Not until now. Seeing him like this, vulnerable before her.

His arms snaked around her waist, his face buried against her chest. His sobs were silent, but she felt each one loudly through every tremor of his muscles. She clung to him and he to her. "Shhh..." she cooed. "Shhh. I've got you."

She began to rock him, combing her fingers through his dirty, matted hair. Their baths were seldom. Feowen and the others visited less and less oven over the months they'd been stuck down here. Nearly a year had passed since the king's departure and now he was finally back. He'd rescued the queen. They had returned to the kingdom.

"He'll never...never....forgive me," Reyr managed. "I don't... deserve it."

"Stop that. Of course he will. You did splendidly—until everything with Kane, of course." That only made him sputter. "Besides, *I* have forgiven you, for how you treated me. So I'm sure he will do the same."

There was a long pause. Reyr lifted his head to look at her, eyes red and inflamed. His arms remained firmly in place. "You have?"

Seeing his broken expression cracked something open in her chest. "Oh, Reyr," she breathed. He looked at her with such hope that she couldn't help but reach forward and wipe at the tears staining his cheeks.

Reyr was one of the most powerful drengr in the kingdom, but here he was overcome with grief. She didn't imagine the king's shields cried often, if ever. "I forgive you," she said, because she knew he needed to hear the words, if only to have one less weight hanging over him. "King Talon will, too."

"Thank you," he managed. His throat bobbed.

"Come here," she murmured, pulling him close again. He complied, though his body no longer shook. She merely held him, stroking his hair.

A fierce protectiveness flared in her chest. She didn't want him to hurt—she might have once, but not now. Her arms tightened around him. She rather liked having him like this. Maybe he did, too, because his crying had stopped but he hadn't pulled away. She squashed the thought as quickly as it came. He was upset. Now was not the time to think about the feel of him clinging to her.

Besides, he was a king's shield and she was...she was no one. Months ago, she'd hated him. There was no way she'd let her feelings run wild, so she pushed them down and locked them away.

"What do you think will happen now?" she wondered, trying to distract herself from the feel of him.

He exhaled but didn't pull away, so she continued to stroke his hair, pulling gently at the tangles to comb them. "I want to believe that they will fix this, that everything will be all right in the end. But..."

"But?"

"But Kane has all five dragonstones. I don't see how they can work around that kind of leverage without a great sacrifice. Talon loves his kingdom but he won't risk turning to stone, turning all his drengr to stone. What if Claire can't turn us back? What if she does but we lose ourselves in the process? What if we're stuck as dragons after that, like the first who turned from stone? There are too many *what ifs*."

"True. But if anyone can fix this, it's them."

Reyr huffed. "Talon is an exceptional king. Claire, an exceptional queen. I want to believe you.  I just wish... It never should have come to this. They're here to clean up the mess I made. Had I been more observant, I might have known Kane was coming to the capital, might have noticed the Osheans arriving with him. Talon trusted me to hold his kingdom together and I did a poor job of it."

"Stop. That's enough." She gave his hair a gentle tug. "You did the best you could. You did an excellent job, as a matter of fact. I don't think many could have put up with the rigors of the position for as long as you did. Nearly eight months, Reyr. That is no simple feat."

He scoffed. "Yes, but I could have done better. I could have treated you better, for a start."

"Yes, true."

"I really am sorry," he croaked. "So godsdamned sorry. You didn't deserve that. You didn't deserve any of this—"

"Enough." She pulled him up, cradling his face in her palms. "You've already apologized and I've already forgiven you. What's done is done. Just because you made mistakes with me doesn't mean you were a poor ruler. Nor does it mean Talon won't forgive you. Thinking like this only adds to your burdens. Put it from your mind, yes?"

His eyes darted between hers, searching. His throat bobbed. "You're right," he said at last, his tongue darting out to wet his parched lips. She followed the action without realizing it then looked away. He exhaled, then repositioned himself to sit beside her.

Part of her wanted to cry out at the loss of him. The other part silently chided herself for letting him affect her. "Let's think of something better," she decided. "Now that it looks like we might survive this, we might even be free of this cell, let's think of what we'll do once we are."

He huffed. "All right. What will you do?"

"Me?" She hesitated, but she didn't need to think over the answer. She'd already fantasized about it many times. "The first thing I'll do is check in on all the poor houses, shelters, and orphanages in the city. Gods only know what Kane has done in our absence. I'll make sure they are taken care of. Then, I think I'd like to travel. This city isn't the only one housing the less fortunate. I've always wanted to see more of the kingdom. Maybe I'll travel to all the big cities and help where I can—"

"I'll come with you."

"What?" She jerked to look at him, sending a sharp pain up her spine. "What are you talking about?"

"I'll come with you. I'll help you. We can establish better funding for those in need. The gods only know Talon's coffers are large enough for it. There are approvals and such, signatures and documents and all the rigamarole that comes with diverting funds, but I can manage that. Then we can set out together and..." He frowned. "Why are you glaring at me like that?"

"This isn't a daydream, Reyr. This is actually what I plan to do when—*if*—we get out of here."

"I'm aware. I'm not making light of it."

"You're serious?"

"Of course I'm serious," he scoffed. "If you think I'd let you run off on your own to do something like this, then you are seriously mistaken."

"I'm not a queen. I don't need a babysitter."

He chuckled. "No, I'm sure you don't, but you are one of us now whether you like it or not, and we protect our own."

She blinked. Something warm filled her belly. Was *that* what this was about? She chewed on the inside of her cheek. Part of her had hoped that maybe he wanted to come because he wanted... well...never mind. It didn't matter. She knew enough about the hardship of life to never decline the offer of charity. If he was willing to do this for her—for the people who needed it—she would gladly take it.

"All right. But just so you know, I'm not exactly keen to be one of you, knowing all it entails." She gestured at the cell around them.

Reyr laughed. The sound made her chest feel lighter. She couldn't remember the last time she'd heard him laugh, if ever. "No, I cannot say we're making the best impression. But I promise you, things will get better. It's not always like this, working for the king. Assuming we get out of here, that is."

"We will," she said, because she needed to believe it. She hesitated. "What about you? I've said what I want to do when we're free. What about you?"

"Aside from coming with you on a tour of the kingdom?" She nodded, but refused to let herself believe he'd actually come with her when the time came. "I plan to hug everyone I hold dear. After being stuck in here, you realize how much you take for granted."

"Maybe hug them *after* a bath, though?"

He laughed again. "Yes, definitely after a bath. No, actually, before *and* after. And then, I think I just want to spend time with them. My shield brothers, the girls, Claire and Talon. I'd be happy simply to sit in the same room with them and just...exist."

"That sounds nice," she mused.

"You'll be there too, of course."

"Oh?" She lifted a brow, her voice teasing.

"Oh yes. I'm not letting you out of my sight once we get out of here." His words made her skin feel stretched tight. "Something tells me if I do, you'll run as far and as fast as possible."

He wasn't wrong. She had an urge to flee from him, from his inner circle. To never look back. And yet...

"She'll want to meet you, you know."

"Who? Claire?"

"Claire. She'd be devastated if you ran before she could. I'd have to drag you back, kicking and screaming," he teased.

"You'd have to find me first."

His eyes locked on hers and a shiver raced down her spine. "I'd find you."

She felt those words deep in her bones. He would. If he truly wanted to, there wasn't a single place in this world she could hide.

Especially not when he was looking at her like he was now. Like she was something...precious.

Oh, gods. She turned away, hoping he didn't see the heat in her cheeks. "Where should we travel first on our tour of the kingdom?"

"Oh." A long pause. "How about north? We could go east from there, then south, perhaps through the forest, to Esterpine, if you'd like—"

"Esterpine?!" she sputtered. "I highly doubt the sprites have need of my mediocre healing abilities. Not when they all do a far better job of it."

"No, but you'd like to see it, wouldn't you?"

"Outsiders aren't permitted."

He scoffed. "They are when they're friends with the spriten queen."

"Right." She hadn't considered that bit. She let the thought take hold. The idea of visiting the famed spriten city of Esterpine, a place few outsiders had ever seen. "I think I'd like that very much."

"Good." Reyr sounded smug.

They continued to fantasize over all the places they'd visit. He told her about the cities he'd been to and the ones he hadn't. They talked about the funds they might set aside, and how they would spend them. With every word, their cell felt a little less bleak. For the first time in months, it was the brightest it had ever been. Freedom might be possible, after all.

# CHAPTER 39
## A FATED SURPRISE

*The Gable Mountains*

Leah blinked against the morning light, shouldering her pack. Just a few more days and they'd reach the capital. "You can tie that to my harness once I'm in form," Jovari said, striding by. He didn't stop to look at her. She watched him seek out Talon, speaking to the king in low tones. His gaze darted in her direction, then quickly away again.

She frowned. Things were better between them. Sort of.

Whatever the king said made Jovari huff and stomp off. Was he trying to get out of flying with her? To be fair, she was apprehensive about it too. It meant they'd be closer than ever. She'd be *touching* him. For days.

"I'm fighting the urge to run back inside." Claire came to a stop beside her, shouldering her own pack. "I'm not ready."

Leah reached for her hand. "Aren't queens supposed to be fearless?"

Claire scoffed. "I'm not. Never have been."

"Well then, let's go back inside. I'm not all that eager to fly with a certain someone, and you're not ready to return to the capital. Might as well slink back into the safety of the cavern."

"Gods, that sounds so tempting."

"Not having second thoughts, are we?" Saffra came up beside them. "Because if so, I vote for more baby dragons."

The three of them laughed. That was definitely a better alternative than facing Kane, not that Claire would face him immediately, or alone. They would meet with the operatives in hiding, first.

Around them, the drengr began to transform. She homed in on Jovari's blue form and sighed, her shoulders dropping. Best to just suck it up and accept it. This would be her life for the next few days, then she could get far, far away from him and merely pretend to be friends. She wasn't actually going to survive being *real* friends. Better to be amicable acquaintances.

It was summer, and though it was early morning, the sun was well above the horizon. It had taken longer than expected to say goodbye to the baby dragons. Irelia was staying. She'd worked with Claire over the past few days to better control her ability to hear the dragons speaking—because apparently that was a thing, and everyone had all these magical abilities, and she didn't.

She took a deep, steadying breath. She didn't need to be special. She just needed to be herself. She just needed to be strong and get through the next few weeks, then she could start fresh, no strings attached. Plenty of people were normal. Plenty of people *longed* to be normal, she reminded herself.

"Well, I guess we'd better get going," Claire said, giving Leah's hand a final squeeze before walking over to Talon. She nuzzled Talon's forearm with her face before climbing up to secure her pack.

"Talk to you soon," Saffra said, walking off to do the same. Taylynn and Koldis were already settled and waiting.

"Right," she muttered, going over to Jovari. She slung her pack off her shoulder. She'd done this plenty now, though she'd always flown with Talon.

"Let's get this over with, yeah?" she meant to sound teasing but it came out slightly scoffing.

Jovari snorted, narrowing his eyes.

She stopped in front of him to regard him, then went to his proffered foreleg, gripping the strap of her pack. She reached for him and felt the warmth of his scales—

And everything disappeared.

No. That wasn't quite right. She blinked. Suddenly her feet were sinking into soft sand. She frowned. What the...?!

*"No."*

*"Jovari?"* She spun at the sound of his voice, finding only waves. The ocean lapped at the shore, vast and unrelenting.

*"No. It's not possible. Can't be. This is some kind of joke."*

*"What's not—?"*

Something, some invisible force, pushed her backwards. When she blinked again, she was staggering away from the dragon in front of her. Her foot caught on a root. She dropped her pack, arms cartwheeling, and fell on her rump. There was a growl, and then Jovari sprang from the forest floor, catapulting into the air. He cleared the treetops, beating his wings in a strong downward sweep that had forest debris swirling around her.

"Wait! What the hell?!" she shouted up at him. "What was that for, asshole?!"

But he had already disappeared.

"Leah?" Claire dismounted and rushed over. "What's going on? Did you say something to him?"

"Why would you think *I* said something? That it's *my* fault?"

"Because...he can't exactly form words with his dragon tongue?"

"Oh. Right. No. He just... He just left. I don't... I don't understand. There was a beach and the ocean..." She frowned.

"Oh. Oh, gods." Something shifted in Claire's expression. "What *exactly* happened when you touched him?"

"What do you mean?"

"When you touched Jovari's scales just now, what happened? You said there was a beach and the ocean."

Leah glanced around, trying to make sense of it herself. Talon was crouched nearby, his keen eyes boring into her. Koldis and

Taylynn were patiently waiting. Saffra stood next to Bedelth, her pack secured.

"I..." She rubbed a hand over her hair, pulling out a few pine needles. "I don't know. I touched him and then I was standing on a beach? But that doesn't make sense. I imagined it, obviously. I thought Jovari was there because he kept saying no, or something about it not being possible? I'm not quite sure. Then he pushed me, I think, because I tripped and fell. Why would he do that?"

"Oh, gods," Claire said again, her lips parted in shock.

"I don't get why you're making this a big deal. Obviously he's in a mood. He clearly didn't want to fly with me. I saw him talking to Talon just a few minutes ago. He didn't look happy."

"Do you think...?"

"Do I think *what*?" she snapped. But Claire was facing Talon, some kind of silent conversation passing between them.

Taylynn dismounted, then strode past them and said, "Well, this will take a while." There was a smug smile on her face before she retreated back into the caves. Like she knew something, whatever that something was.

Claire blew out a breath, turning back to her. Talon sprang into the air.

"Where is he going?" she demanded, her confusion and irritation growing by the moment.

"To speak with Jovari. Well, to track him down first."

"Can't he just speak with him from right here? Or summon him back? We're wasting time."

"Jovari has closed his mind. Looks like he's taking the revelation harder than I would have expected."

"What revelation?" She glanced around at the others. Her voice was a loud demand as she said, "Can someone please tell me what's going on because you clearly know something I don't!"

A laugh burst from Claire's chest. "Gods, I hate that I'm the one who's going to break this to you. It should be him. The two of you are supposed to navigate this together. But..."

"But *what*?" She climbed to her feet, leaving her pack behind.

Saffra quickly mounted and said, "We're going flying. Be back in a bit!" They wasted no time in taking off. Koldis sprang into the air after them. Suddenly, she and Claire were the only ones left.

Concern made her stomach squirm. "Okay, now I really want to know what's going on."

"We should probably sit down for this. Come on." Claire dragged her to a boulder near the cave's opening, pulling her down.

"You're starting to scare me. What the hell? Is something wrong with Jovari?"

"Nope. No. Just...well..." Claire blew out a breath. "You're mates."

Leah stared at her. "I'm sorry, but what?"

"You're mates."

This time, a laugh burst from her chest. Once she started, she couldn't stop. She hopped off the boulder, then doubled over, bracing her hands on her knees. She sounded deranged. When she could finally speak, she said. "That's funny. Really funny. Ha ha."

"I'm not joking about this. I wouldn't joke about something like this. That would be cruel."

Leah froze, her arms going slack. The corners of her vision sparked with light, dancing with stars. She doubled over again, taking a deep breath. "I think I'm going to pass out."

Claire hopped off the boulder to rub her back. "You're fine. Just...deep breaths."

She managed a few, then stood. "We can't be mates. I don't even..."

"What do you mean you *can't be*? Of course you can be. You are—obviously. That's the only reason he reacted like this. Now, tell me exactly what happened. Don't leave anything out."

"Fine. If that's what it takes to make you understand."

Because they weren't mates. Claire would see that soon enough. Why should they be? Things like this didn't happen to her. Never her. Things like this only happened to *other* people. She always watched from the sidelines.

She sat down again. "I touched his scales. They were warm, like scales always are. That was the last thought I had before I blinked and found myself on a beach? But obviously that's impossible. But I felt my feet sink into the sand. It seemed real. The waves were lapping at the shore. I heard Jovari's voice—"

"What did he say?"

"Uhm. He just said, 'No.' That was it. So I called for him, because obviously standing on the beach and hearing his voice but not seeing him is weird. Then again, standing on the beach in the middle of nowhere when I'm technically in the forest is already weird."

"What happened next?"

"He started saying that it couldn't be possible, that it was some kind of joke—"

"He was having trouble believing you're mates."

"Well, obviously, because we're not."

Claire huffed. "Oh, you very much are. What came after that?"

"Well, he pushed me, I think. I don't know. I stumbled backwards and was in the forest and tripped. You know the rest."

"You broke contact with his scales," Claire murmured. "That's what happens when you make contact with your mate for the first time. Your minds connect. Your brain makes sense of it in the best way it knows how."

"So when you touched Talon's scales, you were transported to the beach?"

"A lava field, actually. And sometimes I still see it depending on how my mind puts together the pieces."

"A…a lava field? Then why was I at the beach? See, not mates."

"Oh, you very much are. It's different for everyone. I asked Saffra. She saw the rolling hills of her home."

"Okay, then what about for Koldis and Taylynn?"

"The forest."

"Hmm. That seems fitting, actually." She let herself consider the truth of it. "Let's say— hypothetically speaking—that you're right, that we're mates. Why did he fly off like that? Shouldn't he be happy?"

"I ran off when I discovered my mate bond with Talon."

"You didn't!"

"I did. But mostly it was because I was mad at him for hiding it from me. And anyway, he came after me."

Leah scoffed, glancing up at the sky. "Well, I can't exactly go after him. Besides, that doesn't explain why he wanted to run away in the first place."

Claire frowned. "Talon just found him. They're talking."

"And?" A sour taste filled her mouth. "Is it because he…he doesn't want me?"

That had to be it. If he'd wanted her, he wouldn't have run off. Why would he want to risk more heartbreak after what he'd been through? Except, this was different. Before, Ora hadn't been his mate. But apparently, *she* was.

"It sounds like he's…afraid," Claire said.

"Afraid? Of what? I can't exactly run off and marry a rich noble when we're mates." She covered her mouth, realizing she'd accidentally spilled a little of Jovari's secrets, but Claire wasn't even paying attention. Her eyes were unfocused, obviously deep in Talon's mind.

"He thinks you won't want him…permanently, that is."

"That's ridiculous."

Wasn't it? *Did* she want him? Like, really want him? Forever? The enormity of it barreled into her. Being mates wasn't a temporary thing. It wasn't courting. This wasn't like trying on a garment for size. This was permanent.

"Well?" Claire studied her. "Since we're talking hypotheticals here, do you want him?"

She hesitated. "Everyone I ever loved died. What's to stop that from happening if I let myself fall in love with him?"

"I'm not dead," Claire pointed out. "Unless you're saying you don't actually love me."

"Don't be absurd. You know I love you."

"Got it. Scared, then. Funny—you're both scared. Well then, I'm sure the two of you will work it out. Talon—" She said the rest of her words silently, switching into conversation with her mate.

"Right, work it out. Look, there's no need for our problems to hijack this whole operation. Tell Jovari to come back. Tell him he has nothing to worry about. Since it's clear he doesn't want this thing between us, I'll happily honor his decision."

Claire's eyes came into focus and she snorted. "I'm not even going to dissect all the bullshit you just gave me." Leah's lips parted. "Just know that I'm here for you. Tell me what you need."

"What I need is to not be the center of drama. We should get going. I don't want to be the one holding everything up."

"Oh, believe me, you're not. Jovari is the one who started this. Anyway, Talon is commanding him to return. They should be here shortly."

"Great..."

Claire exhaled. "Look, if you're not ready to face this, there are ways you can avoid it."

"Really?"

"Gloves, for one. I think Saffra still has a pair. It will allow you to fly with him without touching him. It's the skin to scale contact that creates the connection."

"Good. Excellent. I'll take the gloves—"

"Actually, I have a pair," said a voice from behind them. Taylynn strode into view. "Here. I got these for you. They're extras. I don't wear them anymore."

"Thanks," she muttered, taking the proffered gloves and examining them. They were soft, made from some kind of fleece. They'd be warm as hell in the summer, but the sky was much colder, and it was better than being in Jovari's head.

She heard the wingbeats before seeing them. Koldis returned, Bedelth and Saffra on his tail. Then Talon. Finally, her eyes locked on Jovari's glittering blue form. None of them transformed, and she felt a pang of frustration over that.

Then again, it was better this way. Otherwise they'd have to talk. And who knew how long *that* would take.

Jovari watched her out of the corner of his eye, but didn't bother turning his head to acknowledge her existence. So much for mending the bridge between them. Now there was a new chasm of...whatever. Her chest gave a painful squeeze.

Fine. If that's how he was going to be. She marched over to him and climbed up his forearm. She attached her pack, then settled into the harness on his back.

"Ready?" Claire called, mostly for her benefit since all the others could communicate.

She nodded, but said nothing as Jovari launched them into the sky.

# CHAPTER 40
## WEARY TRAVELERS

*Southern Sky*

Claire pressed her cheek to Talon's scales and sighed. Below them, the mountainous region gave way to wide open grasslands ideal for hunting grazers. *"I missed this,"* she sighed.

*"I missed it more."* Talon's words made her smile. *"It wasn't easy watching you fly with Jovari."*

*"Jealousy doesn't suit you, my king."*

*"I have nothing to be jealous of,"* he growled, but his tone revealed the lie for what it was.

She was his, and he was hers, but that didn't eliminate his possessiveness. He was a dragon at heart, and she was his most precious jewel. Dragons hoarded treasure as greedily as goblins.

She pressed her lips to his glassy scales. The muscles in his neck rippled. She did it again and he twitched with pleasure. She'd never kissed him in his dragon form. She'd nuzzled and cuddled against him but...

A wicked thought came to mind and she ran her tongue over him.

*"Stop that,"* he growled, growing immediately eager. *"I can't focus with your mouth on me."*

*"As if you need to focus on anything but flapping your wings, beast that you are,"* she teased.

This time his growl was louder, catching the attention of the others.

*"All is well, Your Majesty?"* Bedelth asked.

*"Fine,"* he snapped.

She suppressed a giggle and rested herself against him. It was so easy, riling him up.

*"As if you're any different,"* he huffed.

That made her grin. He was right. All it took was a single touch from him to set her on fire. Gods, she wished they could have stayed at the hatching cave longer. The next four days would be trying. Whatever came after would be even harder. There would be few, if any, stolen moments with Talon from here on out. Not until they reclaimed their kingdom.

The others were in the sky, flying in formation around them. She glanced over and caught sight of Leah. She gave her a wave and Leah returned it with a gloved hand.

*"I still can't believe it,"* she mused. *"Mates. Of all the people in the world, and they're mates. What if she hadn't come with us? What if Kane hadn't sent me back?"*

*"Then we'd still have the kingdom and would not be in this mess."*

*"Oh, come on. Aren't you just a little glad things worked out like they did?"*

*"Stop."* His temper flared, shutting down her playful mood.

*"I'm sorry,"* she said, needled with guilt. *"I didn't mean to make light of it. You know how important our kingdom is to me. I just..."*

*"You are happy for your friend. I understand this. A part of me is happy too, but our kingdom takes precedence. It is more important than anything."*

*"More important than chasing your queen into another world?"*
Her attempt to lighten the mood failed.

*"You are my queen,"* he said with the utmost seriousness. *"You*

*belong to me, but you also belong to this kingdom. You are this kingdom, in a way. Therefore, you are as important—more important."*

"I love you."

"And I you, mih cralla."

*"Show me again,"* she said, wanting to witness what had happened a little while ago between him and Jovari. He sighed. She could have pressed herself into his memory and done it herself, but it was always easier when he fed them to her.

She watched through his mind as he landed beside Jovari and transformed.

"Jovari, wait," Talon commanded, putting a hand on his shield's shoulder before he could stalk off into the woods. "Talk to me."

Jovari's jaw flexed. "You told me to stay away from her. That I would break her heart. All this time and she's been my mate."

"How was I to know?" Talon demanded. "How were any of us to know?"

Jovari blew out a breath. "Does this change things? Or am I still to keep my hands off her."

"Belligerence doesn't suit you." Were it anyone else, he wouldn't tolerate such a tone.

He and Jovari had grown closer these past few weeks. It was hard to believe that he could get closer than he already was to any of his shields. But Jovari was the youngest—or, had been until Dallin. Traveling to Claire's world had been good for them.

Jovari's shoulders slumped and he found a place to sit, his back against a tree. Talon joined him. "I'll tell you the same thing I told Bedelth and Koldis. Times change. I don't want to keep you from your mate. I would like to keep you as my shield. You already know of my plans to amend the law. Is this what you want?"

Jovari picked up a twig and began breaking it into pieces. He tossed them away. "I don't know."

"Well, that's a first. Too worried about settling down with one female?"

"No," he scoffed.

"Then what?"

Jovari hesitated. "I'm not interested in getting my heart broken again."

"Ah."

"The last human I loved was rather good at it," he added. "Breaking my heart, I mean."

Talon hummed. "You think she will reject you? Wasn't she the one who kissed you first?"

"I suppose, yes."

"You do realize that fighting a mate bond is nearly impossible. It can be done, but with her living in the capital, you'd have to put distance between you. You'd have to leave and wait it out. Even then..."

"I know." He tossed another broken piece of twig away. "I should be rejoicing. I want her. I want her more than I've ever wanted anyone or anything. More than Ora, even."

Ora must have been the human that had broken his heart.

"Then what is the problem?"

"She's human. She is unfamiliar with our ways. I bet if she understood what it means to be tied to someone forever, she'd run in the opposite direction."

"Just because someone you loved once rejected you, doesn't mean Leah will."

"I'm being a coward, I know. You can just say it."

"Okay. You're being a coward." Jovari glared at him. "What? You asked for it." Jovari huffed and Talon fought a grin as he added, "You know, you should be thanking Claire for dropping into my life. I don't think I'd be half as tolerant, otherwise."

At this, Claire smiled. *"Not even a fourth,"* she told him and he chuckled.

"Going through the mate experience has softened you," Jovari agreed. "Suppose I will thank her, but maybe once this is all over."

"So what's your plan then?" Talon asked.

"I don't have one."

"Sounds like you need some time to think. Fortunately we have four days of flying ahead of us."

"I don't want her in my head while I'm thinking about this."

"Ah. Not a problem." Talon saw at that moment that the girls had procured a pair of gloves for Leah. "Her skin will be covered. Now, as much as I'd like to delay, we have a kingdom to reclaim. Are you with me?"

"Always, my king."

"Good. Then let's get back." He stood and offered his shield a hand. Jovari took it, letting Talon pull him up. Most days, his shields were the ones talking *him* off a cliff. But occasionally, during times like these, he was the one doing the talking. It felt good to offer support to those who supported him so selflessly.

Claire extracted herself from the memory and sighed. She had confidence that Jovari would get past his fear. That Leah would, too. This was new and scary for both of them. They'd come around.

*"They'll have to come around after we take care of more pressing matters,"* Talon said. Because they had a kingdom to reclaim.

The rest of the day passed at a snail's pace. They stopped only to stretch their legs and relieve their bladders. None of the drengr transformed—there was no need. When the girls were tired, they slept in the sky. Leah wore a face covering to keep from touching Jovari's scales.

Claire wanted to talk to her again, but there wasn't ever time.

One day blurred into two and then three. They passed a few settlements but didn't dare land. It wasn't until the evening of the fourth day that they located the small woodland outside Kastali Dun. The city was still too far to spot on the horizon.

It was here that the drengr transformed. She all but laughed with glee when she saw Talon's face for the first time in days. She pressed his cheeks between her hands and gave him a sloppy kiss. "Missed me, have you?"

"I missed kissing you," she said. "Obviously."

He nuzzled her and pulled her in for another, this time setting their pace.

"Ack. Get a room, you two," Koldis muttered, as if she hadn't spied him kissing Taylynn in much the same way only moments ago.

"Lu'ah faah likah!" a voice called, making them freeze. *It's about time.*

Talon pulled away and spun around, drawing his sverak. "Sig ayasah," he commanded. *Show yourself.* He'd switched languages without realizing it.

A shadow detached from the trees and she blinked.

"Ah, that would be Tasar," Koldis said, putting a hand on Talon's arm, lowering his weapon. She relaxed. This was the spriten spy they were supposed to meet, the head of the *Eastern Ghost Unit*, a force she never knew existed, which was something she intended to discuss with Feowen when she got the chance.

"Tasar," Taylynn said, striding forward unruffled. "Nua bual-ta." *Well met.*

"Sanleeh, Sarihon," he said.

"Were you waiting long?" she asked, switching languages so the others would understand.

"Ni."

"Good." Taylynn stepped aside and Tasar's eyes fell upon Claire.

She took this as her cue and strode forward, shoulders back, chin held high. "Nua bualta, Tasar."

He stared at her, his expression unreadable, then dropped into a low bow. His voice was gruff as he said, "Nua bualta, Ayas Drol-laya. Mekvelli an barah nin an morviah sinahaya." *Well met, Your Majesty. May the peace of the forest be upon you.*

"Edah sinahaya." She gave the customary response. "Luae," she added, bidding him to rise.

They regarded one another.

"We have a kingdom to reclaim. I am told you can get us into the capital undetected."

"We can do better than that." Another shadow materialized and Feowen stepped into the moonlight.

"Feowen!" Before she realized what she was doing, she launched herself at him.

He caught her up, laughing. "Cousin," he said, spinning in a circle before setting her on her feet. "You are well? Yes, I can see that you are. Good."

"Well, Prince, this is a pleasant surprise." Talon stepped up beside them. Feowen held out his hand to clasp Talon's forearm, but Talon pulled him into a hug, slapping him on the back. "It's good to see your face."

"Welcome back, Your Majesty. I see you were successful."

"Indeed."

The others stepped forward to greet Feowen similarly.

"This is all very touching," Tasar said after a couple of minutes, "but we should be going. It isn't good to linger, even this far from the capital."

"What's the plan?" she asked before Talon could voice the words.

"We will travel to the capital disguised as human travelers. There's a passage that leads into the city from Fort Kastali."

"You're kidding!" Claire breathed.

"Found it while we were exploring," Feowen said, grinning. "Wasn't much else to do while we waited for your return. We've got every passage in the city mapped out."

"Glad to see you've used your time wisely," Talon said. "What of the others?"

He disguised his worry, but Claire felt it gnawing at him. He was afraid of what Feowen would say.

"Good, all good. Well, Reyr is a little worse for wear, but he's hanging in there. Verath and Dallin too. We have kept them sane in these trying times. I'm sure they're ready to be free of their cells."

Claire blew out a breath. The thought of Talon's remaining shields stuck in the dungeon all this time... They must have been going mad. She couldn't wait to hug each of them.

But, first things first.

"Let's get going," she said, nodding at Tasar.

He produced a sack from a nearby shrub and began handing out clothing. It was rough, homespun fabric in shades of brown and black. They separated and changed, packing away their finery.

She wistfully slipped out of her shimmering gown into the brown dress. It scratched against her skin.

When they reassembled and set off, they looked like weary travelers with dusty packs. Tasar assured them that if they kept up a strong pace, they would reach the fort just before morning. It was important to do so under the cover of darkness. "Kane's got Oshean guards everywhere," he explained. "They've all but overrun the capital."

Talon's anger rose but he stayed silent. She reached for his wrist, giving it a squeeze. He threw her a grateful look.

"Tell us what we've missed?" she asked. "How many people have joined the resistance? Who is in charge? What have you all been doing in our absence?"

"One thing at a time, Majesty." Feowen bumped her shoulder.

He started at the beginning, with Reyr acting as Talon's body double. She was still surprised that Taylynn had later enchanted a woman named Merrian to stand in for her.

"Did she do a good job?"she couldn't help but ask.

"Quite. You'll like her," he said, continuing.

Reyr and Merrian had held things together until Kane showed up and ruined the charade. After that, her spriten guard gathered those they could and fled into the passages. From there, they began mapping them out until they found a way into the dungeons. Helping Dallin, Merrian, Reyr, and Verath was one of their riskier tasks. Kane threatened to use the dragonstones should he suspect anything.

Feowen told them about the various resistance Kane faced within the keep, missing cutlery, guards uniforms, furniture, and the like. The false king had his hands full. No one had made it easy for him.

As a result, Kane didn't hesitate to imprison whomever he wished. Those prisoners were then given to slavers.

"You cannot be serious?!" she cried, bile rising in her throat. "He's selling our people?"

"Trying to," Feowen said, and a vicious grin spread across his lips. "We've had some allies helping on that matter."

"Allies?" Talon sounded intrigued.

"Captain Bennett—remember him? We didn't know about it at first. Not until we received word that Byron had contacted him. Together, they arranged a way to go after slave ships carrying our citizens to Oshea. Byron's got some of his drengr aiding in the efforts. From the missives, they've rescued thousands already."

"Gods," she breathed. Heat welled in her chest. It felt a lot like pride—her people were fighting back. She couldn't wait to fight for them, to end this once and for all.

# CHAPTER 41
## FORT KASTALI

Leah took in Fort Kastali through wide eyes. It was just nearing dawn, the first vestiges of light spilling over the horizon. They entered through a portcullis, beneath a thick stone wall. She'd never been inside a castle, though they frequented books she read. This one smelled like rock and mildew. It was more a fortress than anything. The cobbles beneath her feet were a better alternative to mud.

She'd caught a glimpse of the vast city of Kastali Dun a mile or so away, looming. It sent a shiver of excitement racing down her spine. None of this felt real.

The fort was already filled with activity, people rushing to and from their duties. Servants, she supposed? Never mind the number of dragons she'd seen coming and going. It looked like the kind of place that stories were written about.

She kept to the back of the group, not wanting to get in the way. It allowed her to observe everything silently. Claire walked up front with Prince Feowen and the spriten spy they'd met, Tasar. They'd been talking nonstop. She had listened out of curiosity, tucking away every bit of knowledge. She wanted to learn as much as possible about this new life she was soon to begin.

Jovari dogged her steps. Were it not for Saffra's presence by her side, which was both a blessing and a curse, she might have said something to him. As it was, there hadn't been a moment alone to discuss the elephant in the room. Four days of flying with him, four torturous days alone with her thoughts trying desperately to avoid touching him. He never transformed, choosing to stay a dragon because, *conveniently*, dragons couldn't talk. She wanted to say it was on purpose, but the others hadn't either. Still, it felt a little like he was avoiding her.

Were they going to continue ignoring it?

As they strode through the fort's massive courtyard, they caught the attention of passersby who stopped to study them. Dressed as they were, no one seemed to recognize the king and queen. That was fortunate. According to Tasar, Kane had spies in all the forts to ensure the drengr behaved.

They continued through a maze of corridors lined with torches before reaching a set of double doors. Talon knocked and they were immediately ushered into a large receiving room.

"Thank the gods!" someone cried. A female. She must have been a rider. A male appeared beside her, greeting Talon warmly. They looked to be in their fifties, at most. The others gathered around them while she hung back.

"That's Karanth and Eva." She jumped at the sound of Jovari's voice so close to her ear. She could smell the smokey scent of him; she tried to ignore what it did to her. "They're Fort Kastali's leaders."

"Oh," she managed, swallowing. A quick glance showed the two of them were relatively alone. Her heart kicked up a notch. "Are we going to talk about us?"

"Do you really think now is the time?"

His words made her muscles tighten. She didn't turn to look at him. Hopefully he couldn't see the heat flushing her cheeks. "Right. Well, you've obviously been avoiding me."

"I'm not—"

The doors behind them flew open and she whirled. Jovari's expression softened and he strode forward. "Mother, Father."

Her lips parted. His parents?! Jovari hugged them in turn.

He'd mentioned parents and that he had a good relationship with them, but she'd never expected to meet them. Before she could process, he reached for her, taking hold of her wrist and pulling her forward. She sputtered in surprise. "We picked up an outsider on our trip through the gate, would you like to meet her?"

She blinked.

"Oh, my!" Jovari's mother studied her, making her stomach squirm under the scrutiny. She was vaguely aware of the others gathering behind them. She cleared her throat and managed a weak, "Hello."

"Well, I've never seen hair quite like yours. Is that natural? Do people have pink hair in your world?"

She patted her hair, suddenly self conscious. "No it's...fake. I dyed it."

"Well, it suits you—very much. Welcome to our kingdom. I'm Nieven and this is my mate, Durlan."

"Leah," she said, finding her courage and offering her hand.

Nieven grabbed her forearm instead, then pulled her into a hug. It made her warm all over. There were some people you couldn't help instantly liking, and Nieven was one of them. "I'm sure it's hard to leave your home behind. You'll let us know if you need anything at all?"

Her eyes burned. "Of...of course."

She'd been terrified that Jovari's parents would dislike her for whatever reason. As she pulled away, she noticed the way Durlan's gaze darted between her and his son, a suspicious gleam in his eyes. Eyes the same brown as Jovari's. A laugh burst from her chest and her shoulders relaxed. He might have been intimidating but— "You look like you could be brothers. You definitely don't look like you're his father."

Durlan smiled, transforming the hard lines of his face. His hair was auburn, too, just like Jovari's. "I'll take that as a compliment. It is an absolute pleasure to meet you, Leah. Welcome to Dragonwall. I assume you're a friend of our queen's?"

"Her best friend," she said, lifting her chin. "Basically sisters."

"Good. Good!" He was utterly genuine. She felt a pang of longing. Jovari's parents were wonderful people. No wonder he had a good relationship with them. It made her wish, now more than ever, that hers were still alive.

King Talon stepped forward, arm outstretched. "Durlan, Nieven, it's good to see you again. Your son got me through a pretty difficult time. I'm lucky to have him." They exchanged cordial greetings before Jovari facilitated introductions with everyone else. It was obvious that the other shields already knew his parents, but Claire, Taylynn, and Saffra did not.

"They moved down here from Fort Edge when he became a shield." Koldis appeared beside her, keeping his voice low. "So they could be closer to him."

"Okay?" She wasn't sure why he bothered to tell her, even if she did find his information heartwarming.

"Just thought you'd want the extra intelligence," he said, a wicked gleam in his eyes. "You know, seeing as you're his—"

"Enough, Koldis." Taylynn appeared beside her mate, jabbing him in the side.

Koldis only grinned.

Leah let out a loud sigh and turned away from them, only to find Claire watching her intently. They shared a silent look and Claire mouthed, "You okay?" To which she nodded, chewing on the inside of her cheek. For all intents and purposes, she was physically okay, even if the inside of her mind was a chaotic mess of feelings and confusion.

"Well," Talon said, interjecting, "As much as I love a good reunion, there are matters of grave importance awaiting. Planning that must be done. Karanth, Eva, if you will show us to your meeting room, we can get started."

"Would you like us to remain?" Durlan asked.

"No, Durlan, but thank you. Inner circle only." Talon clapped Durlan on the shoulder.

The older male didn't look the slightest bit put out. Actually, he looked relieved. "We'll leave you to it, then."

Leah caught Nieven's gaze and the woman offered her a wide, inviting smile. She took a step towards her, then blurted, "Can I go with you?"

Nieven's blink was her only show of surprise. "I would love that. We can better acquaint ourselves. I've always wondered what the queen's homeland is like."

"Oh, I have plenty of stories."

"She's needed here," Jovari interjected, his voice turning a shade possessive.

"Nonsense," Leah said, throwing him a glare. "I'm hardly part of the inner circle, just because I'm Claire's best friend." It was a poor excuse. The truth was, she was a touch wary to be in Jovari's company, especially right now. And more than that, she needed a change of pace.

He opened his mouth, then closed it. She waited for him to say something—to announce that they were mates, and therefore she had every right to join them, but he only looked uncomfortably between her and his parents.

Right.

Well, that was answer enough.

Jovari's father shrugged. "How about a tour of the fort, Leah? There's a good view of the city from the fort's walls."

Her chest felt immediately lighter. "I'd love that."

Claire stepped up beside her. "Are you sure?" She kept her voice low.

"Positive. I doubt I'll be much help for any of this. I'm sure you'll fill me in on everything you need me to know."

Claire nodded, wearing a look of understanding. Like she knew exactly why Leah would rather be out in the fresh air than holed up in a room with Jovari for hours. She reached over and gave her best friend's hand a quick squeeze, then added in a whisper, "You got this."

Claire smiled. "Thank you. I'll see you later."

She followed Jovari's parents out of the room, imparting a final glare on Jovari before disappearing.

DINNER WAS HELD in the fort leaders' private chambers. It was a warm affair. She sat beside Jovari's parents on one side and Saffra and Bedelth on the other. Jovari sat on his father's other side, just far enough that they could continue avoiding each other.

"How was your tour?" Saffra asked, scooping out a healthy serving of roast chicken and potatoes.

"Oh, wonderful! I got to see where the drengr take their meals, where they train, the archery range—one of the riders let me shoot my first bow!—the cookery, and the fort's walls. The city looks incredible. I can't wait to see it up close."

"We'll definitely give you the grand tour, take you to the market—when we reclaim the kingdom, that is."

"Right, about that. How did the meeting go?" she asked in a lower voice.

"Oh, you know." Saffra sighed. "Lots of back and forth about the Oshean forces and how we plan to confront Kane. Trust me, you were better off not being there."

"I figured." A small pang of uselessness tugged at her gut. She was under no misgivings. As a human and an outsider, there was very little she could do. She was here for Claire, but she was also here for herself. She'd help in whatever way she could, but so far, no one had needed her for much of anything.

In a way, it felt good. She might have gone as far as to say it was a massive relief. She'd been her father's crutch during much of her life, even if he hadn't wanted it that way. Being needed—especially for critical care of a cancer patient—carried a heavy weight that she knew all too well.

Now, she felt freer than ever.

Once the food was cleared, they said their goodbyes. She gave Durlan and Nieven hugs. They promised to visit her in the city once Kane was removed from power. "Take care of my son," Nieven whispered, almost like she knew they were mates and just wasn't saying it.

"I will," she managed, not bothering to deny that there was something between them.

Their group made their way through the fort and descended to an unused corridor leading into a storage cellar. Tasar and Feowen guided them around crates and sacks of foodstuffs, to the corner where an invisible latch opened up a space in the wall. "Took us months to find it," Feowen explained to King Talon as they disappeared into darkness. Claire and Tasar followed, then the others.

She stood at the rear of the group, watching as everyone disappeared.

A tug on her wrist made her hesitate. Jovari's eyes glittered with seriousness in the torchlight. They were alone—finally alone. She glanced around, wondering if she should just bolt. "You all right?"

"Fine," she said, taken aback by his soft question.

He hesitated. "We'll talk. When there's a free moment that affords it, we'll talk."

A lump formed in her throat. "You mean that?"

His expression softened. "Yes. I... I have just needed time, that's all."

She understood, she really did. "Me too, I think. It's a lot."

He dropped her wrist and lifted his hand, hesitating. When he brushed his fingertips over her cheekbone, she shivered. Her eyes fixed on his lips, and she remembered exactly what it felt like to kiss him.

He cleared his throat. "We should probably..."

"Oh, yes, right." She stepped forward, then allowed the darkness to swallow her up. Jovari followed behind her, taking up the rear of the procession. He muttered a word and the section of wall moved back into place, sealing them in.

Ahead, she spotted the glow of several mage lights as the others traversed the narrow passage. A warm pressure at the base of her spine made her breath catch. "Just me," Jovari said. He was nearly pressed against her, coaxing her forward.

"Is it bad—that I'm excited?"

Jovari made a thoughtful humming sound. "It's not bad."

"I really can't wait to see the city. I know... I know it will be a while but..."

Jovari's lips were close to her ear as he said, "Promise me...?"

"Promise you what?" Her heart drummed against her chest.

"Promise me you'll let *me* be the one to show you the city. Not Claire, no matter how much she wants you to. *I* want to show it to you."

"Oh." It was the last thing she'd expected. Her knees turned weak and she forced herself to keep walking, following the glowing light ahead. "I promise," she managed.

And she meant it.

# CHAPTER 42
# REUNITED

*Kastali Dun*

Claire heard the murmur of voices growing louder with each step through the passage tunnel. They were close. Her nerves ratcheted up, as did Talon's. She'd been away from her people for so long, even if it hadn't felt long for her.

Talon was a steady presence at her back as she followed behind Feowen and Tasar. Having him close made her braver; she felt the same mirrored within him. Which was why she lifted her chin and squared her shoulders when the mouth of the passage widened, letting them out into the massive cave deep beneath the keep.

Feowen came to an abrupt halt, then cupped his hands around his mouth and announced, "Our queen has returned! All hail Queen Claire!"

Silence.

And then—

"Claire!" Gasps, shrieks, and cries of elation erupted into the massive space, followed by a rush of people surging towards them. A single breath later, she was engulfed, passed around for hug after hug. She had a brief moment with a tearful Desaree, breathing in her familiar scent, before she was passed to Jocelyn, and then her spriten handmaidens and guards. She was vaguely aware of the others engaged in similar greetings and introductions.

Talon's amusement vibrated across their mate bond as he watched how eagerly she was received. "All right, all right. Back up, all of you. Give my mate some room to breathe," he growled at the bodies pressing in around them.

Everyone scampered backwards at their king's order, assembling in a semicircle around the newcomers. Her eyes caught with Desaree's from across the gap. "I missed you so much," she mouthed.

"I missed you too," Des mouthed back, tears streaming down her cheeks.

"My queen?" Feowen looked at her. "Would you like to say a few words? Address your people?"

"I..." She glanced at all the hopeful faces. She recognized so many of them. Even Mikkin and Jamie, and the dwarg and goblin who had traveled with them. There had to be close to a hundred people hiding out in the cave. Hiding from Kane's reach.

The feel of Talon's hand slipping into hers offered her renewed strength. *"I'm with you—always."*

She cleared her throat. "Thank you—all of you—for your loyalty during this dark time. Kane's tyrannic rule cannot be allowed to continue. I am here—*we* are here—to take back the throne." She shared a meaningful glance with Talon and he nodded, encouraging her to continue. "We will not rest until it is in safe hands. I hope you are all ready, because it's time to act."

Cheers and clapping erupted, even several whoops. Not a single person looked hesitant. Not a single one doubted their ability to reclaim what was stolen. Talon gave her hand a quick squeeze and added, "My queen is right. We've got some work ahead of us. Let's get some rest tonight, and in the morning, we begin."

Murmurs met his words as everyone in the crowd began speculating over what would come next.

"You heard your king," Feowen shouted. "Clear out and get some rest."

She threw the prince a look. "Seems like you've got everything under control."

"Indeed. Now, we've cordoned off a section over there for you, so you have your privacy. Follow me." He set off at a brisk pace, leading them through the cavern. Everywhere she looked were signs of the strength and endurance of their people. Cots and cook fires, makeshift tables, furniture, and more. They'd been living here for months—that much was evident.

She felt a hand in hers and looked over to see Desaree walking beside her. They shared a grin. "I know it's the middle of the night," Des said, "but maybe we can make some time to catch up tomorrow?"

"We will. I promise."

"Good, then I'll see you in the morning." Desaree dropped her hand and turned. "Leah? Would you like to come and bed down with us females?"

"Oh. Yes, that would be fine." Leah had a dazed look on her face, taking everything in.

Claire turned to her best friend. "You are in excellent hands with Desaree, trust me."

"She's right. I've got you." Des linked her arm through Leah's and they wandered off. She watched them go, thinking about how difficult this must be for Desaree, knowing Verath was locked up in the dungeons.

She turned to Talon, keeping pace beside him as they made their way across the cave. "When can we see Reyr and the others?" She ached for the male who held a special place in her heart. He'd been with her since the very beginning and she needed him here.

"Soon, love. I'll arrange something with Feowen for tomorrow."

Her chest gave a painful squeeze. She hated the thought of him stuck in a cell for months on end. She would be forever grateful to Feowen for all he'd done to make Reyr's life—and the others— easier while imprisoned.

"Here we are." Feowen stopped beside a massive tent that had been erected, the only one of its kind in the cave. "The floor wasn't even so we used magic and smoothed it out a bit and set this up, knowing you'd be here soon."

It was smaller than the royal tent she was used to in their war camp, but still, it would offer them the kind of privacy others in the cave didn't have.

"You'll find a surprise waiting inside," Feowen added, piquing her interest. "Along with everything else you might need." He hesitated and then, "Luth utah heilah eah saphi aya zanih, Ayas Drollaya." *It is good to have you back, Your Majesty.* He gave a small bow then departed, leaving her and Talon alone.

She glanced around, noticing a few of Talon's shields mingling. "They'll find their own beds," Talon said, reading her thoughts. "Don't worry over them. Now, shall we see about this supposed surprise?"

"Do you have any guesses?" But she knew that he didn't. She could see that clearly enough in his mind. So she parted the tent flap and stepped inside, looking around. There was a streak of black, followed by a loud *meow*. She gasped. "Batty!"

Her little kitten was a kitten no longer. Talon pressed in behind her then made a humming noise. "The cat."

"Look at him," she cooed, bending to lift Batty into her arms. "Look how much he's grown. Yes you have, haven't you? Look how big you are! Such a handsome boy. My goodness." She rubbed her cheek against the top of his head, cuddling him to her.

Talon huffed. "Suppose I must share my bed with the cat now."

"Oh, don't be such a grump. He's such a grump, isn't he? Don't listen to him. He can't wait to cuddles with you. I bet he's going to love it, isn't he? Yes he is. Yes he is!"

*Meow.*

"I know. I was thinking the exact same thing."

"Gods above," Talon muttered, moving past her. "Are you going to talk to our child like that, too?"

Their child?! Her stomach dipped and she looked up. Their eyes locked, minds linked. He wanted a child—desperately. She could see that plainly now. It wasn't a desire he'd allowed to the forefront of his thoughts before.

Motherhood wasn't something she'd thought about much, or worried over. Pairs struggled to conceive and it could take hundreds of years just for a single child, which made the likelihood of them conceiving anytime soon extremely slim, even if they hadn't used protection. She wasn't sure if she was quite ready yet. With all that was happening, it wasn't safe, not until Kane was defeated.

"Let's talk about it when everything is sorted," he said, his expression soft and vulnerable. She gave him a nod, holding Batty tight as Talon began shedding his clothes. She'd seen him naked many times now, and yet she couldn't take her eyes from his shirtless torso, from the bulge of muscles as he moved around the tent. He kept his pants on, removing his socks and boots.

She gave Batty a final kiss before setting him on the floor, moving to do the same. She discarded her boots first, letting her feet sink into the plush rugs. There was a chest with several familiar clothing items, including a nightgown. "They must have snuck into the keep to grab all this stuff for us."

Talon grunted in answer. He was tired, she could see it in the set of his shoulders, the way he moved about. It wasn't the kind of physical tiredness that came from lack of sleep, though there was that, too, but a bone deep weariness that came from too much stress, from the weight of an entire kingdom pressing in on him.

The small tent was just large enough for their belongings, a little table and two chairs, which currently held a pitcher and basin for washing up, and a pallet piled with blankets and furs. She immediately went to the basin and filled it with water, using one of the cloths to wash up before pulling on her nightgown, then she went to the pallet, pulling the covers back and motioning for Talon to join her. He washed up too, then slipped in beside her, groaning. The sound and feel of his pleasure mixed with hers.

"Feels nice after so many days of travel, doesn't it?"

"Yes," he huffed. Unlike her, he'd had to fly for days on end. Days without sleep. They were too exhausted to do more than tangle their limbs together and gaze at one another. A single candle burned on the table, casting a dim yellow light into the tent. Neither of them had the energy to get up and put it out.

"We finally made it back," she whispered, almost surprised that they'd come this far, not that she'd ever doubted it.

"Indeed." He released one of her hands to brush her hair back. "Finally."

A thump sounded, followed by the pressure of a cat as Batty stalked between them before finding a dip in their conjoined bodies planting himself there. Talon emitted a low growl, more dragon than anything. Batty's ears perked.

"Oh, stop," she whispered before giggling. "We can share."

It was no surprise that when she woke, the pallet was empty with the exception of Batty. A quick brush of her hand told her Talon had vacated a while ago, his body heat long gone. She'd slept like the dead, tangled in his embrace for most of the night. Now, Batty occupied the space on his pillow where his head had been.

She brushed a loving hand over the cat's head, massaging his ears. Batty opened a single eye, then immediately closed it again.

*"Good morning, love."* Talon's voice was the barest whisper of a caress.

She stretched and yawned, loving the way it felt to stay nestled beneath the blankets. So warm and comfortable. *"Good morning,"* she echoed.

A quick glance into his mind showed that he was already at the cave's command center, a number of guards gathered around. He hadn't wanted to wake her; in typical Talon fashion, he'd made sure everyone stayed quiet for their queen. As much as she wished she could remain abed all day, there was too much at stake. Queens didn't have the luxury of sleeping in, which only made her huff in annoyance.

*"No one is demanding you get up,"* Talon said, amused. *"Let me handle things. You rest."*

*"Absolutely not."*

*"Fine, then at least go and spend some time with your friends. Desaree looks a little lost, lurking outside our tent. I'm sure she missed you. I've got things handled here."*

Her heart immediately felt lighter at the thought. Giving Batty a quick kiss, she yawned loudly once more, then got up and began shuffling around, cleaning her face and teeth. "I can't wait to have my bathing chamber back," she groused aloud.

"Knock-knock," came a familiar voice. She whirled as Desaree poked her head in, then entered. She wasn't alone. Miera and Selphie followed behind, the latter carrying a tray laden with breakfast, which she set on the small table. "We're here to prepare you for the day."

She eyed each of them crammed into the small space, then sighed. "I really missed you guys." Even though she hadn't missed them for very long, since she'd only regained her memories after reaching Esterpine, she'd felt their absence. Which reminded her— "We have so much catching up to do. You go first. Tell me everything I missed, and then I'll tell you everything that happened to me."

"Why don't you start on your breakfast then," Desaree said, motioning her to one of the two empty chairs. She eagerly sat, eyeing the fare before her. Porridge with raisins and cinnamon and sugar. "There's not a lot of variety down here."

"No, it's totally fine. I wasn't complaining. I'm starving." She lifted the cup and took a sip of water before mixing everything together and digging in. It was hot and delicious, and that was all that mattered. "How do you even get food down here, anyway?"

"Tess," Desaree said. "Though, I suppose I should start at the beginning, yes?"

Miera and Selphie shuffled around, producing a gown and setting it out before finding places to sit on the end of the pallet.

Desaree filled the small tent with her voice, weaving her words together. Claire already knew a lot of the biggest details, like how Reyr had been disguised as Talon, how they'd hired a woman to become her body-double, and how Kane had taken over months into their charade. Feowen had filled in a lot of the missing pieces when they reunited yesterday.

Still, hearing it from Desaree offered a fresh perspective. Like, how Desaree and a few others had organized a mission into the king's tower to reclaim some of the more important things, and how they'd found Batty hiding away in one of the lower chambers and rescued him. "That's how we managed to spirit away some of your gowns in the chest. We knew that when you returned, you would want a few familiar items from your wardrobe."

"That was...that was really thoughtful, thank you." She refrained from scolding them for taking a risk like that, mostly because she was so relieved to have Batty.

Once Desaree was finished, she recounted her own tale. There was a lot to get through, and by the time she'd finished, it was high time to get dressed and see how things were going in the cave. Her ladies helped her into a royal blue gown, then fixed her hair into a simple coiffure before placing a crown atop her head.

Scooping up Batty, she stepped from the tent and out into the cave, which was bustling with activity. A few people nearby saw her, paused, then offered respectful bows before continuing on. She studied everything, taking in more than she had last night now that she wasn't half-asleep.

Her ladies filed out behind her.

"You wouldn't happen to know where Leah is, would you?" She'd been a little disappointed that her friend hadn't appeared with the others. Something was going on with her, and while she'd wanted to give Leah space and time to deal with it, it was high time they confronted whatever it was. This was a discussion that had been brewing for days, perhaps even weeks. Ever since they had reached Esterpine.

With the way things were balanced on the tip of a blade, she didn't want to wait any longer. There was no predicting the future. No telling what could happen.

Perhaps she should have brought it up the other day, when Leah had discovered the mate bond between herself and Jovari. But it hadn't felt like the right time. Not when Leah had just been smacked in the face with such a big discovery.

"Leah stayed with us last night," Desaree said. "She wanted to help with the food preparation duties this morning. She's probably cleaning up now."

"I see." It wasn't surprising in the least. Leah was used to caring for people. She'd spent a good chunk of her latter teenage years caring for her father before he'd died. It was ingrained in her. But it might also have been a good excuse to keep away, and this avoidance needed to end.

She handed Batty off to Selphie to return to the tent. "Take me to her, if you wouldn't mind."

"Of course." Desaree set off, leading the way into the heart of the cavern.

# CHAPTER 43
## LEAH'S FEELINGS

*Kastali Dun*

Leah laughed as a spray of soapy water shot up into the air. Saffra swore under her breath, but it was too late, there was already water covering both their gowns. "Well, I tried," Saffra said, looking at the large pot that now bobbed in the big tub of sudsy water.

They were washing dishes now that breakfast was over.

She lifted her forearm to brush a strand of hair from her face that had come free, then together with Saffra and Jocelyn, they fished out the large pot and maneuvered it over for easier washing. She went back to the remaining stack of plates, cleaning each with a soapy cloth before handing them off to Jocelyn to dry.

A group of people passed by and thanked them for breakfast, their eyes lingering over her the longest. It had taken a little getting used to—everyone's stares. Pink hair hadn't attracted too much attention back in Esterpine. Sprites were eccentric, some sporting unique hair colors of their own. Hers hadn't exactly shocked them.

What concerned her more was what she would do when it started to grow out. She hated her roots showing. But...did they have hair dye here?

"They're just curious," Saffra said, noticing the way she watched the gawkers as they slipped past.

"What? Oh." She handed another plate off to Jocelyn. "Maybe I should just let my natural color grow out. It will attract far less attention."

"Nonsense!" Saffra hunched over the large pot, scrubbing. "I think bright hair suits you. I'd almost find it weird, now that I'm used to seeing it on you."

"Well, unless I can find more hair dye, I probably don't have a choice."

"I'm sure we could concoct something." Saffra hesitated, expression turning thoughtful.

"Saffra is excellent at magical brews," Jocelyn explained. "I bet she could make you whatever you need."

"Do you think you could make it purple instead of pink?" She sucked her lower lip between her teeth.

"Certainly. I'll have to experiment, but I'm confident I can come up with something."

"Come up with what?" Claire appeared and all of them paused.

"Hair dye," she said, taking in her friend's appearance. "You look better. Did you sleep okay?" She'd be lying if she said her bestie hadn't looked extra exhausted lately. It was a relief to see her looking slightly less exhausted.

"I did."

"Good!" She hesitated, then added, "Sorry I didn't come see you this morning. Saffra and Jocelyn looked a little frazzled and I wanted to help."

"She was a great help," Saffra said, finally wrestling the pot out of the water and back onto the table where she could dry it.

"No need to apologize. Hey...can we take a walk? Just the two of us?"

"Of course." She quickly dried her hands then looked at Jocelyn. "You'll be okay?"

"Certainly, I can handle the rest of this. You've already been a great help."

She couldn't help the soft smile that spread across her lips. "Good. I'm glad."

Linking their arms together, they said goodbye to the others and set off through the cavern towards the emptier areas around the perimeter. She caught sight of the command center, King Talon and several others including Jovari, hovering over the giant table of maps as they discussed strategy. Claire followed her gaze and sighed.

"How are you holding up?" She bumped her bestie's shoulder.

"Oh, I'm managing," Claire said. "I was actually going to ask you the same question. You've seemed distant lately."

Leah opened her mouth—

"I don't mean the mate thing. I noticed even before that. Something is bothering you. Something you aren't telling me."

She should not have been surprised Claire picked up on it. They'd known each other far too long—could read one another far too well.

"At first," Claire continued, "I thought to leave it alone, but I think it would be better if you talked about it, whatever it is."

"You're right." They neared one of the passages that split away from the cavern. Claire guided them into the dark mouth. Only a sliver of light spilled in, casting them into shadow and offering a bit more privacy. "I guess I've been a bit of a mess ever since coming here. Grappling with a bunch of feelings I know I shouldn't have. I'm trying to turn them off. I guess I kind of hoped they'd go away, that I wouldn't have to burden you with them."

"I'm your best friend, that's what you're supposed to do."

"I know it's just—"

"You're worried about adding more to my already overloaded plate."

"Exactly."

"Talk to me—tell me what you're feeling."

She blew out a breath, her shoulders sagging. There was nothing for it. She might as well get it all out in the open. "Well, I'm feeling a bit of Jealousy, for starters, because you have this amazing circle of people around you who adore you, love you, and support you. I barely know what that feels like. You're the only person I have left. It's not the bad kind of jealousy, because I'm so happy for you I want to cry. It's more of a personal jealousy, and I've been trying—so hard—to shut it off."

Claire nodded, a look of understanding on her features that made her want to reach out and hug her. "What else?"

"Inadequacy." She took a steadying breath. "I look at what you've accomplished so far, at what the future holds for you—because let's face it, you're a badass and I have no doubt in my mind you're going to beat that asshole Kane—and I'm reminded that I've accomplished nothing. Don't get me wrong, it's motivating, and I can't wait to make something of myself here. I'm hungry for it, you know? But it's also...overwhelming."

"Leah." Claire reached for her arm, squeezing it gently. "In all the years I've known you, you've never shied away from hard work. When I watched you caring for your dad, there were so many times I wanted to cry for you. So many times I looked at the way you helped him use the bathroom. Helped feed him when he was too weak to feed himself. Drove him to every oncologist appointment, even if it was hours on the road. All I could think about was how I would break—that if it was my own dad, especially if my mom was already gone, I wouldn't be able to handle it."

"You could have done it."

"No, I don't think that I could. Or, at least, not with as much grace and fortitude as you did. Gods, Leah. You gave up your entire portion of inheritance money just to care for your dad. You made so many sacrifices, your future."

"There wasn't any other option."

"Yes, there was! Other people in your shoes would have self-ishly kept it and accepted that nothing else would fix him. Instead, you invested in research medicine by getting him the pills he needed, just hoping something would fix him."

"I would have paid anything to keep him here." Her voice choked and tears spilled down over her cheeks.

"I know, bestie. I know."

A sob erupted and she pressed a hand over her mouth to stifle it. When she finally got control of herself, Claire said, "Anything else? You know you can tell me. I would never judge you."

She swallowed, growing suddenly self conscious. "I think the real reason I'm feeling all of this is because I'm afraid. I'm afraid of what will happen with my future when it's finally time to make a life for myself. When I start over with a clean slate, there will be no more excuses. Nothing holding me back. I'm in a world I barely know anything about, with very few marketable skills, and a hunger to make something of myself, to satisfy this need for fulfillment burning in my chest. I feel like it's something I should be excited about, not scared about. And I look at you, and see so much fearlessness, and I can't help but admire that."

"Oh, Leah." Claire pulled her into a big hug until they were crying. "No judgement, see? In fact, everything you're feeling makes perfect sense! You make it sound like it's wrong to feel all of these things, but feelings are feelings. Whether they're right or wrong, positive or negative, we're humans. Controlling them isn't easy to do. In fact, I think you're better off overcoming them than controlling them."

She let out a laugh in agreement, already feeling lighter. "I think you're right."

"Sure I am. I'm the queen, remember?"

They both burst into tearful laughter. "Remind me to have you settle every argument I ever have with Jovari from now on. You can use that and he'll have to agree."

"Done." Claire sighed, taking hold of her shoulders so they could lock eyes. "I love you. I'm not going to leave you. No matter what you decide to do with yourself, you will always have a place with me, in my closest circle, so please stop avoiding me."

"You're right. I'm sorry."

"Apology accepted." Claire hesitated then said, "Leah, you're my best friend. I want you to continue being my best friend. We can even turn it into an official title. Best Friend to the Queen. I'll put you on my payroll and everything."

"Stop. You never need to pay me for my friendship."

Claire chewed on her bottom lip. "I know. You've always been there for me, no matter what. And I want to be there for you too. Being queen might have its obligations, but I want to be there when you need me. If I'm ever busy and you feel like I'm ignoring you, just slap me or something. I promise I'll snap out of it."

"Deal." She was surprised to realize that her chest felt lighter than it had in weeks. Why hadn't she done this sooner?

Claire grinned. "Feeling better?"

"I think so." She sighed. "I never imagined this would be such an emotional journey. Was it like this for you, when you came here?"

"Oh. You have no idea. An absolute roller coaster."

"Well, that makes me feel a little better."

"Good!" Claire linked their arms again and pulled her back out into the cavern. "Now, tell me the latest on Jovari."

She groaned. "Ugh. Don't even get me started with him."

"Well, you met his parents so..."

"So?"

"You know, it's probably a done deal and all that. I mean, meeting the parents is *huge!*"

"Oh, stop. This isn't our world. And it's not like he purposefully took me home to mom and dad or anything."

"True. But...well, did you like them? You seemed to hit it off."

"I do, actually. I really do, his mom especially. I feel like I've known her all my life. I know that is weird to say since we come from completely different worlds—"

"It's not weird at all. In fact, since you were talking about jealousy, I have to admit I'm a little jealous of you."

"What do you have to be jealous of?" It seemed ridiculous that Claire could feel that way.

"You got to meet Jovari's parents. Talon's are long dead. All I have is memories of them. But I'd have liked to meet them, you know?"

"Oh. I... I'm sorry. I guess you'll never have to worry about arguing with your MIL? That could be a plus, right?"

They both burst out laughing, attracting several curious

glances. They passed along the outskirts of the cavern, dodging the activity taking place.

"Jovari said we would talk when there was some time. I think when all this stuff with Kane is over."

"Do you want to be his mate?"

The question caught her off guard and she hesitated. The answer was simple, really. "Yes. But, I think I'd like to take things slow. I want some time to find myself before we're officially mated and all that."

"That makes perfect sense. I admire that. This is your chance at a new life, one you can live for yourself. No caring for your parents or loved ones. Just something for you. I think that's important."

"You do?"

"Of course."

She nodded, if only to reassure herself. It was a relief, truthfully. She half expected everyone to judge her for not immediately jumping into Jovari's arms. She didn't see any reason to rush straight into something, especially since she wanted him in the long run. But this would make it easier to settle down and find herself without having her mind immediately linked to someone else's. If she couldn't be happy as she was now, how was she supposed to be happy with someone else?

"Thank you," she blurted, looking at Claire. "For pulling me aside and forcing me to have this conversation. I probably would have been a coward about it and let it stew."

"You're welcome." Claire's smile was soft. "And since we're on the topic of thanks. Thank you, for dropping everything and coming with me. I know you didn't love your life before. I know you didn't have anything tying you to it, but you still dropped everything to follow me when I needed a familiar face. I really don't think I would have felt half as safe trusting Talon and running off to a new world if I hadn't had you with me."

Her chest swelled. "I'm glad I was able to do that for you."

"Me too." Claire squeezed her arm. "Now, I think I ought to head over to the command table. They're talking about organizing a small group to visit Reyr. I, for one, cannot wait to give him a big hug. Not to mention, meet this mysterious imposter queen who managed to fool everyone into thinking she was me for months! Can you believe it? Months."

"I think I'd like to meet her too," Leah admitted. "Though, I don't need to be a part of the group that goes. You can just tell me all about it once you get back."

"Deal." Just before they reached the table, Claire gave her arm a final squeeze, then dropped it and moved towards Talon's side. Jovari caught her eye, lifting a questioning brow. She pressed her lips together before offering him a small, friendly smile.

Then she quietly disappeared to rejoin Saffra and Jocelyn and help with whatever new tasks were needed.

*Kastali Dun*

Claire and Talon followed Feowen, emerging into a dark corridor that was very obviously part of the dungeons. She shuddered, remembering her fear all too well during those dark days when she'd first come here. Talon's fingers brushed down her back, accompanied by a wave of self loathing. He hated that he had ever thrown his mate in the dungeon, locking her up for days inside a filthy cell like a criminal.

*"It's all right,"* she soothed. She'd already forgiven him for it, but he'd never truly forgiven himself, nor the fact that he hadn't apologized directly afterward, that it had taken him too long to make things right.

"Just down this way," Feowen said before stopping before a cell door. There were many along this corridor. "The guards won't make another pass for about fifteen minutes, so we need to make it quick. I usually heal his mind so that he can communicate, then spend a few minutes filling him in on everything."

There was a loud click, then the door swung open.

"Feowen," a familiar voice greeted.

Her breath caught. She couldn't wait another moment.

Pressing past the prince, she burst into the small cell. There was a shocked gasp, and then she was swallowed up into the embrace of Reyr's arms. "Claire!" he breathed, burying his face in her neck as he lifted her off her feet, holding her tightly. "Is this truly you?"

"I'm here," she managed, a sob breaking free of her chest. Her eyes blurred. She squeezed them tight to keep the tears from falling. "I missed you so much."

"I missed you more," he growled before setting her down, framing her face with his hands.

The dim mage light cast him into shadow, but she saw enough. A laugh burst from her chest. "You've grown a beard!" Without thinking, she reached up and ran her fingers over it. It made him look older—much older. Or was that the expression in his eyes, the fatigue lurking there? Gods, he'd been here months, stuck in this tiny cell. Just thinking about everything he'd been through, before and after...

Her heart squeezed tight. "We're going to get you out, I promise. But not yet."

His gaze darted over her face. They stood staring at each other, cataloguing everything, making sure the other was unharmed. She was aware of Talon, quietly standing by to give them their time together—

A throat cleared. "I hate to rush things, Your Majesty, but..."

"Right. Sorry." She threw a glance at the prince.

It was then she noticed the woman beside Feowen. She'd been speaking quietly with him. The woman's eyes kept darting to Reyr, softening each time. She was of a similar age, with black hair and bright blue eyes. Her expression was wary.

"You must be my body-double," Claire said, stepping away from Reyr. "Merrian, right?"

"That's right." The woman's voice was little more than a whisper.

Because they shared minds, she was aware of Talon and Reyr embracing behind her, of Talon's immense relief as he held his best friend, then clapped him on the back. They moved away and began whispering.

"You're even more beautiful than the disguise they placed on me," Merrian said, a guarded expression on her face.

"Oh." She felt her cheeks flush, not having expected that. "Thank you."

Merrian's throat bobbed. "Did you really mean that? That you're going to get us out of here?" The words came out high pitched and desperate.

"I did. Now, come here." Before Merrian could protest, she pulled the woman into a tight embrace. Merrian's muscles locked up, but she didn't release her. If anything, she only squeezed tighter. She didn't care that Merrian's clothes were disheveled and dirty, that she probably hadn't bathed properly in ages. She only cared about comforting someone who'd been stuck down here all because of her.

"Thank you—for what you did, standing in for me in my absence. I know things didn't quite work out but, I know what it's like being down here. Only, I can't imagine being stuck here for months."

"You're welcome." Those simple words were a relief.

She released the woman and looked her over. "I cannot wait to hear all about what it was like being me and having to deal with that." She gestured towards Reyr.

A laugh burst from Merrian's chest and her features softened. "It wasn't easy. Who knew the drengr were so broody?"

"Oh, you have no idea. Well, I'm sure you do, now that you've been stuck with one for so long, I don't need to tell you." They both shared a quiet laugh.

"We need to get moving," Feowen said, breaking up the party. While she'd been acquainting herself with Merrian, Feowen and Talon had been filling Reyr in on everything. No doubt he'd pass everything along to Merrian after they left.

Her heart gave a painful pang. She'd barely even gotten to see Reyr.

She glanced around and noticed several bundles hidden in the shadows. Provisions and things Feowen had brought to keep them more comfortable in captivity. She couldn't wait to get them out of here.

"Soon..." she breathed, giving Merrian a final nod, a promise.

Then she went back to Reyr, pushing past Talon to wrap her arms around his waist and squeeze. He lifted an arm and wrapped it around her shoulders, squeezing her back.

"My healing should last you until your next dose of dragon's bane," Feowen was saying to him. "We'll be able to keep you up to date during that time."

She looked up at him, hopeful. "We can communicate?"

"Until my mind is locked down again."

She knew exactly how that felt.

They gave their final goodbyes, then slipped out.

There was even less time to visit Dallin and Verath. Only enough for a few quick hugs so that Feowen could cleanse both their minds, allowing them to speak telepathically. Then they were rushing away before the guards caught them.

*"I'm so relieved you made it back safely,"* Reyr's voice followed her out of the dungeon. She was thrilled to be able to hear him. *"And I can't wait to hear all about what transpired after Kane sent you away."*

She spent their walk back to the cave sending him projections and rushed explanations of everything, from waking up in France, to all the news stories, to Talon showing up. Reyr was excited to meet her parents through some of the projections she sent him, but she could tell that he wished he could have met them in person. He was also amused by the scenes that included Leah, even more so when she let slip a few that showed the tension between Leah and Jovari.

What would he do when he found out they were mates?

Gods, she was so glad she could talk to him like this. It made the sting of his captivity a little easier to bear. And she fully intended to take advantage of every moment they could communicate together until his next dose.

When they emerged back into the cave, there was a swarm of people and loud voices from the direction of the small building in the center. Her breath caught at what she saw. Had they...?

"There you are!!" Desaree and Saffra rushed over, grabbing her and dragging her through the cave. "They got it open! You won't believe what we found inside."

"What?!" She took in the parting bodies as people made way for her, the opening at the front of the little mysterious building. The yellow torchlight spilling out of it.

After learning about Irelia's history, she realized now why it had looked so familiar. Irelia had appeared in Greece after fleeing. That meant the portal had served as a gateway to and from Greece long before Dragonwall was established as a kingdom.

"What's inside?" she demanded, her voice breathless as they ascended the steps and made their way to the door.

"You'll have to see for yourself."

Her heart began to race. With everything going on since its discovery, finding a way to open the mysterious building had taken a back seat. Yet, she couldn't help but wonder if this was all meant to happen. If whatever was inside was something they'd need in the days to come.

She was engulfed in warm, orange torchlight as she passed over the threshold. There were several people inside already. One of them was Berbik.

"We have Berbik to thank for figuring it out," Saffra explained.

"Berbik?" She looked at him in question.

"Your Majesty." He bowed. "It was a simple matter of finding the catch. My people built this, and once I knew it was our handiwork, I knew there'd be a way to open it—more than one. Magical words, obviously. But since we dwargs would need another way to get in and out to complete construction."

"He found a secret lever on the side of one of the pillars."

"You're joking?!" A laugh burst from her chest as she took in everything before them.

It was a crypt. That much was clear from the sarcophagus dominating the center of the room. There were pieces of elegantly carved furniture, vases, jewel boxes, and coins—a treasure trove of things. But it was the walls that caught her attention.

"What is all that?" she breathed.

"It looks like murals—to tell a story." Talon was behind her. He hooked his arms around her waist, holding her back flush to his front as they surveyed everything.

"What do you think they mean?" she wondered.

"We think they tell a story," Saffra said. "Look there, and there, and there. Each depiction shows the same man, like it's showing a story of his life."

"You're right." Excitement buzzed through her as she took in each depiction. There was a scene showing the gate just outside, the one Isabella had destroyed. Another showing others. Then there was a scene showing that same man gathered around other people. Her stomach dropped with fear as she realized something. "Their eyes—they're all red."

"Yes, about that." Saffra was chewing on her bottom lip. "We think maybe this could be the first asarlaí."

Claire's lips parted. She glanced around at the other murals, scenes that surely depicted magical deeds, eyes coming to rest on the final image of the same man on his knees, head back in pain as swirls of black appeared to flow from his body. That was where the paintings ended.

*Cyrus?* She reached for his presence in her mind. He alone had delved into the mind of an asarlai and would have the deepest understanding of their capabilities. *Are you seeing this?*

*I am,* he replied. She sensed a deep thoughtfulness radiating from him as they processed what they were seeing.

Her eyes landed on the sarcophagus in the middle of the room. Pulling free of Talon's grip, she walked over to it. Her hand hovered nervously over the lid. Talon snatched her wrist, making her freeze. "Are you sure?"

He already knew what she intended.

"I need to know."

He released her and ordered the others to stand back. She pressed her hand to the stone's cold surface and everything around her disappeared. She gasped. It was always jarring to find herself witnessing another time.

She wondered—now more than ever—if this was some kind of

gift she'd inherited from Isabella, or even, perhaps, from the first sprite they'd descended from. This ability to look back over the span of time when there was something old enough to warrant it.

A flash of movement caught her gaze as robed figures—asarlaí—carried the body of one of their own, lowering it into the open sarcophagus. She looked at the male's face, studying it, then looked up at the walls, at the murals that had only just been finished. It was the same male, the same asarlaí, which meant these paintings were a telling of his deeds. The heavy stone lid slid into place and her surroundings faded.

She came back into herself with a gasp. Talon was there, a steadying hand on her shoulder. "All right, *mih cralla?*"

"Yes, just give me a moment."

She felt his unease. He'd been there with her.

Nearly everyone here was part of her inner circle. Though Mikkin, Jamie, Berbik, and Unka weren't, she trusted them.

Quickly, she relayed these new findings to Dallin, Reyr, and Verath.

"We should study everything we can," Koldis said.

She frowned. "Where's Taylynn?"

"In the tunnels with Tasar, gathering intel."

Taking a deep breath, she said, "Asarlaí can be killed. I mean, I already knew they could because we know that the first dragons killed their makers, plus they're virtually extinct here, but it's reassuring to see proof that—"

"Kane *can* be killed," Talon finished for her. The room was silent as the truth sank in.

Until then, it had only ever been a possibility. She'd made a promise to end him, never really knowing if it was possible. She'd done everything she could to give herself the best shot at it. What they'd found today was exactly the reminder she needed.

"I'm ready to face him," she murmured, looking first at Talon, at the hope in his gaze. At the fear. She cleared her throat, turning to the others. More loudly, she said, "I'm ready to face him."

It was time.

# CHAPTER 45

# CONFRONTING KANE

*Kastali Dun*

Claire placed a calming hand over her stomach as her ladies fussed. *"Breathe, mia cralla,"* came Talon's soothing voice. She closed her eyes, inhaled, then exhaled. *"If it's too soon, we can wait another day."*

*"Another day will not make a difference,"* she said.

Desaree pinned the remainder of her hair in place as Selphie settled a golden crown atop her head. It didn't weigh much, and yet, the moment it sat atop her brow, she felt the entire weight of a kingdom settle on her shoulders.

"I think I'm going to be sick," she muttered.

"Aya atiah bahka einshaah." Miera held her hand and rubbed circles on the back of her palm. *You should eat something.*

"Ni. Then I truly will vomit."

Miera sighed.

"All done," Selphie said, stepping back to admire their work.

She glanced down at herself. They'd dressed her in a long, embroidered tunic and pair of pants. She wore pieces of spriten plate mail over her clothes. Both her spriten blade and Cyrus's sword were buckled across her back. While there was little concern of weapons piercing her body, today she was a warrior. Today she would stand beside Talon to reclaim their kingdom.

"Wait—one more thing." Desaree stepped forward and lifted the lid of a small box. There was an emerald ring nestled inside. The jewel was small and wouldn't get in her way. "We want you to have this. It belonged to Princess Lena—Queen Lena. You should wear it today."

"Queen Lena? I don't—" Claire stopped herself. The name *did* sound familiar. And there in Talon's mind, she gathered a vague explanation of who Lena was and why she'd heard the name before.

Still, Desaree said, "Queen Lena was born of the royal line eight generations in. The first princess to live to adulthood. The first female to ascend to the throne. The first to oversee a tournament for the crown, which would later expose her mate to the world. The first to marry and mate a drengr who would be crowned king all because of her. She was the first for a lot of things—just like you. I think... I think she would want you to wear this today."

"Oh, Des!" She flung her arms around her friend, pulling her in tightly. Her eyes burned, but she kept her emotions in check. There wasn't room for tears today. "However did you get this, anyway? Have you been holding onto it all this time?"

"We grabbed it when we snuck back into the tower, when we got some of your other things—and Batty." Desaree shared a knowing look with Miera and Selphie. "While we were there, I took a quick look around and saw it in this box embossed with her name and a note, left behind for someone who would appreciate it. Here—"

Desaree pulled free of her embrace and removed a small bit of folded parchment. Like everything else in the tower, magic had preserved it. Otherwise, it would probably be dust by now, seeing as the date placed it at some forty thousand years old.

Claire skimmed the note.

*To a future queen of Dragonwall: This ring was a gift to me from my beloved Triston after the successful birth of our son, Theodred. It is dear to me, just as they are. I have lived a long and full life. I have the kind of family mothers can only dream of. The kind of love ballads are written for. Only now do I remove it from my finger, in hopes that another queen might come along someday and need a reminder. You are enough. You will always be enough. Never let them make you feel otherwise.*

So much for not crying! She felt the tear spill down her cheek before she could stop it. When she looked up, it was to find three sets of loving eyes staring back at her.

"You will wear it?" Selphie asked in a tentative tone, as if there was any question.

"Yes!" she breathed. "And when this is all over, I want a history lesson on Queen Lena and all of her accomplishments."

*"There are entire books written about her in the library,"* Talon chimed in. Only now she realized he'd stopped what he was doing to snoop on this entire interaction.

When she emerged from her tent, she was calmer, every bit the queen her people expected. The cave was a rush of activity. She found Talon with several of his shields at the command table. "The others are already in position. As soon as you are ready, we will depart."

She and Talon had already shared many quiet moments together before the start of the day. Sleep had been nearly impossible, her nerves too chaotic. Talon had made sure to keep her thoroughly distracted with his mouth and body most of the night.

"I'm ready," she said. "The sooner we get this over, the better. If I wait any longer, my nerves are going to get the better of me."

She was already this close to slinking away somewhere.

"I understand." He reached for her hand, twining their fingers together. She felt his apprehension, too.

"Everything is ready." Taylynn appeared beside them wearing spriten armor of her own. She looked like a vengeful warrior goddess. Koldis immediately moved to her side. He acted protective, but it was unlikely Taylynn needed protection. "Spriten forces are in position. Tasar's operatives are in place in the keep and city. Saffra and her team have their orders. The moment you reach the throne room, Feowen will be there. I must get to the barracks."

"Good." Talon nodded. "Then let us go."

Taylynn offered Koldis a brief kiss before disappearing; he watched her go, eyes lingering.

Before they moved out, Claire shared a final hug with Leah and her ladies. Miera and Selphie had orders of their own. Plus, they had plenty of spriten magic. They would protect Desaree and Leah. Verath—and even Jovari—wouldn't have allowed them to accompany her sprite handmaidens otherwise.

"We'll be careful, I promise," Des said, giving her a final squeeze.

"You'd better." She looked at each of them as she said this.

Leah offered her a grin and said, "Just think, when we next see you, you'll be on the throne."

"Don't jinx us," she teased, trying to lighten the moment, trying to keep her stomach from spilling its contents.

"I would never!" Leah said, turning serious. They shared a secret smile that was borne from years and years of knowing each other.

"Let's move out," Talon called. The command was repeated through the cave. Everyone had a part to play.

They'd spent the remainder of yesterday finalizing preparations. There wasn't just Kane to contend with. Osheans had settled in the capital, too. Ships had been arriving for months. Nearly all the guards on Talon's payroll had been replaced by people Kane trusted. Those guards had to be eliminated. Foreign soldiers now occupied much of the barracks.

She thought about the rebuilding that needed to happen once this was all over. Everything they would have to fix. Even the things that couldn't be fixed, like the lives lost in Kane's pursuit for power.

The tunnels below the keep smelled like damp dirt. She kept her breathing under control as they walked, climbing higher and higher. She clenched her spriten staff in her left hand, clutching it like a lifeline.

*Cyrus, are you ready for this?* She nervously reached for him.

*I'm ready,* he said. *I will be here with you every step of the way.*

Those comforting words left both her and Talon feeling

emotional. She loved that Talon could hear everything Cyrus said. That he was no longer cut off from his beloved shield.

She took a deep breath and said, *I can't believe it's finally happening.*

*I can,* Cyrus replied. *I knew you would get here eventually. I'm honored that I witnessed every moment of your transformation.*

*I'm honored that you chose me to be transformed,* she said.

The rocky walls gave way to stone passages.

Talon's thumb brushed over Lena's ring on her finger. It felt like fate, that ring. It was the reminder she'd needed. That she was enough. She *would* get through this.

"*I'm free—we're free.*" Reyr's voice filled Talon's mind. She caught a projection of Feowen using his magic to suck the dragon's bane from his body, then another of them moving through the dungeon to free Verath and Dallin. They freed others too. Many of Talon's guards that Kane had imprisoned, along with people he hadn't trusted. While the sorcerer had killed plenty of subjects, he also liked to keep the cells full. She received one final projection from Reyr, though this one was riddled with doubt. The final person Feowen freed was a wild card. The idea had come to her near dawn. She just hoped she wasn't making a colossal mistake in sanctioning it.

"*Focus, mih cralla.*" Talon pressed his hand at the base of her spine in warning. They were nearing the exit to the secret passage. Talon's shields were silent, each of their minds pressing in on her. She felt their presence, knew they were a mere thought away should she need them.

Koldis stopped before the door and fell still. It clicked open, light spearing into the dim passage. Their mage lights winked out. She blew out the breath she'd been holding.

Koldis stepped out into a narrow servant's hall running adjacent to the throne room's atrium. The murmur of voices meant court had not yet started. It was almost comical, knowing that Kane kept court. As if people had any kind of power here.

No, he just wanted to preen like a peacock on a throne.

"Disguises in place?" Koldis looked at each of them. They wore court attire, with elegant cloaks covering their clothes in case they were spotted. Hers was a gorgeous black cloak that shimmered with iridescence to mimic Talon's scales.

They waited in the shadows for the courtiers to make their way into the throne room. When things quieted down, they strode forward. From across the atrium, Feowen strode into view accompanied by Merrian and Talon's other shields. Behind them, she caught a flash of the man who had tried to kidnap her. Eagle stood at the back of the group, a sword in hand, already dripping with blood. Their eyes caught and he nodded. It was all the thanks she would receive.

Eagle had remained locked in the dungeon all this time. She'd never quite figured out what to do with him. So when the idea came to strike a bargain with him, she'd informed Feowen of the terms. It looked as if Eagle had accepted. In exchange for his freedom, he was to kill as many Osheans as possible.

The two groups converged and she breathed a sigh of relief. *"Glad you made it,"* she said to Reyr.

*"I wouldn't miss this for the world,"* he said. *"I would have clawed my way free if necessary."*

The doors leading into the throne room were shut, four guards standing watch.

One of them stepped forward, eyeing them beneath their hoods. "You're late. Court already start—" The guard's words cut off in a gurgle as blood gushed down his throat. Feowen had a blade in hand, already moving to the second guard. Talon slit the throats of the other two before they could protest.

She blinked. In less than five seconds they'd eliminated everything standing between them and the throne room doors.

*"It's time."* Talon sent the silent command to the fort leaders of Fort Kastali. They waited until the count of five and then—

A distant bell began to toll. Then another, closer. And another.

Talon stepped over the bodies, positioning himself at the doors. She stepped up beside him. "Together?"

"Together," she confirmed, throwing a nod at the others behind them to get ready.

*"Whatever happens, mih cralla, I love you."*

*"More than I could ever put into words,"* she finished for him.

Talon reached for the doors, pushing them open. Silence fell. They waited several beats before striding forward. Whispers erupted.

"Guards!" Kane's voice rang out, irritated by the disruption. "You were supposed to watch the doors."

Two Oshean castle guards rushed forward. Feowen lashed out, his blades glinting. Screams sounded as both bodies struck the floor. A surge of courtiers backed away, scrambling over one another to put distance between them. She and Talon continued forward, Feowen beside them, their shields behind them, Eagle in the back. Merrian had slipped away to safety.

"What is the meaning of—?!" Kane surged to his feet right as they lifted their hoods, cutting him off.

Boots pounded on the floor as nearly fifty Oshean soldiers broke away from the perimeter and formed ranks around them, swords drawn, keeping their distance as they awaited Kane's orders. They were outnumbered, but it didn't matter.

"We're here to reclaim our kingdom," Talon called from beside her, ignoring the blades pointed at them. "Your days of playing king are over."

The sorcerer's eyes fell on her and widened briefly. That small look of surprise sent satisfaction surging through her. "You," he hissed. "I *knew* I should have killed you."

"But you didn't," she said, taking a step forward. "Your mistake."

"Don't come any closer." He lifted his fist. She caught the glint of a dragonstone there. Her gaze dropped to his breastplate where four were already embossed into the metal.

Her heart began to pound. "What are you going to do, hmm? Turn every drengr to stone?" The mere thought made her limbs tremble. Today had been a gamble, but she trusted Taylynn.

"You don't think I will?" Kane snarled. "I'll turn them before you can so much as blink. Try me."

"I don't think you will," she said, calling his bluff. "Because the second you turn them to stone, I *will* kill you. Right here in front of the entire court. The game is up, Kane. You've lost."

She slammed the butt of her staff into the flagstones, the sound reverberating through the hall. It wasn't wood against stone. It was a pure, spriten sound, ringing chime that reminded her of trickling water and chirping insects. Of times spent surrounded by greenery.

"I have lost *nothing*," Kane shouted. She was vaguely aware of Feowen and the others preparing to fight off the soldiers surrounding them. "You couldn't kill me before. What makes you think you can now?"

"Because I am not the same girl you banished," she taunted. "And I would love nothing more than to show you. To *end* you. So go ahead. I dare you."

"No... You wouldn't risk your king." A flash of something crossed his features. Doubt? He descended lower on the dais until he was just three steps from the floor. "Surrender now, and I will let you leave here alive."

"No." She scoffed and said, "We both know that will never happen."

Kane glanced at his soldiers, as if contemplating his next move. "Very well, but do not say I didn't give you the opportunity."

Her muscles coiled, waiting for him to give the order to attack.

He didn't.

Instead, he lifted the dragonstone. Her lips parted, eyes widening. He was going to do it—he was *really* going to do it. Gasps rang out. Kane positioned the stone just over the missing divot in his breastplate, then muttered a word of power to secure it.

It clicked firmly into place.

CHAPTER 46

# THE FINAL DRAGONSTONE

*Kastali Dun*

Talon's stomach lodged in his throat. He couldn't move, couldn't think. There was a chance—there had always been a chance. Taylynn said it likely wouldn't work like the others, but they'd never had proof.

Still, when nothing happened...

He couldn't help his sigh of relief. Koldis let out a whoop from behind him. Claire's elation bled into his mind, mixing with a premature sense of victory.

Kane's eyes widened and he looked up. It was the first time the sorcerer displayed a human emotion other than anger or malice. His confusion was obvious. After all, he'd used magic to fuse the stone into place.

It should have worked.

"Well, that's a shame," Claire announced, her voice bright.

"What have you done?" Kane snarled.

"You used the wrong stone."

"What are you talking about?!" His lip curled downward.

"That stone you already had there—it's white. The two stones protected by the sprites were black and gold. But you wouldn't

398

know that, because you never got your hands on them until you forced Taylynn to hand them over. She switched the white for the black."

"But that's…" Kane's eyes darted down to Fright's dragonstone. "That's impossible. I can feel the magic coming off this stone."

"Oh, it's definitely a real dragonstone. Just…not one of the original five." Claire lifted a shoulder.

Taylynn had told them exactly what she'd done when they'd visited her cottage that day in the forest. Of how Kane had confronted them. How he'd demanded she hand over the stones as she retrieved them. How he'd killed Pelwynn anyway.

The sprite princess had done the only thing she could think of. She'd taken Fright's stone and quickly swapped it with the black one. "All this time," Talon said. "All this time you thought you had the ultimate power in the palm of your hand."

"To be fair, so did the rest of us," Reyr muttered from behind him.

Talon knew that Reyr would forever feel guilty for this, even if he shouldn't. Kane hadn't exactly allowed the imposter king a good look at the stone before having him carted off to the dungeon. Besides, Reyr had been a bit more preoccupied with everything else going on during those disastrous moments in the throne room.

"It's over, Kane." Claire reached behind her for a sword. She pulled Cyrus's blade free. "I told you what would happen if you used that stone."

"No! Kill them!" Kane screamed at the guards. "Bring them down!"

Claire lunged. He went to follow but was immediately beset with blades. Drawing his own, he worked to fight free. He was barricaded in—cut off from his mate. "Protect her!" he shouted at Feowen, who had somehow broken free of the circle trapping them. "You are her captain of the guard! Protect her!"

Feowen gave him a brief nod while lifting his twin blades.

Kane saw her coming. He reached for something, removing it from his pocket. Talon was forced to split his attention between his attackers and Claire's movements. He felt her eyes widen as Kane popped open the cork on a vial of clear liquid before muttering an incantation. The liquid poured over the dais stairs creating a window—a portal.

"As if I'd let you kill me," he scoffed at Claire before jumping.

"No!" she screamed, lunging for him. She managed to grab hold of his cloak before he dragged her with him.

Talon froze. "Claire!"

Feowen jumped in after her, right as the portal of water closed.

No! He couldn't lose her again. He couldn't let this happen again.

His scales began to flicker across his skin, fury bleeding through his mind. He lunged for the nearest guards, removing three heads in rapid succession. The only thing that kept him moving was the knowledge that Claire was still alive. He could feel her in his mind, distant, but there. Her thoughts were mere whispers.

If she died, he would too. He would fall to his knees right here and beg Kane's guards to end him. He couldn't live in a world that didn't have her in it.

There was a weak press of affection against his thoughts. *"I'm all right,"* she seemed to whisper, even if he couldn't really hear the words.

The fighting was over in minutes. When he next blinked, the ground was littered with Oshean guards. The doors to the throne room opened and Taylynn swept in, a mob of sprites behind her, including the rest of Claire's guards, who had been charged with eliminating the hundreds of Oshean soldiers occupying the barracks. Behind her, Saffra walked with her team of operatives, escorting the remaining mages Kane hadn't killed. Claire's hand-maidens, her ladies, her best friend all took up positions behind them, taking in the carnage with wide eyes. Behind him, he was vaguely aware of Eagle slipping away. He didn't blame the assassin, who had fulfilled his end of the bargain.

Silence fell, deep and profound, punctuated by his panicked beating heart.

Taylynn took a quick look around, ignoring the courtiers

cowering against the walls. Her expression relaxed when she noticed Koldis standing in one piece, then tightened again when she realized something was wrong.

"They went through a portal," Talon growled, stalking over to her. "You must take me to her. I need—"

"No." Taylynn lifted a hand to silence him. She appeared to wrestle with her emotions for several moments before she schooled her features and very calmly said, "Your Majesty, it is out of my hands."

"No!" The word was a snarl. He advanced on her, crazed, half ready to strangle her if necessary.

Koldis appeared beside him. His shield's hand latched around his wrist, halting him. "My king," Koldis warned.

He growled, not taking his eyes from Taylynn. "I need to go to her."

"And how do you expect *me* to make that happen? The snap of my fingers? A couple of magical words?"

"I don't know," he cried, growing more frantic. "You're a sprite. You can do things we drengr cannot."

She scoffed a laugh. "If I could travel like that, I would have saved much time throughout my life."

"Then how have you been getting around to do whatever meddling you've done over the years?"

"By unicorn, how else?"

His jaw ticked. He could feel Claire's peril. Could feel the danger she was in. "She could be—she could be fighting against him right this instant!"

"And that would be all right."

He lunged as a menacing growl erupted from his chest, this time barely missing Taylynn's throat as Koldis wrapped both arms around him, keeping his mate safe. "Let me go," he snarled, bucking against Koldis's tight hold.

"Have you forgotten her promise?" Taylynn said, still unruffled. "Or Saffra's vision?" She cocked her head to the side to study him. His chest heaved, but his body went limp in Koldis's arms. "Claire is doing what she was always meant to do. You will be of no help to her. You are needed here. You have a kingdom to stabilize. You are Dragonwall's king. Put your emotions aside and start acting like it."

He bristled. If she wouldn't help him, he'd fly there himself. "Where is she? I know you know. You've seen it, haven't you? Where is she?"

"She is beyond our reach," Taylynn said. He glared at her and she sighed. "She is in Shadowkeep."

"Shadowkeep?!" he roared.

But that was...half a world away.

"She did not go alone, my king." Reyr stepped up beside him.

Taylynn glanced around again and then her eyes widened. "My brother?"

"Yes," Reyr said.

"Good." Taylynn nodded, as if to herself. "That's good. He will see her home safely."

"What?" Talon balked.

"You heard me, *Ayas Drollaya*." Clearly her patience was at its end. "Your queen has her own quest ahead of her. It is time you trust her to do that which needs to be done. Trust that we have all prepared her as best as we can. Trust that she is strong. That she is capable. That she is the woman, the mate worthy of you. She is not some fragile thing so easily broken. But you already know this, don't you?"

Talon swallowed, clenching his jaw.

"Turn your focus towards rebuilding your capital and securing your kingdom. Even now, asarlaí are pouring in from Oshea, attempting to claim the lands Kane promised. Your work here is not yet done."

Koldis gave him a firm squeeze and said, "Feowen loves her like a sister. He will let no harm come to her."

Talon shrugged him off and straightened. He flexed his neck, cracking the joints, then said, "You're right. Taylynn is right. My queen is powerful. She can take care of herself. Forgive me, Taylynn. I overstepped."

He could have sworn in that moment, he felt a thin slip of

amusement travel through his bond with Claire. Like she was proud of him for admitting this. Proud of him asking for forgiveness.

"It is forgiven." Taylynn waved a hand. "I believe my mate would react much the same had I disappeared like that."

Beside him, Koldis huffed and said, "You'd better not or there will be hell to pay."

Talon scrubbed a hand over his face. "I can barely feel her, but she is alive and...unharmed."

"Good. Then you have work to do."

~

WORK WAS AN UNDERSTATEMENT.

He spent the remainder of the day assessing damages, delegating tasks, and organizing small groups of drengr to weed out the remaining Osheans around the city.

He sent drengr messengers to the other forts, letting them know that Kane had retreated. He put measures in place to rebuild his military. He oversaw the cleansing of the throne room, erasing all signs of Kane.

There was no rest to be had. He didn't even eat, even though he was famished. The thought of food in Claire's absence made his stomach sour.

By the time his shields forced him to retreat to his tower for their evening meeting, it was already well past midnight. He sagged in his favorite armchair, thanking the gods Kane hadn't mutilated his tower the way he had the throne room.

Desaree, Jocelyn, and Leah had organized a team to remove their belongings from the cave and move them back into the tower. The place was glowing with warmth. It smelled as if it had been freshly cleaned. He was grateful for the work they'd put in, offering him a quiet place to retreat.

Only, it wasn't a retreat, nor would it be. Not until Claire was here, tucked safely in his arms where she belonged. He stroked Batty, the cat curled in his lap. His shields recounted each of their efforts in the city, while Claire's spriten guards shifted uneasily, perched along the perimeter of the room. He'd offered them places to sit, extra chairs if they wished, but they'd formally declined. Taylynn was off doing the gods only knew what. Koldis didn't seem bothered by it. Perhaps he was growing used to her antics.

His focus was split between listening and reaching for his mate. It wasn't like normal drengr communication. That would have been impossible, especially with an entire forest between Kastali Dun and Shadowkeep. It was only because of their mate bond that he could feel her at all, steady and alive. Beyond that, who could say?

He had no idea if she was with Kane. If she'd fought him and won. No idea if she was hurt. Nothing.

Not knowing made him feel ill.

But Taylynn was right. He needed to trust that she could do this. Trust that she could fulfill her unbreakable promise. He'd done everything in his power to prepare her during their journey to the capital, testing her mage magic, helping her hone it.

This wasn't like before, he reminded himself. When she'd been ripped from him and sent back to her world. This time she had her memories and magic. Her abilities remained intact.

She could do this—

"My king?" This, from Jovari.

His head snapped up. "What?"

"I asked if you would like us to accompany some of the drengr departing for the coastal cities tomorrow afternoon."

"I'll do it," Verath volunteered. Desaree was nestled in his lap. She sat up straighter, like she was ready to protest. She knew better than to interfere with a shield's duty, but she'd only just gotten him back.

"No," Talon said. "You've been in the dungeon. I want you to recover."

Verath grumbled something under his breath, but slouched back into the sofa. No doubt he'd been feeling useless, caged for so long. He'd get over it.

"Koldis, Jovari—both of you can go. Reyr, I want you to fly to

Fort Squall, pay your nephew and his mate a visit. Find out what became of all those captives that he had freed. Make sure they have everything they need to make it back home safely. Then find the ships responsible for freeing them and set them up with a fine sum of money. Enough for their entire crew to retire, if desired."

Reyr and Merrian shared a look. Talon was tempted to ask Reyr what was going on between him and Merrian, but later. He didn't care to know right now. "It will be done, my king."

"What of us, Your Majesty?" Saffra looked at him. She sat with Jocelyn and Leah on the rug beside the fire, a pile of pillows scattered around them.

"Continue working with Tess to get the keep back up in working order, if you would—"

"I—" Leah opened her mouth, then snapped it closed when she realized she'd interrupted.

"What is it?"

"I noticed today that the royal library was in severe disarray," she said. He stared at her, waiting. "I would like to help there, if that would be all right."

"There are already librarians for such a job," Verath pointed out, ever the logical one. Desaree swatted his chest and whispered something to him. He shut his mouth and pressed his lips together, dropping the subject.

Talon sat up straighter. The library was indeed in a sad state. Kane had, in his thirst for more power, swept through and taken whatever books he pleased, destroyed those he saw fit, and more. There would be no fixing some of the damage he'd done, but they would rebuild as best they could.

"You used to work in a library?" He knew far more about Leah than necessary. Claire loved the young woman like a sister, so in a way, he did too.

"Yes."

"What did you do?"

"At the library?" He lifted his brows. "Oh. Well, I organized events, helped manage the keeping of books, that sort of thing. I've even done a bit of book binding and restoring," she announced proudly.

He nodded. "Good. I will introduce you to the master librarian myself. You will apprentice to him, and perhaps someday, take over his position. I'm sure he could use the extra help in repairing the damages done."

"What?!" She gawked.

"Shall I repeat my—?"

"No! I mean. Sorry. I just..." Her cheeks flushed. "I don't need special treatment."

"It isn't special treatment if you are qualified. I'll let the master librarian make that decision once you begin working with him."

She lifted her chin. "I will do my best. Thank you—for the opportunity."

They spent the remainder of the meeting finalizing plans for the next several days. It was the kind of work that would have been better done with two monarchs rather than one. It made the pain of missing Claire that much worse. And yet, her job was the most important one of all.

If she managed to fulfill her promise, to kill Kane and return to him victorious, he would never be able to repay her for such a monumental task. But that didn't mean he wouldn't spend the rest of their days together making it up to her. Every single moment.

# CHAPTER 47
# A DO OVER

*Kastali Dun*

Jovari slipped into the royal library, keeping out of sight. The main floor was a bustle of activity. Carpenters rushed around to repair shelves, the noise of their hammers ringing throughout the vast space. Books were piled high in stacks, some waiting for repairs, others waiting to be shelved. A servant swept up a pile of broken glass by a display case that had been ransacked, probably by some of the Oshean guards looking for valuable trinkets.

Libraries were places of knowledge, of power. It was no surprise that Kane and his constituents had mistreated this place. The sorcerer had mistreated much of Kastali Dun. At least the library could be revived. What of the people he'd killed?

He caught a flash of pink and his breath stilled. Leah swept across the atrium, her arms full of books, then ascended the staircase to begin shelving them. She was wearing a pair of spectacles. It shouldn't have made her look so damned cute, but it did. He silently crept after her. She disappeared down an aisle and he followed, watching as she lifted each book, squinted at the title, then placed it back where it belonged.

His chest swelled. He found his hand lifting unconsciously to rub away the pressure. To relieve it. This was his mate, the woman fate had chosen for him. The woman he was destined to spend his life with.

In those final moments when Kane had used the white dragon-stone, when everyone held their breath hoping beyond hope that Taylynn was correct, he realized how hard-headed he'd been. If things had gone differently, he could be a stone statue right now. And then what? He'd never get to face Leah, to talk about what was between them. All because he'd flown off in a fit of fear.

She was his *mate*, godsdamn it!

The thought frightened him. He'd been hurt before, by a human no less. He knew what it felt like to be rejected. It made him question his worth.

Leah could very well reject him. She was an outsider. She didn't understand the importance of mates the way those of his world did.

She could decide she didn't want to tie herself to the male who had embarrassed her.

The thought stifled the warmth in his chest, replacing it with the burn of acid. He swallowed, pushing the possibility of her rejection far from his mind. Because he knew one thing with certainty. If she rejected him, he would work to convince her to change her mind. There was no reality in which he would go mate-less when his mate was standing *right here*!

"Leah." He stepped from the shadows.

She gasped, clutching what remained of her book stack to her chest. "Oh! Jovari. I... I didn't see you there."

"I apologize. I didn't mean to startle you."

"You didn't," she lied, quickly pulling her spectacles off and stuffing them into her pocket, like she had a reason to hide them.

"Don't." He stepped forward and reached for them. "I didn't realize you wore glasses."

"I don't usually need them unless I'm reading things up close. I haven't had a reason to wear them since...you know."

"I like them on you."

"Oh." Her cheeks flushed. "You do?"

"They make you look learned and scholarly. But not like the old folk who usually occupy the library here, pouring over ancient texts. More like a young, vibrant—" She was grinning now. "All right, I'm babbling."

"No. Do go on. Don't let me stop you."

He bit back a grin. Silence fell between them and she shifted her weight. "Oh, here. Let me take those."

"I can—"

He had the stack in hand before she could further protest. His actions earned a glare, but truth be told, he didn't want her holding it while they simply stood there. He found an empty area of shelving and set it down.

"So, how are you holding up?"

She blew out a breath. "I can't stop worrying about her."

"Me too," he admitted. "Talon swears that the bond remains intact, that she feels alive and unharmed. But...it's the *not* knowing that's killing me."

"Same." She tucked a strand of hair behind her ear, her delicate ear, and he felt his fingers itch to reach out and trace the shell of it.

He cleared his throat and said, "I promised you we'd talk, when things calmed down."

Her throat bobbed. "Things haven't exactly calmed down."

"I know, but I'm set to leave with Koldis today, as per the king's orders. I don't know when we'll be back. I don't want to leave this unfinished between us."

"What's to finish?" She lifted her chin, a challenge in her gaze.

"The fact that we're mates."

"So?"

"So. I want to get a few things off my chest. And then I want to hear your thoughts." She continued to stare at him, so he took that as his cue to continue. "I wanted to apologize. I behaved rashly that day, when we discovered our bond. I can see how my behavior might be taken negatively. I don't want you to think I don't want you. That I didn't want you and thus, didn't want the bond. I know it came across that way and I'm... I'm ashamed of that."

She watched him, motionless.

He blew out a breath. "My mother would probably box my ears if she knew I'd done that."

Leah pressed her lips between her teeth, fighting a small smile. "Nieven doesn't strike me as the type."

A laugh burst from his chest. "Trust me, she tanned my hide plenty of times when I was a child. Raising an unruly boy will test even the most patient of mothers."

"Right." This time, she let her smile free.

"Anyway," he continued, fighting the flutter in his chest. Was his chest supposed to flutter like this? Was that normal? He'd have to ask one of his shield brothers. "So, yeah, I'm sorry about that. The truth is, you know my history, what I've been through. I would be lying if I said I wasn't frightened by all of this. But I want it. I want this bond. Us."

"You do?" She licked her lips and he couldn't help but be drawn to the action.

"I do. That is...assuming you want it too?"

"I..." She twisted her fingers together. Someone passed by their aisle and they both waited for them to retreat. "I do."

He felt his breath rush out of him—

"But, I don't know that I want to rush right into things. I mean, Claire explained what it all means. I know we've kissed, but I feel like we've barely gotten to know each other, you know? Plus, I need time to figure myself out, to find my place in all of this."

His throat felt thick. She wanted this. She wanted *him*.

"What do you suggest, then? You wish for me to court you first?"

Her cheeks flushed again. Gods, she was so cute when she was being shy. He loved that he could take this intelligent, strong, bright young woman and make her blush.

"I think that's a good start."

"Then that's exactly what we'll do." He took a step closer.

Her eyes darted to his lips and darkened. He felt that look straight down to his groin. "I've been thinking a lot about our first kiss."

Her brow furrowed, eyes finding his again. "That wasn't my best moment. I was in a weird place emotionally and looking for comfort."

"You shared your vulnerabilities with me and I gave you another reason to feel vulnerable. It was poorly done." She lifted a shoulder, as if hoping to appear nonchalant. "We've both shared secrets with each other. You, your difficulty grappling with Claire's success and me, my pain of rejection. I like that neither of us is perfect. I like the idea of growing together. Of facing our difficulties together. That's how it should be for mates."

"I've... I've lost a lot of people I loved."

"Your parents." She nodded, even though it wasn't a question. "I cannot say I won't die on you, Leah. No life is certain, especially in these times. But I can say it's going to take a hell of a lot to rip me from this world, from you. I'm right here. I plan to continue being right here—for you."

A look of hope betrayed how she felt.

"*You ready to go?*" Koldis's interruption reminded him that he needed to wrap this up.

"*Give me a moment.*"

"You said you were frightened by all this," she said. "I am too, because like you, I know what it feels like to love someone and lose them, even if it was in a different way, a different kind of relationship."

"I know." He swallowed. "But that's part of why I think we'd be perfect together. We understand one another in that way. Right?"

"Right." She blew out a breath.

Without thinking, he reached for her hand, flattening her palm over his chest. "I'm right here, Leah."

"I know," she managed, her voice a whisper. "I know.

"Good. Then, about that kiss. I'd like a do over, except without all the stuff that was said afterward."

Her shoulders seemed to relax. "Oh." The word was breathy.

Reaching for her waist, he pulled her even closer and said, "You can stop me if you're not ready for this. But just know, I need food for the road. Something to think about while I'm away."

She snorted. "I had a feeling there was more to it."

"Call me selfish if you must." His heart began to hammer against his chest. He'd kissed plenty of women, but none of them had ever made him this nervous. None of them had ever made him ache this much.

Their eyes remained locked, hers dancing with eagerness. He lowered his head, giving her time to lean away. She didn't.

Their lips met, softly brushing at first. He moved his mouth over hers, coaxing a sweet sigh from her. She kissed him back and he turned greedy, swiping his tongue along the seam of her lips. She opened for him and he swept in, clutching her more tightly to him.

Dragons—*drengr*—were ever possessive creatures.

He felt sparks burst along his skin. The sensation made him shiver against her. He could only press her hips more firmly to his, reluctant to ever let her go.

Her fingers twisted in the hair at the nape of his neck. The pressure made a growl rise in his throat. Gods, now he never wanted to leave.

He pulled her even closer, lifting her to get a better angle, devouring her mouth. Their breaths mingled, hungry and ragged. The kiss morphed from sweet to passionate.

"Leah I—*oh*."

He froze and she squeaked, but he didn't release her. A warning growl burst from his chest at being disturbed.

"Forgive me, Lord Jovari. I didn't—"

He angled his head to see Roland, the master librarian standing at the mouth of the aisle, wringing his hands.

"It's fine. She'll be with you in a moment."

"Jovari," Leah hissed. She pushed at him, albeit uselessly. He set her back on her feet reluctantly.

"I'll just be...downstairs." Roland shuffled away.

. . .

IF YOU WOULD LIKE to stay up to date with book news, new releases, spoilers, and bonus content, sign up for my newsletter mailing list at https://www.authormelissamitchell.com/newslettersignup

# ABOUT THE AUTHOR

Melissa Mitchell is a fantasy romance author and creator of the seven-book *Dragonwall* series. Her love of fantasy began with *The Dragonriders of Pern*, and she now writes stories full of dragons, magic, hidden royalty, and slow-burn romance. She holds a PhD in physics and lives in Atlanta, Georgia with her husband, a husky, and four very spoiled bunnies. When she's not writing, she enjoys baking cookies, bullet journaling, and figure skating—usually while plotting her next book.

Visit her online at: authormelissamitchell.com

# Also by Melissa Mitchell

**The Arcane Artifacts**
Bound by the Blood Ruby

**The Dragonwall Series**
Talon the Black
Reyr the Gold
Verath the Red
Koldis the Green
Bedelth the Orange
Jovari the Blue
Dallin the Violet

**The Lady Witch Series**
Wielder's Prize
Wielder's Bond
Wielder's Might
Witch's Ruin
Witch's Heart
Witch's Crown

**Royals of Dragonwall Series**
For the Crown

**Stand Alone Titles**
Blood and Ballet